P9-CAM-155

EXTREME MEASURES

EXTREME MEASURES

ELISABETH NAUGHTON

Montlake
Romance

This is a work of fiction. Names, characters, organizations, places, events, and incidents are either products of the author's imagination or are used fictitiously.

Text copyright © 2014 Elisabeth Naughton
All rights reserved.

No part of this book may be reproduced, or stored in a retrieval system, or transmitted in any form or by any means, electronic, mechanical, photocopying, recording, or otherwise, without express written permission of the publisher.

Published by Montlake Romance, Seattle

www.apub.com

Amazon, the Amazon logo, and Montlake Romance are trademarks of Amazon.com, Inc., or its affiliates.

ISBN-13: 9781477822562
ISBN-10: 1477822569

Cover design by Eileen Carey

Library of Congress Control Number: 2013921709

Printed in the United States of America

.

For my good friend Darcy Burke,

the queen of the coolest names.

Thanks for letting me borrow this one.

chapter 1

Guatemala
ETA to extraction: twelve minutes and counting.

Zane Archer scanned the darkened compound from the trees just beyond the perimeter wall and tried to ignore the sweltering jungle heat.

Too bad it didn't work.

Sweat gathered under his fatigues and beneath his helmet, but he knew that soon the temperature would be the least of his worries. Wiping a hand over the moisture dripping into his eyes, he looked through the scope. At this hour—nearly three in the morning—the only lights flickering were in two windows on the second floor of the Mediterranean-style mansion. A guard roamed the portico outside the first floor, and other than a few howler monkeys chirping in the jungle canopy nearby, no other sound besides rustling leaves and palm fronds met his ears.

He glanced at his watch again. *ETA to extraction: eleven minutes, twenty-five seconds.*

Nerves fluttered in his belly, but he ignored those too. Keeping the M4 carbine rifle trained on the guard, he tipped his head toward the com unit near his shoulder. "Look alive, boys. We're coming up on go time."

1

In his earpiece, the radio squawked. "You're sure he's in there?"

Jake Ryder's skepticism was nothing new. But on this, Zane was confident. "Carter's intel is sound."

"It'd better be," Jake muttered. "Our balls are dangling out here in the breeze, Archer."

Zane bit back the smart-ass comment because Jake had let him take the lead on this one, and then looked through his scope again, scanning the perimeter once more.

His heart picked up speed, and adrenaline flooded his system. Ryder and Hedley should have their men in position on the far side of the compound by now. Though Zane was confident this extraction was going to go down without a hitch, he knew Jake Ryder—CEO of Aegis Security, the private company comprising Zane and a handful of elite specialists from around the globe—wasn't so sure. Jake didn't know "Carter" from a fart in the wind. And though he was aware Zane and Carter had teamed together during Zane's five years with the CIA, he still questioned the fact that this whole op hinged on the intel Carter had passed along to Zane. Intel that said one Adam Humbolt, PhD and specialist in chemical weaponry, was being held in this Guatemalan compound by a gang of thugs who worked for Central American drug lord Roberto Contosa.

"Humbolt's in there," he said into his com unit. "Trust me, Carter and the Company want this guy free as much as we do."

Not as much. *More.* Humbolt didn't 'officially' work for the US government, but word on the street was that the scientist knew some super top secret shit the United States didn't want shared with anyone—Central American drug lords included. And though logic said this extraction probably should have fallen to a SEAL or Delta team, because the State Department didn't want this op on record, the job had been handed off to Aegis, with its superior track record. Aegis's orders were simple: get the job done quietly and quickly and with no link back to the US government whatsoever.

Ryder didn't respond, and Zane knew his boss was thinking, *We'll see,* but facts were facts. Sure, there were a whole lot of people who wanted the science percolating in Humbolt's genius mind, and another bunch who'd like to see him dead, but the ones who mattered just wanted him back in the States alive and in one piece.

Time ticked by slowly in the oppressive early morning heat. Zane could all but feel the adrenaline from his teammates stationed around the compound. And though he tried to stay focused as he waited, he couldn't stop his mind from drifting back to the last time he'd worked with Carter. To being stuck in that run-down apartment in Beirut he'd shared with Carter and Juliet. To the months of running surveillance, blending in, fighting back the boredom. To the nights he'd been alone with Juliet when Carter had been out. To the laughs, the looks, the heated moments that never should have happened.

"Holy hell," he whispered. "You are such a fucking moron."

"You say something?" Hedley piped in his ear.

Shit, he was talking to himself. He cleared his throat, peered through the scope again, and put all thoughts of Juliet out of his mind for good. "Remember, boys," he said. "Slow is smooth, smooth is fast."

"Ooh-rah," Landon Miller murmured, the only communication the former Marine had uttered since they'd set up the perimeter.

As the team went black, Zane said a quick prayer they'd be in and out in seconds rather than minutes or hours. Said another that no one got dead.

He shifted his finger from guard to trigger. Lined up the compound sentry in his crosshairs. And just as the last second passed on his watch, he fired once, killing the south-end sentry with a barely audible pop. On the north end, he was confident Ryder had just accomplished the same.

He was out of the tree and across the wall before the sentry's body hit the ground, rappelling the cement structure as quickly as possible and bracing his rifle against his shoulder as he crossed the dew-covered grass. At the southwest corner of the compound, he caught up with Hedley's group coming in from the side and pointed up, signaling the hostage room they'd identified earlier on the second floor.

Miller and Stone tossed ropes up and over the second-story balcony, the grappling hooks catching the balustrade and securing tight. Zane followed Hedley to the second floor, waiting in silence as the other two men climbed up and over the railing. As a silent unit, they made their way across the balcony and lined up outside the hostage room.

Hedley signaled with his finger, counted to three, and then pulled an M84 flash grenade from his pack. When he got the nod from Hedley, Zane used his rifle to blow open the door of the compound. Hedley jerked the pin from his grenade and tossed the explosive into the room.

A roar shook the building and echoed through the darkness, followed by a blinding flash of light, intended to disorient those inside.

Zane was the first through the door, sweeping the right side of the room with his gun. Hedley came in on his tail, scanning the left, while Miller and Stone followed through the middle zone. Shouts echoed around them. Zane caught sight of two hostages, tied in chairs in the center of the room, then the tangos, two on the right, one on the left, all three scrambling for weapons in their confusion.

He fired two double-taps, shifted his weapon to the second target, and fired again. The shots hit dead center in the chest, dropping the captors with quick pops. "Clear right," he said into his shoulder.

To his left, he heard two more pops and saw the last captor go down. "Clear left," Hedley echoed in his earpiece.

"All clear," Miller followed from the middle of the room.

"Who's there?" The man in the chair turned his head from side to side, his vision obstructed by a black bandana tied at the back of his head.

"The cavalry." Zane yanked the blindfold from Humbolt's head. The man blinked several times. He was thin from weeks in captivity, and he looked like he'd taken a major beating. Bruises and dried blood covered one whole side of his face.

In the chair beside him, the brunette vibrated with fear. Zane shot her a look and then refocused on the job at hand. "Mr. Humbolt, we're here to get you out."

"Thank God," Humbolt breathed.

Hedley cut the hostages' ties while Zane and the other two got them to their feet.

"How did you find us?" the woman asked in a shaky voice as Zane ushered her toward the door. She didn't look much steadier on her feet than Humbolt, but at least she wasn't black and blue.

Zane didn't know who she was, but there'd be plenty of time for intros later. "We'll fill you in once we're secure. Right now just focus on keeping up."

The woman nodded, and Zane glanced at his watch. Time from start of op to apprehension of hostages: three minutes, thirty-seven seconds.

They were ahead of schedule.

"We're on our way out," he said into his com unit. "Plus two."

"Roger that," Ryder echoed back.

Slow is smooth, smooth is fast. Zane repeated the phrase in his head as he lifted the rifle to his shoulder again and turned back for the door. Miller and Stone took up position on either side of the hostages. Hedley brought up the rear.

They moved with stealth back to the balcony, where Zane and Hedley provided cover and Miller and Stone took the hostages over the railing and down to the ground. In the jungle around them, nothing moved, just like they'd planned. The lack of noise from the front of the compound confirmed Ryder's team had taken out their targets and that everything was smooth sailing from here.

When they were safely on the ground, they resumed position and headed for the southwest corner of the compound again, where Ryder's team of four waited.

Just as they rounded the corner, an explosion rocked the compound. The force of the blast shot Zane's body backward. He landed on his back with a crunch, his ears ringing. Coughing through the smoke pouring out of a giant hole in the first floor, he rolled to his stomach. Gunfire lit up the night sky. Something sharp ripped through his left quad.

He struggled to his feet. Swayed but found his balance. Disbelief rushed through him as he held up a hand to block the smoke and dust from getting in his eyes while he scanned the blown-out building. His entire body went still when his gaze caught sight of Humbolt, five feet away on the ground, blood oozing from multiple cuts and scrapes over his arms and face and seeping like a river from the man's ears.

Humbolt's eyes were wide and lifeless, his body limp. Draped over his torso, the woman also lay dead, her eyes staring out into space, a hole the size of a melon in her abdomen.

No. Disbelief churned to panic, then boiling rage. *No!*

"Goddammit, Archer!" a voice yelled from somewhere close. "Get back!"

A hand grasped his fatigues, dragging him tight to the side of the blown-open building. He stumbled, then fell to his ass. His back hit the crumbling stucco. A burn like dynamite lit up his left leg, and his vision swam. Struggling to see, he found Miller through the smoke, covered in soot, pulling Stone back in the same manner.

The ringing in his ears prevented Zane from hearing shit going on around him, but he recognized the ricochet of bullets hitting dirt, thought maybe he'd been hit—somewhere—but he still couldn't focus on anything except Humbolt lying dead against the earth.

His principal. Four minutes, twenty-three seconds after the start of the op.

"Humbolt's fucking dead!" Hedley hollered into his com unit. "No. One man down. Leg. I don't know. It's gushing. We need to get the bloody fuck out of here!"

In Zane's earpiece, Ryder's muffled voice rattled off commands, but the words were too dim to make out. They always had a backup plan ready to go in case things went wrong. Their backup in this case was to haul ass out before anyone else got dead, then reconnoiter two klicks south of the compound and rendezvous with the chopper.

How had it gone so wrong? Zane had led the planning phase of the mission himself. They'd known exactly how many guards would be on-site, what kind of weapons they'd be up against. The firepower raining down around them and the carefully timed explosion signaled they'd been compromised.

Hedley dragged him to his feet, bracing an arm under Zane's to hold him up. Through the smoky haze, Zane saw Hedley's mouth moving as the Aussie screamed directions, but that fucking ringing was growing louder, drowning out most sound. In the distance, two bodies rushed toward them through the smoke. Zane lifted a hand that held no gun. Shit, where was his rifle? He pointed, had no idea if he screamed or not. Hedley whipped around with his weapon just as Jake Ryder and Pierce Bentley appeared through the debris.

Zane nearly went down as soon as Hedley let go, but somehow he managed to prop himself against what was left of the wall. Dirt and sweat slid into his eyes and messed with his vision. His lungs burned. The scent of searing flesh and rubber was all he could focus on. Ryder signaled the roundup as the rest of his team fired back at the tangos spraying bullets from the second floor and the outer wall where Zane and his team had just been. Hedley wrapped an arm around Zane's waist, pulled Zane's wrist over his shoulder, and forced him low as they moved under the balcony and stayed out of the line of fire. Behind him, Stone hauled Humbolt's body through the debris and followed.

Zane lost track of time, wasn't sure how the hell they made it through the jungle and to the chopper alive. All he knew when he got there was that he was sweating like a motherfucker, he couldn't feel his leg anymore, and his principal was dead.

Dead.

Hedley threw him in the Huey, turned, and yelled at the others behind them. The chopper's blades whipped everything around them—trees, grass, palms. Seconds later they were loaded, and the chopper lifted off, banking to the left into the inky darkness. Zane shifted where he was lying on the chopper's floor and glanced out the open door down to the compound below, alive with flames and billowing smoke.

It looked like the world was on fire. One simple extraction had gone violently wrong. His gaze strayed to Humbolt's lifeless body.

Nausea rolled through his stomach. He dropped onto his back again, stared up at the Huey's ceiling, and worked not to lose his dinner. Somehow, he clawed himself free of his helmet, dropped it on the floor, and focused simply on sucking air into his suddenly too-small lungs. It took several seconds before he realized someone was screaming his name over the whir of the blades. His gaze shifted to the side where Ryder held a sat phone out to him.

"Says they want to talk to you!"

Zane took the phone and pressed it to his ear while Stone cut through his fatigues and started work on his leg.

"I need a tourniquet!" Stone yelled.

Hands moved in unison. Blood spurted. Someone tied a strip of cloth or rubber—or, holy *fuck*, that felt like metal—across his thigh. Pain returned with the force of a Mack truck moving at a hundred and twenty miles per hour. Zane gritted his teeth to keep from screaming just as the familiar voice said, "Sawyer? You survived?"

He knew that voice. He recognized the breathy cadence and the use of his CIA alias. But more than anything he understood the sound of victory.

Juliet.

In that second, he knew. He knew just who'd fucked their mission and why.

"How—?"

"How is not important." Her voice hardened. "It's the why you should really be concerned with. But then, you know the why, don't you?"

He pushed up to sitting, even though Stone pressed against his shoulder with one bloody hand and hollered at him to lie down. The pain in his leg morphed to a blinding red, which erupted behind his eyes. "When I find you—"

"You won't. I trained with the best, and I never lose." He could almost see those amber eyes of hers when she was in black ops mode, hard and cold and as soulless as any terrorist's. No wonder she'd made such a good operative. She was just like them. A venomous black widow, waiting to strike.

The phone went dead in his ear before he could respond. As dead as Humbolt on the floor beside him. Zane dropped back to the ground with a groan. The phone fell from his fingers to roll across the floor. And as they flew over the jungle and Stone packed his leg wound, Zane vaguely heard their medic tell the pilot to haul ass or they were gonna run out of time.

But he didn't care. As his vision blurred and darkness threatened, only one thing revolved in Zane's mind. Only one goal remained.

No matter what it took, no matter how long, he'd find her. He'd find her, and he'd make her pay.

chapter 2

One year later.

Evelyn Wolfe appreciated good music. Though she couldn't play an instrument to save her life, that didn't stop her from recognizing talent when she heard it. The guy with the violin two tables over, though, staring at her on the warm Seattle street as he played a medley that literally hurt her ears? He wasn't one of those talents. Not even close.

She avoided eye contact like she'd been doing since he came over twenty minutes ago and bugged her to request a song. She might look like a tourist enjoying the summer sunshine, but looks could be deceiving. She knew that better than anyone.

With her back to the café windows, she scanned the busy street again, her gaze shielded by dark sunglasses as it skipped past trendy boutiques, cars whizzing by, and multicolored flower baskets hanging from light posts to give the area an upscale feel. The salty scent of the Sound drifted on the breeze along with that of fried foods from street vendors, but she blocked it all out, instead focusing on the contact she was about to meet. She didn't have a picture of the man, but she remembered how he'd depicted himself: tall, dark, blue eyes, dimples.

That could describe anyone, she knew, as four different men, all matching that tall, dark description, walked by the outdoor café at various intervals. Each time one would pass, anticipation curled in her stomach and then dropped like a stone when he moved away.

Come on already. I don't have all damn day.

Eve's frustration grew to exponential levels. A quick glance at her watch told her Smith—which wasn't his real name by a long shot—was now twenty minutes late. Scenarios and options for what the holdup could be raced through her mind.

She brushed a strand of shoulder-length blonde hair back from her face and tucked it behind her ear. She missed her long, dark locks already. But the change, like everything else she'd done to prepare for this meeting, was important. In a few weeks—hopefully, if all went as planned—she'd hit her stylist in Monterey and dye it back.

If all goes as planned . . .

She nearly snorted. She'd learned long ago that things in this business never went as planned. But that didn't stop her. Or make her think of leaving. She'd considered leaving once, a long time ago, but that seemed like a different world now. And it was probably a good thing her plans hadn't panned out then. She could barely remember what life was like in the real world.

Her rambling mind froze when she caught sight of a man across the street heading her direction. She narrowed her eyes to see him better. He wore jeans, a gray T-shirt, fancy boots, and a baseball cap to cover his head so she couldn't decipher his hair color. But he was definitely tall. And dark, judging by the stubble on his jaw. And his gaze was locked solidly on her.

Her adrenaline shot up as she watched him cross the street a block down. As he maneuvered around tourists and locals. But she calmed herself, just as she'd been trained, when she realized his gaze hadn't once wavered from her face.

The fingers of her left hand tightened around the napkin in her lap. The Glock pressing against her lower spine reminded her just what was at stake.

The man slowed as he approached. She caught his eye color. Blue, definitely blue.

He stopped in front of her. Smiled. Two deep dents creased his youthful face.

He was her guy.

"Juliet?"

Eve smiled. Using an alias came as easy as breathing. And this one . . . well, she'd been using it for years. "You're late."

He slid into the seat opposite her. "Couldn't be helped. You brought it?"

American. Definitely. But Eve couldn't tell which part of the country he hailed from. Not that it mattered. Though there was something . . . familiar about him.

She scanned his face but was sure she'd never met him before. However, that tickle in the back of her throat told her she knew him from somewhere, and she needed to be careful.

"First I'll need proof you have my"—she paused for a moment, just to show him he didn't hold all the cards—"package."

Smith shot her a devastatingly handsome grin, leaned back in his chair, and stretched his long legs in front of him. Anyone walking by would think they were old friends. But she knew different. "And what if I said no?"

For some reason, at that second, a long-ago conversation with Sawyer ran through her mind.

"Bluffing is 90 percent of the game," she'd said. "You know that. If they believe you, that's all that matters."

"It's different for a woman, though," he'd countered. "Are you ever scared?"

"Always. But that's part of the risk we take."

It'd been one of those quiet nights in Lebanon when they'd both been on duty, monitoring the run-down drugstore across the dusty road through their apartment's crappy windows while Carter had been snoring in the next room. Why the conversation popped into her head now, she didn't know. But she definitely didn't need it. Or thoughts of the man who now hated her with every fiber of his being.

She pushed aside the memory and reached for the bag at her feet. Her chair scraped the sidewalk as she stood. "Then I guess our meeting's over."

She turned to leave.

"Juliet?"

She glanced back over her shoulder and followed Smith's gaze as it shifted across the street to a white van now parked against the curb. A burly man dressed in jeans and a tight-fitting T-shirt climbed out to stand in the road. He folded his arms over his massive chest and stared right at her.

"That move is not advised." Smith nodded toward her chair. "Sit."

Eve scanned the street for other threats, for something she might have missed earlier. Didn't see anything other than the van that had appeared during their conversation. But the hair on her nape was suddenly standing straight, telling her the power of this meeting had shifted. And not in her favor.

Slowly, she eased back down into her chair. Smith smiled and signaled the waiter. A server darted over and listened as he ordered.

He was gloating. This most definitely wasn't going as planned. Eve's adrenaline ratcheted up.

When the waiter left, Smith pulled a cell phone from his pocket, pressed a button, and slid it across the table toward her. "Take a look."

Eve expected to see a photo of the file she'd been tracking, but what flashed on the screen was an image of a woman, lying on her side, hands bound behind her, ankles tied together, feet bare, and a black sack covering her face. Eve lifted the phone, watched as the woman struggled against the bonds, trying to free herself. When she rolled toward the camera, a purple butterfly on her right ankle came into view. The same tattoo her sister Olivia had gotten during her freshman year of college.

No.

Eve's gaze shot to the man across from her, and any pretense of bluffing disappeared. "Where?"

He nodded toward the van across the street. The burly driver was now gone.

Her heartbeat shot up into the triple digits. "How do I know for sure she's in there?"

"Look closer."

In the background, Eve could just make out the floor of the van and the rear cargo doors with a smattering of daylight illuminating the black sack over her sister's face.

Fear pushed in from every side. Risking her own life was one thing, but her sister . . . Olivia was a schoolteacher. She didn't know the first thing about espionage or terrorist factions or traitors.

"What do you want?"

His smile widened. "I think we both know what I want."

She set the phone down, pulled the envelope from her bag, and slid it across the table. Smith looked inside, smiled at the currency he saw, and then tucked the envelope into the back pocket of his jeans. "Sometimes even the best laid plans go awry. Very nice doing business with you, Ms. Wolfe. I wish you and your sister all the best."

Smith rose and tipped his hat. He moved around her and headed away from the outdoor café, his whistling slowly disappearing on the breeze. The waiter appeared and set a mimosa on her table. "Enjoy, ma'am."

The noise of the café rose up around Eve. People chatting, silverware and glasses clinking, all melded with the traffic on the street to signal normal. Peaceful. A regular day in a beautiful city. Not a thing out of the ordinary.

Except this wasn't ordinary.

Olivia.

She hadn't talked to Olivia in months. Not since their father's funeral. And then they'd argued over Eve's gypsy ways and the fact that Eve was never around for the important things, like their father's last days. Eve already felt guilty enough over that, and Olivia's rant had only deepened that guilt, which resulted in Eve leaving early and Olivia not returning any of Eve's calls when Eve had contacted her days later and tried to apologize. But as frustrated as Eve was with her little sister, a tiny place inside knew Olivia deserved an explanation—about all the missed holidays, the months of no contact, and, most important, what she really did for a living. To repair the rift between them, to salvage the last blood relationship she had left, Eve had been ready to confess all to Olivia. Only now it was too late. Olivia's life was in danger all because of her, and her sister might never even know why.

Ignoring the drink in front of her, Eve eyed the van, then the bustling four-lane traffic. She'd get herself killed if she rushed right out there. Plus, if anyone was watching, she didn't want to draw extra attention. Pushing back from her chair, the legs scraping cement with a sound that echoed in her ears, she tossed the cell in her purse and then swung the strap of her bag over her shoulder and walked slowly but intently through the outdoor tables toward the streetlight half a block down.

She stopped at the corner with a handful of people waiting to cross and worked to keep her expression neutral. Tried to keep her nerves from giving her away. A child—no more than four, holding his mother's hand—looked up at her with big hazel eyes.

Eyes, Eve thought briefly, that seemed to look through her, all the way to her soul. Eyes that reminded her of Sawyer.

She glanced quickly away.

Come on, come on, come on . . .

Just when Eve thought the light was never going to change, it signaled Walk, and she stepped off the curb onto the street with the child and his mother and the rest of the pedestrians.

The van exploded in a fireball that shot flames thirty feet into the air.

Eve's body went sailing. Screams echoed around her. She hit something hard, registered a sharp stab in her skull, knew consciousness was leaving her. But before she blacked out, she saw the shops lining the street, the van, even the umbrellas outside the café she'd just been sitting in, all engulfed in flames. Flames that looked like they signaled the end of the world.

And in the middle of it all, the body of the child, lying still as stone in the rubble around her.

Zane Archer could pick Juliet—*correction*, Evelyn Wolfe—out of a crowd with barely a look. Didn't matter that she'd cut and dyed her hair. He knew her walk, recognized those sexy legs in the slim black skirt that hit just below her knees, and, thanks to three months he now wished had never happened, was more than familiar with every inch of that toned body.

He'd watched her interactions from the shadows of an outdoor table at Starbucks a block down. After six months of searching, he'd finally found her. Meeting with a contact, in the United States, in broad daylight.

Man, the woman had balls of steel.

The throb in his thigh kicked up, a result, the doctors said, of the scar tissue and nerve damage he'd sustained from that bullet he'd taken in Guatemala, but he wasn't popping another pain pill. Not yet. He watched as Juliet handed the man an envelope, as the man rose and left, as Juliet looked around cautiously and then swung her bag over her shoulder and hoofed it for the crosswalk in those ice-pick heels that drew his gaze toward her legs. Long, slender, muscular legs he remembered wrapping around his hips, drawing him in, shutting out all other thoughts.

Fake, he reminded himself. Whatever he *thought* they'd shared was nothing more than a lie. Just as she was nothing more than a traitor. The lone woman responsible for Humbolt's death and all the shit he'd been through during the last year.

The red rage of revenge swirled behind his eyes. He pushed to his feet, tossed his paper cup in a trashcan at the edge of the building, and then stuffed his hands into his pockets and headed toward her.

He'd made it half a block before the van exploded into a thousand pieces and a fireball engulfed the street.

The explosion knocked him back to the ground. His head hit the concrete with a crack. Around him, screams and panic rose up to join the smoke and debris raining down. He coughed, rolled to his side, and pushed up to his feet, gritting his teeth at the pain reigniting in his thigh. He'd lost his sunglasses in the chaos, but he barely noticed. All he could focus on was Eve. He wasn't losing her. Not this time. Not when he was so close.

Squinting to see through the smoke, he searched the sea of running bodies. And caught sight of her on the ground, fifty yards away.

Panic closed in. Panic that she was already dead. That he wouldn't get the revenge that had been driving him. That she'd never have to pay for what she'd done.

He pushed his way through the crowd. Screams and sirens echoed in his ears, and burning smoke filled his lungs. The heat of the flames singed the hair on his arms as he drew close to the point of impact. Someone knocked into his shoulder, sending him spinning. He stepped on a chunk of cement with his bad leg and nearly went down. Blinding pain shot to his skull, but he pressed on, pulling his T-shirt up over his mouth to stop the smoke from pouring into his lungs.

He felt like he'd been dropped into a war zone. When he finally reached Eve, she lay motionless on the ground, covered in a layer of dust and bleeding from multiple scrapes and cuts across her skin.

He knelt at her side, leaned in close, and listened for her breathing. Hoping, praying.

There!

She wasn't dead. He checked her body and found—luckily—that the wounds weren't life threatening. She'd have a hell of a headache when she awoke, and a few of her cuts needed stitching, but she wasn't dead, just unconscious. Relief rippled through him. Relief and a pressing reminder that they needed to get the hell out of there before the situation changed. Glancing around, he spotted her bag five feet away, covered in soot. He reached for it, then hefted her into his arms.

She was dead weight as he carried her past rescue vehicles now flooding the street, past police and fire crews racing to the devastation. The burn in his leg flamed all over. A paramedic called out to him, motioning for him to bring her to him. Zane ignored the guy and darted behind a burning car lying on its side.

He didn't doubt the explosion had been for her. As he shifted direction and headed down a side street for the waterfront where he'd parked earlier, he ground his teeth together. Someone was obviously sending her a message. But then, what the hell did she expect after dealing with terrorists and selling out her country? He'd caught her red-handed, and even that hadn't stopped her. The woman should have known it was only a matter of time before her actions caught up with her and someone put a hit out on her.

Someone besides him.

chapter 3

Every inch of Eve's body hurt. She tried to roll to her side but couldn't. A moan echoed somewhere close. A moan, she realized, that had come from her.

"You're finally awake."

Eve stilled at the sound of the voice somewhere close. She tried to pry her eyelids open, but they weren't working. And doing even just that made her whimper in pain.

Something soft brushed her forehead. A haze had descended on her brain. She couldn't place the voice, but she recognized it. And she still couldn't move. Why couldn't she move?

"Don't try to get up, beautiful. Wouldn't want you hurting yourself so early now, would we?"

Little by little, her brain came back on line. The haze slowly dissipated, clearing from her mind in wisps and curls. She gathered her energy and was finally able to break her eyelids apart. Pain radiated through her skull, but she focused on the fuzzy orange light ahead. Tried to see through it.

"Always were an overachiever," the male voice said. "Guess that hasn't changed."

Who was he? Why couldn't she answer him? And why weren't her arms and legs working? She struggled. Managed to move her foot, just a fraction of an inch, but at least it was something. Footsteps echoed, fading in the distance. Eve stilled, squinted to see more clearly. A dark shape seemed to move somewhere ahead. Then the shape grew larger, and the sound of footsteps increased in intensity.

"Here," he said. "Drink this."

A straw pressed against her mouth. Her throat suddenly dry, Eve drew the straw between her lips and sucked.

Juice. Apple.

She moaned at the taste. Sucked again. God, that was good.

The straw was pulled from between her lips before she was ready to let it go. A click echoed as the cup was set down. Eve rolled her head from side to side. Her neck was moving now. And the orange blur was sharpening. The dark shadow in front of her becoming clearer.

"That's it," the man said, his voice closer, the heat of his breath sliding over her cheeks. Mint and musk. Those were the scents that bombarded her. Familiar scents. She just didn't know from where. "You've been out for quite a while. Thought maybe I'd been wrong and that I should have taken you to a hospital. Glad to see now that I wasn't. A hospital would just cause all kinds of problems we don't need."

Eve stilled at the bite she heard in his last words. A bite that indicated he was not friendly.

Dread curled in her stomach. She didn't know where she was, but she needed to get away. Basic instinct told her staying would lead to something bad.

She tried to reach for her gun, only her arms weren't working. Her legs, yes. Her head, yes. But not her arms. Why weren't her arms working?

"It amazes me you were this careless, beautiful." Fingers brushed over her temple, pushing hair back from her face. "After all, you trained with the best, didn't you?"

Everything inside Eve went cold. Those words were familiar. She tried to focus the blur into a single image. Could only see dark hair, dark eyes, and a fuzzy face. Tried to remember where she'd heard those words before.

"Of course," he went on, "you don't work with the best anymore, do you, Juliet? Should I even call you Juliet anymore? No, why don't I call you by your real name? What do you think, Evie? Think that'll work? Yeah, I think it will. I think for what I've got planned for you, tossing out all the old shit is the best way to go."

Eve's pulse shot into the stratosphere. Her hazy vision cleared just as the sound of his voice registered. She sucked in a breath when Sawyer's—no, Zane Archer's—face came into view. A tanned, scraped, and extremely pissed Zane Archer.

"You," she managed in a raspy voice. "How . . . ?"

"How is irrelevant, isn't it?" His brow lowered, and a dark look crept into his eyes. "What you should be concerned with is the why. But then, you know the why, don't you, Evie?"

Memories of her phone call to Zane nearly a year before spiraled through her mind. As did the weeks and months they'd spent together on that op in Beirut.

"Some of it's coming back to you now, isn't it?" He eased away. Behind him, dark wood beams came into sight. "I have to run out for something. I'll let you think long and hard until I get back."

He leaned close again, and she sucked in a breath. Something sharp stabbed into her arm where it was pinned above her head. Metal jingled. His fingers rubbed the stinging spot on her arm, and then his face came into view once more. "This should work pretty quickly." Before she could turn her head, he slapped duct tape over her mouth. "I'll be back in a few, beautiful. Don't get into any trouble while I'm gone."

Footsteps echoed. Keys clinked, followed by clicks. Three.

A door pulled open but didn't close.

"By the way, sweetheart," Archer said from a distance, "you look good. Better than I expected. Even banged up, you're still beautiful. My damn luck, huh?"

The door snapped closed, the sound echoing in Eve's mind, followed by three clicks again as she was locked in. She didn't know how she'd gotten here or why she was with Archer, but something in the back of her head told her she needed to remember before it was too late.

She struggled, tried to sit up, still couldn't. Metal clanked behind her head. Pain raced along her wrists. Her hands were cuffed above, she realized, and . . .

Her vision grew dark along the edges. The wood beams above blurred once more. Her heart raced as she drew deep breaths through her nose and tried to calm herself. He'd drugged her. The son of a bitch had drugged her.

Pay attention to your surroundings. Think, dammit.

She was lying on a bed. The room was big. She could tell from the way sound echoed that it was larger than a regular apartment and that there were no carpets on the floor. Was she in a barn? A loft apartment, maybe? A warehouse?

Before she could decide, darkness spiraled in, and that fuzzy, light feeling that signaled her time was almost up fogged her brain.

She had no idea where she was, but one thing was clear. If Archer was here, it was someplace she shouldn't—*couldn't*—be. Her stomach twisted, hard. Considering how much he hated her, she'd be safer with a group of jihad terrorists than she was now with him.

Zane wanted to give the drug time to work. And he needed to get away from Juliet—*shit*, he had to stop thinking of her as that and call her by her real name—before he forgot what the hell he needed to do next.

Evelyn. Eve. Fitting name considering a temptress with the same name had been Adam's downfall in the Garden of Eden.

His leg throbbed as he leaned against the dreary hallway wall, tugged a bag of M&M's from his pocket, and ripped off one corner. Shaking a few into his hand, he popped them in his mouth and chewed. Not the pain pill he wanted, but enough. For now. And at least out here he didn't have to listen to those sex-kitten mewing sounds she'd been making when she'd awakened. The ones that reminded him way too much of the sounds she'd made when he'd been inside her. God knew, the last thing he needed to remember right now was how good that had felt. How tight she'd been. How—back then—she'd been the only thing he'd wanted.

The familiar anger he'd lived with the last year rippled through his veins. He shoved the bag back in his pocket and chewed. Man, he'd been a class-A pussy back then, hadn't he? He'd fallen for her ruse like a teenager ramped up on hormones. Even with all the training and instruction and the knowledge that he shouldn't trust anyone. He just hadn't expected the "anyone" to include his colleagues in the CIA, living in his own fucking house.

His phone rang, and he pulled it from his back pocket without looking at the screen, hit Answer, and pressed it to his ear.

"Archer?" a familiar voice said. "Is that you, you dumb shit?"

Fuck. Zane tipped the receiver away from his mouth and rubbed his aching forehead. If not bothering to check his cell screen before answering wasn't proof Eve was fucking with his head again, nothing was.

He was just about to quietly end the call when Jake Ryder added, "Are you in Seattle, you moron? I'm staring at a news report right now that's got your name written all over it. Goddammit, Archer. Fourteen injured? Are you fucking insane?"

Zane's temper flared. Of course Ryder, his ex-boss—although technically the guy wasn't an ex anything since he'd refused to accept

Zane's resignation from Aegis six months ago—would assume he'd had something to do with that little explosion.

"I'm sorry," Zane said, working not to clench his teeth, "but the party you're trying to reach is unavailable. *Adiós.*"

"Archer, you son of a bitch, don't you dare hang up on—"

Zane hit End, powered down the phone, and shoved it back in his pocket. Fuck Ryder and his intel. Fuck Ryder telling him not to go after Eve in retaliation for what she'd done to their team in Guatemala. To Ryder it wasn't personal. To Zane it was everything.

He checked his watch, knew he needed to give the drugs a few more minutes to work, and moved over to the dirt-streaked window at the end of the corridor. It looked out over the construction site of a waterfront warehouse next door. Thirty feet separated this building from the naked beams of the next, and a tower crane between the two loomed above like an ominous threat. Zane leaned forward and glanced to the end of the building, toward the parking lot beyond, and noticed a man dressed in black, looking from one building to the next as if searching for something. Or someone.

Zane's already tightly strung nerves kicked up a notch. His spine stiffened as he watched the man take three steps into the construction chaos, look up and around again, pause for several seconds, and then jog back to the street and disappear from sight.

One of Eve's lowlife partners? The terrorists she'd pissed off who'd blown up that street? Or just a dumbass schmuck who didn't realize what the hell was going down around him?

Zane waited to see if the dipshit returned, the SIG Sauer cool and heavy where it was holstered at his lower back. When several minutes passed and the guy didn't return, Zane told himself to stop being so jumpy.

Jumpy, however, had saved his life on more than one occasion, so he didn't push the incident totally from his mind. He remembered the look of the man. And the location of the crane. And the fire escape on this building. And the empty floors of the one next door.

He headed back down the hallway toward the loft he'd rented, slid the key into the first lock, and turned. It opened with a click. After repeating with the other two, he pushed the heavy steel door open and stepped back inside.

The building was used mostly for storage. This loft was nothing but a wide, empty room consisting of a handful of pillars holding the ceiling up and a bank of windows that gazed out to the parking lot. There was one small bathroom off to the right that looked like it hadn't been cleaned in a year, and a table that held Eve's gun and all the supplies he'd need. There was also a bed. A bed where Eve lay snoozing.

He crossed to the bare mattress and stared down at her. Her head was tipped to the side, resting against her updrawn arm, her eyes closed, her chest rising and falling with her shallow breaths. Her face was bruised along one side, and small nicks and cuts marred her perfect complexion, but they didn't take away from her beauty.

Man, he hated that she still got to him, but even he couldn't deny the woman was gorgeous. The shoulder-length curly blonde hair wasn't bad, but he missed the straight chestnut locks she'd had when they'd been together in Lebanon. Had loved to wrap the strands around his hand when they'd made love.

Fucked, he corrected himself, that familiar sense of betrayal whipping through him the longer he stared at her. There'd been no love on her side. And on his . . . just a stupid-ass fool's gullibility.

He unlocked the cuffs from the rusted bed frame and brought her arms down by her sides. Her breasts pushed against the dirty, white button-down blouse she wore as he slipped one arm under her back, and the familiar scent of peaches wafted to his nose.

He used to love peaches—peach ice cream, peach cobbler, peach preserves. Hell, he was from Georgia. Peaches were practically a food group where he was from, and before his mother had died from breast cancer, her specialty had been peach pie. But ever since Beirut, he couldn't stomach peaches. And he hated that now, even after all this time, just the scent of that peach lotion she still obviously slathered all over her body fresh from a shower brought a host of memories he'd rather forget.

He clenched his jaw until it hurt and hefted her into his arms. As he carried her to the chair he'd set up earlier, he ignored the toned muscles in her arms and legs and the tightness of her ass where her body pressed against his. Reminded himself—again—that she wasn't the sweet and innocent California girl she'd pretended to be.

She was a traitor, one who'd let a known arms dealer walk when they'd been in Beirut, a man who'd gone on to kill innocent women and children. A traitor who'd set his team up to be killed in Guatemala. Who even now was plotting with terrorists—for what he didn't know, but he'd soon find out.

How many other guys had she fucked to get what she wanted? How many others had died trusting her? How many more lives would be lost—civilians, soldiers, children—before she was done?

He set her in the plastic folding chair and made sure she was propped up. Her head fell forward as he hooked her arms around the back of the chair and cuffed them together. Using zip ties, he strapped each foot to the chair's legs, then pushed to his feet and stared down at all that curly blonde hair hiding her face.

A sliver of guilt crept into his chest. If there was a hell, he was surely headed there. But he didn't care. Someone needed to put a stop to her. And it looked like that someone was now him.

- - - - - - - - - - - - - - - - -

"Stupid fucking son of a bitch!" Jake Ryder slammed the phone down on his desk. "Marley! Get in here!"

The door to his office at Aegis headquarters pushed open just as he was tugging off his tie, and Marley Addison, his assistant, stuck her head into the room.

"That doesn't sound like happiness to me," she muttered.

Jake threw the tie onto the corner of his desk, scrubbed his hand through his hair, and then leaned both palms on the aged mahogany, ignoring her sarcasm. Seven years with SEAL Team Six had taught him plenty about patience, but all that training was currently flying through the window as his mind raced over what to do about Zane Archer.

He had a soft spot for America's best. Though Archer had left the CIA for his own personal reasons, his track record there had been stellar. Jake had enough contacts within the organization to know who was worth recruiting and who wasn't, but had he known then that Zane was going to be a major thorn in his side, he'd never have hired the son of a bitch. He hadn't spent years building Aegis into the best black ops security company in the world for nothing, and he'd be damned if he was going to let Archer fuck it up for him now.

In the corner of the room near a grouping of leather couches, CNN flickered with images of the Seattle bombing and updates on the number of injured, but he ignored those too. "Who do we have in the Pacific Northwest?"

Marley moved fully into the room. Her blonde hair was pulled back in a neat tail, and the wire-rimmed glasses Jake was used to seeing on her face were pushed up to the top of her head. The door snapped shut behind her as she paged through screens on her smartphone, knowing better than to comment on his mood. "Landon Miller just finished an assignment near Bellingham. He's scheduled to be off the next two weeks."

"Get him on the line. ASAP. His vacation's been canceled until further notice."

"That's not going to go over well," Marley said as he turned to look out at the rolling Kentucky hills lined with neat white fences. "What do I tell him is the reason for this callback?"

Jake watched a stallion race across the field. He'd set up Aegis's headquarters here, in one wing of the twenty-thousand-square-foot mansion he'd inherited from his louse of a father when the bastard had finally keeled over. Partly because the scenery always relaxed him. Partly because it reminded him of where he'd come from and where he was going next. But mostly because he got a sick sense of satisfaction knowing he was dancing on his good-for-nothing father's grave.

The view today, though, didn't help. It only pissed him off, because being *here* meant he was too far away to wrap his hands around Zane's fucking neck. "I want Archer brought in before the Feds get a hold of him."

"You think Zane's involved in the bombing in Seattle?"

Jake turned toward Marley. The black slacks were standard for her. The red blouse was new. He'd thought about mentioning it earlier but had decided not to. Their relationship was structured and professional and had been for going on four years now. She was the best damn assistant he'd ever had. The woman monitored his team of operatives better than Central Command, *and* she put up with his ass on a daily basis, which, he knew, wasn't easy to do. If he started tossing out compliments now, it'd all turn to shit. And he'd had enough shit relationships with women to span a lifetime. He wasn't going there with Marley no matter how pretty she might look today.

"I think Archer's thinking with his dick and not his brain. And even if he didn't set that bomb—which I hope to God he didn't, because it's going to fuck Aegis if he had anything to do with it—I have a feeling he's knee-deep in the shit. Send Miller Archer's last GPS location and have him pick the son of a bitch up before he causes any more trouble."

Marley was already dialing as she stepped toward the door. "You got it, boss man."

She left the door open in her wake, and in the silence, Jake's headache kicked up to the beat of a marching band. He reached into the pocket of his slacks for the bottle of Motrin he kept there, flipped the lid, and shook the contents over his palm. When nothing spilled out, his frustration shot to a whole new level.

"And get me some more grunt candy before my fucking head explodes!"

A small white bottle flew through the open door and nearly nailed him in the head.

- - - - - - - - - - - - - - - - -

"Come on, beautiful, naptime's over. Wake up."

The tapping on Eve's cheek brought her around. She jolted.

"That's it. Open those pretty amber eyes for me."

Lifting her head, she tried to see through the haze. Confusion mixed with the grogginess. "Saw-Sawyer?"

"There's my girl. Can't have you sleeping on the job, now can we?"

What was Sawyer doing here? And where was here anyway? She looked around, narrowed her eyes, couldn't see anything more than fuzzy shapes that seemed to bounce back and forth as if the world had been set on spin cycle.

"Over here, baby." She followed the sound of his voice. "That's it. Yeah, I think things are working well enough for us to get started now."

Get started? Eve had no idea what he meant. Or what was going on. But a niggling thought in the back of her mind warned, *Be careful.*

Metal scraped the floor. Eve focused long enough to see Sawyer's fuzzy shape pull a chair in front of her and sit. "We'll start with something easy. Tell me your name."

Her name? He knew her name. "What is this? What's going—?"

"Your name, beautiful. And where you live."

"J-Juliet."

"No, not your CIA cover, sweetheart. Your real name."

Eve's mind spun, and before she thought better of it, she said, "Ev-Evelyn Wolfe. I live in . . ." Crap, where did she live? "Monterey. I live in Monterey." That was right. On the beach. She had this great bungalow that overlooked the Pacific. It was small and had cost a fortune, but it was so worth it. "In California."

"Good," Sawyer said. "Very good. Now, how about who you work for?"

Why was he asking her these questions? Eve couldn't seem to think straight. "I work for . . . the CIA. You know that."

"Wrong." Sawyer leaned forward. A snap echoed in the room, followed by a whisper of air across Eve's skin and the soft clink of something hitting the floor. "Try again, Evie."

Eve blinked twice, tried to clear her watery vision. Sawyer was sitting in front of her, and in his hand he held something silver. A knife? Eve tried to see through the fuzziness.

No, not a knife, a pair of scissors.

Scissors? What the hell would he need scissors for? He—

She looked down, and even though everything still seemed to be moving as if underwater, she noticed the top button of her blouse was missing. Her breasts all but spilling out of her once-white top.

Her gaze shot back to his face, and inch by inch, it came into view. Dark hair in need of a trim, several days' worth of beard on his sculpted jaw, a thin scab across his forehead, and piercing, unfriendly, more-brown-than-green familiar hazel eyes. "Try again, Evie."

She swallowed. Hard. Tried to make sense of what was happening. Couldn't. Couldn't seem to stop herself from talking either. "I . . . I work for the CIA. Counterintelligence. I'm—"

"Wrong." Sawyer leaned forward again. Another snip. Another whisper of air across her stomach. Another clink as the button hit the cement floor. "I'm not interested in your lies."

Eve's stomach tightened. The venom in Sawyer's words was new. And bone-chilling. She tried to move, to get away, but her hands were locked behind her. She tried to stand but couldn't because her legs weren't working. Too late she realized he'd tied her to a chair.

Panic pushed in, mixed with the drug still wreaking havoc on her brain to make things seem surreal. "Sawyer—"

Sawyer leaned back and rubbed a hand over his face. "Okay," he said more calmly. "Let's try something else."

Metal scraped the floor again. Eve held her breath as he stood and moved around behind her, where she couldn't see him. "What were you doing in Beirut?"

Beirut . . . The word mixed with fuzzy memories. Fuzzy, heated memories of the two of them locked tight together. In their apartment. In the shower. In that crappy car when she'd been sure no one could see them. "I . . . my job."

"Yeah, I know that, beautiful." He leaned close to her ear, his warm breath rushing over bare skin to send tingles down her spine. This close she could smell him. Musk and mint and man. She'd always loved the smell of him. "But you weren't working for the CIA then."

She had been, though. Synapses slowly started to fire, like links in a chain firming up when pulled tight. And oh man, he wasn't going to believe her. But the truth . . . the truth was the only thing that seemed to be condensing in her mind. Where were the carefully orchestrated covers? Where were the lies she so often rattled off without a second thought? "I . . . I was working undercover."

"Spying."

She nodded. "Yes."

"For whom?"

"The CIA."

"Oh, Evie." *Snip. Whoosh. Clank.* "I didn't realize how eager you were to get naked."

Eve gasped as her blouse fell open all the way to her belly button.

Frustration, fear, and panic all coalesced in the bottom of her stomach. "I'm telling you the truth!"

Blinding pain lit off behind her eyes. Before he could ask her another question, she slammed her lids closed and groaned. "Oh God, my head."

"You took a nasty hit on the noggin, beautiful. Breathe through it."

She did. But not because he told her to. Because it was the only thing she could do.

"That's better," he said when her face relaxed. "Now, back to what we were discussing. You said you were spying. Are you implying you were spying on the CIA *for* the CIA?"

"Yes," she managed, gritting her teeth through the pain that was, thankfully, now easing. "I mean . . . the Pentagon—"

"I'm not buying it, honey." He snipped another button from her shirt. Only one remained.

A red haze lowered over Eve's vision. He was trying to intimidate her. But this was Sawyer, not some terrorist. He wouldn't really hurt her. Would he?

She struggled against the chair. "This is bullshit."

"Ah, but you like bullshit. You spin it so well."

Pain shot up her arms. "Why are you doing this?"

"Why? You tell me, Eve." He leaned close to her ear. So close she could feel his lips brush her skin when he whispered, "Think hard. About the phone call you made to me. Just after the raid. When I was lying on the floor of that Huey bleeding out. Remember what you said?"

Eve's whole body went cold. And that day—a year ago— flashed in her memory. Not fuzzy and watery as everything else, but crystal clear.

"'*I never lose.*' Ring a bell, Evie?"

Bile rose up in Eve's stomach. This was not the same caring man she'd once thought of leaving the CIA for. Whatever gentleness used to be inside Sawyer—no, Zane Archer—was gone, thanks to what she'd done.

"There are all kinds of ways to go about getting the answers I want," Archer said softly in her ear. "If you cooperate and tell me what you know, I'll try to make it . . . pleasurable. You remember how nice I can be, don't you, Evie?"

Unfortunately, she did. She remembered everything. Every secret touch, every stolen kiss, every nip and lick and suck and thrust. And she remembered how he'd made her feel. Not dead inside as she'd felt since Sam's death, but alive.

Only this, what he had planned for her here—something in her gut told her this was not going to end up being sweet or romantic or anything like she remembered. The man she'd once known was nowhere to be found in the one at her back. Fear—true fear—slithered into her chest. Unless she found a way to make him listen, this was going to be bad.

Think, dammit. Archer knew all too well how important control was to her, and he was taking that from her now. Exposing not only her secrets but her body in the process, using that to intimidate her. This was a mind fuck, nothing more. He wouldn't really hurt her.

Or so she hoped.

"I-I didn't compromise your team in Guatemala, Archer. I-I wasn't the one who turned you over. I found out the raid had been compromised after it was too late to get in touch with you."

"You always were good at the lies, Evie." He snipped the last button on her blouse. It hit the floor and rolled away, leaving the two halves of her shirt to swing open and a chill to slide over her bare skin.

His boots echoed on the floor as he came around to sit in front of her again. Eve's adrenaline amped all over. "I'm not lying," she said quickly. "When I called you after—when you were in the chopper"— she glanced at his leg and realized he'd limped around her chair. "I didn't call to gloat. I called to make sure you were still alive."

"Lies, Eve," he said calmly, way too calmly, "come so easy to you." He opened the blades of the scissors, positioned them at the hem of her skirt, and sliced through the black fabric.

"I'm not lying," Eve said again. "I only acted like I was gloating because I didn't know who might be listening. Archer, there are moles in the CIA. My unit hunts them down. That's what I was doing in Beirut. What I've been doing since."

He opened the scissors and sliced again. Her skirt opened to just above her knee. But unlike before, when he'd yelled at her, there was too little emotion on his face. As if he'd already decided she wasn't going to tell him what he wanted to hear and that nothing she had to say would change his mind. Goddammit, being caught by a terrorist was one thing. Being caught by someone who hated you and *knew* your weak spots was an altogether different horror.

"Archer—"

The cool blade of the scissors brushed her inner thigh, and she jumped. Panic pushed in and rippled through every inch of her body. And with it, in the background, something—a memory, a thought, a picture she couldn't quite bring into focus—telling her there was an important element to all of this that she was forgetting. Something personal. Something from earlier. Something that would make what he was doing here seem like nothing.

Why couldn't she remember?

"Archer, listen to me." She swallowed again and tried to stay calm. Through a haze she fought the effects of the drug and focused on the here and now. "It killed me that I couldn't tell you the truth in Beirut. It killed me that I couldn't tell you on the phone that day I called. Someone inside the CIA set Aegis up to take the fall for that scientist's death in Guatemala. Someone who wasn't me. I swear it."

His eyes stayed locked on her skirt. He opened the scissors and sliced through the fabric again. "It's really too bad you chose to work in espionage. You'd have made millions in Hollywood."

"Archer, dammit! I loved you, you son of a bitch! Why would I try to get you killed? I was trying to save you!"

The scissors stilled. His head lifted. Stormy hazel eyes locked on hers. Eyes that didn't seem so sure anymore.

Her heart pounded hard. Her palms grew sweaty. "Archer—Zane—I-I'm not lying. I'm telling you the truth. Just listen to me. Listen to what I have to say—"

A roar of metal slicing through metal echoed from the doorway. Sparks flew into the room, spraying across the floor.

Eve swiveled in the direction of the noise so fast she knocked the chair off balance and hit the concrete. Pain radiated through her shoulder, echoing in her head.

"Fucking fabulous. Your goons found us." Archer was at her side in a flash.

The whir of a saw continued to snarl through the room. Voices echoed on the other side of the door. Voices that sounded even more hostile than Archer's.

"Hold still."

Something cold pressed against her ankle, followed by pressure and release.

Zip ties. Not handcuffs. He'd zip-tied her to the fucking chair.

He cut the tie from her other leg, grabbed her arm, and hauled her to her feet. The room spun. The cement was cold against her bare toes but solid. Shoving her around, he reached for her arms, bound at her back. "If you're lying to me again, Eve, I swear to God this will pale in comparison to what I'll do to you."

The cuffs released from her wrists and clattered against the floor. The roar of the saw cut off, and a banging sounded from the direction of the door. As if whoever was out there was about to blow into the room.

Fuck that.

The need to escape grew to exponential levels. But the here and now overrode her flight response. As soon as she was free, Eve whipped around and plowed her fist into Archer's jaw. "That's for threatening me, you bastard."

He stumbled back a step. She hauled off and kicked him as hard as she could in the thigh of his good leg. His weight went out from under him, and he dropped to the floor with a grunt.

Temper boiling, she leaned over and added, "And that's for drugging me, you son of a bitch."

chapter 4

He'd underestimated her. While that thought pissed Zane off, the reality of what was bearing down on them overrode his need to retaliate.

He rolled to his side and pushed up on his hands. Ground his teeth against the pain throbbing in his leg. Eve's hands yanking on his arm surprised him more than if she'd hauled off and kicked him in the head just for the fun of it.

"Dammit, hurry your ass up, Archer. They're going to be in here any second."

They. Whoever the hell was after her. Which, considering her associations, were likely al-Qaeda terrorists. Holy hell, he'd dropped himself into a fucking nightmare.

Way to go, dumbass.

He stumbled to his feet and brushed off her hand still pulling on his arm, hating the fact her touch ignited heat all along his skin, even now when he knew what she was and they were about to be overrun.

Shit.

Eve twisted the skirt to the side so the slit he'd cut hit at her thigh and rushed to the window. She muscled it open with arms that flexed to show she still worked out. A lot. Her shirt hung open at the front, but she didn't seem to care. "There's a fire escape. Did you check the surrounding area?"

The drugs had obviously worn off. She was thinking clearly. Why the hell wasn't he?

He reached to the small of his back for his SIG and hobbled toward the open window. Before she got both legs onto the fire escape, he grasped her arm at the biceps, dragging her attention his way. "Don't get any funny ideas, Eve. We're not done."

"No, we're not, are we?" Her eyes sharpened, but she didn't try to wrench her arm from his grip. "Just try to keep up, Archer. If you fall behind, I'm not coming after you."

She scrambled out on the fire escape, feet bare, shirt flapping open, that damn slit in her skirt showing a distracting amount of thigh. Zane followed and pulled the window down behind him, hoping to give them a few minutes' head start at least, and called himself ten kinds of stupid. What kind of dumbass thought he could intimidate someone like Eve into talking? Now he was stuck looking at her toned legs and those amazing breasts all but spilling from her bra, and he was still nowhere closer to knowing who she really worked for.

The door crashed open into the loft at his back, the sound pushing him into overdrive. One glance down and he realized the goons had men on the ground, heading their way fast. He shoved Eve toward the roof. "Haul ass, dammit!"

Zane grabbed the railing, pulled himself onto the roof of the warehouse after Eve, and squinted into the Seattle early evening sun. Eve stood still, looking around for an escape. He rushed by her, snagged her arm, and yelled, "Move!"

They skidded to a stop at the far end of the roof. Across the thirty-foot distance, the other building mid-construction stood like a steel skeleton against the setting sun. If they could get to it, they could escape. The problem was, it was too far away. A tower crane, bolted to the ground, sat between them and the construction site, the crisscrossed bands of metal that made up its tower a good five or six feet out. They could jump for it, but then what? Odds were good the thugs on the ground were already heading to this side of the building.

He glanced up at the arm of the crane, pointing away from the construction site, sticking halfway out over the water of Puget Sound.

Voices grew louder on the fire escape behind them. They had seconds to decide. Zane looked north, to the ConEx containers piled high beyond the construction site at the Port of Seattle, then to the huge shipping cranes and the miles of water. They were out of options. He pushed Eve toward the edge of the roof, hoping they could reach the ground before the other men barreled their direction. "How are your Superman skills?"

Eve's eyes grew wide. "Oh my God, you're kidding, right? You're going to get us both killed."

"I don't see any other alternatives, do you?"

"Holy crap." She wiped her hands on her skirt and then pushed that mass of blonde hair that didn't match her coloring back from her face. "This is the dumbest idea you've come up with so far."

He eyed the thick metal bars of the crane's tower, set at a diagonal. If they jumped and couldn't grab hold or if the metal sliced their hands and they slipped, they'd fall to their deaths.

Shit, she was right. This was a really dumb idea.

"Wait—"

Pounding footsteps and roaring voices exploded behind them. He turned to look. A curse rushed out of Eve's mouth. He turned back and reached out for her, but before he could stop her, she moved back several steps and then took a running leap off the roof, arms and legs flailing as she jumped toward the crane's tower.

His heart lurched into his throat. "Eve!"

For a second, all sound evaporated. He watched her legs kick out midair, her arms outstretch and fingers flex as she neared the tower. Then her scream echoed in his ears, followed by the grunt of her body hitting metal.

Oh shit . . .

He might want her stopped. He might want her to pay for what she'd done to that scientist and to him, but he didn't want her dead. Scared, yeah. Promising she'd clean up her act, absolutely. Making amends for betraying her country, you bet. But not dead. Never dead.

Every muscle in Zane's body contracted. He inched toward the edge of the roof, willing her fingers to wrap around the angled metal. "Come on, baby."

A yelp slipped from her mouth. Her bare feet grappled for footing. Her hands tightened around a metal bar, and the muscles in her arms flexed as she pulled herself up.

Thank you, God.

"Holy *shit*!" Eve yelled. "I fucking hate you, Archer!" Her knuckles turned white as she held on for dear life. "Behind you!"

Instinct had him lifting his gun. He turned just as a man cleared the fire escape, a handgun clenched tightly in his grip. Zane braced the butt of his SIG against his palm and fired. Gunshots echoed in the air. The bullet hit the man in the chest before he could get off a round. Two more rushed the roof, but Zane dropped them just as quickly, just as efficiently, with two perfectly placed bullets.

He waited a breath to see if anyone else came charging up. When the coast seemed clear, he holstered the gun at his spine and then whipped back to Eve. "Watch out!"

Her eyes grew wide. He didn't wait for her smart-ass response, just hurled himself out onto the tower after her.

"Archer!"

Eve's scream mixed with voices from somewhere below. Zane's body slammed into the crisscrossed metal, his stomach and face taking the brunt of the impact. The tower rocked. His hand slipped, and his adrenaline shot even higher. He felt himself falling, tried to hold on. Pain ripped across his right palm. Just when he thought he was done for, he managed to hook his boot on the intersection between two bars and wrap his fingers around a strip of metal. Pulse racing, he pulled himself up until he reached Eve, then just worked to suck back air.

Holy hell. He'd gotten lucky.

"You son of a bitch, Archer. What the fuck was that?" She let go with one arm, then slammed her fist into his left biceps.

A burst of pain rushed across his skin, and he winced. Why the hell was she pissed? He was the one who had nearly fallen, not her.

She shook her hand. "You could have been killed, you idiot."

The fact she didn't seem relieved by that thought hit Zane right in the sternum. And clamped on tight.

"We have to get off this tower," she said.

He gave his head a swift shake. Told himself not to read too much into her comments. The woman had been trained in the art of lying. Extensively. One glance around, though, confirmed she was right. Now was their best chance to get off this damn thing.

"Go," he said, already reaching down with his foot for another foothold. "And hurry before your boyfriends show up."

She huffed and started the climb down, but before either of them made it a good foot, shouts from the ground echoed up, mixing with the unmistakable *ping, ping, ping* of gunfire ricocheting off the tower's metal.

"Up!" Zane screamed, already shifting direction and pulling himself toward the sky. "Goddammit, go around to the other side!"

Eve muttered a curse he could barely make out, but she listened, climbing around the tower to the far side and hauling herself up toward the arm of the crane without looking to see if he followed. Sweat poured down his forehead and dripped along his spine. The metal dug into his hands. His muscles screamed from the effort, and pain spiraled all through his bad leg. When they reached the slewing unit—the gear and motor just beneath the crane's arm—Zane grasped Eve's hand and pulled her next to him.

The goons below had stopped firing and were now pointing in their direction and hollering in a language Zane couldn't make out. He glanced down just as three men took off from the group and ran around the far side of the building, likely toward the fire escape on the other side. One man headed for the operator's cab at the bottom of the tower.

"We're about to have company," he said to Eve. "Come on. All the way up out onto the arm."

Eve let him help her up onto the arm, then waited as he pulled himself up next to her. Once on top, she leaned forward to suck back air and gripped the railing to her right. "Smooth move, smart guy. We're sitting ducks up here."

Yeah, no shit. The arm didn't even come close to the construction site, as if the operator had swung it away from the building at quitting time so no one could mess with the thing. Options rushed through Zane's mind, but the only plausible one solidified when he heard voices on the roof of the warehouse behind him. He grabbed Eve's hand and pulled her with him. "Come on! Toward the water!"

"What the fuck? Archer!"

Automatic gunfire ignited in the air. Eve gripped his hand and ran. A whirring sound echoed, followed by a jolt as the arm of the crane began to swivel.

Holy God, they'd turned the damn crane on. Zane grasped the railing with his bloody hand and pulled harder on Eve's arm with the other. "Fucking run!"

She was right. This was easily the dumbest thing he'd done to date. When was he going to start using his fucking brain like Ryder had told him to do?

Eve pulled back on his hand as they neared the end of the jib, her face awash with horror. The entire arm slowly rotated away from the water. They had seconds before they'd be out over dry land instead of the Sound. Zane gripped Eve's wrist tightly. "Jump!"

"Goddammit, Archer. I really hate you!"

Her last word echoed up as they pushed off, the sparkling water of Puget Sound hovering below. The jib bounced under their feet. As cool air rushed over Zane's skin and bullets pinged off metal at their backs, he said one quick prayer that the water was deep enough off these docks so they didn't kill themselves when they hit.

But before he heard the splash, a burn like the heat of a thousand suns lit up his left arm. Then he was sucked down in a black, wet, ice-cold abyss. Where he heard nothing at all.

Eve came up gasping.

The frigid water cut like a knife, and she was sure her heart had taken up permanent residence in her throat. The scents of fish and algae filled her nostrils, nearly making her gag. She treaded water and breathed deep as she turned a slow circle to catch her bearings. As she tried to clear the cobwebs from her head still lingering from the drugs Archer had given her.

Holy shit, she'd made it. No way she should have survived that drop. Voices echoing from above reminded her she needed to get out of sight. She swam toward the dock, grasped the slimy wood of a post, and looked back for Archer.

The low light of dusk made it hard to see off the water. She should leave his ass. After what he'd done to her, she didn't owe him a damn thing except a swift kick in the balls. And yet, something held her back. Where the hell was he? He should be up by now. Why wasn't he breaking the surface, yelling at her to move her ass?

Panic closed in. She looked up at the crane's arm, stopped now, no longer rotating away from the water. The men who'd chased them up onto the roof hadn't ventured out on the steel themselves, and they obviously hadn't seen her yet. They were pointing down at the water, waving their guns, yelling things she couldn't quite make out. She looked back to the water again and flinched when something brushed her leg.

Come on, Archer . . .

He broke the surface a good ten yards out and gasped, a pained expression across his face.

"Dammit, Archer." Relief rushed through her chest even though he didn't deserve it. He looked like he was having trouble, so she swam out to him, grasped his arm, and helped pull him back toward the safety of the dock. "I thought you were fish food. That was the dumbest fucking idea you've ever come up with."

"Worked, didn't it?"

He hooked one arm around the pillar of the dock and paused to catch his breath. And that's when she saw the blood running down his biceps. That panic formed all over again. "You're hit?"

He glanced at his arm and then wrestled his way out of his shirt. More shaken than she wanted to admit, Eve helped free him from the wet garment, then tied the T-shirt around his arm to slow the blood loss. But her stomach rolled as red seeped into the cotton.

She swallowed hard and glanced up. The thugs had left the roof and were likely on their way down to the docks. Her brain switched to action mode. "We have to get out of this water."

He nodded, his tanned chest rising and falling as he sucked back air and pointed toward what looked like a ladder. "There."

She swam that direction and told herself she was a fool for being relieved he followed. He'd tied her up, drugged her, and then nearly gotten her killed with his Superman stunt. But instead of being pissed, all she could think about was the fact he'd saved her life. He could have left her tied to that chair in the warehouse when those men came in, but he hadn't. Instead of offering her up to save his own ass, he'd put himself between her and danger. And he'd taken a bullet as a result.

Water sluiced off her body as she climbed onto the dock and ducked into the shadows of another warehouse, wishing for her gun. *Don't be stupid, Eve.* Archer hadn't saved her because he cared about her. He'd done it because he still wanted answers. Answers she couldn't give him. Not if she wanted him to live.

They inched around the building, making their way toward the road that led to the Seattle waterfront. If they could get to the tourist area, they could blend in and find safety in numbers. These guys wouldn't gun them down in broad daylight. At least she hoped they wouldn't.

An engine roared somewhere behind them.

Archer grabbed her arm and jerked her back against his body into the shadows of the building. She gasped. Then his wet chest pressed against hers, and there was nothing but her dripping bra separating their skin.

His whispered "shh" mixed with the warmth of his breath drifting over her chilled flesh to heat her in ways she didn't expect. She looked up into those familiar hazel eyes and couldn't help but remember the hundreds of times she'd looked into his eyes when they'd been in Beirut together. Heat arced between their bodies. A heat she couldn't help wonder if he felt as strongly as she did.

The vehicle sped through the parking lot, the sound of tires crunching over loose gravel echoing in the air. Long seconds passed before he wiped a hand down his face and nodded north. "We need to get into the city. They're going to be looking for us. And then you have a hell of a lot of explaining to do."

Explaining. Right. Not if she could help it.

She looked past the shipping yard toward the Seattle waterfront beyond, just now coming alive with light, and tried to think clearly. But her head was too full of memories and missed opportunities and lies that had finally caught up with her. "If we can make it onto a ferry without being noticed, they won't know where to follow."

"The key word in that phrase is *if*. You're not exactly dressed for Seattle foot traffic."

She glanced down at her open shirt, soaked bra, and torn skirt. She'd dressed the part for her meeting earlier today, hoping to coax out as much information from her contact as she could. While sleeping with an informant was out of the question, she'd never been against using her God-given assets to get what she needed. Today, however, the push-up bra and formfitting skirt hadn't done a thing to help her cause. In fact, now they deterred them.

And damn, there was something from that meeting she was forgetting. Something important she needed to remember . . .

Her gaze strayed to Zane, bare-chested and gorgeous, even with that blood-soaked T-shirt wrapped around his arm. Neither of them was dressed for Seattle foot traffic, but she wasn't going to let that hinder her. And she was determined to get them on that ferry, no matter what it took.

She gripped the tails of her ruined shirt and tied them at her midriff. It left her belly way too bare for her liking, but at least her breasts were now covered. "Lack of appropriate attire has never stopped me from getting the job done."

Heat flared in his eyes. A wicked, knowing heat that told her he was remembering the night in Beirut when they'd been locked in that van together, running surveillance on a safe house where they suspected an arms dealer linked to the Taliban was holed up. And without warning, a tingle ran down her spine and shot between her thighs. She'd been draped in cloth that night—as was customary for women in the culture—and they'd been so bored, sitting there hour after hour after miserable hour with no movement, that he'd challenged her to a dare: to see who could break the other's concentration first.

She'd won, of course. She hadn't even needed to remove the first scarf. He hadn't seen her coming. But he'd definitely felt her, especially when she'd leaned over his lap and slid the zipper of his jeans down.

Stupid move. Stupid risk to take in a country that didn't value women. They'd been lucky they hadn't been seen. Or that nothing had gone down at that safe house while they'd been distracted.

If she were honest, she'd admit that night was part of the reason she'd walked away from Archer without an explanation. It hadn't just been about her career. It was about the fact that when she was with him, she forgot what she was supposed to do and gave in to what she *wanted* to do. And for a woman in her position, in some of the places around the globe she traveled, that wasn't just idiotic, it was deadly.

Her cheeks heated at the memory, and a pain she didn't want to acknowledge took up space in her chest.

"Just keep up, Archer." She headed for the parking lot as dusk turned to darkness, careful to keep her expression neutral and pick her way over rocks and leftover construction materials so nothing tore up her bare feet. "And try not to bleed everywhere. That, more than my shirt, is bound to get us noticed first."

"Beautiful," Archer said at her back, his voice low and warm and so damn gruff she felt it all the way in her core, "it's not your ripped skirt or my bleeding arm that'll make us stand out. It's those world-class breasts of yours. Damn things should have a warning label on them. We won't get far with you dressed like that."

An idiotic warmth unfurled in her stomach. That he'd looked. That he'd noticed her breasts at all. A warmth she wasn't going to give in to this time. They'd become unlikely allies for the time being, but that didn't mean they were on the same side. Zane Archer had very clear right and wrong boundaries. He'd never understand or condone the things she'd done, but she justified them by knowing she was making a difference. A difference she couldn't see today but someone else would feel tomorrow.

Or so she hoped.

The smartest move for her right now was to play along, not be confrontational, and then ditch his ass the first chance she got.

Which, for her, was harder said than done. Because regardless of what he'd done, this was *Zane Archer.* The only man she'd never truly gotten over.

"These breasts might just save your life. Watch and learn, Archer."

Zane's arm was on fire, and his leg hurt like a son of a bitch. Somewhere between the top of that warehouse and the bottom of Puget Sound, he'd lost his pain pills, and he was cursing his shitty luck because in another hour he was going to be seriously hating life. More than he already was.

He followed Eve away from the port and toward the pier, the two of them careful to stay in the shadows and dart into crowds whenever they could. They got looks—especially Eve in that Daisy Duke top and obscenely ripped skirt—but Seattle was an eclectic city known for bringing out all kinds. Though every car that sped by on the busy street sent Zane's already-soaring adrenaline into the ozone. No way those goons had given up looking for them.

Who the hell was she working for? She'd disappeared from the CIA a year and a half ago, after he'd caught her playing double agent in Beirut and told her to get lost. Since she'd screwed his mission in Guatemala, he'd been trying to find her, waiting for the moment to strike, but the woman knew how to disappear. She'd only just recently popped up on his radar.

Shit, he should have turned her in back in Beirut. He knew that now—knew it then—but something had held him back. Something inside him that had wanted to believe she wasn't the traitor she appeared to be. Guatemala had changed his thinking for good, though. And now . . . Holy hell, people had likely died today in Seattle—on American soil—all because of her. All because he hadn't been able to do what needed to be done.

This time was different. This time he wasn't letting her get away. This time she'd answer for everything she'd done.

She drew up short on the sidewalk in front of him, shoved a hand against his chest, and pushed him into the wall of a building. "Stay here. Don't move. I'll be right back."

Before he could grab her, she disappeared into a tourist shop. His head was foggy, the pain messing with his reflexes. Just as he was about to go after her, she reappeared and handed him a navy-blue T-shirt that read I RODE THE SLUT (SOUTH LAKE UNION TROLLEY).

"Here. Put this on."

He was still trying to process the fact she hadn't taken off when she helped him drag the shirt on so it covered his wound. "Where the hell did you find money in that getup to pay for these?"

She dropped flip-flops on the ground, slid her feet into them, and then tugged him back into the crowd. "I didn't. Move fast."

Great. Now he could add theft to her list of crimes.

He followed as she quickened her pace, gritting his teeth with every step that sent pain spiraling up his bad leg. Rounding the corner, he spotted Pier 52 and the ferries that linked Seattle with Bremerton and Bainbridge Island.

She was right. A ferry out of here would get them far enough from the city where those goons couldn't find them, but getting on one wasn't going to be as easy as it sounded. Security guards roamed the area, peering into cars, stopping pedestrians. Of course security would be on heightened status after that bombing downtown. He scanned the area, then realized that could work to their advantage.

He reached back for his wallet, but Eve's hand on his arm stopped him. "No, don't. Drenched dollar bills are going to get us stopped, and if those guys figured out who you are, I guarantee they're now tracking your credit cards."

"We have to get tickets."

"No, we don't. Because we're going through there."

She nodded toward the passenger reentry gate on the Bainbridge side of the lot. Two security guards manned the entrance. One was talking to passengers as they passed in and out of the gate, and the other was searching a woman's bag. Beyond the gate, cars were lined up, those of passengers who'd already bought tickets and were waiting to board the ferry that hadn't yet arrived.

"How the hell do you plan to get through there?"

"With a lot of BS and my world-class boobs."

When he shot her a look, she added, "The kiosks don't work, and they don't give out tickets anymore. Security has definitely waned the past few years. Passengers park in line and then wander out because the wait can be up to forty-five minutes. Normally, there isn't even anyone in the booth, but today they're obviously being more cautious."

She'd clearly been in Seattle awhile. That thought didn't settle his nerves. "So how—"

The warmth of her palm against his chest rather than the way she tugged on his shirt cut off his words. "Just play along."

They waited in line until it was their turn, then stepped up next to the guard with the thin moustache manning the gate. Thankfully, their clothing had dried enough so they didn't look like they'd just crawled out of the Sound. Eve turned a charming smile the Moustache's way and waited as he focused on her breasts, squeezing her biceps at her sides, Zane noticed, to push them out even more.

No way the guard would fall for that.

Moustache stared a moment too long and, realizing his mistake, looked up at Eve's face with a scowl. "Stamp?"

"Oh, we didn't get one." Eve's brow furrowed, and she looked toward Zane, then back at the guard. "Were we supposed to?"

"Only stamped passengers allowed back through the gate."

"In all the chaos, someone must have forgotten to stamp our hands." She nodded toward the parked automobiles without looking. "That's our baby-blue Volkswagen."

She rattled off the Oregon license plate number, then stepped close and gripped Zane's bad arm, right above the makeshift bandage, rubbing that delectable breast against his skin in the process. Pain shot through his arm, followed by a heat that felt way too damn good.

"We drove up from Eugene yesterday. We're on our honeymoon. Davey here already got us in a little fender bender and dented the back wheel well when we parked over at Lake Washington to go jet-skiing, and it's going to cost a fortune to fix. We'd hate to get stuck here in Seattle when we have a beach rental waiting for us. We just went to get a drink while we waited for the ferry. Can't you make an exception just this once?"

Moustache frowned, and when Eve let go of Zane and pushed her breasts out again, his gaze dropped to her cleavage once more.

Dumbass. A major bombing only miles away and this guy had boobs on the brain instead of his fucking job.

Eventually, Moustache looked from her to the other guard, then nodded for him to go check the vehicle.

The ancient VW bug was parked six cars in, hard to see among the other vehicles. The second guard jogged over to look, then came back and nodded at Moustache. "Looks like they hit a pole. License matches."

Moustache eyed her again, from her flip-flops to her bare midriff and tied shirt, hovering a little too long on her breasts once more. After several seconds' hesitation, he reached for a stamp from the window counter behind him. "Hold out your hands. And the next time you come through, make sure you get stamped before you leave, or you won't be allowed back in."

Eve smiled a sickly sweet grin. "Thank you so much. You totally just made our day. Right, Davey?"

Zane worked for a smile but knew it came out more as a scowl. If she didn't let go of his arm, he was going to scream. And if that guy leered at her breasts once more, he was gonna pop the bastard in the nose.

Eve tugged Zane through the gate and finally let go of his arm. "See? Told ya."

He wiped the sweat from his brow and followed her out onto the dock. "Your talents are staggering."

She leaned back against the hood of the VW while they waited for the ferry. "Photographic memory comes in handy now and then. As you know."

He did know. It was part of the whole spook gig. "What now? The real hippie owners are bound to show up at any time."

"True, but we're not staying here. We're heading there." She nodded toward a camper RV perched on the back of a beat-up truck in line four vehicles up. "And eventually, we're going for that." She pointed toward an ambulance parked two rows over. "I gotta get that arm of yours bandaged before infection sets in."

Zane's gaze drifted to the out-of-service ambulance, which looked like heaven to him. There had to be narcotics of some kind in there.

He glanced past the ambulance. Guards with bomb-sniffing dogs moved between vehicles. They waited until security moved past the ambulance, then wove through cars until they reached the back of the RV. Lights from above shone down over the pier in the early evening light. Far off in the distance, the approaching ferry grew bigger on the horizon. Luckily, the driver wasn't in the cab yet, but they had only minutes before he or she returned.

Eve slinked around the back of the camper, reached up for the door handle, and whispered, "Yes!" Zane checked to make sure no one was watching, then climbed into the back after her and closed the door.

The camper was musty and dark. A bathroom closet gave way to a kitchen sink on the left. A too-tight table and bench seats sat to the right. Ahead and up three steps, a bed loomed above the canopy of the truck, and thick denim curtains covered the small windows.

Fatigue settled in as Zane eyed the messy comforter and mattress he knew couldn't be comfortable but right now looked like an inviting cloud. He'd been awake going on twenty-four hours, fueled by revenge and adrenaline, and as light-headed as he felt, he knew the blood loss from the wound in his arm was catching up with him. He swayed on his feet.

Eve's hand landed against his chest. "Whoa, big guy. Careful there. Archer? Are you okay?"

No, he wasn't okay. Her hand felt way too damn good, even through the thin T-shirt. And he knew he was seriously losing it if he was reacting to her. He'd gotten over Evelyn Wolfe the day she'd turned her back on America. Had gotten *way* over her the day she'd set his team up in Guatemala. He was only with her now because he wanted answers. And then wanted to see her pay.

I work for the CIA. Counterterrorism.

Her words crept back into his brain, and with them, doubt. She'd been under the influence of amobarbital then. There was plenty of literature to say truth serums didn't work, but amobarbital had a tendency to make people ramble even when they wanted to stop, which was why it was still used. That didn't mean she'd been telling him the truth, though. She'd been trained in the same tactics he had. And she'd convincingly lied to him for months while they were in Beirut. She'd even gone so far as to screw him to keep him from finding out the truth. She knew how to beat the system. And yet . . .

As he stared down at her in the dim light coming through the thin curtains, he couldn't stop hearing her voice in his head. The only words she'd said in that warehouse that had brought him to a stop.

I loved you, you son of a bitch! Why would I try to get you killed?

"Archer?" She looked up at him with those big amber eyes. Eyes that had drawn him in from the first. "What is it?"

He forced himself to look away. Tried to break the spell she was using to suck him under all over again. Failed because he still felt her hands on his chest and wanted—dammit—those hands everywhere. Even after everything she'd done.

"I . . . I need to sit down," he managed. "I'll be fine in a minute."

She shifted so he could move past her to the bench, her body brushing his in the process, igniting heat all along his skin. He ground his teeth so he didn't reach for her and focused on the pain lighting up his biceps and thigh. She bumped into the bathroom door and swore under her breath. The camper rocked.

"As soon as we get on the ferry and the coast is clear," she said, rubbing her elbow, "I'll get supplies from that ambulance."

He didn't care how she was going to do that; he just wanted some relief. And to get his head back in the game so he'd stop reacting to her. Stop thinking of her. Stop second-guessing himself like he was doing now.

"Archer? Did you hear me?"

He didn't look at her, but when footsteps echoed outside the camper, his head came up, and he froze.

"All right," a voice said. A male voice. Just beyond the camper door. "I know you're in there. Open up."

chapter 5

Eve froze with her hand against Zane's shoulder and peered toward the door. Her heart rate jumped, and beneath her palm, Zane went still as stone.

"I said come out," the male voice repeated. "I know you're in there."

Eve glanced quickly around the small camper. There was no other exit. The windows were too small to climb through, and in the middle of all these cars, they'd never escape without being seen.

"Fuck me," Zane mouthed.

Perspiration dotted Eve's forehead, and her adrenaline surged. She was not going down like this, minutes to freedom. She squeezed Zane's shoulder.

"Payton," the man said, "if I have to come in there after you, I won't be smiling."

Payton? Eve's gaze darted to Zane. His confused expression mirrored her own. Muffled giggling echoed from the front of the truck, followed by heavy footsteps moving around the vehicle, then the cab door opening.

"I told you to stay with me," the man said. "Don't run off again, or I'll put you down for a nap in the back of the camper."

More giggling echoed from the front of the vehicle, followed by a small voice exclaiming, "I win at hide-and-seek!"

"I hate hide-and-seek," the man mumbled. Then louder, "Move over, Freckles. The ferry's about to load."

The kid clapped wildly, then the car door slammed shut, and the truck roared to life.

Eve released the breath she'd been holding. When Zane moved over on the bench, Eve eased onto the seat next to him. Heat immediately enveloped her, followed by the sweet, masculine scent of his skin, and too late she realized she should have sat across from him, not beside him. But when he closed his eyes and leaned his head back against the wall, she glanced his way and was glad she'd sat where she had. He was pale, and blood from the wound in his shoulder was starting to seep through the T-shirt she'd snagged downtown. He looked like he could pass out at any moment.

Worry tightened her chest. A worry he didn't deserve, but which consumed her. She glanced over her shoulder toward the bed above the canopy of the truck.

The vehicle rocked, and what little light had seeped through around the edge of the curtains grew dark. They were moving into the belly of the ferry. They both sat still, unmoving and silent as the vehicle stopped and the ignition died.

A door opened.

"Let's go, let's go!" the kid said in an excited voice.

"Hold my hand," the man yelled. Then quieter, "Your mother so owes me for this."

The door slammed shut, and footsteps echoed away.

Eve didn't move until the sounds around her quieted and she felt the ferry engine come to life. Only then did she breathe again and push to her feet.

"Come on, Archer," she said quietly, gently tugging on his good arm.

"Just want to sit here."

"I know. But I think you'll like this better."

It took a lot of coaxing to get him to his feet, and when she did, he swayed. "Whoa," Eve muttered, placing a hand against his chest, another around his back to hold him upright. Heat seeped from him into her, penetrating her skin, warming places she didn't want to remember had gone cold. "Don't fall."

"I'm not gonna fall," he groused. "Just . . . tired."

She helped him up the three small steps, and when his head hit the ceiling, she bit her lip to keep from laughing.

"Son of a bitch," he muttered, rubbing the spot. "This is the worst fucking day ever."

"Tell me about it." Eve knelt up on the mattress above the cab. "Watch your head. The ceiling's low."

"Now you tell me."

Yeah, he was a breath of fresh air, this man. She should totally ditch his ass, but she couldn't. At least not until she got him out of Seattle.

He grunted and grumbled as he got situated on the mattress, and when he was finally lying on his back, he breathed out a long sigh. "I'm just . . . gonna close my eyes for a minute."

Eve looked down at him and had a memory flash. Of him sound asleep on his cot in Beirut. Of her slinking into his room in the middle of the night when Carter had been on watch and thought both of them were catching a few winks. Of stripping him of his pants and taking him into her mouth. And the satisfied groan that had echoed from his chest when he'd finally awakened.

Her chest grew tighter, and she turned quickly away, hating the lump forming in her throat. "I'm getting something to close your wound. I'll be right back."

"Don't go far, Evie," he slurred. "We're not . . . done."

No, they weren't done. Eve blinked back the sting behind her eyes and drew a deep breath. They'd never truly be done, at least not for her.

A quick scan of the camper gave her nothing useful. In a cabinet, she found a metal coat hanger and a screwdriver and figured that would have to do. The car deck was empty of people when she stepped out of the RV and softly closed the door at her back. Just rows and rows of empty vehicles. Breathing easier, she maneuvered through the lanes until she came to the ambulance.

Her heart rate ticked up, but relief filled her chest. The ambulance was old, which meant it likely didn't have an alarm system. She moved around the passenger side and peered inside the window. Then jerked back.

One lone EMT sat in the driver's seat, reading a book.

Shit. *Shit . . .*

Eve's mind spun, and she bit her lip, contemplating. The coat hanger trick was never going to work now.

Quietly, she peeked through the window again. The EMT was so engrossed in her book, she didn't look up. Eve's gaze slid over the interior of the vehicle and locked on the fob hanging from the key ring. A remote locking system she could work with.

She moved back to the camper and gently eased the door open.

Archer pushed up on his elbows and peered in her direction. "That was fast."

Dammit, he was just as handsome as ever—more so now, all rumpled from their run across the waterfront and scruffy from days without shaving. She faltered coming up the two steps into the camper, and more questions raced through her mind, but these had nothing to do with what she needed to do next. They had only to do with him—where he'd been this last year, what he'd been doing, and with whom.

She knew his background, not because he'd told her long ago in Beirut, but because she'd investigated him thoroughly before being stationed there. His father had never really been in his life. His mother had come from old Southern money. He'd been raised primarily by his mother and maternal grandparents in Savannah, though his mother had instilled a strong work ethic in him and taught him what it meant to be successful without the help of her parents' wealth. He had no siblings, had excelled in school, and in the summers, instead of hanging out on his grandparents' estate with his friends, he'd manned the register in his mother's small bookstore. He'd gone to college on an academic scholarship, and after graduating from Duke University at the top of his class, he'd joined the CIA.

Their backgrounds weren't the same, but their single-minded focus on success was. He was a lot like her, she realized now. A loner who'd been more fixated on his career than on marriage. And maybe that's why she'd been drawn to him from the start. Because with him she'd felt a compatibility—a closeness she hadn't felt with anyone since Sam. With him she'd been able to push aside memories of the past and everything she'd lost the day Sam had died and just focus on the moment. And with him she'd started to feel again.

But that *feeling* had only gotten her into trouble, hadn't it? Just like it was threatening to do here, by making her wonder who he'd turned to after he'd been injured in Guatemala and who warmed his bed at night now.

Off-limits . . .

She gave her head a swift shake. Even if he didn't hate her guts, he would forever be off-limits, and she needed to remember that fact before she did or said something to make this entire situation worse.

She closed the door slowly at her back. "We have a slight hiccup. I'm going to need your help to get past it."

His hazel eyes narrowed in speculation. "What kind of hiccup?"

"A pretty blonde, from what I can see. About five foot eight and one hundred and thirty pounds. Should be no problem for you, Superman."

Zane stood in the shadows at the rear passenger side of the ambulance and swiped the sweat from his forehead. He'd let Juliet—correction, *Eve*—talk him into this only because he wanted the narcotics on that vehicle. Not because he was letting her run the show.

Superman . . . He sorta liked that she'd called him that. He couldn't remember the last time he'd been anyone's hero.

He ground his teeth against the pain in his shoulder and the stupid thoughts running through his head. No way was he giving her any kind of control over where they went or how they got there, and he definitely wasn't letting her get under his skin. She wanted to be all cute and sassy? Well, tough. She was still his prisoner whether she thought so or not.

Reaching for his cell phone from his pocket, he pulled it out and then frowned at the blank screen. No sense turning it on right now. The insides were probably waterlogged. He'd need to pick up a new one soon.

A tapping echoed from the far side of the ambulance. Zane shoved the phone back in his pocket and went still.

"May I help you?" The EMT's question to Eve drifted through the open door.

"I'm sorry to bother you," Eve said in her sweetest voice. "The lock on the trunk of our Honda keeps sticking, and my boyfriend hurt his hand trying to get it open. I was wondering if maybe you could come help me. He's bleeding."

Fabric rustled, followed by boots hitting the car deck. Seconds later, the back end of the ambulance swung open, triggered by remote. "Show me where," the EMT answered.

Well out of view of the driver side door, Zane darted into the back of the vehicle.

A muffled grunt echoed from outside, and the locked storage cabinet in the ambulance popped open, indicating Eve had hit the fob.

"Be fast," Eve hollered from beyond the ambulance wall. "You've got about nine seconds before she wakes up."

Perspiration slid down Zane's spine. Pain radiated from both his injured arm and leg. The sleeper hold worked wonders at immobilizing and knocking a person out, but the effects lasted mere moments. He thanked his shitty luck for remote locking mechanisms.

He pulled the tub in the compartment open and pawed around until he found the vials. Then nearly cheered when he discovered it was Dilaudid and not morphine. After grabbing four vials, he swiveled and opened a drawer. Grasping whatever bandages he could wrap his hand around, he shoved the drawer closed with his hip, closed the narcotics compartment, and darted out of the back of the ambulance.

He paused in the shadows on the passenger side of the ambulance, hidden behind the back door, and breathed deep. The pain in his shoulder and leg throbbed, but he pushed it from his mind and waited.

"Miss?" Eve said. "Miss? Are you okay?"

"Wh-what happened?" the EMT responded in a dazed voice.

"I don't know. You were about to help me with my friend, but you passed out as soon as you got out of the ambulance."

Zane fought from smiling. The sleeper hold shut down blood flow to the brain, which left a person with memory gaps, and as he remembered, Eve was good at administering it. He'd been on the receiving end of it a few times when they'd been killing time, sparring in Beirut. This poor girl would never know what hit her.

When he heard shuffling, he darted around a parked car so he'd be out of the view of the ambulance's mirrors.

"Here," Eve said. "Why don't you sit down? You don't look so good."

"I'm . . . I'm fine," the EMT replied. "Wow. That was weird. I don't remember anything except getting out of the vehicle."

"You could have low blood pressure. You might want to get that checked."

Zane found it mildly ironic that Eve was giving the EMT medical advice, but then, Eve had always been confident in everything she did. The woman could fake it with the best of them. His lips turned to a frown when he thought about how she'd used those incredible acting skills to play him from the start. And that only reminded him of just why they were here in the first place.

He waited while Eve helped the EMT around the back of the ambulance so she could sit. From his position, he couldn't see much of the EMT except her boots perched on the bumper. But he could see Eve, standing next to the open back doors, looking concerned and . . . stunning in that ridiculous outfit and wild blonde hair.

Blondes had never really been his type, but at the moment he wouldn't mind taking that one for a test drive.

Dammit. He ground his teeth when he realized where his fucked-up thoughts were going. She still got to him, after all this time. Even after everything she'd done. But he wasn't a moron. People had died because of her. *He'd* almost died because of her. And he wasn't about to forget that.

I loved you, you son of a bitch! Why would I try to get you killed?

She hadn't been telling the truth. She couldn't have been. A person like Eve didn't know how to love. And he wasn't falling for her fiction even if she was helping him right now.

"Do you want me to get someone?" Eve asked the EMT. "Do you have a partner deckside?"

"No." The EMT lifted a hand toward her head. "No, I'm fine. I—wait. Didn't you say your friend was hurt?"

"He is, but you're in no shape to help him right now. Though if you have some bandages or gauze so I could cover his wound until we dock, I'd appreciate it."

"Sure. Yeah. I can do that for you. Um, bandages are in here."

Eve disappeared into the back of the ambulance with the EMT, and Zane used that as his chance to get away. Staying low, he maneuvered back around cars until he came to the RV. Quietly, he opened the door and slid inside. Dropping the materials on the small table, he pulled the needle guard from the shot, tugged down his pants, and injected the solution into his hip.

Relief would come slowly, but faster than with his pills. And maybe it made him a wuss, but he didn't care. Between the pain in his arm from that gunshot wound and the perpetual burn in his leg from all the scar tissue, he needed some relief right now.

He dropped onto the bench, leaned his head back against the wall, and closed his eyes while the drug began to work. Minutes later, Eve tapped on the door and pulled it open. The scent of peaches reached him, and he drew it in, remembering the hundreds of other times he'd taken that scent in with his eyes closed. Just before she'd touched him, or kissed him, or straddled his lap and ridden him to oblivion.

"Looks like my plan worked." Paper rustled as she dropped supplies on the table. "The EMT gave me extra bandages. Now take off your shirt so I can get at that wound. We don't have a lot of time."

He grunted as he tugged his shirt up and off. Eve's soft fingers landed against his skin, helping him, sending tiny shivers of awareness all through his body. He leaned his head back against the wall again and closed his eyes while she knelt next to his seat and cleaned the wound, afraid that if he looked, he might not be able to look away. And if he saw her on her knees in front of him . . . forget it.

"This isn't as bad as I thought." She packed the wound with gauze, then began wrapping his arm in bandages. "You were lucky."

Zane huffed. "Luck and I are not good friends. You're proof of that."

Eve's hand stilled against his arm, and when he opened his eyes, curious as to why she'd stopped, he faltered because he couldn't read the emotion lurking in her amber gaze.

Guilt? Remorse? Regret? He couldn't be sure which. But something was there. Something he wasn't sure he wanted to see.

"I know you don't believe me, Archer," she said in a quiet voice, "but I wasn't lying to you earlier."

Quietly, she went back to wrapping his arm, and as Zane stared at her, he took in the stubborn set of her jaw, the lock of white-blonde hair that fell across her creamy cheek, the way her long eyelashes curled outward from her deep amber eyes. He'd been with a lot of women in his life, but she was the only one who'd stuck with him, and he wasn't sure why. It wasn't just because of her beauty—though she had that hands down over all the others he'd dated. No, she was forever engrained in his mind because of her brains and wit, and because during one of his most miserable assignments, she'd been his shining ray of light. Until she'd been his darkness.

"No, I don't believe you." He tore his gaze away from her mesmerizing face and looked back at the bandages on the table, only mildly concerned they were blurring against the fake wood. More than anything, he hated that feeling in his chest, those pinpricks of doubt that were growing sharper. She was a traitor, and he needed to remember that fact. Not get lost in her all over again like she obviously wanted him to do. "And this isn't the time to get into it. The ferry's about to dock, and we need to get out of this RV before Boy Wonder and his dad come back."

Sighing, she finished wrapping his arm, then pushed to her feet. "You've changed, you know that?"

His gaze shot to her. "*I've* changed? That's rich, sweetheart. I'm still the same guy I was in Beirut. I just wised up to your game."

She crossed her arms over her chest and glared down at him. "Not everything's black-and-white, Zane. Sometimes there are shades of gray. But you're too bullheaded to see them."

"The only gray I see is you trying to color the situation so I'll drop my guard around you." He pushed to his feet, needing his height advantage so he could intimidate her. Which was a lame idea because Evelyn Wolfe was never intimidated by anyone.

He swayed on his bad leg and caught himself with a hand on the back of the bench seat before he went down.

"Zane—"

He pulled away from her reach, knowing if she touched him he might forget what was at stake here. The RV swirled in front of him. *Son of a bitch.* Either that dose of Dilaudid was too strong, or he was seriously weak from the loss of blood.

Gripping the back of the bench seat, he said, "Once we get off this boat, I'm calling Carter, and you're turning yourself in."

Her face drained of all color, and she dropped her arms. "The hell I am."

"The hell you aren't."

"Archer—Zane," she said more softly, "I wasn't responsible for that bombing in Seattle."

He pushed past her and peered through the curtain toward the car deck beyond. "My gut says otherwise."

"Your gut is as bullheaded as your brain."

"It might be, but it's not falling for your shit anymore." He pushed the door open. "Come on. People are starting to come back down. We need to go topside."

She didn't move, and as he stepped outside the RV, he realized if she wanted to kick his ass and run, she could do it now, no problem. He was weak, in pain, and not operating on all cylinders, and she was clearly none of the above.

He glanced over his shoulder. She stood in the doorway of the RV, staring at him, that white-blonde hair like a halo around her head, and those emotions he didn't want to acknowledge reflecting deeply in her rich amber eyes again. But there was also something else lurking in her gaze now. Something that tightened his chest like a drum and made him wish he'd never looked back.

Something that seemed a lot like fear.

"Archer," she said quietly, "if you were smart, you'd let this go. You'd let me go. You left the CIA for a reason. You don't want to be involved in this."

He steeled himself against the sudden burst of tenderness he felt in his chest and reminded himself that retribution was all that mattered. "You made me a part of this the day you sabotaged my mission in Guatemala. Sorry, sweetheart, but you're not going anywhere but where I say."

chapter 6

Eve looked over the display of fish antibiotics toward Archer on the other side of the small pet store where he was tinkering with his waterlogged cell phone.

The ferry had docked on Bainbridge Island, and they'd stepped off without anyone looking twice at them. She'd been a little nervous about the deck cameras, but the Mariners cap and oversized sweatshirt she'd snagged from the back of the RV hid her from view. And the fact that Zane's phone was dead put a little of her anxiety to rest, knowing he couldn't call anyone this minute. But right now she was focused on making sure that wound in his shoulder didn't get any worse. The light jacket he'd found in the RV's closet covered the bandages on his upper arm, but she was worried about infection setting in, even if he wasn't.

She looked back at the choices in front of her and wished—again—that she wasn't so damn gullible. Yeah, she could have gotten away from Archer at any time, but the way he kept swaying on his feet wouldn't let her. It was because of her he'd been shot. Because of her he was now weak and pale. She was still pissed at him for the way he'd treated her in that warehouse, but before she ditched him for good, she needed to make sure he didn't pass out or—God forbid—die because of her.

The key was getting him someplace he could get off his feet. He still had his wallet, and she hoped he had enough cash for a motel room, because she didn't want to risk using a credit card, even if it was his.

Grabbing a bottle of erythromycin tablets, she rounded the end aisle and headed in his direction. A bell above the door jangled, and a rumpled woman in her midfifties with salt-and-pepper hair rushed in and headed for the front counter.

"Mabel," the sixty-something man behind the counter said, looking away from the wall-mounted TV where coverage of the explosion in downtown Seattle was replaying. "Are you okay? You weren't in the city today, were you?"

Mabel waved a finely manicured hand. "Nothing like that. Just frustrated. This mess in Seattle is already eating into my business. I just had a cancellation on the Walker Road home. They're shutting the ferry system down tonight, and the renters have decided it's too much of a hassle to drive all the way down to Tacoma then up and around for their vacation." She sighed. "I hate these damn terrorists. First Boston and now us."

"Sorry to hear that," the clerk said. "Tourism here's gonna take a big hit because of this."

Mabel frowned. "Any update on the victims?"

"No." The clerk crossed his sun-freckled arms and looked back at the screen. "Fifteen so far sent to the hospital. But they're not listing fatalities yet. Supposed to have a press conference at nine."

"Such a bad day." Mabel sighed again. "I need a couple bags of Pro Plan for Millicent. That dog is going to put me in the poorhouse, I swear."

Eve's stomach clenched, and she tuned out the conversation, not wanting to hear too many details about the bombing. If she did, she'd get lost in them and forget what she needed to do next. And right now all she could focus on was getting Zane settled, then disappearing and calling her department chief at Langley to let him know what she'd seen this afternoon.

She paused at the end of the aisle and had a memory flash. Of sitting in that outdoor café in the city, of her contact looking familiar and smug and victorious. Of a cell phone he'd passed to her, the image on the screen . . .

The image on the screen of *what*?

Her brow furrowed, and she tried to remember what he'd shown her, but she couldn't. The only other thing she remembered was the explosion that had knocked her off her feet and sent her sailing. Then waking up to Zane's familiar voice.

"You look about as pale as I feel," Zane muttered.

His words snapped her out of her trance, and she shook off the strange feeling trying to suck her under. "Just tired. Some asshole drugged me earlier." When he glanced her way with a raised brow, she straightened her spine and sighed. "Look, I've got a bead on a place we can rest."

"I don't need rest." He grasped a bag of zip ties from the shelf.

She eyed the bag in his hand, then plucked it out of his grip and set it back on the shelf. "Don't even think about it, Archer. And if you don't want to rest, fine. I will. You can continue to be a jackass. It's a vacation rental that's not being used."

"How did you come by this info?"

She pointed over her shoulder with her thumb. "That woman's a rental agent. She's bitching about the status of her business, thanks to what happened in Seattle." When he glanced toward the counter and didn't say anything, Eve added, "Look, whatever you plan to do with me can wait until we both have a chance to regroup. Carter will still be there in the morning, and odds are he's so busy with fallout from the bombing right now, you won't be able to get through to him anyway."

He stared at her, and in his dark eyes, she couldn't read his thoughts. Did he believe her? Did he think she was lying? Or did he not really plan to turn her over to Carter like he'd said?

Unease filtered through her stomach. The dark Archer, the one who wanted revenge, who'd tied her to that chair and slowly cut away her clothing, was still in there. She could see it in the flash of distrust in his eyes. But the one she remembered, the one who'd freed her when they'd been found, who'd been worried about her safety on that roof, who'd made love to her so slowly and thoroughly in Beirut, was also in there. And he was the one she needed to draw out if she planned to get away from him with no drama.

"Where?" he asked in a low voice.

Victory pulsed in her veins. "I'm not sure. But it can't be far. I know the street name. We just need to find a pay phone and look at a map."

He glanced at the bottle in her hand. "You're not planning to poison me, are you?"

"Only if my luck's improved." He frowned, and she felt her spirits lifting. "Relax, Sawyer. Fish diseases are treated with human antibiotics. The only thing they lack is a prescription."

"Running an aquarium these last few years between leaking national security secrets?"

"No, I read it in a book." She checked her temper. He obviously hadn't reconsidered his first opinion of her, though why she thought he might left her feeling like an idiot. "A hot and steamy Joan Swan novel. You should try one. You might learn a thing or two about women by reading romance novels."

She turned for the counter, and he snorted at her back like he didn't agree. "Romance was never my problem. Trust? Yeah. Thanks to you."

He was right. Romance had definitely never been his problem. When Zane Archer turned on the loving, he could make a woman go weak at the knees. Thank God she wasn't in any danger of having that happen.

"Don't get any smart ideas about running," he mumbled at her back.

Eve tamped down the urge to show him just what kind of smart ideas she really had. God, he was a jackass. She shouldn't be helping him. What the hell was she doing? Then, from the corner of her eye, she noticed his limp.

He masked it well, but she could tell his leg was bugging him. Her mind flicked back to the empty syringe she'd found on the table in the back of the RV. He was supposed to be looking for antibiotics in the back of that ambulance, not narcotics, but when she'd first seen the syringe, she'd assumed he'd snagged it for his shoulder. Now she rethought that assessment and wondered if it was really his leg that was causing the most pain. A stab of guilt rushed through her when she thought of him injured in that raid in Guatemala.

She forced back the "if only" closing in. Her whole life was a combination of "if only" this and "if only" that. If only she'd convinced Sam not to get on that plane . . . If only her life hadn't been flipped upside down because of that night . . . If only she hadn't been assigned to that house in Beirut . . . If only she hadn't met Zane . . .

She shook off the thoughts as she waited next to Zane and he paid for their items. She'd learned long ago that playing the "if only" game did no good. All it would do was leave her wishing for a past she couldn't change, and she needed to keep her wits about her if she planned to get away before she put Zane's life in more danger.

Darkness had settled in by the time they stepped out of the pet shop. Spotting a pay phone, Eve pushed down her excitement so it wouldn't show. For the first time in hours, she had hope that things were finally going her way.

She grasped Zane's sleeve, tugging him after her. Once they got to Walker Road, she'd be home free.

At least she hoped she would be.

NO SERVICE.

Zane frowned at his cell phone, then powered it off. He'd been surprised when it had popped on, but little good it did him without a signal.

He shoved the phone in his pocket and glanced toward Eve, busy at work on the back-door lock of the rental house. Finding the place hadn't been easy, but since it was the only dark house on the street, they'd decided this had to be it. And honestly, even if it wasn't, he didn't care. He wanted off his feet for a few hours. After he'd rested, then he'd figure out what to do next.

He watched Eve work the lock and frowned. "Where the hell did you get a screwdriver?"

"From the RV. I found it when you were sleeping. Snagged it just in case."

"Just in case you needed a weapon to jam through my carotid artery?"

She smiled in the dim light. "Something like that. I think I almost have it."

A click echoed through the quiet air, and then the door popped open with a groan.

"Got it," Eve said in a victorious voice.

Moonlight reflected off the peaceful water of Puget Sound, and off in the distance, the lights of Seattle lit up the sky, but all Zane could see was Eve. The set of her determined chin, the lock of hair falling over her cheek, the way her whole face lit up when she smiled. And the longer he stared at her, the stronger the buzzing in his head grew, telling him he needed to park it for a few hours before he did something really insane. Like tie her to another chair so she'd stop fucking with his mind. Or kiss her until she fucked with something else.

Turning his back on the view, he followed Eve into the one-level home. The kitchen was dark, but he could just make out a long island, a small breakfast nook, and to his left, a great room filled with plush furnishings.

Relief filtered through his veins. Three hours of shut-eye. That's all he needed. Just enough time to regroup.

Eve moved to the refrigerator and pulled it open. Light spilled over her, highlighting her long, shapely bare legs, the soft line of her jaw, and her tousled hair, framing her face like a halo. She frowned. "Nothing. We should have grabbed food in town. I can head back and find something for us to ea—"

Zane closed the refrigerator door with a snap. "No food. I just need sleep." He grasped her arm at the wrist and pulled her along behind him. "Come on."

She didn't jerk back on his grip, and he was thankful for that, because he wasn't sure he had enough energy to fight her right now if she tried anything.

"I need to look at your shoulder again before you lie down," she said at his back.

He didn't answer, just found the closest bedroom and pulled her inside. Closing the door with his boot, he tugged off his jacket and tossed it on a chair to his right, then did the same with his T-shirt and pulled her toward the bed.

"Impatient, aren't you?" she mumbled. He set the bag of supplies they'd picked up on the bed beside him while she shrugged out of her sweatshirt, dropped it on the ground, and then began gently peeling away his bandages.

Zane closed his eyes. "I'm a man, darlin'. We're always impatient."

"I remember. This actually looks pretty good. I'm just going to change the dressing."

He didn't want to think about what she remembered. He had enough memories pinging around in his brain for both of them—and most were the X-rated variety. He sat still while she removed the soaked bandages, added antibiotic ointment, and covered the wound again. But his stomach clenched every time her soft fingers grazed his skin, and with every breath he drew, a whiff of that sweet peach scent bombarded him, amping his awareness and sending blood straight to his groin.

"There," she said, placing the last piece of tape over the wound. "Now you just need to take these before you pass out, and you should be good." She handed him two pills from the bottle they'd picked up at the pet store and stepped away.

He snagged her by the wrist. "Where do you think you're going?"

"To get you a glass of water."

"No water." He popped the pills in his mouth and dry swallowed them.

There was just enough light coming through the window to see her exasperated expression. "Wow. What a stud you are."

He ignored the sarcasm and patted the mattress beside him. "Get comfortable, sweetheart."

She sighed. "Look, Archer. I—"

He jerked her toward him. A yelp slipped from her lips just before she fell into his body. Heat immediately enveloped him, but he quickly flipped her to her back, then climbed over her.

"Archer—"

Her warning was laced with just a touch of fear. Just enough to tell him he'd surprised her. And considering nothing seemed to surprise this woman, he was using that to his advantage.

He grasped both of her arms at the wrists and pinned them above her head. Pain ricocheted from his shoulder down his arm and back up again, but he ignored it. Just like he tried to ignore her trim hips locked between his knees and the way the light from the window spilled over her breasts and bare abdomen in that revealing top. "Here's how this is going to work, sweetheart. I'm going to close my eyes for a few hours, and you're going to stay right here beside me where I know you can't get into any trouble. Then, when I wake up, I'll call Carter, and we can both be rid of each other for good."

She pursed her lips and lifted her chin, a clear challenge glinting in her eyes. "I'd like to be rid of you right now."

"Too bad. You're stuck with me." He lowered his weight onto her, let go of one arm, and cinched the zip tie hidden in his hand around her wrist.

"Archer . . . *What the hell?*"

Zane looped the second zip tie through hers, tightened it around his own wrist, and then rolled off her onto his back.

"Oh my God." She sat upright. "You did not just do that. Where the *fuck* did you get more zip ties?"

He yanked on her arm until his lowered back to the bed. "I stole them. You're not the only one who can filch goods unnoticed, beautiful." He relaxed back into the pillows and closed his eyes. "Now lie down."

"You are so gonna pay for this."

He didn't need to see the smoke pumping from her ears to know it was there. He could hear it in her voice and feel it in the heat radiating from her skin. A wry smile curled his lips. "I figure I'm already doing time in purgatory, thanks to you. A few more years won't kill me."

"And to think," Eve snapped as she flopped back onto the bed, "I was actually worried about you."

Zane's humor faded. "We both know you weren't worried. You were just biding your time until you could run. I'm not a stupid Southern hick, sweetheart. Now shut up so I can get some sleep."

"Don't mind me," she muttered, crossing her arms over her chest and dragging his hand with her. "I'll just be sitting here plotting all the ways I can murder you in your sleep."

He chuckled. Now that was the feisty brunette he remembered. "Just do it quietly. I'm beat."

She let out a long, frustrated sigh, but the sound didn't irritate Zane like it should; instead, it relaxed him. And man, either he was seriously losing it, or all those drugs had finally fried his gray matter. Because lying next to his archenemy, feeling her heat, and smelling her soft, arousing scent, he suddenly wasn't focused on revenge. Losing himself in all her softness sounded a hell of a lot better. And more fun. And, holy hell, way more fucking erotic.

He just wasn't sure what to do about it.

- - - - - - - - - - - - - - - - -

The sound of metal scraping metal roused Olivia Wolfe from a restless sleep.

Pushing up on aching muscles, she looked toward the sound. Bright light blinded her, and she lifted a hand to shield her eyes.

"Wh-who's there?" she asked in a voice rough from screams that had gone unanswered.

A silhouette moved in front of the light, but she couldn't make out more than fuzzy shapes, light and darkness. Fresh air seeped into the blackness around her, and she drew it in, afraid it might be her last breath.

"Shh," a voice said softly. A familiar voice. "I'm not gonna hurt you."

Terror consumed Olivia, and she scooted back until her spine hit the cold metal wall.

"It's just food," the voice—the male voice—said in the same easy tone. "You need to eat."

A scraping sound echoed, and nerves humming, Olivia looked down at the metal plate he scooted across the floor.

Her gaze darted up to where he was kneeling, feet from her, but she couldn't make out more than shadows. "Eat," he said softly.

The scent finally hit her. Not filth and metal and mildew like she'd been living with these last few hours—or had it been days already? She had no concept of time—the smell was of something sweet and rich and cheesy.

Her stomach rumbled. She grasped the plate and pulled it toward her. She hadn't eaten since dinner with Karl. And she'd been so repulsed by the amount of grease the awful Mexican restaurant had cooked everything in that she'd barely eaten then. Not that Karl's company had been a whole lot better, but what did she expect, going out with a chemistry teacher?

Carefully, she scooped two fingers into the food and lifted it to her nose. She sniffed, and when the smell didn't repulse her, she brought it to her lips. Then groaned at the taste. Pasta. Some kind of cheesy, tomatoey dish. She swallowed a mouthful and went back for more. She didn't even care that it wasn't something she'd normally eat. It was hot and fresh, and right now it tasted like heaven.

She downed the entire plate like a starving animal before her brain kicked over from nourishment to wondering where Karl was and what he was doing. Surely he had to have told someone what had happened when he'd dropped her off at her house. Surely the authorities had to be looking for her right this very minute.

Her captor chuckled, and the sound was like ice, drenching her heart and soul and mind. She swallowed the last bite and looked up. The plate rattled against her broken fingernails.

"Be sure to drink." He set a plastic jug of water on the floor, then pushed himself to his feet. "We don't want you getting dehydrated. It's almost over. Just hold on a little longer."

He backed out the way he'd come, and then the metal hinges groaned and the door slammed shut with a crack that shook the entire room.

Silence and utter blackness swirled around Olivia like a vortex. Her stomach rolled, and the food she'd just eaten felt like a mound of lead in her gut. Pushing the plate away, she tugged her legs up, wrapped her arms around her head, and leaned against the corner of the cold room while she fought the rush of tears suddenly choking off her air supply. She didn't know where she was. She didn't know who was doing this to her or why. And she had no idea how long she'd be here or if she'd ever break free. All she knew was that she was alone.

Alone and tired and cold and afraid. And there was no one to hear her scream.

chapter 7

Okay, enough was enough. Eve cut her gaze toward Archer in the dim bedroom and clenched her jaw.

The bastard had fallen asleep like he didn't have a care in the world while she sat here fuming and wishing she had a hatchet so she could chop off his arm and get away from all his manly heat.

Anger simmered under her skin as she watched light from the window fall over his bare muscular torso, his bandaged shoulder, and his scruffy jawline. His hair was a rumpled mess, his face tipped her way on the pillow. Moonlight made his eyelashes look longer and his lips too damn kissable.

She didn't want to kiss him, dammit. She wanted to get the hell away from him. Her gaze strayed to the hand of his bad arm resting against his chiseled stomach, then to his jeans, riding entirely too low for her taste right now. Warmth bloomed in her stomach and trickled between her legs. Even in the dim light, she could see the hollow of his hip bones and that dark patch of hair leading south like a giant arrow.

She blew out a frustrated breath that lifted her bangs. She so didn't need this. His body heat was already doing a number on her libido. And having to look at *that*—at something she'd swear was photoshopped if she wasn't staring at it in the flesh? So not what she deserved right now.

Escape. She needed to think about getting away from him before things got out of control.

She looked back down at the plastic zip tie around her wrist and twisted until pain shot up her arm for the hundredth time. *Fucking Archer . . .*

A thought hit, and she glanced toward the nightstand. It was a long shot, considering this was a rental, but maybe the last person who'd stayed here had left something in the top drawer that would help her.

She tried the one on her side of the bed first, reaching carefully away with her free arm so as not to rouse him. When she found the drawer empty, she sighed in disappointment, then scooted back to the middle of the bed. She glanced past him toward the nightstand on his side. One look told her he was still sound asleep, his chest rising and falling in a gentle rhythm. She bit her lip, slowly—carefully—rolled onto her side, and pushed her weight on one knee.

Her hand, connected to his, landed against the mattress down by her leg. She couldn't lift it any higher for fear of waking him. Balancing her weight on one knee and wrist, she slowly straddled his hips, then pressed her other hand against the pillow near his head.

That heat intensified, and his scent drifted in, making her light-headed, reminding her of the dozens of other times she'd straddled him like this. In the middle of the night. Silent so Carter wouldn't hear them. Naked.

She closed her eyes and fought back the wicked burst of arousal coursing through her veins. Escape. She needed to focus on escaping and not the X-rated sex she suddenly wanted to have with the man between her legs.

Quietly, she reached for the drawer on the nightstand. Her fingertips grazed the knob, but she couldn't quite pull it open. Gritting her teeth, she shifted her weight to the knee closer to the side of the bed and leaned a little more.

Her fingers wrapped around the drawer, and she tugged it open. The wood creaked, and she stilled, holding her breath as she looked down to see if it had awoken him. But his eyes were still tightly shut, his head still tipped away, and his chest still rose and fell with his deep breaths.

Relaxing, she reached inside the drawer and felt around. Then cursed her stupid luck when she found the drawer empty.

This so wasn't her day. Wasn't her year either, apparently.

Frustrated, she closed the drawer and then shifted her hand back to the mattress and looked down at Zane. Just her luck he was hotter than he'd ever been. The bastard. She didn't doubt he'd gotten better looking on purpose, just to irritate her.

She shifted to push off him, when she felt something hard in the pocket of his jeans. Curious, she leaned her weight back on her knees and placed her free hand over the object. Then nearly jumped for joy when she realized it was a pocketknife.

Her pulse sped up. Maybe her luck wasn't so bad after all.

Watching his face, she leaned forward and slid her fingertips into his pocket, moving slowly. When he grunted and rolled his head to the other direction, Eve went still as stone. Her heart hammered hard while she waited to see what he'd do. Long seconds passed, and his breathing lengthened once more. Blowing out a breath of relief, she slid her hand deeper into his pocket and wrapped her fingers around the metal object.

His hand landing against her bare thigh stopped her cold. "Hm. Like that."

Adrenaline pumped through her body, and perspiration broke out on her forehead. She pulled her hand free of his pocket and placed it back on the pillow next to his head. "Um . . . I . . . ." She swallowed. "I was just . . ."

His other hand—the one still joined with hers—landed against her other thigh. And heat sparked from the spot and spread straight between her legs.

"Mm . . ." He wrapped his big hands around her hips and squeezed, then forcefully dragged her down to meet his body. "Was dreaming about this."

Oh holy hell. He was hot. And fully aroused. She bit her lip and reached for his hands to try to pry them away. But they were like steel, holding her in place. Then he lifted his hips and rubbed that massive erection across her already-swollen clit, and pleasure ripped through her pelvis and sent a shudder through her entire body.

Her eyes slid closed. She groaned. She knew it was wrong, but she couldn't seem to stop herself from arching into him. His free hand slid up to her breast and squeezed. And she felt all common sense slipping away. Felt her resistance wavering with every rub and tug and sinful grind.

This was why she needed to get away from him. Not just for his own damn safety, but because when she was close to him, she couldn't think straight. Couldn't rationalize things. And when he touched her like he'd done before, like—God help her—he was doing now, she lost all ability to focus on the job at hand and gave in to temptation.

"Mm . . ." he mumbled as he pressed himself against her. "Want to taste you."

Oh God. She wanted that too. Knew she shouldn't but couldn't seem to stop herself.

Her body fell forward. Her weight landed on her hand near his head. The movement caused his heavenly erection to press against her clit from a new angle, sending tiny sparks of electricity all through her lower body. His free hand slid from her breast, up her neck, and into her hair. Then his fingers tightened on her scalp, and he dragged her mouth to his.

His tongue pushed past her lips and into her mouth. Slick. Hot. So very wet. She opened for him, drew him deeper. His plump, scrumptious lips moved over hers just like she remembered. His tongue flicked again and again, tasting her everywhere. Between her legs, he lifted and lowered, mimicking what he was doing to her mouth with his tongue. What she desperately wanted him to do to her body with his hard, thick cock.

"Zane . . ." she mouthed against him.

His other hand slid across her lower back, dragging her arm with it, and she found herself trapped—one hand locked behind her and one barely holding her up. But she suddenly didn't care. She was teetering on the edge of losing control. And it felt good. So incredibly good after all her carefully constructed years of never losing her cool. Of never letting anyone tempt her. Of never giving herself over completely.

His palm spread, and he pushed down against her while lifting his hips at the same time. His thick erection rubbed again and again at the growing wetness between her legs.

"Want you," he mumbled. "Don't want to wait."

She didn't want to wait either. She'd forgotten how good he tasted. How heavenly he felt. How he could light her up with just one wicked touch. One stolen kiss. One forbidden brush of skin against sweaty skin.

"I . . . Zane . . ."

She couldn't hold back any longer. She gave in and kissed him, licked into his mouth, and ground herself against him. And he groaned against her lips, tightened his arm around her back, and lifted until sweet, heavenly pleasure streaked down her spine. She pulled her mouth from his and moaned. And oh, she was close. So close. If he just rubbed a little more, right there . . .

"Shh," he mouthed against her lips. "Don't want to . . . wake Carter."

Her stomach tightened, and between her legs, the sparks sputtered. She glanced down at his half-lidded eyes and the dazed look and realized that he was dreaming. Caught in that semiconscious drugged state when your body reacts but your mind hasn't quite caught up. He didn't know this was happening now. He was reliving something they'd done a dozen times in the middle of the night *back then.*

The heat in her veins iced. He rubbed against her, groaned into her neck. His hot breath washed over her skin, but the pleasure was gone for her, replaced with a tingly prickling feeling that exploded all along her back. One she didn't like.

The need to run overwhelmed her. This time not for his safety, but her own. She was in too deep with him. Losing not only her common sense, but her identity—everything that mattered. The longer she stayed with him, the harder it would be for her to pull away. And she needed to pull away now, because he clearly wasn't feeling anything for her like she'd stupidly been feeling for him. And that made her the biggest fool of all.

She lifted her arm from the mattress and scooted back, just enough so she could reach into his pocket. His cock was hard against her fingers, and she swallowed, even as he ground that erection against her clit again. Tiny threads of arousal speared through her, tempting her all over again, but she fought them. Pulling her hand free, she quietly rejoiced when she drew out the pocketknife and her key to freedom.

"Juliet . . ."

He groaned. Lifted against her. And Eve bit her lip to keep from crying out when those sparks flared hot and wild all over again, arcing pleasure right back through her pelvis.

She shouldn't . . .

Her body fell forward; her weight perched on her closed fist as she tried not to rub against him.

She couldn't . . .

His lips brushed her neck. His free hand found her breast. Desire shot straight to her core.

Oh God, but she wanted . . .

"Zane . . ."

That haze of arousal was washing everything away again, dragging her back down. Telling her it was okay to let go. Just a few more seconds. Just for a minute . . .

She rubbed her body against his. Felt her orgasm rushing close. Ground her clit against his cock, once, twice, three times before she realized he was no longer moving.

"Zane?"

She stilled. Looked down. But instead of the almost-lover he'd been seconds ago, he now lay still and silent. His head was tipped to the side, and his chest gently rose and fell with his slow breaths, the clandestine memory he'd been reliving long gone as he drifted back into his drug-induced stupor.

She fell against him and groaned—this time in utter frustration.

Disgusted with herself, she rolled off him and flopped back onto the mattress, breathing heavily while she tried to cool her sweat-slicked skin. The son of a bitch didn't even budge and obviously hadn't known what he was doing. Dammit—she'd told herself not two minutes ago that this was a bad idea.

Her fingers tightened into a fist, and the sensation of the warm metal object in her palm finally registered. Opening her hand, she stared at the pocketknife and remembered what she'd been trying to do in the first place.

Adrenaline raced back through her body, and she pushed up to sitting and flicked the instrument open, searching for the small scissors.

Victory flashed in her brain when she found them. Carefully, she slid the bottom blade beneath the zip tie at her wrist and cut.

The plastic gave with a snap, and sweet relief filled Eve's lungs. Quietly, she climbed off the bed, grabbed her flip-flops from the floor, and then tugged Zane's wallet from the jacket he'd tossed aside earlier and pocketed some cash.

She paused when she reached the hall, turned, and peered back into the room. Zane was still totally out, his hair mussed and sexy around his weathered face. In the morning she'd be long gone, and he wouldn't know what hit him.

The space around her heart squeezed tight, and she called herself an idiot for the last time. She was done with him. She'd taken care of his wound, gotten him to safety. Wherever he went from here was his responsibility and not her own. But a tiny place inside wished that she'd been able to explain things to him. That he understood. That he didn't hate her anymore.

Foolish dreams. Wishing ranked right up there with "if only," and she was done with both.

She closed the door softly at her back, headed for the kitchen, and turned into the great room. A flat-screen TV sat against the far wall, and she reached for the remote and flicked it on, careful to keep the volume low.

The eleven-o'clock news was running recaps of the bombing. Before she took off, she just wanted to make sure her face hadn't been caught in any passerby footage or that the men chasing her hadn't leaked her identity and blamed the whole thing on her.

Images of the blown-out coffee shop filled the screen, and Eve's stomach tightened when she remembered the child standing on the street corner next to her. *Please, please, please don't list any children among the dead . . .*

Seventeen now listed as injured. No update on the death toll yet, though.

Frustration warred with helplessness while she continued to watch the coverage. Fifteen minutes passed, but she didn't see a speck about her or what had happened on that warehouse roof. Breathing a little easier, she pushed to her feet and lifted the remote to flip the TV off, when Zane's face filled the screen.

"We have breaking news to bring you," the newscaster announced. *"Authorities are looking for this man, Zane Archer, in connection with the bombing in Seattle earlier today. If you've seen him recently or know his whereabouts, you're encouraged to contact officials at the number on the screen. Do not approach him yourself. I repeat, do not attempt to approach him yourself."*

The room blurred in front of Eve, and her legs gave out. She dropped onto the couch and stared at Zane's face in utter disbelief.

All those thoughts about leaving him came to an abrupt halt. She couldn't go now. Not if the authorities thought he was to blame for all of this. Not when she was ultimately responsible.

Sickness churned and swirled through her belly. And for the first time in years—ever, maybe—she had no plan.

chapter 8

Landon Miller stood in the early morning darkness on the quiet, tree-lined street on Bainbridge Island and cursed his dumbass luck for the hundredth time.

He was gonna wring Archer's motherfucking neck when he found the idiot.

Leave it to the dipshit to ruin the first vacation he'd had in over a year.

He thought of Marissa's long, shapely legs and those stilletos she'd been wearing when they'd met. He'd picked her up in a hotel bar, waiting for his principal during his last assignment. She definitely wasn't anything special, but the woman had a killer rack, and he'd been looking forward to locking her in his suite at the Fairmont and exploring her big tits, that tiny waist, and her luscious mouth from every angle during the next seventy-two hours. Now, though, he wasn't sure she'd even be there when he finally got back. And thanks to this mess with Archer, she'd probably already found some other nameless guy to fuck senseless for the next three days.

Tension gathered in his shoulders, and he rolled his head from side to side as he eyed the white one-story home on the banks of the water. The streetlight above was burned out, the drive was empty, and the windows were dark. But that didn't mean no one was home.

His cell phone vibrated in his pocket, and he pulled it out, then glanced down at the screen.

ADDISON: Find him yet?

His fingers flew over the keys as he typed a response to Marley at Aegis headquarters.

MILLER: Not yet. Located his hideout. Cell phone's on and transmitting a signal, but the place is dark. Pretty sure he's in there tho.

ADDISON: Be careful. Ryder's not sure what you'll find inside.

Landon frowned.

MILLER: Archer's a dumbass, not a psycho.

ADDISON: I agree with you, but Ryder's not so convinced. Authorities put out an APB on Archer in connection with the bombing.

MILLER: Fuck.

ADDISON: Pretty much.

MILLER: Ryder busting a vein yet?

ADDISON: Not yet. But it's close. I've got Jake under control. Just get Archer out of there before the authorities find him. It's not going to be long before they connect him with Aegis. Jake has first dibs on him.

Landon snorted. Yeah, he just bet Jake Ryder wanted to get his hands on Archer before Uncle Sam. Archer had been a loose cannon ever since the raid in Guatemala had gone to shit, not that Landon blamed him. That kind of fuckup wasn't one you bounced back from easily. He hadn't been surprised when Archer had fallen off the grid for nearly a year, nor had he been shocked when the guy had resigned from Aegis with no warning. But showing up in the middle of this fucking mess? Yeah, that was a new one, even for Archer.

MILLER: You deserve hazard pay dealing with Ryder on a daily basis, girlie.

ADDISON: You don't even know the half of it. Call me when you've got Archer. And watch your six.

Landon smiled. Marley was a saint. How she put up with Ryder's grouchy ass day in and day out he'd never know. God knew he couldn't do it.

MILLER: Will do.

He pocketed his phone again and eyed the dark house. Thoughts of Marissa's sinful mouth flashed in his mind, but they dimmed and faded when a shadow moved in front of the window.

If he was gonna go in, he needed to do it now, before dawn hit and before Archer decided to run again.

He just hoped like hell he didn't have to shoot the fucker.

Zane was in heaven. The grinding beat of AC/DC's "You Shook Me All Night Long" echoed through his ears, and against his lap, Juliet ground her luscious body and gasped.

He didn't care that they were in a shithole apartment in the worst part of a crappy city. He didn't care that Carter was in the next room taking his shift on watch. He didn't even care what was happening outside these flimsy walls. All he could focus on was the woman straddling him, whispering naughty words, and doing insanely wicked things with her tongue.

"Zane . . ."

He tugged her mouth back to his, slid his tongue along her lips, and then dipped in for a sinful taste. And groaned when she leaned those full, heavy breasts against his chest and reached back to unlatch her bra.

"Zane . . ."

She never called him by his real name. He was pretty sure she didn't even *know* his real name. Which meant this was special. It was . . .

Fuck. It wasn't real.

His eyes shot open. Darkness surrounded him. Silence met his ears. He rolled his head to his right and found the bed beside him empty.

Son of a bitch. He jerked upright and looked at the broken zip tie around his wrist. The arousal he'd just been feeling fizzled and died. *No fucking way.*

He scrambled off the bed and cringed as pain shot up his leg. Grabbing his shirt from the floor, he tugged it on, then hobbled toward the door, cursing himself for being weak. For needing the drugs to cut the pain. For falling fucking asleep. He never should have dropped his guard with the black widow. Not when she—

His bare feet drew up short on the carpet when he stepped into the living room and found Eve asleep on the couch. Blonde hair fell across her face as she tossed her head from side to side, and her muscles were tensed and bunched, as if she were in the middle of a fight.

"No, don't," she moaned. "Zane, they're taking her . . . Have to get them to let her go . . ."

A tightness took up space in the middle of his chest. He knew a thing or two about nightmares, and from the looks of it, she was smack-dab in the middle of a doozy.

Quietly, he moved into the room and tried to decide what to do while she thrashed from side to side. She definitely didn't deserve any of his sympathy, but the last thing he wanted her to do was fall off that couch and hurt herself. Then she'd just be an even bigger pain in his ass than she already was.

Except . . . she hadn't been. Not the way he'd expected. She'd tended his wound and gotten them somewhere quiet so he could rest. In the state he'd been last night, she could have overpowered him at any point, but she hadn't. And she obviously could have run when she cut those zip ties. Yet she was still here. She was still *with* him.

His palms grew sweaty, and his pulse ticked up. He swiped his hands against his jeans and knelt on the ground in front of her. "Eve."

"No . . ." She tossed her head again, all that light-blonde hair falling over her cheeks and eyes and lips. "Zane. Need help . . ."

He didn't know what she was dreaming about, but unease lodged itself in his chest. Carefully, he placed a hand on her arm. "Eve. Wake up."

She jolted, but he tightened his grip. Then her eyes flew open. Wide, fear-filled eyes that sent a tingle straight down his spine. Slowly, those eyes narrowed and focused on his face. "Ar-Archer?"

"Yeah, it's me," he said, loosening his grip but still keeping his arm on hers, just in case. "You were having a bad dream."

She looked up and around the dark living room like she'd never seen it before, then slowly shifted up to sitting.

He eased back on his heels and let go of her, waiting for . . . hell, he didn't know what. Whatever she'd been dreaming about had rattled him in a way he didn't expect. Especially because *she'd called his name.* "Wanna tell me about it?"

"I . . ." She placed a hand against her forehead and closed her eyes, still obviously rattled herself. "I don't remember."

Bullshit. He fought back the frustration. "Do you have dreams like this all the time?"

"No. I mean, yes. I mean . . . I dream about the past, like they told us might happen, but not like this. I . . . I don't know."

PTSD. Yeah, he knew about it. Working for the CIA, they'd both been educated heavily in the aftereffects of an op. He still had plenty that kept him up at night. He just couldn't help but wonder which one was tormenting her.

He ground his teeth at the pain in his leg as he pushed up, then sat on the couch next to her. He held up his wrist so she could see the one lone zip tie. "Should I even ask how you managed this?"

Her gaze flicked his direction, and something uneasy flashed in her eyes before she glanced quickly away again. "Oh . . . I . . . um . . . found a pocketknife."

Where the hell would she have gotten a pocketkni—?

Zane patted his pocket and found it empty. A frown tugged at his mouth just before a memory flashed.

Heat—everywhere—grinding against his cock. Rubbing against his chest. Licking into his mouth in a sinful, suggestive way. And Eve's breathy voice in the throes of passion, saying his name again and again. Warning—no, *begging*.

"Hold on." His eyes widened. "That *happened* last night?"

Eve quickly pushed to her feet. "Nothing happened. Get your head out of the gutter. I snagged your pocketknife and cut the zip tie. Big deal."

She moved into the kitchen, whatever PTSD she'd been experiencing long gone, but he saw the flash of pink in her cheeks. Confused, he followed and stared at her as she pulled the fridge open and warm light cascaded over her body. "Right. Nothing happened. Which explains why I woke up with a hard-on."

She frowned his way, a sexy turn of her lips that only heated his blood all over again. "How you wake up and with what is not my concern."

Understanding dawned, and his eyes grew wider. "You seduced me to get that damn pocketknife."

"I did no such thing." She slammed the fridge door shut and turned to face him. "I was simply looking for something in the nightstand so I could get the hell away from you. You're the one who grabbed me and started getting all hot and bothered. You made it perfectly clear you don't like me anymore, so why the hell would I *not* try to get free from you?"

"I'm the one who . . . ? How . . . ? What the hell does that . . . ?" Words sputtered from his mouth, and then his memory flashed again. Hot, sexy, erotic memories of her body grinding down against his erection, making him ache. Her gasps. Her moans. The way she pushed her tongue past his lips and kissed him—like she couldn't get enough. Like a woman starved.

He glared at her. "You sure didn't put up too much of a protest."

"I'm not having this conversation with you." She brushed past him for the living room again. "Nothing happened. End of story. Let it go, Archer."

No, it wasn't the end of things, and he wasn't letting it go. Because between her calling for him this morning and what had happened last night, he needed to know just what kind of angle she was working now.

"Stop, Eve." He grasped her arm and whipped her back to face him.

"Let me go, you jackass." She pulled back from his grip.

"For once in your life don't fucking lie." He tightened his grip on her arm. "Why didn't you run last night after you got free?"

She slowed her frantic fighting. Her chest rose and fell with her deep breaths, but she didn't answer.

"Tell me the truth. Why are you still here?"

Her amber eyes slowly lifted to his and held. And something like remorse trickled through those pretty gems.

The tightness lodged in his chest felt like it expanded, cinching down his lungs, making it hard to get air.

"I . . ." Her gaze slid from his and searched the room, searching, he knew, for another lie.

He squeezed her arm. "The *truth*."

"I . . ." She exhaled a long breath. "I was planning to run, you jackass. Then I came out here to flip on the news and make sure there was nothing linking me to the bombing when I saw . . ."

"Saw what?"

She scowled. "Your face. On the news. The FBI's issued an arrest warrant for you in connection with the bombing."

"Me?" Disbelief had the blood draining from Zane's face.

"I don't know how they connected you. Someone must have caught video or stills of you leaving the blast site. It's no big deal, though. I mean, we'll call Carter today like you were planning to do, and I'll tell him everything. He'll be able to help. I . . ." Eve's brow dropped low, and she hesitated, as if thinking through something. But before Zane could ask what she was plotting next, her eyes flew wide. "Oh my God."

"What now?" What could be worse than the FBI being after him? *Fucking fantastic.* His shitty luck was turning to pure crap right before his eyes.

"No. Oh my God." She swayed and gripped the back of a chair.

"Eve?" Something wasn't right. Her face had gone ashen. "What?"

"Oh my God. Olivia. They have Olivia."

"Who the hell is Olivia?" Zane raked a hand through his hair. He'd had enough. It was time she spilled the beans. About everything. "Start at the beginning, and don't leave anything out."

"Olivia is"—Eve dropped into a chair, crossed her arms over her stomach, and began rocking back and forth—"my sister. Oh God, they have her."

Wood splintered, and the front door crashed in. Zane and Eve both gasped and jerked that direction. And looked straight into the barrel of a SIG.

- - - - - - - - - - - - - - - -

"Son of a bitch, Archer," the man in the doorway said. "You're in so much fucking trouble right now."

Every muscle in Eve's body tensed, but she was still in too much shock over what she'd just remembered to react. The man dressed in black pants, combat boots, and a black T-shirt dropped his gun to his side and glared Zane's way. He was taller than Zane, his arms and thighs as thick as tree trunks, and every inch of his demeanor screamed military. "Ryder's ready to blacklist you, and the Feds just issued an APB for your sorry ass."

"Tell me something I don't already know, Miller." Zane strode to the door and shoved it closed. "You nearly gave me a heart attack. You didn't have to come in all Rambo-like. You could have fucking knocked."

Surprise flicked over Miller's rugged face, and he straightened. "I didn't know what kind of scene I'd find."

He wasn't a threat. He knew Zane. Not that that helped Eve's queasy stomach. Memories bombarded her. Ones she'd obviously blacked out after the explosion. The image of the purple butterfly on Olivia's ankle in the window of that cell phone. The van across the street from the café. The smug look of victory in her contact's eyes when he'd said, *"Very nice doing business with you, Ms. Wolfe."*

The explosion.

Eve groaned on a wave of pain so intense it stole her breath. She dropped her head into her hands.

"Shit, Archer. What the hell did you do to her?"

"Nothing," Zane muttered. "I didn't do anything to her. Eve?" Panic filled his voice. A panic she didn't need right now. "Eve? Tell me what's going on."

His hands slid against her arms, and he tried to lift her out of the chair, but the pain caused her to kick out and push against him. "They killed her. Oh God, she was in the van when it exploded, and they killed her." Tears burned the backs of her eyes and turned to fury as they slid down her throat. "And I could have gone after them, but you fucking drugged me, you asshole, and I didn't remember until just now!"

She flailed against him, but he held her tight. Tighter than he had yesterday. "Eve, stop. Stop, goddammit!"

Rage turned a blinding red behind her eyes. She wanted to hurt him the way she hurt. Wanted to make them all pay. The muscles in her arms and legs burned from fighting. She'd given up her life for this? No. *No, no, no . . .*

"They didn't find a body in that van," Miller said from somewhere beyond Zane.

Eve stilled and looked toward the newcomer through locks of stupid blonde hair that had fallen over her face. A scar ran down the left side of his face. One she hadn't noticed before. "Wh-what did you say?"

Miller slid the gun into his shoulder holster. "There was nothing in that van except C4 and a homemade detonator."

"Are—are you sure?" Hope bloomed in her chest, and her fingers, curled against Zane's bare chest, relaxed and flattened.

"Pretty damn," Miller said, leaning back against the arm of the sofa. "Ryder's got a contact at the FBI who's giving us updates."

Confused, Eve turned wide eyes up toward Archer.

"Jake Ryder's my boss at Aegis Security."

"Or was," Miller huffed, crossing his massive arms over his chest. "Until you fucking quit."

When . . . ? How . . . ? A thousand different questions swirled in Eve's mind. "You quit your job? Why?"

"We'll get to that later." He loosened his grip on her arms. "After you tell us what the hell's going on and why you think they—whoever they are—have your sister."

Eve could barely think, let alone breathe. But if her sister hadn't been in that van, then it meant she might still be alive.

She turned to Miller. "Give me your phone."

"What? No way."

"Give me your phone," she said louder. "I need to make sure Olivia's okay."

"Eve." Zane placed a hand on her arm. "Think. They could be monitoring her lines. You call her from here and they could trace it back to this location."

Eve's chest vibrated. He was right. But . . . She looked up at him. "I need to know she's okay."

Zane glanced toward Miller. Eve's gaze followed. Several seconds passed, and then Miller sighed and said, "You so fucking owe me, Archer. Not just for this, but for the hot piece of ass I left alone in my suite to come out here and find you. I'll text Marley and have her look into it." He glanced toward Eve. "What's your sister's full name and address?"

Eve swallowed hard. "Olivia Wolfe. She's a . . . a teacher. In Boise, Idaho."

Eve rattled off her sister's address and waited while Miller typed into his phone. To Zane she whispered, "Who's Marley?"

"Just the heart and soul of Aegis Security." When she looked over, he added, "Ryder's right hand. She monitors and runs all the ops. She'll be able to locate your sister, don't worry."

"Don't worry" were words Eve was used to telling others, not hearing for herself. Nerves vibrating, she waited with bated breath while Miller shoved his phone back in his pocket.

"Marley's on it," Miller said. "She'll call or text when she has news. Now," he said as he crossed his arms over his chest, "why don't you start talking, little lady? What's your sister got to do with all of this?"

Eve looked from Miller to Zane, but when her eyes landed on Zane's familiar hazel ones, her chest squeezed even tighter. She didn't want to tell him the truth, especially after their argument earlier when he'd accused her of seducing him to get away, but she didn't have any choice now, and maybe . . . maybe it would be better if she finally just told him everything.

She dropped into a side chair and pressed her fingers against her aching forehead. "I work for the counterintelligence division under Assistant Deputy Director Roberts. My job is to ferret out moles within the CIA so the government can build a case against them. Three years ago, I was sent to Beirut because someone in the Agency was working with a local munitions dealer funding terrorism throughout the Middle East. Someone on our side was trading secrets for money."

When Archer didn't say anything, Eve swallowed and lifted her eyes to his. Doubt lingered in his gaze. Doubt and distrust. And for the first time in forever, she wished she'd chosen any other profession than this one. Because he so wasn't going to like what she had to say next.

"You and Carter weren't the only team stationed in Beirut, Archer, but you were the only one CI was looking at. I was sent to Beirut to take you down."

chapter 9

Zane had to have heard her wrong. "Say that again."

Eve blew out a long breath and dropped her hands into her lap. "You heard me right. You'd been in Beirut for six months, and the shipments had picked up considerably in that time. My bureau chief was convinced your team was responsible. Carter checked out, but you didn't. Several large deposits had been made to your accounts, and your supervisor was already concerned about your dedication to the team. Your record up until then had been flawless, but he'd sensed something was off with you on that op, and he was nervous."

"I . . ." Zane remembered a discussion with his supervisor about his level of dedication, just before Eve had joined his team, but his lack of enthusiasm hadn't been because he'd been looking for alternate opportunities. It had been because he'd finally realized the life of an undercover spy wasn't what he'd expected. At least until he'd met her.

He glared down at her and felt that rolling anger he'd harbored against her the last year begin to grow again in his belly. "My mother died of breast cancer. And a few months later, my grandmother. I inherited money. I wasn't selling secrets."

"I know that now," Eve said. "But back then . . . they wanted you checked out."

"So you lied to me?"

She looked down at the floor. "About my reasons for being there, yes."

No, she hadn't just lied about that. He could tell by the way she wouldn't meet his gaze. "About everything."

Eve's cheeks turned the slightest shade of pink, and she quickly glanced toward Miller.

Fuck Miller. At this point, Zane didn't care what Miller heard.

Miller held up both hands in mock surrender. "Don't mind me. I'm just here to make sure no one gets killed."

Eve frowned.

"Answer the question, Wolfe," Zane said, his patience growing thin.

Eve looked back to Zane and pursed her lips. "I lied to you about the op. Nothing else."

I loved you, you son of a bitch! Why would I try to get you killed?

He didn't know what to believe anymore. She could lie with the best of them, but those words—spoken so frantically and with such emotion—wouldn't leave him alone. His pulse beat faster.

Focus on the facts, dumbass. Not stupid emotions that don't mean anything now.

Zane crossed his arms over his chest. "What about the arms dealer I saw you meeting with? The one we'd been observing for months?"

"He was an informant, helping us figure out which officers were compromised."

That answer was way too easy as far as Zane was concerned.

At his silence, Eve looked up. "My job was not to bring him down. My job was to stop the leak within. Come on, Archer. You know as well as I do that sometimes in this business bad things happen no matter how we try to stop them."

"Bad things?" Zane's control snapped. He leaned forward and gripped the arms of her chair, every muscle in his body tense and rigid. "We were close to nabbing that son of a bitch, and you let him go. And he went on to bomb an entire school and kill dozens of young kids. That's more than a fucking *bad thing*."

Eve's eyes flew open wide. "I didn't know he was going to bomb that school. If I had—"

She was acting again. She had to be. "If you had, what?"

"If I had, I wouldn't have let him walk away."

Zane stared hard into her eyes, looking for confirmation of the lie. He couldn't see it. But he couldn't see the truth, either.

She clenched her jaw and lifted her chin, her own temper finally bubbling to the surface. "Do you honestly think I'm such a monster that I wanted innocent children to die? I live with that decision every day. I wake up to it at night in a cold sweat. Just like I'm going to wake up to the image of that child lying in the middle of the street next to me in Seattle. Don't talk to me like I don't know the cost of the choices I've made. I know them all. And I carry every single one of them inside me."

"Why don't we take a breather?" Miller pushed a hand against the center of Zane's chest, forcing him back from Eve's chair. To Zane, Miller whispered, "You need to dial it down a notch, cowboy."

Zane's chest rose and fell as he stared at Eve, his brain humming with questions and memories he was too keyed up to focus on. She blinked several times, looked away from him, and then drew a deep breath and let it out. He tried to tell himself she was lying, that she was making all of this up, but the wetness in her eyes and the emotion he'd heard in her barely contained voice wouldn't let him believe it. Yeah, she was a good actress, but he'd never seen her fake emotion like this. Not even when she'd walked away from him.

If what she said was true—if she really was with CI—Ryder could get confirmation for him. But that still didn't explain what had happened yesterday in Seattle or what she'd done to his team in Guatemala.

"I'm fine," he said to Miller, pushing his hand away.

"Really? 'Cause you don't look fine, brother."

Zane glared at Miller. "I said I was fine, and I meant it. Let it go."

Miller dropped his hand in a "whatever" move, then shrugged. He stepped aside but stayed close enough to get between them if things heated up again.

And Zane wasn't sure whether to be relieved or upset by that realization. Because he wasn't sure who needed protecting more right now—him or Eve.

Raking a hand through his hair, he worked to cool his temper. "Okay, assuming you really do work for CI, what were you doing in Seattle yesterday at the site of the bombing?"

Eve's jaw clenched. "I was scheduled to meet a man by the name of Tyrone Smith. Recently, the CIA has seen an influx of opium and other drugs being imported from places like Afghanistan. The money exchange is going to fund terrorism. Case officers are constantly being bombarded with opportunities that didn't exist ten or twelve years ago. Anyway, a contact with CSIS—the Canadian Security Intelligence Services—set up the meeting. Smith has connections all over the globe, and through those connections, he'd supposedly come into possession of a laundry list of compromised operatives collected by MI6. I was posing as the front person for a privately funded defense company interested in the information he'd obtained. He'd agreed to sell it to me."

"Did you get the list?" Miller asked.

"No. Smith was being evasive. I got a bad feeling and decided it was time to turn tail and run. Just as I was about to leave, he pushed his phone across the table and showed me the image of my sister bound in the back of what I assumed was the van across the street. He led me to believe she was in there."

"How can you be sure it was her?" Zane asked.

"Because Olivia has a unique purple butterfly tattoo on her ankle. I saw it clearly in the image. I didn't doubt it was her. This kind of guy doesn't play games. He also knew my real name."

Eve finally met his gaze. And Zane's chest stretched tight as a drum when he saw the fear in her eyes.

She looked back down and gripped the chair cushion. "I gave him the money, he called his goons off the van, then he left and I headed for the crosswalk to get to the van and get my sister out. But it blew before I could cross the street. And the next thing I remember is waking up"—she lifted her gaze once more—"with you."

Zane's heart beat hard against his ribs. First slow, then faster with every pounding blow. *She lies. She lies for a living . . .*

"What—" He cleared his throat because there was suddenly a huge lump blocking his words. "What about Guatemala? You knew my team was compromised."

Eve sighed and looked back down at the floor. "I didn't know your team had been set up until it was too late to warn you. Someone in the CIA has a personal vendetta against the CEO of Aegis Security. I don't know why, and I don't know who. I just know he wanted to see Aegis taken down."

Miller looked Archer's way. "Ryder told the State Department to go fuck itself when Aegis didn't get that contract in Egypt."

Yeah, Zane remembered. Ryder had been pissed when Aegis had been passed over for the Egypt job, even though his guys were the more qualified team. That had been a few months before the Guatemala raid. Aegis hadn't originally been awarded the Humbolt contract in Guatemala. It had gone to a different defense contractor, but at the last minute they'd backed out and the government had come calling.

At the time, Archer had been psyched. Especially when Ryder had allowed him to use his CIA contacts to aid with the planning. Now it seemed like one major-ass setup.

"I was in Istanbul at the time," Eve went on. "But when I caught wind of what was happening, I called to make sure you were still alive. Not to gloat like you thought."

"It didn't sound like you were just checking to see if I was alive."

She frowned up at him. "We're talking about a spy organization, Archer. We spy on others, but we sure the hell spy on each other. I'm living proof of that. I didn't know who might be listening on some back channel, so I pretended not to care. I couldn't care, because if I did, who knows how many others might have been compromised. I also couldn't let them know—"

She closed her mouth, and Zane found himself waiting for more. "Know what?"

She clenched her jaw and looked away. Irritation, anger, and something else lingered in her gaze. Something he couldn't read but that caused his pulse to beat even faster. She crossed her arms over her chest. "Know that I'm an idiot. That's all."

That wasn't all, though. There was something else. Something she wasn't saying.

Zane opened his mouth to ask, but the ping from Miller's cell phone cut him off.

Eve's wide-eyed gaze immediately shot to Miller, who was already pulling the phone from his pocket. "Is it about my sister?" She pushed out of the chair. "Did they find her?"

Miller frowned as he stared down at the screen. "She didn't show up for work two days ago. She's been listed as officially missing. No signs of foul play at her house, though."

"Oh God." Eve closed her eyes and turned away.

Zane's stomach churned, and contradicting thoughts raced through his mind.

"There's more," Miller said, shoving the phone back in his pocket.

"More what?" Eve swiveled back to face him.

Miller crossed the room, picked up the remote from the coffee table, and flipped on the TV. A young female reporter's face filled the screen. Followed by a not-too-recent picture of Zane.

In the photo, his hair was short and neatly trimmed, and he was wearing a white button-down and black blazer. An ID badge hung off his jacket pocket.

"Oh shit," Eve whispered.

"While no group has yet claimed responsibility for yesterday's bombing in Seattle, sources confirm this man, Zane Archer, also wanted in connection with the tragedy, is a former case officer with the Central Intelligence Agency. Archer left the State Department a year and a half ago under questionable circumstances."

Eve whipped toward Miller. "Give me your phone." When he only stared at her, she said in a frantic voice, "I need your phone now."

"Who are you planning to call?" he asked skeptically, reaching for his cell.

"My supervisor. Someone leaked Archer's CIA photo to the press."

Zane's mind was a swirl of contradicting information, but Eve's anxiety got through. "Wolfe," he said, more for himself than her. "Take a breath."

She yanked the cell from Miller's hand and started dialing. "I'll take a breath when I figure out what the fuck is going on." Into the phone she said, "Yes, I need you to patch me through to 1-5-7-8-4." She hesitated, then muttered, "My security clearance is . . ."

She wandered into the kitchen with Miller's phone, and Zane let her go, knowing she couldn't get far, too rattled to think straight. At some point, Miller had hit mute on the TV, but all Zane could do was stare at the younger image of himself on the screen, a stupid rookie who thought he'd been making things better in the world when he'd only been making them worse.

Now it felt like the world had just been blown to shit and he was in the center of the fallout. With Eve's words from the warehouse continuing to ring in his ears.

I loved you, you son of a bitch. I loved you . . .

"Dude. You okay?"

Miller's hand slapping against Zane's shoulder shocked him out of his trance. "What?"

"I asked if you were okay. You look like shit."

Zane felt like shit. He rubbed a hand down his face. "Yeah." Dropping his hand, he looked toward the kitchen. He could hear Eve's low voice but couldn't make out any of her words. "Do you believe her?"

Miller shrugged and dropped into a chair. "I don't *not* believe her, if that helps. She could totally be telling the truth. I mean, her story makes sense."

Perspiration dotted the back of Zane's neck. Yeah, it made sense to him too. What didn't make sense was why *he* was being tagged in this mess and not her.

"Why don't you tell me how you found her yesterday and what you've been up to since," Miller said. "Maybe then I can figure out how to help you. Because the Feds aren't the only ones who have a hard-on for you, buddy. Ryder's got one too, and that's not exactly a good thing."

Zane rested his hands on his hips. Yeah, he bet Ryder had it in for him. Before Eve could come back into the room, he launched into how he'd tracked her to Seattle and caught up with her just before that bomb went off. Then he relayed what had happened since.

Miller crossed his hands over his chest, kicked out his legs, and shook his head as he looked up at the ceiling. "God Almighty, but you know how to screw up a wet dream, don't you? What the fuck were you planning on doing with her, man?"

Frustration welled in Zane's stomach. He punched the Off button on the TV and began pacing. "I don't know. I wanted to find out what she'd been up to. And I guess I wanted to scare her a little."

Miller chuckled. "Looks to me like you all you did is piss her off. That woman does not like you. And if what she told us is true, then with good reason."

Zane stopped in the middle of the floor and looked toward the kitchen. Eve was quiet now, but he knew she was still in there. How, he wasn't sure. He just . . . felt her.

His heart beat faster, and a tingling spread across his neck and down his spine, then wrapped itself around his abdomen until it tightened every muscle in his torso.

"Life is tough," Miller muttered. "But it's tougher when you're stupid."

Zane's gaze snapped Miller's way, and Miller grinned. "John Wayne. Smart man. You could learn a thing or two from the Duke."

Zane frowned and was just about to tell Miller what he could do with his smart-mouthed advice when Eve stepped back in the room. Her face was pale, her hands were shaking against the phone, and a dazed look reflected in her normally clear and confident eyes.

"Eve?" Concern immediately spread icy fingers through Zane's chest. "What's wrong?"

"I . . . I couldn't get through. My security clearance has been . . . revoked."

"Shit." Miller pushed to his feet. "They've linked you two together already. If they were waiting for you to call in—"

"No," she said quickly. "They won't be able to track me. I . . . I cut the call before that could happen." She lowered herself onto the couch. "I need to get in touch with my supervisor and figure out what's going on. But first I need to find my sister."

"You're not getting anywhere near downtown Seattle with all of this going on," Miller said. "The entire city's looking for Archer, and security cams on the ferry will link the two of you together soon enough. You two need to get the hell out of the Pacific Northwest, like fast."

Surprise trickled through Zane. "I thought Ryder sent you here to bring me in."

"He did." Miller tugged keys from the front pocket of his jeans. "Call me crazy, but I hate to see a dumb shit take the fall for something he didn't do. Especially when the government's behind it." He looked toward Eve. "I'll find your sister. You two just get the hell out of Dodge and figure out who's behind this, because if you don't, it's going to link back to Aegis, and that'll just fuck things up for all of us."

"You . . ." Confusion clouded Eve's eyes. "How do you think you can—?"

"Miller used to be DIA," Zane told her.

"Defense Intelligence Agency," Eve muttered. Her gaze shot to Miller. "You worked for the Pentagon?"

"Four years," Zane said, answering for him. A surge of brotherhood filled his chest as he glanced Miller's way. He'd left Aegis a year ago without a word to any of the guys, and he'd shunned their attempts to get in touch with him since. But the bond they'd formed, all coming from similar backgrounds, was still strong. It was still there. "Isn't that right, Bull?"

A wry smile curled one side of Miller's lips when Zane used his nickname, but it faded when he glanced toward Eve. "How did this contact get in touch with you?"

"Cell phone."

"Where is it?"

Eve pressed a hand to her head. "I lost it, in the explosion."

"No, you didn't," Zane said. "It's in the loft at the warehouse."

"What loft?" Miller asked.

"Where I took her. After the bombing."

When Eve's shocked gaze darted Zane's way, he shrugged. "I didn't know what was in it, so I grabbed it when I pulled you from that rubble." He glanced back to Miller, not wanting to remember what Eve had looked like then, or how relieved he'd been to find her still alive. "It's probably still there, unless the team that came after us picked it up."

"It's a start." Miller tossed the keys in his hand to Zane. "I've got a truck outside, registered under a different name, so it'll take quite a bit of digging for anyone to find you in it. Just don't get a speeding ticket, dumbass. Come outside with me. Got a few other things you might find useful."

Miller headed for the door, and Zane moved to follow, but Eve stopped him with a hand on his arm. "How do you know he can do this?"

The fear in her eyes was stark and fresh, and it told him loud and clear her biggest concern right now was for her sister. She wasn't lying. All of this—everything she'd told him—was true. He felt it in his chest even if his mind still wanted to believe the worst. "Miller wasn't just a case officer for the DIA. His specialty was finding people who didn't want to be found. And eliminating them."

Understanding dawned in Eve's eyes.

"If anyone can find your sister besides you, it's him. Trust me, Evie. He's your safest bet right now."

Eve dropped her hand and slowly nodded. "I . . . I need a minute to clear my head."

For a second, Zane considered the fact that she might use the opportunity to run. After all, it was his name associated with the bombing right now, not hers. Then he pushed the thought aside. She hadn't run yet, and the Eve he knew—the one he remembered, at least—was smart enough to know when she needed help.

"I'll get supplies from Miller and be right back."

Dawn was just creeping over the island when he closed the door at his back. Miller was two blocks down the quiet road, standing at the open passenger door of black Ford F150. From a dark gray duffel bag, he handed Zane a fresh cell phone and placed a SIG P250 and a Glock 9mm on the seat cushion, along with ammo magazines. "These should tide you over. You got supplies somewhere?"

Zane picked up the SIG, checked the chamber, and holstered the gun at his lower back as he thought of the car he'd parked in Everett. "Yeah, getting to it might be a problem, though."

Miller snagged a piece of paper from the glove box and jotted down a name and number. "This is a document guy I've used in the area. He's in Bellingham, which might be a drive, but worth it if you two have to get out of the country fast."

"Thanks." Zane pocketed the number and the phone. "What about Ryder?"

Miller shrugged. "Ryder fucked my vacation, which caused me to lose out on three days locked in a suite at the Fairmont with a hot, leggy brunette. He can chill it on this one for all I care."

The corner of Zane's lips curled. "No wonder you were so eager to help us."

"Not *us—you*." Miller nodded toward the house. "Watch your six with her. Just because I think she's telling the truth doesn't mean she won't screw you the first chance she gets. Everyone in the spy game fucks everyone else, one way or another. You and I know that better than most."

Yeah, Zane did know that better than most. And with Eve, he was already walking a fine line between love and hate. He honestly had no clue what she'd do next. And that made him more nervous than when he'd thought she was a traitor.

"I owe you, Bull."

Miller frowned. "Sure as shit you do." He handed the Glock and extra ammo to Zane, tossed the duffel over his shoulder, and then slammed the passenger door. "And if I get my ass blown off by some freakin' terrorist over a homely looking schoolteacher, I'm gonna come back and haunt yours from here to DC." He pinned Zane with a look. "Don't fuck this one up, Archer."

Miller didn't wait for Zane to answer. Didn't say goodbye either. Just turned and headed off into the early morning light without another word.

Alone, Zane pulled the cell from his pocket and punched in the number of the one person he hoped could shed some light on this whole clusterfuck.

"Dietrick," a voice answered on the first ring. "Talk to me."

"Carter? It's Sawyer."

"Sawyer?" Surprise registered in Carter's—correction, James Dietrick's—voice. "Is that really you? Holy fuck, man. Do you have any idea what kind of mess you're in?"

"Yeah." Zane couldn't even see Miller anymore. The guy was a like a shadow. Here one minute, gone the next. But that was the way it usually worked with the DIA's best. Right now, he just hoped Carter was half as good. "And I'm calling in that favor. I need your help."

Bracing her hands against the counter in the bathroom, Eve looked up at her reflection and barely saw herself.

All she could think about was Olivia, who had her and why. And every time she pictured Olivia's butterfly tattoo on that phone screen, her mind flashed back to the Agency. To her security clearance being revoked. To the operator's voice on the line when she'd called—too calm, too cool, too collected. Eve knew that was the way they were trained, but something in her gut said things weren't right. This wasn't a technical problem with her clearance like the operator had wanted her to believe. It was a setup, just like the Guatemala raid.

A red haze covered her eyes, and her blood pumped hot.

"Eve?" Archer's knock against the bathroom door brought her head around. "You okay in there? We need to get going."

Eve looked back at her reflection. Was she okay? She didn't feel okay. She felt . . . betrayed. And pissed. And . . . reckless. The years spun in front of her as she stared at herself, starting with the night Sam had been killed. At first, joining the Agency had been an escape from the pain and a way to do something to prevent others from being innocently murdered like Sam, but somewhere along the way—in all the things she'd done to that end—she'd lost sight of the big picture. She'd given everything to the Agency in the name of national security, and she'd kept nothing for herself. And now they were repaying her by blacklisting her, turning their back on her, and setting her up to take the blame for something she hadn't done.

She had not sacrificed her life for this. To be thrown aside like she was expendable. And she wasn't about to let them blame her for something she had no hand in.

"Eve?" Archer knocked again, and Eve's pulse shot even higher. "Come on, open the door. Don't make me come in there after you."

Against the sink, Eve's fingers turned white where she gripped the counter. She didn't trust herself near Archer right now. Not with the way she was feeling. She was already pissed at him for what he'd done to her, and feeling guilty about his getting dragged into this mess at the same time. And every time she looked at him she saw the old him, the one she'd nearly given up her career for. And right now she couldn't help but think that maybe if she had, she wouldn't be in this current mess.

"I . . . I need to be alone right now," she managed. "Go away."

Wood splintered, and the door to the bathroom flew inward, knocking against the wall with a crack. Shocked, Eve whipped toward the opening and stared at Archer with wide eyes. "What the hell was that?"

Archer glanced around the small room with its tile floor and granite counter, then focused on the small, rectangular window high over the shower wall. "Just wanted to make sure you weren't planning on doing anything stupid."

Like running. Her temper skyrocketed. He thought she was going to bail. He still didn't trust her. Even after everything she'd told him.

"Fuck you, Archer." She pushed past him and moved into the bedroom, trying to settle her raging temper.

It didn't work.

"Fuck me? You seem to forget I'm the reason you're still alive, missy."

Her eyes focused on a Glock, sitting on the dresser. One he'd obviously gotten from Miller. She moved toward it. "And how do you figure that? If it were up to you, I'd be in handcuffs. If it were up to you, I'd still probably be tied to a chair in that fucking warehouse."

He stepped into the room and heaved out a sigh. "Eve—"

"You don't want to believe a single thing I have to say." She lifted the Glock and checked the chamber. The thing was loaded. Stupid move on his part. She turned to face him. "You want to blame me for everything. And now I'm your way out. Well, I'm not going in. Not until I figure out who's trying to set me up."

"Set *us* up."

Her eyes narrowed. "What?"

He took a step toward her. "I'm in this now too."

"That's your own stupid fault. I didn't ask you to follow me. I didn't ask you to get involved in any of this. You're the one with trust issues."

His gaze shifted to the gun in her hand. "With good reason."

Power rippled through her veins. "Afraid I'm gonna hurt you, Archer?"

"Evie, you've always been able to hurt me."

"Bullshit. You believed the worst about me from the very start. It never even occurred to you there could be more. Because you only see things in black-and-white. It's why you couldn't cut it with the Agency. Because you're weak."

The anger was roiling now, and she couldn't stop it. Couldn't seem to rein it in either. She'd spent the last year feeling guilty over what had happened to him in Guatemala. The last eighteen months missing him and wishing she'd been strong enough to leave the Agency for him. And for what? To be made to feel like she didn't matter? It was bad enough knowing he thought she was a traitor, but to stand here and see that he didn't care anything for her anymore? It was too much.

"You think I'm weak?" Challenge flared in his hazel eyes. He pulled a SIG from the back waistband of his jeans and set it on the dresser next to him. "I dare you to prove your point. But not with the gun."

Something hot rolled through her belly. Something wicked. Something reckless. She shouldn't. Her emotions were way too close to the surface. But she needed to do something to get rid of this roiling anger and bubbling adrenaline. And maybe kicking his ass right now would do it.

Eyes locked on his, she set the Glock on the dresser next to the SIG, dropped her arm, and stared at him. "You don't want to do this, Archer. You've got a bad shoulder and a bum leg. It's not a fair fight."

A cocky smile slid across his lips. "You're good, Eve, but you're not that good. Even with my bad leg I can still take you."

Beirut flashed in her mind. All those hours locked in that house. When they'd sparred together in one of the empty rooms, just to pass the time. When their wrestling would turn to the X-rated kind as soon as they were both breathless and panting.

Warning flags went off in her mind. Big ones. Signaling this had bad news written all over it. And she'd better wise up and listen before it was too late.

She reached for the gun and turned away. "Nice try, Archer, but I'm not interested."

"I *let* you win in Beirut."

Eve froze. And inside her chest, something pinched tight. "Don't bring up Beirut to me. Don't even mention it."

His hand landed on hers, resting on the gun, and his body heat washed over her just before she felt him brush up against her back. "Why not?" he whispered close to her ear. Too close. A shiver ran down her spine as his warm breath slid across her skin. "Because it wasn't good for you? Or because I was nothing but a job?"

Her breaths sped up. He was using sex against her, the bastard. Making her remember. Making her want. That was a low blow, even for him. "You don't know anything about me, Archer. You never did."

"I know you're pissed about what's happened, and you're too stubborn to ask for help. And I know you don't trust me, which is why you're trying to tick me off so I'll walk away. But that's not gonna happen, Evie. I'm in this now with you, whether you like it or not." He closed his hand over hers and lifted it off the gun. "So go ahead and take your best shot at me right now, so we can get over this and move on with what we need to do next."

"Get over this?" He thought she could *get over this?* Like she'd *gotten over him?* He didn't know what she'd been through this last year. Didn't have any clue how she felt.

Her temper shot through the roof. Before she could stop herself, she shoved her elbow into his gut, twisted, and lifted her knee to catch him in the groin.

117

He grunted at the first blow but caught her leg before she could nail him in the balls. Twisting quickly to her right, she swiveled out of his grip and landed on her bare feet.

"You've been practicing."

She didn't like the condescending tone of his voice. Or the way his hands felt against her skin. Warm. Electric. Alive.

Tempting.

Eve forced back the arousal and stepped to the right. *Remember how you felt in that warehouse. Remember what he did to you.*

Her adrenaline pumped, and the blood roared in her ears, but she was focused solely on him. On his low-riding jeans, his chiseled shoulders, and that smug look on his scruffy, way-too-damn-handsome face. "And you're about to get your ass handed to you."

He chuckled, and the sound was—*fuck*—it was sexy as hell. "You always did like my ass."

That was it. All she could take. She kicked out with her foot and nailed him in his bad leg. His knee gave, and he hit the ground with a grunt. Eve swung out with her arm to hit him in the side of the head, but he caught her wrist in his massive palm and yanked her down. She fell against him with a yelp, but before she could wriggle free, he rolled her to her back and pinned both arms over her head against the carpet.

His chest rose and fell with his rapid breaths. His shaggy hair was a mess around his face. And his cheeks were flushed with both exertion and pain. But victory flared in his hazel eyes when she struggled and couldn't break free. "Had enough yet?"

She clenched her jaw. Both because he had her pinned and because—*dammit*—he felt so good against her, sinking his weight onto her, pressing his hips—*oh shit*—tight against hers. "Never."

She wrapped both legs around his hips, slid them higher to his waist, hooked her feet together, and squeezed as hard as she could.

"Dammit, Eve . . ." His face contorted in pain. She knew she was hurting him, but she didn't let up. She squeezed harder, both to get him to back off and because she couldn't stand being this close to him again. Not after last night. "Gonna make you . . . pay . . ." His grip tightened on her wrists.

She flexed her muscles on her right side, intent on rolling him over. "Try it, you son of a—"

His mouth covered hers.

Synapses misfired. The electrical message from her brain to her muscles shorted out. He dipped his tongue inside her mouth, and she tasted him, like she had last night. Except this wasn't a drug-induced dream. It wasn't a hallucination. And it wasn't the least bit sweet and gentle.

She froze. Thought was replaced by a hazy, thick cloud while he ravished her mouth, while he stroked his tongue against hers again and again and pressed his body down onto hers. Heat brewed in her belly and shot south between her legs where she held him tight, and she realized he was hard. Hard and thick and already rubbing against her in a way that brought every cell in her body to life, making her feel things she hadn't felt in years.

"Stop fighting me, Eve," he whispered against her lips. "I'm not your enemy."

But he was. He always would be. The one person she didn't want to live without and the one she'd never been able to fully commit to.

He tipped his head to the other side and kissed her again. This time without the insane pressure. This time with long, slow, deep strokes that sent a shiver down her spine. She opened to him, took him in, kissed him back as the muscles in her legs relaxed around his waist, and slid to his hips.

"That's it, Evie," he whispered. "Let me in. You have to trust me so we can help each other."

His words cut through the sexual haze coloring everything, and she suddenly realized what he was doing.

Intimidating her hadn't worked. Tying her up hadn't either. So now he was resorting to using her stupid feelings against her so he could run the show and tell her what to do next. Well, she wasn't going to let him. He thought he could use sex to manipulate her? He didn't know what was about to hit him.

She tightened her muscles, shifted her weight, and flipped him to his back. Then she pinned his hands above his head, pulled her mouth from his, and stared down at him. "Do you really want me to trust you, Archer?"

Desire filled his dark eyes and flushed his cheeks. A desire she remembered well from Beirut. One she'd dreamt about seeing again on his face. But not like this. "Yeah, I do."

She leaned forward and brushed her breasts against his bare chest. The movement forced her sex into tighter contact with his erection. Tingles spread all through her lower body. Tingles she wanted to savor but couldn't. "It takes a lot for me to trust someone. I need to feel something for them." She did it again, and she knew he felt those tingles too by the way he sucked in a breath. "You made me feel once. I wonder if you could do it again."

"Eve—"

She flexed her hips, this time intentionally rubbing against his swollen cock. "Do you want me, Archer? Tell me you want me."

"Eve . . ." His eyes rolled back, and he lifted his hips to meet hers. "Yes, I want you."

Anger pulsed through her once more. She tightened her grip on his arms and then pushed quickly off him. "Well, tough shit. In this business we never get what we want. And you just proved to me you're a bigger liar than I am."

chapter 10

Zane's blood ran hot. Before Eve could get a step away, he grasped her by the ankle and flipped her onto her back on the bed.

"What the—?"

Her surprised gasp met his ears just before he climbed over her on the mattress, straddled her hips, and pinned her arms near her head. "Stop, Eve."

She thrashed beneath him, but he was stronger than her, even with his injuries, and all her struggling did was shake the bed. "Let me go, you stupid son of a—"

"Bitch. Yeah, I know. God, you don't know when to quit, do you? I'm not lying to you. I do want to help you, but you're too goddamn stubborn to see it. And if I didn't still want you, I wouldn't have had a hard-on these last twelve hours, and I sure as hell wouldn't have spent the last year trying to track you down."

She jerked against his hold but couldn't break free. "You tracked me down because you wanted to turn me over to the Feds."

"Partly. But I didn't, did I?"

"That's your stupidity, not mine."

His temper flared. "You're right, it is. Because I wanted to know if you felt anything for me or if it was all just an act. You cut me when you left me, Eve. Not because of what I thought I'd caught you doing, but because you turned your back on me without a second look. Like none of it mattered. Is that all I was to you? Just a job? Tell me the truth right now and this ends here. You want to go? I'll let you go. Just tell me the fucking truth."

She stopped her struggling and stared up at him with wide amber eyes he couldn't read. Eyes that had haunted him for way too long. Her chest rose and fell with her quick breaths, and the pink hue to her cheeks screamed of arousal—he just couldn't tell if it was for him or for some stupid job that turned her on more than he ever had.

"I . . ." She blinked several times, and her hands curled into fists against the mattress on each side of her head, but she didn't try to wriggle free.

"Come on, Eve. You've never been speechless before. Tell me the truth. Tell me I never mattered to you and it was all about the job. I'll walk away and you'll never have to see me again."

"The government—"

"Fuck the government." Why was she stalling? Because she liked torturing him? God, he really was a dumb fuck. For concocting this whole plan, for spending the last year searching for her, for think-ing—after she'd finally told him the truth earlier—that she'd done any of it because she cared about him. "I know how to disappear and not be found. I did it this whole last year, and I can do it again. Just tell me the damn truth. Tell me you don't give a shit about me."

"You're a complete jackass," she whispered.

Zane stilled above her. The air caught in his throat, and his chest drew tight as a drum. Not because of what she'd said, but because of what he saw in her suddenly damp eyes.

Fury—yeah, there was still plenty of that—but behind that, something else. Something vulnerable. Something hot.

"I don't care about you," she whispered. "I really don't. You don't deserve it. I hate you. I—"

He let go of her wrists, lowered his mouth to hers, and kissed her. But unlike when he'd kissed her before, when he'd been trying to distract her from crushing him to death, this time she kissed him back. Her tongue found his, and she arched up into him while she wrapped her arms around him, opened her legs, and made room for him between her thighs.

The taste of her was something he hadn't forgotten. Not even in the dead of night when he'd been plotting ways to string her up and torture the truth out of her. Sweet, spicy, so fucking forbidden. Her fingers slid up into his hair and fisted, pulling on the strands until pain shot through his scalp. Kissing her again and again, he tasted her deeper, drew her in even though he knew he shouldn't. Even though he knew it would only fuck with his mind even more.

"Evie—"

"Shut up. Just—" She hooked a leg over his hip, flexed, and flipped him to his back in one smooth move. The mattress bounced. "Don't talk."

She closed her mouth over his again. Kissed him hard. Tongues tangled. Teeth scraped flesh. Her fingers found the edge of her T-shirt, and she pulled away from his mouth long enough to drag the cotton up and over her head. It landed somewhere behind her, and she yanked his shirt off, then lowered her mouth back to his and kissed him until all thought—all reason and common sense—disappeared into the ether.

He trailed his hands up her ribcage to the underside of her breasts, hidden behind the soft, nude-colored bra. Classic Eve. Functional, not seductive. But he liked that about her. There was something so damn hot about a woman who could rock a simple bra and panties and look like a Victoria's Secret model, and Eve had the body to do that. Toned, muscular, so freakin' perfect it made his cock throb with the thought of getting inside her.

He flicked the front clasp of her bra and groaned into her mouth when her bare breasts spilled into his hands. His fingers cupped the soft flesh, and he dragged his thumbs over the sensitive nipples, already hard and aching for his touch . . . for his mouth. But before he could break away from her greedy kiss so he could give them what they desperately needed, he realized she'd already undone his pants and that her clever hands were inside his boxers, pushing them and his jeans down his hips.

Cool air washed over his cock as it sprang free. Then her hand was there—hot, tight—wrapping around the base and sliding up the tip to squeeze and stroke his shaft until he couldn't take it anymore.

His hands fell against the mattress, and he gripped the comforter in a tight fist as he jerked his mouth from hers. Something way in the back of his mind warned this was a bad idea, but he couldn't seem to listen. "Eve, wait, you have to—"

"Shh. Don't talk to me. Put your cock in me." She shimmied away and came back. Her knees bumped into his hips. She hiked up her skirt. Then her mouth was back on his. Needy, aggressive, devouring his until she was all he could taste. Until a slick, hot vise closed over the tip of his cock, drowning out every other sensation.

He groaned. Or maybe it was her, he couldn't tell. All he knew was that her tight, slippery sex was sliding down his aching cock, sucking him in, making him see stars.

"Oh *fuck*, Sawyer." Her palms landed against his bare chest, and her fingernails dug into his skin as she stretched around him, taking him all the way in. And he didn't even care because she felt so fucking incredible. He loved that she was using his alias, that she was remembering what they'd once had.

His reasons for trying to get her to stop slid to the back of his mind. He let go of the blanket and gripped her hips. Thrust up to get deeper inside her. She gasped, pressed against his shoulders, and lifted, the movement dragging his cock against her walls, making them both shiver. She clamped down with her sex as she did it again, and he helped her by squeezing the skirt bunched around her hips and lifting with his hands, by clenching his ass and thrusting up on her every downstroke.

"Fuck . . . oh *fuck* that feels good." Tiny tremors racked her body. Her eyes slammed shut as she lifted and lowered. As his cock pressed deep and then slid back out. Her hands slipped from his shoulders to the mattress, lengthening her body over his. Her hard nipples abraded his skin, and he knew by the way she was rocking, by the way her eyes were clenched tight, that she was grinding her clit against him. That she was close. "So big. So good . . ."

Warmth infused his chest. Made his blood pump hot. The need to feel her release overrode every other thought. "Do it, Juliet. Come all over my cock."

She grunted. Lifted, lowered. He captured her mouth and thrust into her with his tongue just as he was doing with his cock. Grabbed her knees and slid them wider so she could rub her greedy sex harder against him with every deep thrust. Her hips picked up speed. She rocked against him faster. Harder. Wrapping both arms around her waist, he pulled her tight and met her speed. Then ravished her mouth and let his body take over.

Thought dissipated. Need took over. He thrust deeper. Harder. Faster. Every muscle in Eve's body contracted while he fucked her. While sweat slid down his temples and dripped onto the mattress. Then her sheath clamped tight around his cock, and she tore her mouth from his and cried out as her body jerked and shivered.

Her orgasm made her even tighter than before. But he didn't ease up. Couldn't. He continued to drive into her again and again while the wave dragged her under. Continued to hold her tight so she couldn't get away from the pressure on her clit. To plow into her with all the loss and frustration and sexual need he'd been saving this whole last year.

More. Harder. Deeper.

He grunted with every thrust. Heard her cry out again and didn't know this time whether it was in pleasure or pain, but he couldn't stop himself to check. Electricity raced down his spine, gathered in his balls, and then shot through his cock like a rocket. Followed by stars exploding behind his eyelids as pure bliss radiated down his legs and up into his chest.

Eve's body jerked, and she cried out again, her slick sheath tightening once, twice more, pumping him like a velvet fist before she collapsed against his chest. His own body quaked from her mini-orgasm, and tingles spread all along his skin.

She was breathless, panting against his chest, and something sharp was sticking into his ribs, but he didn't care. All Zane could focus on was that sweet, weightless feeling gliding through his limbs like a feathery soft touch.

"Oh God," Eve managed. "That was . . ."—her hand pressed into his good shoulder, and her hot breath ran across his neck, sending a shiver down his spine—"such a bad idea."

He trailed his fingers down her bare spine, across the skirt still bunched around her waist, and finally down her muscular ass, which he squeezed. A bad idea? He wasn't so sure anymore. "For the record, I didn't start it. Not *that*, at least."

"No," she breathed. "You just pushed me up to the edge where you knew I'd go right on over."

She rolled off him and dropped onto the mattress at his side. The loss of her heat was like a cold blanket draping over his skin. She tossed a hand over her eyes as her chest rose and fell and she tried to catch her breath, but she didn't sound pissed. If anything, she sounded . . . unnerved.

Which didn't help because he was unnerved too. He hadn't planned that, but hell if he was about to regret it. His gaze ran over her nakedness, and as the dim morning light highlighted the curves and angles of her muscular body, his stomach tightened with the reality of what they'd just done, and her reason for being unhinged.

"Shit. Eve. I didn't mean for—"

"Don't say it." She pushed up quickly to sitting, grabbed both sides of her bra, and clasped it around her breasts in front. "You may have pushed the matter, but I could have stopped it. So it happened. Big deal. It's not like we never fucked before. Where the hell is my shirt?"

She rose to her feet, glanced around the room, and then moved for her T-shirt, which was hanging halfway off the nightstand lamp.

But it was a big deal. A huge deal. More so now when Zane thought of the consequences. His nerves strung tight, he tugged on his jeans and buttoned them. "I didn't plan . . ." Shit. He raked a hand through his hair. This had never been anything he had to worry about because he was always safe. Except with her. She'd made him lose his mind more than once in Beirut. It was just worse now because he couldn't tell where they stood. Or where he even wanted them to stand. "Look, I'm clean. You don't have to worry about that. I—"

She tugged the shirt over her head and whipped his way. "Oh geez, Archer. The Feds think you set off a bomb in the middle of Seattle and you're worried about screwing me without a condom? Your priorities are really fucking twisted."

He stared at her, completely unsure how to take her reaction. Unsure of everything right now. Somewhere between the time he'd seen her on that Seattle street and now, things had changed, and he didn't know what he wanted or what to do next. The only thing he knew was in that moment when they'd been locked together, everything had felt . . . right.

"I'm clean too," she said with a frown. "And I won't get pregnant from this, so stop worrying. A woman in my line of work takes precautions against that kind of thing."

He watched her pick up her panties from the floor and wondered when she'd ditched them, but he was too curious about her statement to ask. "What kind of precautions?"

She tugged them on and smoothed her skirt. "Nothing permanent, though not by my choice. My doctor's sure I'll regret something permanent since I'm still so young." She huffed and turned away. "Right. Can you see me with a family? That'd be hilarious. I've got the whole birth control thing covered, so stop stressing."

He wasn't stressing. As he watched her twist her skirt so the slit was back against her left thigh, he couldn't help but imagine her with a family. A kid. A dog. A house on the beach with a white picket fence. She'd told him once she loved the beach. She could do anything she wanted if she put her mind to it. If she wanted it enough. He just couldn't see himself in that picture with her. And wasn't sure whether he wanted to be there or not.

His chest tightened as she turned to face him. "Eve—"

"Okay, that?" She pointed at the bed. "Clearly not happening again. Once we get out of here and I get in touch with my director, we'll get this all straightened out, and you can go wherever the hell it is you go." She picked up his shirt from the floor and flung it toward him. "We'll just chalk that up to stupidity and not talk about it again. God knows we were stupid before."

He caught the shirt in both hands and tugged it on, but something inside him didn't want to drop the subject, even if he wasn't entirely sure where he wanted it to go. "Eve—"

Gunfire exploded from the back of the house, the sound of wood and glass shattering drowning out his voice and thoughts and reactions.

He dropped to the ground behind the bed. Eve hit the carpet next to him and rolled to her back. In her hands she held both guns from the dresser. "Holy fuck. How did they find us?"

He plucked the SIG out of her hand and checked the magazine, then snapped it back into place. "Miller was right. Your call to the Agency—"

"No way they tracked us from that call." She ducked her head as the doorjamb to the bedroom splintered into a hundred pieces. "I know how long it takes to track a call."

Zane angled his head around the leg of the bed and looked toward the open door. He couldn't see anything besides carpet, walls, and splintered wood. "Then how the hell did they—" Understanding hit, and he froze. His eyes fell closed. "Oh *shit*."

"What?" Eve asked.

More glass exploded in the other room. From the direction of the kitchen. He ducked his head back behind the bed and looked her way. "I called Carter's cell. Outside. Before I came back in."

"You son of a bitch." Eve smacked the butt of her gun hard against his bad arm. "Are you fucking brain dead?"

"Son of a—" He shoved her hand away. "Knock that shit off. Carter would never rat us out."

"No," she snapped. "But that doesn't mean they're not monitoring him to get to us." She moved to her belly and stilled. The gunshots had stopped. "How many do you think there are?"

Zane tuned in to his hearing. Footsteps were moving around the side of the house. Faint ones. "From the number of shots fired," he whispered, "five. At most."

"They've split up," Eve whispered back.

He nodded and pointed two fingers to his right.

"Fuck that," Eve whispered. "I'm a better shot than you any day. You get the two moving around the south side of the house; I'll take the other three."

She was gone before he could stop her, sliding around the end of the torn-up mattress and disappearing into the hallway without a single look back.

"God, you're a moron," he muttered to himself. "Why can't you be interested in a normal girl? One whose idea of an adrenaline rush is parasailing on some Mexican beach? But no, you gotta go and fall for Jane fucking Bond."

He ground his teeth while he pushed to his feet. Then wished for a dose of that Dilaudid again. He had no idea where those stupid syringes had even gone.

Pausing near the doorway, he waited and listened. A quick shot of remorse trickled in when he thought about the fact these could be fellow agents, but it faded when he realized they weren't here for a garden party. They were here to kill them, no questions asked. There was no remorse on their side, and if he wanted to stay alive, there couldn't be any on his.

Fear gripped icy fingers around his heart and squeezed when he realized Eve was somewhere near the kitchen, walking into . . . he didn't know what. If she got herself killed right now, before he'd decided what the hell to do about her—about them—he'd never forgive her.

A twig cracked just outside the window at the end of the hall. He swiveled, lifted his gun, and fired.

chapter 11

The gunshots echoed a split second before Eve cursed Archer for his bad timing.

The soldier decked out in black ops gear with an assault rifle poised at his shoulder swiveled in the kitchen and aimed her way. Her fingers closed around the knife she'd quietly pulled from the butcher block, and she hurled it hard.

A grunt echoed as the blade sank into his neck. His finger hit the trigger as he fell backward, and gunfire lit up the kitchen, tearing into the ceiling.

Eve ducked behind the cabinet. Plaster and wood rained down around her. She bit her lip and kept her curse to herself while chunks of wood cut into her shoulder. Her pulse raced. As soon as the gunfire cut off, she pushed to her feet. Broken glass dug into her foot, but she tiptoed through the kitchen as carefully as she could and stepped over the man choking on his own blood. He was wearing a black ski mask—not that she'd expected to see his face—and she wasn't tempted to look beneath it. Averting her gaze, she holstered the Glock at her lower back and picked up the rifle.

Footsteps pounded from the direction of the living room. Adrenaline surging, Eve opened the steel fridge door, slung the strap of the weapon over her shoulder, and reached for the chilled bottle of champagne.

Not the welcome-to-your-vacation gift the management company had anticipated, not that Eve cared. Backing into the cold chill, she grasped the top edge of the open fridge door for balance and lifted her feet onto the bottom ledge, out of view, and waited.

Glass crunched under boot steps, and Eve tensed. When the tip of a rifle passed the edge of the open door, she shoved the door open hard with her shoulder, then swung out with the bottle.

Glass shattered against bone. The man grunted. Arms flailed out as his body weight pitched backward. Dragging her arm away, Eve shoved her fist into the man's throat, collapsing his windpipe. He dropped to the ground with a thunk.

Eve stepped over him, shifted the first rifle to her back, and picked up the second.

Glass crackled from the living room, and Eve froze.

Her pulse shot up all over again. She ducked behind the edge of the wall and lifted the weapon.

"Don't fucking shoot," Archer announced. "It's me."

Eve released the breath she hadn't realized she'd been holding and lowered her weapon. "Dammit, Archer," she whispered. "There's still another one lurking."

"No there's not." He rounded the corner into the kitchen and glanced down at the two unmoving bodies lying among broken glass and splintered wood on the kitchen floor. "I got the other three."

She wasn't going to be impressed. She straightened and frowned. "Just had to show me up, didn't you?"

His dark gaze lifted to hers. Blood splatters stained his cheek, sweat beaded his forehead, and his shirt was torn at the shoulder. And though he had two weapons slung over his shoulder, much like her, and was holding one assault rifle in his hand, his feet weren't torn to pieces from the broken glass like hers. The man hadn't just taken out three black ops assassins in the time it had taken her to drop two. He'd already snagged their combat boots. "It's not a competition, Evie."

"Everything's a competition, Archer. Especially when you're a woman." Why was she so irritated? She'd worked with men on ops before. She'd even worked well with Archer—and not just in the bedroom. She didn't have to prove herself to anyone. But the way he was looking at her set the fine hairs on her nape standing straight, and something uncomfortable rolled through her belly.

She shook off the strange feeling, slung the second rifle over her shoulder, then knelt and tugged the boots off the closest body, refusing to look at the soldier's face. "That was a wet team. Not the same untrained thugs who chased us at the docks."

"Yeah. But this insignia isn't US government."

She looked down at the patch on the sleeve of the man at her feet. A wolf encased in a circle, surrounded by stars. "I noticed that too. Hired mercenaries?"

"Could be. Or something else."

The "something else" didn't leave Eve feeling all rosy inside. "The Agency wouldn't have sent a wet team just for you. They'd have sent the Feds in, along with the press to catch it all on camera so they could brag to the world they caught the mastermind behind the Seattle bombing."

"I know."

Eve's stomach tightened as she pushed her feet into the boots. That meant someone besides the US government and a group of terrorist thugs was after them. She cringed at the pain in her left foot. There was still glass in there. She'd get it out later.

"They came in by boat," Archer said. "There's a Bayliner tied to the dock."

Eve knelt to tie the laces. The boots were three sizes too big, but big was better than nothing. "That's probably our easiest way out of here."

"Yeah. Miller left his truck, but it'll take us twice as long to get to Everett that way."

Eve stood and ground her teeth against the pain. "What's in Everett?"

"My car." When she stared at him, he added, "Supplies."

Money, ID, passports, fresh weapons. Eve knew the drill. "Fine. Let's go."

She turned for the back door, but Zane's hand gripped her T-shirt and pulled her back. Before she could catch her footing, he pushed the weapon to his side, shoved her up against the wall, and closed in at her front. Then his mouth was on hers. Hot. Hard. Demanding.

He kissed her with those sensuous lips and pressed his muscular, sweaty body into hers until all thought slipped from her mind, then pulled back. "You're not alone, and you don't have to do everything on your own. I'm here with you in this. Try to remember that."

He stepped past her, out into the morning light, and, dazed, Eve stayed right where she was, pulse racing and mind spinning.

He was offering help. Help for something she'd dragged him into. No, she corrected herself, for something he'd stumbled into all on his own. He could leave, take off and get his team at Aegis to help him clear his name, but he wasn't. Her gaze strayed out the shattered window toward the dock. He was staying. Waiting for her to join him.

Her heart picked up speed, and pain gathered beneath her ribs, where it beat hard and fast. Their rendezvous—okay, fuck session— in the bedroom replayed in her mind, and her stomach and chest grew tight all over again, just like it had the moment she'd realized what she'd done and climbed off him.

Sweat broke out all along her forehead, and she swiped at it with a shaky hand. A pissed Archer she knew how to handle. One hell-bent on revenge and retribution? Way easier to deal with than the one currently standing out on that dock. Offering to help. Trying to protect her. Because he cared.

"Tell me I never mattered to you and it was all about the job. I'll walk away and you'll never have to see me again."

She squeezed her eyes tight. Stupid, stupid—so fucking stupid. He'd given her an out, and she hadn't taken it. And now he knew her biggest weakness.

She braced a hand against the wall and tried to settle her quaking stomach. But it didn't work. Because what waited for her out there scared her more than anything the CIA could throw her way.

- - - - - - - - - - - - - - - - -

Metal scraped metal, and Olivia braced a hand against the cold, dingy floor as she pushed up from where she'd been trying to sleep.

Bright light blinded her as the door to her cell was pulled open. A silhouette blocked part of the light, and she blinked several times to see more clearly, but she couldn't make out any distinguishing features. "Who—who's there?"

Fresh, blessed air drifted to her nostrils, pushing aside all the stale filth she'd been wallowing in these last days, and she drew it in deeply, as much as she could before they closed her in again. Heavy footsteps crossed the dirty metal floor as she was filling her lungs, and then a firm, large hand wrapped around her biceps and hauled her to her feet. "Time to go, little lady. The powers that be have decided you just might be useful to us after all."

Pain raced down her arm and back up again. She yelped as she was dragged across the grimy floor and tried to find her footing. This wasn't the same man who'd brought her food before. It was someone else.

Bright sunlight washed over her, blinding her, bringing her limbs to a stop in the warmth, and halting all questions about who had her now.

Freedom. Her body shook with sweet relief. The sun was still there. It hadn't disappeared. There was still hope. Her legs went out from under her.

"Son of a bitch," the man holding her arm muttered in a thick accent. He tugged hard again, and pain spiraled through Olivia's body, but she couldn't move her legs. They weren't working. And the sun felt so good. She didn't want to leave it. Couldn't . . .

"Get up." He yanked hard again.

Olivia yelped. Tried to stand. But her legs felt like Jell-O, and the sun . . .

"Fucking bitch." He hauled her up and tossed her over his shoulder like she was nothing more than a sack of potatoes.

Pain echoed all through her weak body, but Olivia braced her hands against his back and lifted her head, blinking into the sunshine as he moved, trying to see—see something, anything.

Large shapes closed in around her. Blocking out the sunlight. She blinked over and over, trying to get her eyes to work, and then, slowly, the shapes came into focus.

Large metal containers. Hundreds of them, all around her. And above, angry-looking claw-like hooks. Big ones.

A seagull cried somewhere overhead, and Olivia realized it wasn't just sunlight she was drawing in; it was salt as well. From seawater. They were at a port of some kind. And around her . . . those were ConEx containers. The kind that were shipped on barges from one country to another.

Gravel crunched under the man's feet below her. He spoke to someone nearby in a language she didn't understand. Spanish? German? Arabic? She couldn't tell.

Focus, Olivia. Focus on anything you can so you can remember.

She was a teacher. Nothing special. And she was too weak to try to overpower these two and still live. But she'd watched enough crime movies to know that when she got out of this—*if* she got out of it—she needed to pay attention to every detail if she wanted them to be caught.

The man carrying her stopped. Words were spoken—more she couldn't make out—then a car door opened, and the man holding her set her down on her feet.

He let go of her for a split second, and her legs wobbled, but she braced a hand on the edge of the white van to steady herself.

Then she realized *he'd let go of her.*

The flight response kicked in without her even searching for it. She shoved her arms hard into the cargo door. It hit one of the men, knocking him off balance. She turned and pushed her legs forward as hard as she could.

She was a runner. She might be weak from days in isolation and very little food, but she dug deep for the strength she'd gained from hours and hours running trails back in Boise.

"Dammit. Get her!"

She darted around a car. Didn't even care that her feet were bare or that gravel was digging into her soles. She pumped her arms and ran as fast and hard as she could. Away. She had no idea where she was going—just away.

She scurried behind a truck and turned to her right. A body slammed into her hard. She grunted, sailed through the air, and hit the packed gravel on her side, sliding through rocks and dirt that embedded into her skin.

"Stupid fucking bitch." A man—not the same one who'd carried her, this one was smaller—grabbed her by the front of her blouse with both hands, lifted her upper body inches from the ground, and then slammed her back into the gravel.

Blinding pain ricocheted through Olivia's skull, and she gasped.

"You're gonna pay for that." Chest heaving, he yanked her from the ground and tossed her over his shoulder.

Stars fired off behind Olivia's eyelids. And the pain . . . She groaned as he jostled her bruised and bleeding body.

When they reached the van, he tossed her into the back. She hit the floor with a grunt and tried to pull her legs up to her chest to alleviate the burning pain in her hip and shoulder. Only nothing helped. She breathed through her mouth and cradled her aching arm close, but then he was there, climbing into the back, pulling the cargo doors closed, and yelling, "Let's go!"

The van's engine turned over, and Olivia braced herself as the vehicle whipped around and bounced over the uneven ground, but it did nothing to stop the pain thrumming through every cell in her body.

"Stupid bitch," the man growled. "We were nice to you before because of your sister. But not anymore."

Olivia's eyes tore open, and she stared up at his dark face, twisted in a fury she'd never seen before.

"My—my sister?"

He chuckled, a dark, menacing sound that condensed into a knot of terror in her belly. "What? You thought this was all for fun? No. You're leverage now."

He dropped to his knees and leaned over her, and his scent— sweat, spice, and danger—filled her nostrils. A scent she'd never forget. "Too bad she won't find you in one piece. Not after that little stunt."

It took Landon longer to locate Archer's warehouse than he'd thought. The ferry system had been shut down, which meant he had to drive all the way down to Tacoma and back up and around. Then, when he'd finally made it back to Seattle, the damn traffic was being rerouted all over the place because of the ongoing investigation.

Frustrated, he climbed out of the rental car he'd picked up on Bainbridge Island after leaving Archer and slammed the door shut. An abandoned warehouse stood to his right, the skeleton of a building under construction on his left, and between the two a tower crane sat unmoving, its long arm angled out toward the waters of Puget Sound in the distance.

Damn, but the guy really was a moron to bring her here, not even three miles from the bombing site.

Landon rubbed his aching forehead as he moved for the warehouse doors. Obviously, the dumb fuck hadn't been thinking. But then, when it came to a woman, he wasn't the first man to lose all common sense. Landon knew that lesson well himself. The difference was, he'd never repeat his stupidity, and after seeing Archer this morning, he knew the idiot was bound to repeat every single stupid-ass thing he'd done because of Evelyn Wolfe. Archer might not be able to see it, but Landon could. Up close and personal. The idiot was still in love with her.

The door handle didn't turn, but picking the lock was easy enough, and Landon was inside in a matter of minutes.

The warehouse was cut in the middle by a long hallway and doors that led to what looked like large storage units. Uncovered, dim bulbs hung from the ceiling every twelve feet. Landon paused to listen. Hearing nothing out of the ordinary, he moved for the metal stairs that ran up to the second and third floors.

He knew when he'd found the right loft. The steel door was cut in two, as if whoever had wanted in had used a buzz saw to get inside. Landon pushed the right side open the rest of the way and moved into the loft.

His gaze scanned the empty room. A chair was turned over on its side. A broken table sat upside down. A metal tray and three hypodermic needles lay scattered across the floor. His gaze strayed to the bed against the far wall. To the mattress stained with blood and other things he didn't want to focus too much on. Then to the metal handcuffs hanging from the metal headboard.

"Stupid-ass dumb fuck," he muttered. Oh yeah, Evelyn Wolfe had every reason to kick Archer's ass from here to Mount Rainier, and at the moment, Landon kinda hoped she did.

He shook his head as he turned away and looked around for the purse Archer had told him he'd brought back with him. Whatever happened between Archer and Wolfe was not his problem. The only thing he cared about was finding Wolfe's sister. Then he was taking a monthlong vacation, and his boss Ryder could suck it if he didn't agree.

He checked cabinets along the wall and finally found a woman's black purse hanging behind what had to be Archer's denim jacket on a hook in the bathroom.

He set the bag on the dirty counter and pawed through it until he found a cheap cell phone. He powered it on and saw a video on the home screen. His fingers hit Play, and he watched as a woman, her hands tied behind her back and her face covered by a black sack, thrashed on the floor of what looked like a van. The purple butterfly tattoo on her ankle was clearly visible as she struggled.

There was no sound. Landon replayed it three times, looking for anything that might help him identify the van. Fury rolled through his gut. He didn't have a problem taking down anyone who deserved it, but he had a major-ass problem when innocents were drawn into the mix. He knew that was why he'd washed out at DIA. Not because he couldn't stomach what he was asked to do, but because he refused to do it to civilians.

He clicked the video off and paged through the contacts. Nothing showed on the phone. He turned it in his hand and remembered Wolfe's explanation of what had happened at that outdoor café. This was the phone her contact—Smith—had slid across the table to her.

He tucked the phone into his pocket and resumed searching her bag, looking for another one. He finally found it—an iPhone, the most recent version—and turned it on. A white apple appeared on the screen, followed by a tropical image of a beach, hammock, and swaying palms. Apps appeared, dotting the screen. He waited until service clicked in, then hit the Phone button and paged through her recent calls. DC numbers. One he recognized belonging to Langley. Another that was labeled "Olivia Wolfe." And a few blocked calls he'd have to try.

He hit Close and scrolled back to the home screen to look through her messages. The one at the top was from another blocked number.

BLOCKED NUMBER: 2:00 p.m. You have the location. Bring the envelope. Don't be late.

"Bingo," Landon muttered.

He was just about to hit Dial when his cell buzzed. Tugging it from his pocket, he held it up to his ear. "Miller."

"It's Marley. I have some information on Wolfe's sister."

Landon grabbed the purse and moved out of the bathroom, back into the main portion of the loft. "Let's hear it."

"She's a drama teacher in Boise. Has worked at one of the local high schools for about five years. She was last seen four days ago at a Mexican restaurant downtown with a man named Karl Stetson, a teacher at the same school where she works."

"What does he teach?"

"Biology, physics, chemistry. Claims he drove her home after what was—by his words—an uneventful date, and two men jumped them when he pulled into her drive."

"Did he get a look at either of them?"

"Not really. Said they were big. Dark-skinned. He described them as either Hispanic or Middle Eastern. And they were speaking a language he didn't recognize."

Landon frowned. "Observant, isn't he?"

"It's not his most charming quality," Marley muttered, "trust me. According to his story, they snagged Olivia Wolfe, roughed him up a little, and then let him go. And here's what has me all warm and gooey for the guy. He didn't report her abduction to the cops for a full twenty-four hours."

"Bastard."

"Yeah, well. There are a lot of them out there. I should know. Ask me about my last date sometime. Anyway, Stetson claims they threatened him, but I got the impression he just didn't want to get involved."

Landon clenched his jaw. "Someone needs to abduct his ass."

"I agree, but he's not our problem. Cops are handling him. Did you find Archer?"

Landon looked out the broken window toward the fire escape. "Sort of."

"Sort of? What does that mean?"

"It means Ryder isn't going to like what's coming next. Listen, Marley, I need a favor."

"I'm here to help."

"I need to know who at the State Department has it in for Aegis. Evelyn Wolfe hinted that the raid in Guatemala was a setup, and Aegis was the target. I need you to do some digging, without Ryder knowing."

"Why can't Jake know?"

"Because if what Wolfe said is accurate, then Ryder was the target, not Humbolt. And if that's the case, I'm thinking it's possible that blaming this whole bombing in Seattle on Archer is a setup too, not to take him down per se, but to get at Ryder. You and I both know Ryder's pissed off more people in Washington than he should have. What better way to guarantee Aegis doesn't score another defense contract than to charge their operatives with treason?"

"Don't you think that's a stretch?"

"I worked for the Pentagon. Trust me, sugar. Nothing's a stretch."

"Okay," Marley said. "I'll see what I can find out. I still don't understand why Jake can't know, though."

"Because whether I'm right or wrong, it'll just get him fired up, and he'll start making calls. And if someone at the State Department finds out Aegis is asking questions about black ops, they'll clam up. Or worse, leak shit to the press. Ryder's not exactly a people person."

Marley huffed. "You can say that again."

Landon smiled. Marley was a saint. She really was. Ryder didn't realize the gold mine he had in her. Landon just hoped she didn't get fed up with Ryder at some point and walk away from the company. Because if she did, Ryder would lose more than just his right hand. He'd lose the majority of his operatives, who'd follow her anywhere if she asked. Him included. "Thanks."

"Okay, my turn to ask you a question. Is Archer okay?"

"Yeah, he's fine."

"Is he with Evelyn Wolfe?"

Landon hesitated, then figured the more Marley knew, the longer she could keep Ryder in the dark. "Yes. And neither's killed the other yet, so I think we're safe."

"That doesn't leave me feeling all tingly inside."

"That's why you get the joy of dealing with people like Karl Stetson on a daily basis."

Marley laughed. "Okay, point taken. So, tell me this, smart guy. If you're no longer tracking Archer, what are you doing?"

"Looking for her sister. Something tells me Olivia Wolfe knows a hell of a lot more about what's going on here than anyone else."

"And Archer and Evelyn Wolfe?"

"Running down other leads. Wolfe's security clearance with the CIA has been revoked. It's only a matter of time before her name shows up in the press as being linked to the bombing as well."

"Fabulous. Just watch your six. My gut says there's more going on here than meets the eye."

Marley's gut was usually right. And on this one, Landon agreed. He looked back out at the water again. "Speaking of . . . if Ryder ever fires you, you've got a freebie from me. I wouldn't mind being the one to take that bastard out."

"He's your boss."

"That's never stopped me before."

Marley chuckled, then sighed. "Firing me isn't the worst thing he could do to me." Her voice strengthened. "I'll call you as soon as I have news."

chapter 12

Eve stood near a rack of workout pants in Macy's while Archer paid for new clothes for both of them. She glanced around the quiet store in the middle of the afternoon in Everett as her pulse ticked up another notch.

Come on, come on, come on . . .

The young girl behind the counter was the slowest clerk ever. And either exhaustion was finally settling in, or Eve's blood sugar was at an all-time low, because her patience was nearly at the breaking point.

Archer pocketed the change, said thank you, and took the bags. He was careful to keep his ball cap pulled low so his face was shadowed, but Eve's gaze strayed to the ceiling and the security cameras for the hundredth time, then darted toward the doors where a security guard stood still as a gargoyle.

She didn't like the way the guy kept glancing in her direction. Just her luck they'd get a GI Joe wannabe. An ambitious rent-a-cop was the last thing they needed right now.

Archer moved next to her and placed a hand at the small of her back, right over the Glock nestled in the waistband of her skirt, then herded her toward the exit. "Relax. That girl had no idea who I was."

The guard near the door stiffened as they approached, and Eve had a vision of everything going straight to the shitter, all because Archer had left his supply bag in a locker near an ice-skating rink instead of somewhere more easily accessible and out of sight of the public.

She turned quickly, wrapped her fingers in the fabric of his shirt, and tugged him into her. "Baby, I'm not done shopping yet. I want those crotchless panties you promised me."

Archer's eyes widened, just a touch, and Eve rose up on her toes and kissed him. Then she mumbled against his lips, "That security guard has got his eye trained right on you."

Archer wrapped the arm holding the shopping bags around her back and tugged her in tight. Then he smiled and said, "Anything you want, sweetheart," before pressing his mouth to hers.

It was an act. Eve knew it was an act. But oh man, the guy could kiss. He pushed her lips apart, then dipped inside for a wicked taste. And tingles shot straight to Eve's core as soon as his slick, hot tongue touched hers.

She arched into him, tangled her fingers in the fabric of his T-shirt, and kissed him back while her mind replayed what they'd done this morning. Behind her, the security guard sighed. The door opened and closed, and voices bounced off the store walls, but Eve was suddenly too light-headed to care.

Minutes passed—or maybe it was only seconds; she couldn't be sure, since her brain seemed to short out every time Archer kissed her—and then he eased back. A twinkle lit up his hazel eyes when he smiled down at her. "Crotchless panties? Oh baby, I'm all over that. Come on."

He let go of her, grabbed her hand, and pulled her back to the middle of the store, then turned down the aisle that led to lingerie. A quick glance over her shoulder told Eve the security guard was no longer watching them and had moved on to staring at another man, lurking near a display of men's belts.

Eve followed Archer into the lingerie section and glanced around. Another security guard—this time a woman—was walking through this end of the store, but her gaze skipped right over them as if they weren't even there.

"These?" Archer held up a pair of black boy-short panties, open along both hips, with crisscrossed ties holding them together.

Eve's brow lowered. "For you? I doubt they'd fit."

Archer picked up a second pair from the table display—this one in red. "I can't wait to see you in these."

He pulled her toward another register, and Eve's adrenaline kicked up again—but this time not from being caught. "Hold on. I was kidding about the panties."

"I wasn't." He set their bags on the floor, pulled cash out of his wallet, and slapped it on the counter, careful to keep his head tipped down so the clerk couldn't see his face. Not that she would notice even if he looked right at her. The girl was barely eighteen and bored out of her mind. The place could probably get robbed and she'd barely notice.

She bagged the panties, then handed Archer the receipt. "Thanks for shopping at Macy's," she said in a monotone voice, without even looking their way.

Archer took the bag and muttered thanks, then herded Eve toward the unguarded exit. "Friendly girl."

"I'm not wearing those," Eve said as they stepped out of the store and moved into the parking garage.

"You were right." Archer nodded up toward the ramp. "You need underwear. Should have thought of it when we were grabbing new clothes."

"Not those kind," Eve huffed. "I was just trying to fool the security guard."

Archer shot her a wicked grin. "I bet you'll look totally hot in these."

They stopped behind a Ford Taurus parked on the third level, and Eve crossed her arms over her chest while he opened the trunk. "Well, then you'll lose the bet, because I'd rather go commando than wear those."

That spark flared in his eyes all over again as he glanced sideways at her. "Oh, baby. Stop talking like that or you're gonna make *me* hot."

Eve's skin grew warm, and she glared at him under the orange parking lights. Why was she letting him get to her? The Archer she remembered had a wicked sense of humor, and it was clear he was just razzing her like he'd once done. And she'd obviously started this by kissing him as a cover, so she needed to suck it up and deal with it. So why was she feeling so . . . frustrated and out of sorts?

It wasn't because of this morning. She wouldn't let it be. Yeah, they'd screwed each other in a moment of complete insanity, but life-and-death situations often pushed people to do things they wouldn't otherwise do. They'd both been trained on the effects of adrenaline, and she was smart enough not to fall into the relationship trap again anyway—any kind of relationship for her was a dead end. So that's not what this was about.

He closed the trunk and turned toward her. And a frown cut across his lips when he said, "Relax. There are security cameras out here too, you know." Then he moved in close and rubbed his thumb across her cheek. "You've still got some dirt or blood there from earlier."

Warmth spread across her cheek where he touched her and shot a wicked blend of heat and need straight to her abdomen. And in an instant, she knew what was bothering her. Not just the fact he was staying and helping her. Not even the fact he'd admitted earlier that he cared. What was freaking her out was this feeling growing in the center of her chest, the same one she'd had in Beirut and which had ultimately caused her to walk—no, *run*—away from him the first time. This sense of security telling her she could have this. That there could be more. That if she reached out and just took, she could have him and everything she'd stopped wanting so long ago.

The air clogged in her lungs, and the walls seemed to close in around her. Turning away from his touch, she moved around the side of the car and reached for the passenger door. "We need to go."

She felt him looking after her, wondering what the hell was up with her, even after she climbed into the car and closed the door, but she didn't care. As she breathed deep and tried to steady her racing pulse, she reminded herself that crazy thoughts like that were the reason she'd ended up with a broken heart in the first place. And she wasn't going back there again. Some people weren't meant for happily ever after, and she'd learned long ago that she was one of them.

Archer climbed into the driver's seat and closed the door, and she steeled her nerves and looked his way. "I need to call ADD Roberts."

He started the car and glanced into the rearview mirror. "I want you to wait until we hear back from Carter."

They both trusted Carter. When someone put his life on the line—like Carter had done for both of them more than once in Beirut—it solidified that trust. Eve knew Carter would do whatever he could to help them, but she didn't believe that about the organization he—and she—worked for.

"Carter isn't going to be able to help us the way Roberts can."

He backed out of the parking spot and shoved the car into drive. "And what if Roberts is in on all of this?"

"In on what? This conspiracy you've cooked up?"

He frowned sideways at her as they wound through the parking garage. "Someone leaked my name to the press. Someone sent a wet team after us. And your security clearance has been revoked. I think it's safe to say I don't have to cook anything up."

She looked out the front windshield and frowned herself. None of this made sense. "You yourself said that wet team probably wasn't government sanctioned. There could be a logical explanation."

"Yeah. That the Agency wants us both dead."

Archer's cell phone rang before Eve could tell him he was higher than a kite. He glanced at the screen, then lifted it to his ear. "Dude. Tell me this is a secure line and that you have good news."

He was silent as he listened, and Eve found herself digging her fingernails into the seat while she waited.

"When?" Archer asked. Then, "And you're sure about that?"

They pulled out of the parking garage and turned right onto the city street. Eve had no idea where Archer was heading, and right now she didn't care. She just wanted answers.

"Okay," Archer said. "We'll do that. Yeah. Thanks. I'll tell her."

"Well?" Eve said as he hung up.

"That was Carter."

"Duh. I got that. What did he say?"

"He said not to piss you off."

"Smart man. Keep going."

Zane sighed. "Your contact? Smith? He's been linked to a Chechen terrorist group with ties to al-Qaeda. And that laundry list of compromised agents he was supposedly selling you? It wasn't a list. There was something bigger on that drive."

"Like what?"

"Carter doesn't know. But he said shit's hitting the fan at Langley. Four of the terrorists were picked up at a safe house in Seattle. None is talking. Smith is still unaccounted for. Along with you. According to Carter, the Agency's launched a full-out search for you, and Assistant Deputy Director Roberts is heading it up."

The knot in Eve's stomach grew even larger. "They think I was involved in whatever Smith was doing."

"Or that you double-crossed him."

"Perfect." Her stomach twisted. "Someone's setting me up to take the fall for whatever's on that drive."

"They're setting *us* up to take the fall."

The way he said "us" made that feeling grow in her chest again, and she looked quickly away to avert her gaze.

They passed a fast-food restaurant, and her stomach grumbled. Distracting her—thankfully—from other things she didn't want to be feeling. "Where are we going?"

"Someplace we can lay low for the next few hours. We need to figure out what was on that drive if we have any chance of clearing our names. Which means you need to set up a meeting with your CSIS contact."

"She already told me what she thought was on the drive. I doubt she'll be much help."

"She lied to you." Zane glanced her way. "I want to know why."

The hard look in his eyes told her loud and clear what he'd do to anyone who lied to them again, and as she stared at him, Eve was reminded of the sweaty, sexy man who'd met her in the kitchen of that vacation rental this morning after taking out three black ops soldiers in only a matter of minutes. Yeah, he'd washed out of the CIA, but not because he wasn't skilled. He'd left because he actually had morals. Something most agents lost after a few months on the job.

Herself, obviously, included.

They headed up Highway 92 and found a small motel outside Granite Falls.

After checking in, Zane left Eve to take a shower and ran to get food. They'd picked up a few supplies from a grocery store earlier—mostly water and medical supplies for his shoulder—but the best he could find for dinner was a mom-and-pop burger joint. The food was hot and smelled good, though, and his stomach rumbled, telling him he'd gone way too long without sustenance.

Granite Falls was a small community in the foothills of the Cascades, and Zane felt confident no one would find them there. It was also close enough to the Canadian border so if they had to make a run for it, they wouldn't be trapped.

Bag of food in hand, he climbed out of the car, slid the key into the door, and turned the lock of their room. The building was an L-shaped structure, with the office on the small arm of the building and no more than sixteen rooms side by side on the longer arm. As he stepped into the room, the sound of water running met his ears, and steam poured from a gap in the open bathroom door.

Relief trickled through him when he heard the water shut off. He'd known it wasn't in Eve's best interest to run, but part of him hadn't totally believed she'd still be here when he got back. Especially not after what had happened between them this morning.

He closed the motel room door at his back, his mind zeroing in on the image of her naked in the bathroom, right this very moment. Blood rushed to his groin, making him hard in an instant.

Not smart. He rubbed a hand over his suddenly sweaty forehead and set the bag of food on the small round table flanked by two cracked plastic chairs. Probably shouldn't have challenged her this morning. Definitely shouldn't have kissed her. And he absolutely should have put a stop to things when she'd taken that challenge and torn off his clothes. But he'd been weak. And emotionally strung out. And it was Eve . . .

His entire body tightened and warmed as memories of her riding him filled his mind. Of the way she'd felt against his overheated skin. Of how tight she'd been around him.

"Holy hell, you're such a fucking loser," he muttered. "Get a grip."

He opened one of the bottles of water he'd bought and downed the contents. The last thing he needed was to get wrapped up in

Evelyn Wolfe again. Yeah, they had a history, but she wasn't interested anymore. He'd gotten that sign loud and clear after the fact
And though he'd played along at the mall—even drawn things out
just to get under her skin—he hadn't kissed her because he felt
anything for her. Not really. He was too smart to get sucked back in
by her again. He'd kissed her purely as cover.

That's right, pussy. Keep telling yourself that one.

The bathroom door pulled open, and a wave of steam spilled
into the room. Eve followed, damp from the shower, wearing nothing but a thin, white cotton towel wrapped around her curvy body
from breasts to midthigh.

Shit.

Zane's blood stirred as he watched her tip her head to the side and
use a hand towel to wring the wetness from her newly dark hair. She'd
cut and colored it when he'd been gone. Instead of shoulder length,
curly blonde locks, it was now closer to chin length, straight, and a
deep, rich brown that made her eyes look bigger and more golden,
made her chin look sharper. Made her look more like the woman he
hadn't been able to stop fantasizing about for the last eighteen months.

"Food." Eve's gaze locked on the white paper bag on the table.
"Thank God. I'm starving."

She tossed the hand towel on the table, eased into the closest
chair, and dug into the bag. Water droplets glistened on her shoulders and arms as she unwrapped her burger. And the slit in her towel
inched up dangerously high to reveal her toned, wet thigh. Watching her lift the burger to her lips, Zane remembered those long
fingers of hers sliding up and down his cock only hours ago, teasing
him to within an inch of his life.

"Aren't you eating?" she asked around a mouthful.

Zane moved toward the queen-sized bed closest to the door and
sat, careful to pull a pillow over his lap to keep his hard-on from
being freakin' obvious. "I'm not hungry at the moment."

Not hungry for food at least. Hungry for her? Yeah. Which he shouldn't be. He wasn't going there. Never again.

He leaned back against the headboard while she ate. Crossed his feet at the ankles and his arms over his chest as he stared up at the water-stained ceiling. *Think about what you need to do next. Think about who's setting you up and why. Think about anything except Eve sitting across the room all but naked like an offering.*

"Did you get a hold of your contact at CSIS?"

Eve swallowed and reached for the second bottle of water. "Yeah. Tomorrow, oh nine hundred. We're meeting her in Bellingham. She was in Vancouver, so it's not that far for her."

Zane nodded and zeroed in on one rather large ring on the ceiling so he wouldn't be tempted to look Eve's way. "Why did she give you Smith? How did that come about?"

Paper crinkled as Eve moved food around on the table. "Um." She swallowed her bite. "We pass information back and forth when it suits us. One of the officers I've been investigating over the last year—Connor Perkins—had worked with a few of her CSIS agents overseas. The last time I talked to her, she told me one of her agents had gotten word that this list had been created by MI6, and that Perkins's name was supposedly on it. We weren't sure who Tyrone Smith—the guy I met in Seattle—worked for, but his organization supposedly lifted the list from a dead MI6 agent in London a few months back and was trying to sell it on the black market."

"Why didn't CSIS make the deal? Why did she bring you in?"

"Because her agents weren't on the list."

That seemed fishy to Zane. "What about this Smith? You're sure you never saw him before?"

Eve was quiet for a moment and then said, "No. I mean, he was vaguely familiar, but I can't remember where I've seen him. He had one of those faces, you know?"

"And he didn't give you the drive or indicate he wanted anything from you besides the money you'd agreed to pay for the list."

"No. He took the money and left."

Zane frowned as his eyes moved to a different stained, yellow circle. "I don't get why they took your sister then."

"If I knew that, we wouldn't be sitting here, now would we?"

Ignoring the sarcasm in her voice, Zane pushed to his feet and began pacing. "A hostage means they want something. But they haven't made contact with you. They haven't made any demands."

"It's not like they can, though. I've been with you since the bombing. If they wanted to contact me, they can't because they never planned on you stepping in and taking me out of the picture."

Zane stopped near the window, pulled the curtains back a touch, and peered out. Dusk was just moving over the small town, and the first twinkle of streetlights glowed across the parking lot and against the steadily darkening sky. "True, but they sent their thugs after you when we were at the warehouse, not in any way to negotiate or make demands. Which makes me think"—he turned to face her—"they wanted you dead in that bombing. You were the target, not your sister, and not innocent people like the news is making it sound. This wasn't a typical terrorist bombing. This was a direct hit."

Eve looked down at the empty wrapper on the table in front of her. "Which means my sister is—"

"Alive." Her gaze shot his way, and his heart pinched at the fear he saw lurking in her eyes. A fear she kept closely guarded. A fear he'd seen this morning, which had bubbled over into the most incredible sex he could remember. A fear that told him the tough girl she wanted everyone to see wasn't the real her.

His heart pounded hard. Because he felt like he was getting his first glimpse of the real her. Not the one he'd fallen for in Beirut, but the one who'd run from him the night he thought he'd caught her betraying their country. The one who'd been afraid for him to get too close. The one who'd admitted in that warehouse that she'd been in love with him.

And holy hell—that Eve was more dangerous to his psyche than the slick, wet, nearly naked one sitting in front of him.

"She's alive," he said, throat thick. "If they want you, they'll keep her alive to get to you. As insurance. Which means this isn't just about a list. It's something more. Something you know too much about."

Eve's gaze slid back to her food, and a dazed look passed over her eyes. "I think I've lost my appetite." She rested her elbows on the table and rubbed her forehead. "Any word from Miller about my sister?"

"No. None." Zane watched her shoulders drop, and he knew by the way she sagged against the table that she had to be exhausted. Then his gaze strayed to her foot and the toilet paper wrapped around it like an ACE bandage.

"What's wrong with your foot?"

Eve cringed and looked down. "I cut it on some broken glass this morning. It's fine."

He moved before he thought better of it, sweeping her out of the chair and into his arms. The scent of soap assailed his nostrils, and her heat immediately seeped into his skin, telling him this might be a bad idea, but . . . screw it. She'd be no help to him injured.

Yep, that's why you're doing it. Keep lying to yourself, pussy.

She pressed a warm hand against his chest. "What do you think you're doing?"

"Helping you. God, you're a stubborn-ass woman. Why the hell didn't you tell me you were cut?"

He set her on the bed, and she scooted back against the headboard, tugging the towel down as far as she could. Her long, shapely legs filled his line of sight, but the red-tinged makeshift bandage was all he could focus on. "Because it's no big deal. I'm fine. I was going to put a bandage on it after I got out of the shower, but I got distracted by the food. Really, just leave it alone."

He pulled a pocketknife from his front pocket—the same one she'd used to cut those zip ties early this morning and which he'd found before they'd left that house—and knelt on the floor near the edge of the bed. One flick and he opened a pair of tweezers from the gizmo. Gently, he tugged the toilet paper from around her foot. "Hold still."

"Archer. Really? I'm fine."

Three angry red cuts formed swollen bumps against the bottom of her foot. The biggest one clearly had something left inside. He ran the pad of his index finger over the largest. She tensed.

"This might hurt. Try not to move."

Her fingers curled into the comforter as he scraped the tweezers over the wound, looking for the glass. Finding it, he pressed the tweezers against the shard and tried to get a grip on it. Her lips compressed, and she sucked in a breath, then let out a small shriek.

Frowning, he pulled the bloody shard from her foot and held it up for her to see. "This doesn't look like nothing."

He dropped the two-centimeter-long piece of glass on the nightstand, then went back to her foot. Eve tensed again and gripped the comforter more tightly. When she jerked her foot away, Zane clamped a hand on her shin and pulled it right back. "Hold still, I said."

Eve's lips turned white as she pressed them together, and her shoulders lifted, her entire body taut and ready to escape. "Oh my God," she gasped as he searched for more glass, "are you trying to fucking kill me?"

Zane pulled out another piece of glass, this one smaller, and held it up for her. "Not kill. Not yet anyway. How on earth did you walk around all day with this in your foot?"

He tossed the second shard on the nightstand with the other piece and moved for the bag of first aid supplies they'd picked up. Eve dropped back into the pillows with heavy, deep breaths. "I had other things on my mind."

He picked up the bag and glanced her way. She lay diagonally across the mattress, her chest rising and falling with her labored breaths, one hand over her eyes, and the towel so damn high, it just barely covered her sex.

Heat rushed right back into his groin, making his cock throb.

Clearing his throat, he focused on her bloody foot and knelt near the end of the bed again. "This part might sting."

He poured alcohol on a sterile pad and pressed it against the wound. Eve sucked in a breath, and then every muscle in her body went rigid. Her hands gripped the comforter once more. Her head lifted an inch off the pillow as she grunted through the pain, and her legs spread, just a fraction of an inch, tugging the towel aside, just enough so he could see the pink lips of her sex.

Holy *hell*. She was bare. Everywhere. His erection pushed against his fly until pain shot through his lower body. She must have been bare this morning, only he'd been so overwhelmed by the feeling of her closing around him, dragging him in, he hadn't noticed.

His skin broke out in a fine sweat, and his balls tightened, making him even harder. Clearing his throat, he looked quickly away from her pretty pink center and told himself to think of anything besides touching her there—tasting her there. He wasn't still with her for sex. *No sex.* They'd gotten that out of their systems. They were here to find answers. Nothing more.

Refocusing on her foot, he swiped the alcohol swab over her wounds again. Eve tensed, moaned, and tightened her muscles once more, forcing her legs open another fraction of an inch.

And holy shit—his blood turned to a roar in his ears, and sweat slid down his spine. She was there—right there—opening for him like a flower. All he had to do was lean forward a few inches, part her with his fingers, slide his tongue down her slick, swollen slit, and feast.

"Archer?"

Her voice shook him out of his sex-induced trance, and he blinked, then realized she'd closed her legs and pulled the towel down until it covered her mound.

Heat erupted in his stomach and shot straight to his face. His gaze jerked to her foot, and he slapped on a bandage and then quickly pushed to his feet. "You're done. I need a shower."

A cold shower. Ice-cold shower. Maybe ten, so he could cool the fuck off.

"Zane?" she called when he reached the bathroom door. "What about your shoulder?"

His shoulder? His shoulder was the last thing on his mind. Every cell in his body was currently condensed behind his fly. "It's fine."

He closed the bathroom door quickly at his back, then braced his hands on the sink and dropped his head while he breathed deep and tried to settle his raging hormones.

Zane . . . Why the hell did it sound so fucking good when she called him by his first name?

Because you're a moron. Because you're still whipped. Because you like getting your teeth kicked in by the viper in the other room.

He looked up at his reflection, blurry from the still-damp mirror, thanks to Eve's shower. A few bruises had formed around his temple where he'd gotten hit—he couldn't remember which time—but it was his eyes he focused on. Dilated pupils, dark gaze, skin flushed and hot from his arousal. His flesh felt tight, like it wasn't his own, and the raging hard-on in his pants screamed, *Get the hell back out there!* but he refused to listen.

His fingers turned white where he gripped the sink tight. He wasn't going down that road with Eve again. This morning was the result of too much adrenaline and way too little sleep, but if he went out there now, it'd simply be stupidity. Clearing his name was now all that mattered. Not how tight she'd be. Or how slick he could make her. Or how fucking good she'd feel when he drove inside her. Freedom trumped sex any day of the week, and she'd be the first to throw him aside to save her own ass. The sooner he remembered that, the better off he'd be.

Disgusted with himself, he flipped on the shower, then tugged off his clothes. And as the hot water cascaded over his sore muscles, he ignored the burn in his shoulder and the ache in his leg and especially the throb in his cock. Instead, he reminded himself of all the shit he'd been through because of her. Nothing—not even the hottest sex of his life—was worth living through that kind of pain again.

And he sure as shit wasn't listening to that little voice whispering that he might already be halfway there.

chapter 13

Eve hobbled to the sack of clothing they'd picked up and tugged on the long T-shirt she'd grabbed to sleep in. She debated putting on a bra and then figured she was only going to bed, so why bother?

She glanced toward the closed bathroom door and listened to the sound of the shower, still running. Zane had been in there for at least fifteen minutes. Her mind flashed to the heated look in his eyes when she'd realized he'd been staring at her bared sex, then to the way he'd bolted out of the room when she'd caught him. Her skin grew warm and tingly when she remembered the arousal flushing his cheeks, and a heavy weight settled right between her thighs. Then an image filled her mind, this one of him standing naked beneath the spray, the water sliding over his chiseled muscles, his hand closed around his cock, stroking the length of his erection, up, down, again and again while he thought of her . . .

Heat exploded in her hips and shot fingers of arousal straight to her breasts. Her nipples pebbled against the thin cotton of her T-shirt, and she sank to the end of the bed, swiped at the perspiration on her forehead, and pressed her thighs together.

It was official. She was an idiot. Her sister was missing, the government thought she'd turned traitor and was right now looking for her, and all she could think about was mind-numbing sex with the man on the other side of the door who still didn't completely trust her. And what was worse—what was really knocking her off her feet—was the knowledge that if Zane had reached for her a moment ago, she wouldn't have been able to say no.

She pressed shaking fingers against her closed eyes and breathed deep. *Keep it together, Eve.*

Okay, so, the reality was, if he'd wanted her, he'd have taken her. Yeah, he'd been turned on—she'd seen his erection when he'd pushed to his feet—but he'd walked out because even he knew a repeat of this morning was a bad fucking idea. Sex—now—would just be a major mistake. It wouldn't help her find her sister, and it wouldn't clear their names. But oh God, it would feel good . . .

Her traitorous mind skipped back to this morning. To the feel of his cock pressing inside her, stretching her, drawing a groan from her lips. To the tight slide and retreat, to the electrical current that had shot through her entire body and the exquisite feeling of coming apart around him.

She braced her hands on her knees, squeezed until pain shot through her legs, and breathed deeply. *Think about Olivia. Think about Roberts. Think about anything besides going into that bathroom, stripping out of your clothes, and joining Zane in that hot, wet shower.*

She needed perspective. She needed someone to slap some common sense into her. Because she'd distanced herself from her family, she'd never confided anything to Olivia, and thanks to her job, she didn't have any close girlfriends to turn to. There was only one person who knew both her and Archer and who'd been a rock for her to lean on when she'd broken things off with Archer the first time. Only one person who could possibly save her from doing something stupid right this very minute.

Her eyes popped open, and before she could stop herself, she reached for the unregistered cell phone Zane had given her and dialed the private number.

"Dietrick."

"Carter? It's Juliet."

James Dietrick sighed. "Eve, where the hell are you? I tried to call Archer earlier, but he didn't answer."

The sexy image of Zane pleasuring himself threatened once more, but Eve forced it back. "Is this line secure?"

"Yes."

"You're sure?"

"I know how to cover my ass, Juliet. Where's Sawyer?"

"He's in the shower. They sent a wet team after us before, when he called you from Bainbridge."

"I know. But it wasn't us. Feds already found the house. Nice work there, by the way."

"Who were they?" she asked.

"I don't know. We're running things now. Think they might have been part of a Chechen militia with ties to the terrorists who set off that bomb."

Eve sighed. "Great. How the hell would they have found us?"

"I don't know." He hesitated. "Hey, you don't sound so hot. Is everything okay?"

No, everything was most definitely not okay. She was danger-ously close to jumping Zane's bones, and she needed Carter to talk some sense into her before she took the situation from bad to worse. Thankfully, Carter had always been the conscience she seemed to lack. He'd been the one to warn her that things with Zane were heating up too fast back in Beirut. And he'd cautioned her to the consequences of getting involved with a fellow officer. Too bad she hadn't listened to him sooner. Then maybe she never would have fallen in love with Archer in the first place.

"I'm fine. Everything's fine. I'm just . . ." She closed her eyes and drew a deep breath. "Remind me again why he's not like us."

Carter chuckled. "You want the condensed or unabridged version?"

Eve's blood hummed, and she hobbled to the window, hoping some of the damp Pacific Northwest air radiating from the glass would cool her down. "I want the sane version."

Carter sighed. "Your soft spot's showing, Juliet."

"I don't have a soft spot, dammit. I'm just . . . tired and stressed and . . . not thinking clearly."

"Does the dumbass know how you feel?"

How could he? Eve barely understood how she felt herself. And she didn't want to feel anything for him, but she knew now that was a pipe dream. The truth was, she hadn't been able to leave him last night like she should have because she still cared about him. And she wasn't walking out now—like a sane person would—because somewhere, deep inside, she was still halfway in love with the guy.

Her heart thumped hard at that realization. "I'm scared," she whispered. "I haven't been scared in a long time, but I'm scared now."

"We'll figure all of this out. Don't worry. You've got Archer there, and I'm here to help, however I can. Did you set up the meeting with your CSIS agent?"

"Yeah. Tomorrow. Oh nine hundred, in Bellingham."

"Good. By tomorrow night this could all be over."

Over . . .

The word hung in Eve's mind, and she chanced a look back toward the closed bathroom door. Yeah, she wanted this nightmare over, but as soon as that happened, Zane would be gone. And then she'd be alone, like she'd been before. Except this time she'd have the fresh memory of what it felt like to have his arms close around her, to have his lips on hers, to remember the exquisite pleasure only he'd ever been able to wring out of her.

"It's gonna be okay," Carter said softly. "You're gonna be fine."

She huffed out a half laugh and looked back out the window. "See, that's the thing. I don't care about me. I just don't want anything to happen to my sister or Archer because of me."

"We'll find your sister. It's what we do. I've got people looking into her disappearance now. As for Archer . . . he's a big boy. He knows the consequences."

"Yeah, but he doesn't see things the way we do. He sees them in black-and-white, not shades of gray."

"Which is what makes him different from us. Look, Eve, I can't tell you what to do about the guy. You walked away from him once before, and what good did that do you? You're right back with him again. Whether that's fate or destiny or just bad luck, I don't know. But I do know, if you still want him, you should go for it. I mean, it *could* work. You two could, like, buy a house together or something. When you run off to play 007, he could . . . I don't know . . . What the fuck does he do these days?"

The absurdity of his words made Eve scoff. "Right. Most case officers get married three to four times, and the majority end up divorced and alone regardless of the number of times they say 'I do.' And that's with someone who doesn't know all the bad shit you've done. I'm not stupid enough to think there's any kind of valentine at the end of my rainbow, especially not where Zane Archer is concerned."

"I think you're getting your holidays mixed up, honey."

"See? Another reason it would never work out. Then there's the very real fact he still hates my guts."

Carter chuckled again. "You really are in a mood, aren't you?"

Eve leaned a shoulder against the wall and pressed still-shaking fingers against her throbbing eyes. "I'm just . . . overwhelmed."

"I know you are, honey, but this is all gonna work out. Trust me. If you're conflicted, keep your distance from Archer and don't do anything stupid. Meet with your contact in the morning, get that damn data drive, find out what's on it, then call me. I'm not gonna let you go down for this, Eve. You're not alone. You've got friends. Remember that."

Friends. Eve wasn't sure what that word meant anymore. She'd spent so many years lying and faking relationships for her job, she didn't think she could recognize a friend even if they hit her over the head with a two-by-four.

"You're not alone, and you don't have to do everything on your own. I'm here with you in this."

Zane's words from the kitchen of that house on Bainbridge Island rushed through her mind. The words he'd spoken just before they'd left. Just *after* he'd kissed her crazy.

Her pulse ticked up again. And when the water finally shut off in the bathroom, she pictured him wet and dripping, his skin warm and glossy as he rubbed a fresh towel all over his muscular body. The blood beat hard and hot in her veins all over again, heading straight for her belly.

"Eve?"

Carter's voice dragged her attention back to the phone. "What?"

"Everything okay? Think I lost you there for a minute."

He had. Eve swallowed hard and closed her eyes. Oh God, she was losing it. And she had a sinking suspicion there was no way she'd be able to keep her distance from Archer tonight. Not the way she was suddenly feeling. "I'm . . . here."

"Good. Get some rest and call me tomorrow."

"I will. And Carter, please let me know if you hear anything about Olivia. Anything at all."

"Done. Sleep well, Juliet."

The line clicked in her ear, and Eve's hand dropped to her side. *Stupid . . .*

She rested her head against the wall and scrunched her eyes. She should leave right now before Archer came out of that bathroom. Before it was too late. But she wasn't going to. No, like the idiot she'd been in Beirut, she was going to sit here and want and suffer. And if he even made one tiny move toward her, she'd probably rock his world, and hers, and fuck everything up for good.

Then hate herself even more in the morning.

Olivia's throat was bone-dry.

She pushed her aching upper body off the frayed mattress she'd been lying on and looked toward the door. The room they'd moved her to felt like the Ritz compared to the box she'd been in before. She was in some kind of house. A high window on the wall let in moonlight, which illuminated the cracked plaster walls and the dirty wood floor, but she had no idea what it looked out at. Aside from the rusted iron bed—bolted to the wall—and the mattress stained with sweat and blood, there was no other furniture to move around so she could climb up to see. And the bars over the windows prevented her from getting out, even if she had the energy to try.

It felt like cotton coated her mouth, and she licked her lips for the hundredth time. She needed water but was too afraid to bang on the door and ask. A shudder ran through her when her mind flashed to the image of that man climbing into the back of the van with her after she'd tried to run. As if he'd hit her all over again, pain ricocheted through her entire body.

Her head throbbed. She was filthy and covered in her own blood, and part of her didn't even want to know where the blood had come from. She'd blacked out in that van—the only plus to the entire ordeal—and she didn't want to think about or do anything to trigger her memories.

Tears welled in her eyes, and she closed them quickly, willing back the self-defeating thoughts. Someone would find her. People had to know she was missing by now. Her principal. The secretary at school. Her mind spun with possibilities, and then she remembered the guy in the van mentioning Eve.

Eve worked as an assistant to some politician in Washington, DC. Surely once she realized Olivia was missing, with her contacts, she'd send someone to come after Olivia.

But even as she tried to convince herself all wasn't lost, a tiny voice in the back of Olivia's head whispered, *No one's coming after you. You're not important. What have you ever done that makes your life worth saving?* And then there was the very real fact she and Eve hadn't spoken in over a year.

Regret welled in Olivia's chest. The last time she'd seen her sister was at their father's funeral, when Eve had breezed in for the service and then breezed right back out again, as she always did. But this time, before she'd left, Olivia had been pissed enough to let Eve have it. *She'd* been the one to visit Daddy every day in the hospital after the cancer had spread. *She'd* been the one to take care of the preparations for the funeral and to oversee liquidating what was left of their parents' estate. *She'd* been the only Wolfe child her parents could depend on in their last years because *she* hadn't disappeared as soon as life got tough.

Unlike Eve. Who'd shed a few tears at the funeral, accepted the condolences from friends and family as if she'd carried some huge burden, and then had taken off again like she always did. And the saddest part was, their father wouldn't have cared. Because—according to him—Eve was doing something important with her life, unlike Olivia, who was simply teaching.

Those who can, do. Those who can't, teach.

He'd never said those words aloud, but she knew he'd believed them. Because she believed them too.

She swiped at the stupid tear falling from the corner of her eye and felt like giving in to a long crying jag. But a groan echoed through the wall, drawing her up short.

Her breath caught, and she listened, afraid her captors were coming for her again. She wouldn't survive another beating. Her body began to shake. She wouldn't make it if—

"Who's there?"

Olivia stilled. The voice hadn't come from the hallway beyond her door but from . . . the wall.

She looked to her right, to the wall opposite the window, and held her breath.

"I can hear you," the voice said. A male voice. A weak male voice, which was . . . oddly familiar. "Don't pretend like you don't know I'm here."

Her gaze locked on a heating vent at the bottom of the wall, near the corner of the room. Slowly, she slid off the bed and crawled toward it, gritting her teeth at the pain in her muscles as she moved. When she was seated on the floor near the vent, her back against the adjacent wall and her knees pulled up to her chest, she finally worked up the courage to say, "Wh-who are you?"

"No one you know."

But she did. Olivia's brow dropped. His voice was very familiar, she just didn't know from where.

"Any idea what time it is?"

"No." She focused on the cadence of his words to see if anything triggered her memory but came up empty. The only thing she knew for sure was that his voice was frail, like hers, indicating he'd taken a beating or two himself. "It's late, though."

He sighed. "I'm sorry I got you involved in this."

"Don't worry. I won't hurt you. This won't take long, I promise."

Words—words *he* had spoken to her the night Karl had dropped her off at her house after that awful date and he'd come out of the shadows to grab her—echoed through Olivia's mind. She gripped her knees and sat straight up. "You—"

"I didn't plan this," he said quickly. "They made me. They told me nothing would happen to you. I believed them. I'm sorry."

Olivia's gaze darted around the barren floor, but she couldn't seem to focus on any one thing. "Who's *they*?"

Silence.

"Who's *they*?" she said again. "I have a right to know who's doing this to me."

"Shh, relax. You don't want them to hear us, do you?"

Olivia stared at the grate between the walls, barely able to think, let alone feel. The man who'd kidnapped her was in the next room. The one who'd started all of this.

"And you don't have any rights," he mumbled. "Not where they're concerned. It's written on the fucking Constitution. You lose all rights as soon as they turn your way."

Olivia didn't know what he was getting at, but she didn't care. All that mattered was finding out what was really going on, so that maybe—somehow—she could figure a way out of this nightmare. Because she wasn't so sure help was coming after her anymore.

"What do they want? Why me?"

"Does it even matter? We're gonna die in this hellhole."

Panic pushed its way up Olivia's throat, but she forced it back. "Yes, it matters. I need to know. Why did they—whoever they are—tell you to come after me? What do they want with me?"

"Nothing."

"Nothing?" That couldn't be right. "If I was nothing, they would have killed me already." She knew from the beating she'd taken that they were capable of it. There was a reason they were keeping her alive. When they'd moved her from that container she'd been locked in, the big guy from the van had told her she was now "useful." "What do I know—?"

"Nothing," he said on an exasperated breath. "You know nothing. Don't you get it? They don't care about you. They made me grab you to draw out your sister. They wanted to take her out, and they used me to do it. But no one ever told me they were going to set off a fucking bomb. I'd never have agreed if I'd known about that. I'm not a murderer, you understand?"

Olivia's breath caught. And images of Eve swirled in her mind. She didn't know what was going on, but a kidnapping, a bomb, this house . . . something big was happening.

"Are you still there?"

Olivia's heart beat so hard, it echoed in her ears. "I-I'm here."

"I'm not a murderer," he said even softer. "I'm not. I just . . . I made a really bad business decision. That's all this is. Business. You understand? I didn't plan for any of this to happen. I was gonna let you go. As soon as I had the money, I was gonna let you go. I swear."

Her mind flashed to that dark box. To the door opening and a man standing in the light. Then kneeling down and sliding a plate of food across the floor to her.

That had been him. The man she was now talking to. Until yesterday—or had it been the day before?—he hadn't been a prisoner. He'd been her captor.

A feeling she didn't know how to define bubbled through her—a mix of rage and disbelief and horror. She gripped her knees tightly. "What's your name?"

He hesitated and then said, "Tyrone."

The name wasn't familiar, not that Olivia expected it to be. "Why do they want my sister?"

"Because she knows too much."

"About what?"

He was silent for a moment. Then finally, he said, "Project Thirteen."

Unease slid through her veins and tightened the muscles in her chest. Against her knees, her palms grew slick. "What is Project Thirteen?" she asked hesitantly.

"It's bad shit. Let's just put it that way. Nothing you ever want to come in contact with."

"And Eve's involved in it?"

"Unfortunately." He was quiet a second, then said softly, "Look, if anything should happen to me and you ever find a way out of here, go to the athletic club on Western Avenue, downtown Seattle. Find locker eighty-nine. It's the only thing that will help your sister."

"What do you mean by 'help' her?" Fear clawed its way up Olivia's throat. "Eve's okay, isn't she?"

"I don't know—"

Wood splintered before he could finish his sentence. A door crashing open. Olivia jumped, then realized it wasn't the door to her room. Through the grate, Tyrone yelled, "Hey. No! I already told you I don't know anything!"

A crash echoed, and Olivia's heart rate jerked.

"Get up," another voice growled.

Tyrone grunted. "I don't—"

A crack reverberated through the grate, followed by another thunk of a body against breaking wood. Olivia couldn't see what was happening, but she could hear it. The distinct thwack of a fist slamming into flesh and bone sounded through the wall, sending her adrenaline pumping.

"The boss wants to talk to you."

More grunting. A yelp. Scraping. Then the door slammed shut, and all that remained was silence.

"Tyrone?" Olivia called quietly into the grate.

Nothing. Silence settled over the space like an ominous black cloud.

Shaking, Olivia wrapped her arms around her knees and dropped her head. And this time she didn't try to stop the tears from falling.

chapter 14

Landon sat in the front seat of his rental in the shadows outside a row of run-down townhomes in the Yesler Terrace district of Seattle. A smokestack rose behind the aged neighborhood, its blinking red light flashing against the dark sky, and the lights of Seattle's skyscrapers downtown twinkled in the distance.

He glanced around the packed street with its dented cars and chain-link fences. It made sense that whoever had taken Olivia Wolfe had wound up here, in one of Seattle's crummiest neighborhoods, but even the Emerald City's worst didn't qualify as a ghetto by East Coast standards, and Landon found himself wondering just how bright these kidnappers could be.

A glance at his phone confirmed the GPS coordinates he'd tracked from the last phone call made on the cell he'd pulled from Evelyn Wolfe's purse had gone to this location. Now all he had to do was wait and watch and see if anything odd stood out.

Two hours passed with nothing more than a few cars sliding by on the street and a couple lights going on and off in the house he'd targeted. Interestingly, no lights flickered upstairs, only downstairs.

His cell phone buzzed.

He pulled it out and looked at the screen, then held it up to his ear. "Marley, you're up way too late."

"I'm always up way too late. I have some intel for you."

"Shoot."

"The FBI picked up four Chechen terrorists with links to al-Qaeda. The Feds are saying the four were involved in the Seattle bombing, but so far all are claiming innocence."

"They always do."

"I also did some checking at the State Department. The Guatemala contract was awarded to Aegis by Assistant Deputy Director Roberts himself. When he found out Aegis had been pulled from the project and that it had been given to someone else, he stepped in and made sure the selection committee handed it back to Aegis."

Landon braced an elbow on the windowsill and looked toward the dark house. The lights had gone off downstairs. "That is interesting."

"According to my contact, Roberts was adamant that Humbolt be brought back alive ASAP. Suspicion is that he knew something about leaks within the counterintelligence division. Roberts told the committee that he had the utmost confidence in Aegis to pull off the job. Whether that had anything to do with Ryder or Archer, whom he must have known from Archer's time with the CIA, I don't know."

Landon rubbed a hand over his mouth. This whole thing was just getting bigger and more complicated. If Assistant Deputy Director Roberts was involved in Humbolt's death, and Evelyn Wolfe had stumbled upon evidence pointing to that, then this mess in Seattle could quite possibly be part of an elaborate cover-up. And if that was the case, and it went way up the chain of command, proving Wolfe's and Archer's innocence was going to be a real bitch.

"What about the connection between Roberts and Ryder?" Landon asked. "Do they know each other?"

"Yep. Went to Notre Dame together. And word is, they weren't exactly friends there."

"Fuck."

"Pretty much. Though I don't know the status of their relationship, it's not looking good. If Roberts wanted to make sure the op in Guatemala was a failure, he could have easily set this up."

Landon considered for a moment. "I think it's time we brought Ryder in on this."

"Agreed. Though this you might also find interesting. Humbolt's specialty wasn't chemical weaponry like we were led to believe. It was biological weapons, and supposedly he'd discovered something big. Though no one will talk about what that something is. All I've managed to get is a name. Project Thirteen."

"Ever heard of it before?"

"No. Whatever it is, it's hush-hush."

Landon stared at the quiet, dark house. So far he'd counted three men coming and going. Two had left earlier, which meant there was at least one left inside. No other movement at any of the windows told him that if he was going to go in, now was his best shot. He could sit here and wait to be sure, or he could make something happen. His gut said waiting wasn't the solution.

"Okay, you talk to Ryder. I've got a bead on Olivia Wolfe. Between the two of us maybe we can figure out how all of this is connected. Archer and Wolfe are meeting with her CSIS contact tomorrow, and hopefully we'll know more about what was on that data drive she was supposed to get when all this shit went down."

"Will do. Stay safe, Miller."

"I always do."

He powered off his phone and quietly climbed out of the car. Pulling the SIG from his shoulder holster, he jumped the chain-link fence to the backyard and quietly moved up the back-porch steps.

A dog barked four houses down. Landon peeked through the windows but didn't see anything. One turn confirmed the back door was locked, so he holstered his gun and pulled out his lock pick.

Minutes later he was in the house, moving silently through the dark kitchen, his gun in his hand again. The small kitchen gave way to a cramped living area with eighties furniture. Stairs ran up to the second level.

He hesitated at the stairs, looked up, and listened. No sound met his ears. Moving past the staircase, he headed for the hallway that ran behind the garage and the bedrooms beyond.

The first room—an office—was empty except for a desk and closed laptop. But blue-green light flickered through the open door of the second.

His adrenaline stirred. No sound echoed. Gun in both hands, he rounded the corner and scanned the room.

A night light shone in the corner of the room. A double bed was pushed up against the wall next to a nightstand, the covers rumpled as if someone had recently slept there. Across the room, a dresser sat under the high window.

He checked the closet, then headed quietly back to the staircase. The old wooden steps creaked under his weight, but he moved up as quickly as he could. Once he reached the second floor, he scanned the hallway and the three closed doors, two off the right and one off the left.

The first bedroom was empty. The one across the hall was the same, but dried blood stained the worn carpet. After checking the closets and finding nothing out of the ordinary, he moved to the last bedroom.

This one held a rusted iron-framed bed and dirty mattress. Nothing else. A high window looked out at the backyard beyond.

Frowning, Landon lowered the gun.

A body slammed into him from behind before he heard the footsteps. Landon hit the wall with his shoulder, staggered, but kept from going down. He pivoted, looked up. The guy who'd hit him was dressed all in black and hard to see. The attacker kicked out, knocking the gun from Landon's hand. It flew across the room and smacked into the wall, then dropped to the hardwood floor with a clap. The man swung out. Landon blocked the blow and slammed his fist in the guy's face.

The attacker stumbled backward, then swiveled quickly and kicked out again. Landon caught his leg and twisted backward. The man screamed. Landon jammed his elbow into the man's thigh, making him cry out even louder, then hurled him back against the wall.

Wood splintered. Bone cracked against plaster. The attacker crumbled against the ground with a groan. Chest heaving, Landon stepped over him and lifted his body by the shirtfront. "I'm looking for a woman. Tell me where she is, and I'll think twice about killing you."

"Go to hell."

He was American. No accent. Landon slammed his fist into the guy's jaw. The man grunted. Blood seeped from the corner of his mouth. "Not the answer I'm looking for."

The attacker spit out a mouthful of blood. "Look, I don't know nothin', 'kay?"

Landon lifted him three inches off the floor and slammed him back against the hardwood. "My guess is, you know a hell of a lot. And you can cooperate and we can do this here, or I can let the Feds beat it out of you. But I've seen the shit they do to terrorists, and trust me, you're a hell of a lot better off with me. Now tell me about the girl."

"I ain't no terrorist," the guy coughed in a defiant tone. "All I did was let some pricks rent the house. That doesn't make me no terrorist. I didn't know who they were until the shit hit the news tonight. I came over here to see what was going on and found you. For all I know, *you* could be the terrorist."

Landon was losing his patience. He jammed his knee into the guy's stomach. "The girl."

The man groaned. "Stop. Dammit, stop, okay? Look"—he coughed—"they had a girl with them yesterday. She was kinda banged up, but it's not my place to ask questions, you know? They must have taken her out of here earlier. I don't know where they went."

"Bullshit." Landon lowered his knee, ready to nail the prick in the balls.

"Wait!" He held up both hands in a frantic motion. "They said something about a place in Fremont."

Fremont was an artsy district of Seattle. Way more upscale than Yesler Terrace. "Where?"

"I-I don't know."

Landon pulled his fist back.

The man cringed. "I-I have a phone number. That's all, though."

A cell number he could track. "Give it to me."

"It-it's in my phone. In my pocket."

Landon reached into the guy's jacket pocket and pulled out the phone.

"It's under 'renters.' The most recent number. They didn't give me a name. I just wanted to get some cash for this dump, you know? You're not gonna report me, are you? I don't know nothin' else."

Landon pushed to his feet and hauled the guy with him. After dragging him toward the bed, he pulled zip ties from his pocket and cinched them around the guy's wrists, anchoring him to the bed frame.

"Hey!"

Landon shoved on the guy's shoulder, forcing him to sit on the end of the bed. "You're gonna sit your ass here and tell the Feds everything they want to know. And if you're lucky, and you're honest, they won't charge you with aiding and abetting a terrorist cell." Crossing the floor, he picked up his gun and holstered it. "How many were there?"

The man slumped down. He was maybe five foot eight and a hundred and sixty pounds. And the missing teeth told Landon loud and clear that he was more interested in money to fuel his drug habit than anything else. "I don't know. Three, I think. I only saw three."

Landon pulled out his cell phone and dialed. Marley answered on the first ring. "Miss me already?"

"Always. Look, I need a GPS track on a number."

"I can do that. Did you find the sister?"

"Almost." He eyed the man on the bed, and disgust rolled through him over what some people would do for a quick buck. "Then I need you to call the Feds for me. I've got some trash they need to pick up."

- - - - - - - - - - - - - - - - -

Eve blew out a deep breath.

This wasn't working. She'd been lying here staring at the ceiling for the last hour and wasn't anywhere closer to falling asleep than she'd been when Archer had come out of the bathroom and climbed into the other bed.

Counting stains on the ceiling, she reminded herself not to think about how fresh he'd smelled or how damp and muscular his skin had looked when he'd walked out wearing only those low-slung jeans he'd picked up at the mall. So they had a past. So she still felt something for him. That didn't mean she was going to be stupid.

She rolled to her side and punched the pillow near her head. When that didn't work, she flopped to her back, the mattress springs creaking as she moved.

"God Almighty, Wolfe. Could you be any louder?"

Great, now he was awake. She heaved out another sigh. "Sorry. I'm just"—*agitated, hot, sexually frustrated*—"keyed up."

From the corner of her vision, she watched as he laced his fingers behind his head, his arms catching what little streetlight was shining in from outside, highlighting the muscles and planes she'd had her hands all over this morning. "Miller will find your sister, don't worry."

Eve scrubbed the heels of her hands over both eyes to block the image of all his sexy goodness. "I'd feel better if he'd just call."

"He will when he has news. There's nothing you can do but wait."

Yeah, she knew that, but she sucked at the waiting game. Which was ironic, because in her line of work, there was a lot of sitting around, watching and waiting. "So Miller was DIA, huh?" she asked, trying to take her mind off how she'd filled all those boring hours with Archer in Beirut. "Not what I expected. I would have thought marine from his demeanor."

"He's that too. Ex–Special Operations Command. In addition to his tactical abilities, they quickly realized he had a certain . . . moral ambiguity . . . that fit in well with DIA, and they recruited him. He signed on. End of story."

But it wasn't. There was always a story with these guys. "Why'd he leave?"

"I don't know. You'd have to ask him. He joined Aegis just after I did."

Which would have been about a year and a half ago, Eve calculated. She knew why Zane had left the CIA, but a man like Landon Miller was wired differently, especially if he'd been trained as an assassin, and she couldn't help but wonder just what had been his tipping point.

Not your concern. You have enough other things to worry about.

Muscles tight, Eve pushed from the bed and crossed the floor to get a bottle of water. She downed half of it, but the cool liquid did little to settle this uneasy feeling growing in the pit of her stomach. She needed to *do* something. Something physical. And since the only physical activity she could think to do in this room meant crossing a line she wasn't about to cross again, she capped the water and began pacing. "Why'd you quit?"

"What?"

Zane's surprised voice drifted to her ears, but she refused to turn and look his way. *Keep walking. Don't look at his naked torso or that damn sexy scruff on his jaw.* "Aegis. When we were at the house on Bainbridge, Miller said you'd quit. You told me you'd tell me why later. It's later, and I can't sleep, so you might as well answer the question now. God knows I've answered enough of yours."

"Motherfucker," he muttered under his breath. "Miller should learn to keep his big mouth shut."

Eve's interest was piqued. Whatever the reason, he obviously didn't want her to know. And focusing on that gave her something to think about besides sex. "I figured you'd like defense contract work way more than Agency work. We both know that wasn't your cup of tea. So why'd you quit?"

"Not my cup of tea? Bullshit. We both know I was a damn good officer."

She frowned. The last thing she wanted was for him to get all agitated. She was agitated enough for the both of them. Reaching the wall, she turned and paced back across the dingy carpet. "Bad choice of words. I didn't say you weren't a good officer. I just meant we both know your heart wasn't in it. You're a doer, not a watcher. So why did you leave? Did you have an argument with your boss?"

"Sort of."

Sort of. That didn't tell her a lot. She glanced his way. His arms were still laced behind his head, but he was now staring up at the ceiling with a serious expression. One she couldn't read. "About an assignment?"

"You could say that."

"What happened?"

"Ryder told me not to get personally involved."

Eve stilled in the middle of the room, and her mind tumbled. *Personally involved . . .* There was only one way you could get personally involved with an assignment.

Her heart picked up speed, and her skin grew cold and clammy. She wasn't sure she wanted to hear more, but some twisted place inside needed to know what kind of woman could get him to quit his job. "And you didn't listen?"

"Nope."

Her heart beat hard. Drumbeats against her ribs. "What happened?"

"He told me not to go after her. Said if I did, I wouldn't have a job to come back to. I told him it wasn't his fucking business and to shove the job."

Ouch.

"Then he told me I needed to cool the hell off and that when I was ready, we'd talk again, but not to do anything in the meantime. I didn't call him back."

Obviously, whoever this woman was, she had meant a lot to him. "Was—" She cleared her throat because it was suddenly thick and sounded funny. "Was she worth it?"

"I don't know." He continued to stare up at the ceiling. "She sure has fucked my life up good, though." He chuckled, but the sound held no humor. "Shot in the leg, shot in the shoulder, and my face is plastered all over the news linked to a terrorist bombing. You tell me. Is she worth it?"

Eve froze. The air caught in her throat. And his words from this morning ran back through her mind. Words she'd heard but had been too angry to process until right now.

"If I didn't still want you, I sure as hell wouldn't have spent the last year trying to track you down."

Her. He'd been talking about her moments ago, not some random woman. Her chest constricted until it was hard to draw air. And somewhere deep inside, a warmth began to blossom, all around her heart.

The room grew stifling, and sweat popped out all over her skin. She needed air. Needed to breathe. Needed—her mind raced back to this morning . . . to stripping him of his pants, to sinking down onto his length, to the exquisite feeling of him filling her.

Tingles shot straight to her center. Oh shit. She needed to get gone before she did something she knew she should never do. Like fucked him senseless until they both screamed.

"I . . ." She could barely think, let alone speak. "I need a shower."

His head came up an inch off the bed, and he looked her way. "You already took a shower."

"Yeah, well . . ." Forcing herself not to look his way, she rushed for the bathroom.

chapter 15

Let her go. Don't go after her. A smart guy would know he's in over his head and leave well enough alone.

Yeah. Good advice. The problem was, when it came to Evelyn Wolfe, Zane had never been anything but a complete fucking idiot.

"Son of a bitch." He pushed off the bed and crossed the floor. Running water echoed from the shower. He listened at the door but couldn't hear her moving around. His skin vibrated. His muscles bunched while he stood still, trying to decide what to do. His breaths picked up speed as he imagined her naked under the spray, her flesh glossy and wet and pink from the heat.

His groin tightened. All the blood in his body seemed to rush due south. He wasn't going to be able to sleep tonight. There was too much energy arcing between them. And when he thought of the surprise he'd heard in her voice moments before—like she didn't *know* she was his own personal form of kryptonite—his resistance where she was concerned crumbled just a little more.

Let her go. Don't go after her.

Fuck it. He was tired of playing this game. Of dancing around each other. Of making himself insane.

He turned the doorknob and found it unlocked. Stepping into the steam-filled room, he could just make out her silhouette behind the white shower curtain. Head tipped up. Hands resting on the back of her neck. Perfect body filled out in all the right places, dripping with water as it hit her chest and slid down the curves and hollows of her physique, drawing him toward her like a magnet.

He waited until she stepped under the spray, and then he pulled the shower curtain open at the back and moved into the tub behind her.

She didn't immediately hear him. But she tensed when she sensed him, and before she could whip around, he caught her arms, wrapped them around her front, and pulled her back against him.

"Archer, what are you—?"

The soft curve of her ass pressed against his damp jeans and his already hardening cock.

"I'm done tiptoeing around this, Evie."

Beneath his fingers, he felt the pulse in her wrists pick up speed. "Around what? I don't know what you're talking about."

"Yeah, you do. This. You and me. You know damn well what I'm talking about."

She swallowed. "Archer—"

"Anytime the conversation gets personal, you run. Tell me, beautiful. Do I make you nervous?"

"As if."

He tightened his grip on her wrists. "I think I do. I think you're scared to death of me."

She turned her head, just enough so he could see her profile and those plump, pouty lips. "Are you taking pain meds again? Because you sound higher than a kite. I've faced down terrorists. You're a cupcake compared to them."

A smile curled his lips. He watched droplets of water slide down the long, sexy column of her neck. "Always with the lies. How about the truth for a change? I think that's what you're most afraid of. I think it's the truth that always makes you run."

She tensed. "What have you been smok—?"

"You wanna ask the questions? Then you have to deal with the answers. Six months, Eve. I was in and out of physical therapy for six months after the raid in Guatemala. I didn't just take a bullet; I took a shitload of shrapnel that tore my leg to pieces. Almost bled out on the helo. And you know what I thought about when I was in and out of hospitals and rehab and dealing with more doctors than any man should?"

"No," she said quietly.

"Too bad. I thought about you."

She was silent, but where his arms were crossed over hers against her chest, her heart pounded hard, and her breaths picked up speed.

"Now who lies?" she whispered. "You weren't thinking about me for any reason other than wanting to make me pay for something I hadn't done."

"You're right. I was. After I told Ryder what he could do with his job, I went to a friend's place in the mountains of Mexico to recuperate. And the whole time I was there I thought about nothing but tracking you and finding out what you were up to. But I also thought about this."

He released one wrist, slid his arm to the side, and gently brushed his fingertips over her soft breast.

She sucked in a breath, and against his arm, her pulse ticked up higher.

"Do you remember this, Evie?" He slid his fingers over her nipple and circled just the very tip.

She wrestled her hands free and gripped his forearms, trying to push him away, but he only held her tighter against him. "Don't."

"Why not?" Her movement gave him better access to her breast and he pressed her ass harder against his groin. Blood pumping, he brushed his whole hand over her and cupped the soft mass in his palm. Then squeezed. She bit back a moan. "Because it feels too good? Or because it reminds you how much you want me?"

"I"—she exhaled a heavy breath—"don't want you, idiot. I'm just stuck with you. What happened this morning was nothing more than adrenaline."

God, she was good. But she wasn't that good. "You know what I think? I think you've told so many lies, you don't know when to stop. It stops now, Eve."

He turned her quickly and pushed her up against the shower wall, face first, dragging her arms above her head. She gasped. Before she could decide what to do, he pulled the belt from the loops of his jeans and wrapped the leather around her wrists, tying them together. Then he pinned them against the cold tile.

"Goddammit, Archer. What the hell do you think you're doing now?"

Water sprayed in his face and soaked his jeans. Keeping one hand pressed against her bound wrists, he reached up with the other and tipped the showerhead down so the spray hit at their waists. "Testing a theory. Time for a little truth or dare."

"What? No way." She twisted her head to try to look at him, but he pressed his hips against her perfectly rounded ass to hold her in place. She sucked in a breath and slowed her fight. Swallowed hard. Again. "I'm not playing some stupid game with you. It's one o'clock in the morning."

"We used to play this game all the time in Beirut." Holding her wrists in his grip, he trailed his free hand down the subtle curve of her spine. "Scared?"

She opened her mouth. Closed it. Seconds beat by in silence. Then her shoulders stiffened, and she tipped her head, shooting a glare that was all challenge over her shoulder. "Never. I can beat you at any game, anytime."

This was the Eve he remembered. The tough girl who always had to prove she was better than the boys. But she wasn't the one he wanted. No, he wanted the girl he'd caught a glimpse of this morning. The one who'd nearly lost it over her sister's abduction. The one who'd leaned on him when she'd discovered the Agency had abandoned her. The one who'd told him, in a moment of honesty, that she'd once loved him.

"Don't move your hands."

He let go of her. To her credit, she didn't turn and knee him in the balls, and he took that as a sign to keep going.

"I think you're at a clear advantage here, Archer." She twisted her hands in the leather binding and pressed her palms flat against the wall. "What are the ground rules, and how do I win?"

Everything was a competition to her. But he didn't care who won. He just wanted to see her finally give in. He glanced down the curve of her wet, pink, glistening body. "I get five questions."

"You mean dares."

"Yeah." He watched the water bead on her skin and slide over her ass to drip down the back of her shapely legs. Of course she'd go for the dares, because Evelyn Wolfe didn't know how to answer a question truthfully. But he'd use that to his advantage. "If at the end of five you can make me believe you don't want me, you win. You can have anything you want if you win, Evie." He brushed a line of water away from her lower spine. She tensed at his touch, telling him this would be a lot easier than he'd planned. "What do you want?"

She was silent a moment, then said, "I want you to leave."

His head came up, and he focused on her profile. But she wasn't looking at him. She was staring at the end of the shower as if it held the mysteries of the universe.

"If I win," she went on, "then tomorrow, after we meet with my contact—no matter what she has to say—I want you gone. You're a big boy. With your connections, you can clear your own name without me. All you're doing is slowing me down."

A hurt he didn't know how to define pierced his chest. After everything they'd been through the past few days, she still wanted to ditch his ass. Even when she knew she was safer with him than without. Then he noticed her gaze. Far off. Resolute. Unwavering as she focused on the tiles behind the showerhead.

She was protecting him. Trying to make sure he didn't get hurt again. He'd seen that look on her face when he'd told her what he'd been through because of her. He saw it now in the way she couldn't meet his eyes.

His pulse picked up speed, and the blood surged to his groin. He glanced back down at her ass, and behind his fly, the erection that moments before had eased, swelled and lengthened. "Done. Spread your feet, beautiful."

Slowly, she inched her feet apart until her lower body formed a sexy upside-down V. The air in the shower grew hot and sultry, vibrating with the sexual charge between them. "Aren't you going to ask me 'truth or dare' first?"

"Why should I? We both know you don't tell the truth." He unlatched the watch from his wrist and handed it to her. Her fingers closed around the band, brushing his in the process, sending tiny sparks of electricity all through his flesh. Then he settled both hands at her waist and leaned close to her ear. "Round one. You get sixty seconds. If you can keep yourself from reacting to my touch in those sixty seconds, you win the first round and we move to the second."

Her head tipped back, and she looked at the watch face. "Is this waterproof?"

He smiled against her neck. "Yes."

"And what do you mean by reacting?"

Same old Eve. Always so technical. He breathed hot over her skin. "You can't come, beautiful."

Eve's eyes slid closed. "Oh fuck."

He chuckled and brushed his hands up her ribcage. "Now if you ask me to do that, I think that definitely counts as you admitting you do still want me. In which case, you lose. Are you ready, Evie? Sixty seconds on the clock."

- - - - - - - - - - - - - - - - -

Stupid. Stupid idea. Why had she agreed to this?

Eve held her breath while Archer's wicked hands ran up and down her ribcage, sending shock waves all through her body. Hot water beat against her skin, but it was the man at her back—the one wearing soaked jeans and a wicked smile she could just barely see from the corner of her eye—that was making her sweat.

She bit her lip as his hands grazed the underside of her breasts, then came around and cupped the masses gently. Against her ass, she felt his erection pressing against her through the damp denim.

Holy shit. *Okay, don't moan. Don't rock back against him. You want him gone for good? Be tough, and you've got your chance.*

She could win this. He'd given her an out, and this time she was taking it. After listening to what had happened to him in Guatemala, after realizing he was sticking with her now because he still felt something for her, after knowing the bullet that had grazed his shoulder wasn't the worst that could happen to him because of her, she wasn't about to put his life on the line anymore.

His fingers brushed her nipples, and air caught in her lungs. She went perfectly still. Warm breath fanned the skin of her neck, sending tiny shivers all through her body.

"How does that feel, Evie?" He twisted her nipples, then pinched each one, ever so slightly.

"Fine."

He chuckled against her neck, the vibration echoing through his chest and hips, right against her ass. "I think it feels better than fine. I remember how much you used to like it when I'd play with your breasts while I slid into you from behind."

Eve swallowed a groan. Tore her eyes open and looked at the watch. *Twenty-five seconds to go . . .*

One hand let go of her breast while the other continued to tease and torture. Then she felt his fingers slowly sliding down her belly, inching across her abs and slinking lower.

The first touch at her mound caused her to suck in a breath. But he didn't press inside like she expected. Instead he cupped her mound and rubbed the heel of his hand against her until she saw stars.

"I like this, beautiful. Bare. It's so damn sexy. Did you shave for me?"

She scoffed, but it came out more as a gasp. "No."

He brushed his fingers across her lips and over her naked mound. "I don't believe you."

Eve focused on the watch face, but her vision swam. He pinched her nipple, and a jolt of electricity rippled through her, sending shock waves to her sex. It took every ounce of strength she had not to arch into his touch.

"Do you want more, Eve? Do you want me to touch you deeper"—he cupped her sex—"here?"

Eve bit down hard on her lip. *Ten seconds. Eight . . .*

He moved his hand up, and relief teased—that he was backing away, that she'd won this round—then two fingers pressed between her folds, sliding along her slit.

"Ooooh, baby. You are *soooo* fucking wet."

His slick fingers glided up and around her clit. And every cell in Eve's body shuddered. She gripped the watch tightly. The second hand blurred in front of her eyes. *Two seconds . . . One . . .*

"Time," she groaned, dropping her forehead against the tile wall.

At her back, Zane chuckled. His fingers fell from her breast and sex, and the pressure eased against her ass. Cool air and the warm shower spray hit her body, but it did little to cool her down. She focused on the droplets splashing against her skin. Focused on her breaths. In and out. Focused on anything to take her mind off the fire growing in her core.

"You ready for round two? This time I get to add my mouth."

Oh God. No, she wasn't ready. The son of a bitch was sadistic. She should have realized that after he'd tied her up and cut away her blouse at that warehouse. And she was even sicker because a tiny part of her *liked* this.

Do not back down from him.

Her stomach caved in. She squeezed the watch in her hand. "Do it."

His soft laughter met her ears. "A hundred and twenty seconds, Eve. Starting now."

Fuck. Two minutes? She'd never last. Swallowing hard, she looked up at the watch. His hands landed at her shoulders, and she felt him move in close all over again.

Think about Olivia. And what Miller's doing right this minute. And the bombing in Seattle. And how ADD Roberts fits into this mess. Don't think about his mouth at your ear, blowing hot over your skin. Or the soft glide of his fingertips down your spine. Or—oh shit—his lips pressing softly against your neck . . .

Her eyes slid closed. Those wicked lips of his moved down her nape, then up to the sensitive spot behind her ear. A shudder rushed through her, one she couldn't contain. He hummed his approval and moved to the other side.

He'd always been able to do this to her. Drive her wild with just one touch. With one press of his lips. It was another reason she'd walked away from him in Beirut. Because he made her forget about everything else and focus only on him.

"Mm . . ." he whispered against her. "You smell good. I bet you taste even better." He nibbled on her ear and worked his way down her nape. Finding an extra sensitive spot, he licked, then sucked. His fingers tiptoed down her back to her hips.

Eve bit her lip again. Forced herself to remain perfectly still. Those sultry lips of his pressed against her spine, slinking lower with every kiss. When he reached her lower back, she gripped the watch tightly and held her breath.

She sensed him sink to his knees behind her. One big hand palmed her right cheek. His lips pressed against the other. He eased an inch away. "God, you've got a sexy ass, Eve. You work out, don't you?"

"Um . . ." Her mind wasn't working. She couldn't think. "Yeah."

"Running?"

He kept one hand cupping her right cheek. The other slid over the curve of her behind and under to brush against her sex. She was just about to answer when she felt his fingers slide between her folds. Her body jolted at the intimate touch, and she pushed her forehead against the tiles. *Oh God . . .*

He kissed the top of her ass and slipped his fingers up and around her clit. "You're drenched, Evie. I can smell your arousal. Sure you don't want to just give in and tell me you want me?"

Eve turned her head and pressed her cheek against the cool tiles. Drawing her eyes open, she stared at the watch. *Forty more seconds . . .*

She swallowed hard and fought back the need raging in her veins. "Piece of cake."

He chuckled again and slipped his fingers up and over her clit, then down to circle her opening. "You never could back down from a challenge, could you? Spread your legs and arch your back, Evie. I want to kiss you here."

Oh . . . God . . .

Eve's heart pounded. Slowly, her legs inched wider apart, and she arched, pushing her hips away from the wall like she knew he wanted.

Twenty seconds . . . Eighteen . . .

His hands gripped her ass cheeks, pulling them open. His warm breath fanned her sex. She gripped the watch tightly in her hand. Stared at the ticking second hand. *Come on, come on, come on . . .*

Fourteen . . . Twelve . . .

His soft, naughty lips pressed gently against her clit. And all thought rushed out of her mind as electrical sensations shot through every cell in her body.

She groaned. Pressed back against him. He answered by humming and kissing her again and again. Slid his fingers down to circle her opening until she saw stars.

Her eyes slammed shut. Her hands pressed against the tiles. The watch fell from her grip to clatter against the shower floor.

She gasped. "Zane—"

His mouth left her sex. He pressed hot, dangerous kisses across her ass cheeks, moved slowly up her spine. But his fingers were still there. Still stroking her wetness. Still teasing her arousal. Still circling her opening, where she ached to feel him most.

His chest brushed her back. Then his mouth was at her ear, breathing heavily. The hard, rigid length of his cock behind his fly, pressing into her ass. His arm wrapped around her body, and his hand closed over her breast, squeezing tightly. "I think time's almost up, Evie. Do you want me to stop?"

She arched back into him. No, she didn't want him to stop. She needed to come. Wanted him to fill her . . .

"Tell me you want me, Evie. I can feel you burning up. I can feel how much you need me."

Oh God, she did need him. But she couldn't tell him. Couldn't give in. Because too much was at stake. Gasping, she shook her head from side to side. "No. Round three."

"Are you sure?" His fingers slid up and over her clit again, sending another shock wave outward from her hips.

She slammed her eyes shut and nodded.

His hot breath dripped down her neck, and he leaned even closer. "This time I get to use my tongue."

Oh . . . *fuck* . . .

"Truth," she sputtered. "I pick truth."

His fingers stopped their relentless torture, and he stilled behind her. "Are you sure?"

She nodded quickly. Clawed for control.

He was silent at her back, the only sound his own ragged in-and-out breathing. Opening her eyes, Eve tried not to move. His hand was still resting against her sex, and his cock was still pressing into her ass, and though he was still behind her, she didn't know what he was thinking. What he was planning.

Very gently he released his hold on her waist and lifted his free hand to brush the damp hair away from her neck. "Truth, Eve," he said softly. "How many men have you been with since you left me in Beirut?"

Eve's pulse picked up speed, and sweat broke out all along her skin. Of all the questions he could ask, he wanted to know *that?*

Lies tumbled through her mind. Anything to keep him from knowing the truth. *Be convincing. Be tough. Son of a bitch, you know how to beat a polygraph. You can beat Zane Archer at this stupid game.*

"I don't know," she said between breaths. "I don't keep track. Four. Maybe five."

His arm circled her waist, and he pulled her back tight against him. The hard length of his cock pressed against her ass once more, his lips right at her ear. "Try again, Evie. You were too tight this morning to have been fucking five different guys."

She gasped. Braced her forearms against the wall. Between her legs he stroked her once, twice. She felt her limbs growing liquid, her body responding to his touch, on the verge of giving in. She pressed back against him. "Zane—"

"The truth, Eve. How many and when? I'm not letting you go until you tell me."

He stroked her faster. Nipped at her ear. Rocked his hips against her so she could feel his cock pressing against her swollen sex.

Sensations bombarded her from every side. Her skin felt like it was on fire. And with every lick and press and touch it became too much. She needed him to stop. Needed him to make her come. Needed . . . him.

"None, okay?" Oh God, she couldn't stand it anymore. Her body took over. She arched back against him. "I haven't been able to be with anyone since you."

He stepped away from her body. His hand lifted from her sex. Startled, Eve's eyes popped open. He grabbed her and whipped her around, pressing her back against the cool shower wall, then moved in at her front.

The dark, hungry look in his eyes supercharged her blood. She tensed. Every cell in her body vibrated in anticipation. Strong hands shoved her bound wrists above her head, and then he lowered his mouth to hers.

She opened for him at the first touch. Drew his tongue into her mouth. Groaned at the heavenly taste of him. His hands found her breasts, squeezing and teasing while he plundered her mouth. He pressed his hips against hers so the rigid length of his cock pressed into her lower belly, and she arched up into him, offering anything he wanted, needing all he could give.

He dragged his lips from her mouth, pressed sinful, tantalizing kisses along her jaw and down her throat. Bent his knees so his cock pressed right between her thighs. Water sprayed over their bodies, splashing up to her face. "Tell me you want me, Eve. Tell me, dammit."

Oh yes. That's what she wanted. Right there. She rolled her hips forward, desperate for more. "Yes. Yes. Yes, oh God, yes."

A tiny voice in the back of her head warned he could be playing her. That he could be doing what she'd done to him this morning and plotting a way to get back at her. But she was too far gone to listen. And when she heard the rasp of a zipper and felt his hands leave her breasts so he could push down his jeans, she forced it from her mind.

His hands landed at her ass, palmed the sensitive flesh, and lifted her off the ground. She lowered her bound wrists over his head while he pressed her back into the wall. His gruff voice met her ears when he rasped, "Wrap your legs around me."

His mouth closed over hers again, and his hot, wet tongue pushed between her lips, stroking her deeply. Between her thighs she felt the wide, blunt head of his cock probing at her entrance.

"Tell me you want me, Evie." He rocked forward, just a touch. Just until the head of him slid inside her. "Tell me."

She groaned. Tightened. Bent her elbows and combed her fingers through his wet hair. "Yes, I want you. Please, Zane. Stop torturing me."

His mouth captured hers. And then he pressed deeply inside her. And they both groaned together as he filled her.

Eve shuddered as she stretched around him. She kissed him, tried to hold on as he drew out and pressed back in even deeper. His fingers dug into her ass where he held her tightly, and he slowly began to fuck into her with longer, harder, deeper strokes.

She dragged her mouth from his and gasped. Water splashed around them, but she barely felt it. All she could feel was the tantalizing drag and glide, the tight friction as he flexed his hips and drove into her again and again.

"Zane—"

"Tell me, Evie. Tell me what you want."

Oh . . . Tingles raced up and down her spine. Her orgasm barreled close. She clamped down around him and focused on that one spot. On the heat gathering deep inside her.

"I want you," she gasped. "I only ever want you."

His mouth claimed hers again, but just before the wave hit, he pulled her away from the wall and slowed his thrusting. One hand tightened under her ass. The other shut off the water, then yanked the shower curtain back. He held her tight as he stepped over the edge of the tub and carried her out into the bedroom.

Cool air sent a shiver down her spine, but the hot man at her front quickly warmed her with his heat, with his tongue chasing hers, with the length of his arousal still so deep inside her. In one swift move he pulled out of her and dropped her on the bed. The mattress bounced, and she looked up to see his face flushed with arousal, his skin slicked with beads of water, and his wet jeans just low enough to free his cock but still bunched around his hips.

Her eyes locked on his beautiful erection, thick, engorged, slick from her own arousal, and her mouth watered. She wanted to taste him there. Wanted to drive him as crazy as he'd driven her. She lifted her torso from the bed.

He shook his head and pushed her back down. "Uh-uh. You do that and I won't last. Roll over, beautiful. I want to be as deep inside you as possible when you come."

Eve's pulse raced, and her body shook with excitement. She rolled to her belly and pressed up on her forearms as he lifted her hips and nudged her knees apart. Slick, wet fingers parted her and rubbed over her clit. She closed her eyes and groaned.

"God, Eve." The head of his cock pressed against her again. "You wreck me, baby. You always have."

He filled her quickly, and Eve groaned, lowered her head to the mattress, and closed her eyes. Yes, yes, yes . . . this was what she wanted. The only thing she ever wanted. Him close. Touching her, taking her, making her his.

He rocked in and out, his strokes growing longer, deeper, faster. His fingers continued to drive her insane, circling, sliding, rubbing. She tightened around him and pressed back into each thrust, seeing stars every time he hit that perfect spot. Closing her eyes, she focused on the orgasm she'd almost reached in the shower. Needed it so bad . . .

He wrapped his arm around her waist and pulled her upper body off the bed, back against his chest. She gasped and tried to push herself up, but with her wrists still bound she had to lean into him for support.

His muscles flexed. His mouth closed over her neck, licking, suckling. Sparks of electricity raced down her spine. Between her legs he slid his fingers back over her clit, flicking again and again while he thrust in and out of her body, sending shock waves all through her flesh. Then she felt his lips at her ear. Felt his cock thicken and swell inside her. Felt his need for her reach its peak.

"None for me either, Evie. I tried. God, I tried. But even when I hated you, you were the only woman I wanted. Come with me, beautiful. Don't hold back from me anymore. Give it to me, Eve."

He groaned against her neck, his hot breath rushing all along her skin, sending tremors throughout her body. And when she felt his release, when she felt him spill eighteen months of frustration and need and longing inside her, it triggered her own intense orgasm that consumed her body, overrode her mind, and blinded her to everything but him.

She felt herself falling. Couldn't seem to stop it from happening. Couldn't make her muscles work just yet. Softness pressed against her belly, her breasts, her face. Dragging in ragged breaths, she turned her head and felt the comforter brush her cheek.

Zane's arms closed around her, and he pulled her back against him, rolling her to her side. His damp chest brushed her spine, his own ragged breaths echoing in her ears. Against her ass, she felt the rough fabric of his wet jeans.

"Holy hell, Eve. You might just kill me yet, beautiful."

Slowly, her eyes opened, and she stared across the dimly lit room while she tried to steady her racing heart.

But it was reality, not his words, that sent a shiver down her spine, and not even his tightening arms, pulling her closer against him, helped. Because thanks to her ever-loving weakness, there was no way she'd be able to walk away from him cleanly now. And that meant not only was his life still on the line; her heart now was too.

He pressed his lips to her nape and reached around to unlace the belt from her wrists. She'd forgotten it was still there. When she was free, he dropped the belt over the side of the bed, then reached down and dragged the covers over both of them. His arms tightened around her once more, dragging her back and into him. The heat of his body seeped into hers, slowly warming her from the outside in. "Promise me you won't run when I fall asleep."

Chest tight, Eve gripped his forearms. And even though pain lanced her heart, she said, "That wouldn't be fair. I lost the game, now didn't I?"

He smiled against her ear. "You didn't lose, beautiful. We both won. Just like I've dreamed more times than I can count. Sleep, baby. We have a big day tomorrow."

The icy walls she'd built around her heart started to crack. She closed her eyes tight. Pinched her lips together. Tried to breathe through the pain. Because in that moment she knew nothing—not the government chasing her, not even the biggest terrorist cell— could hurt her more than the broken heart she was doomed to have when this was finally over.

And it didn't even come close to comparing to how much she'd miss him when she ultimately left him for good.

chapter 16

The gritty intro to Nickelback's "This Means War" roused Zane in the early morning hours. Blinking into the dim light, he rolled to his side and eyed the illuminated cell phone screen sitting on the nightstand.

Fuck. Aegis.

He rubbed at his left eye and pushed up onto his elbow. Muscles in his back and shoulders ached, and for a moment he couldn't remember why. Then his mind flashed to a steamy shower, to Eve's wrists bound above her head, to the sexiest sounds he'd ever heard.

The music died off. He whipped around and looked at the empty bed beside him. Heart pounding, he shot a glance toward the open bathroom door, the room beyond dark and quiet.

Double fuck.

"Eve?"

No answer. No sound or movement from anywhere in the small, dark motel room. When "This Means War" fired up his cell phone again, he grabbed it on reflex. "What?"

"Good morning to you too, grouchy."

Marley. Shit. He should have expected this call. Sitting up, he rubbed a hand over his face and worked for calm when he felt anything but. "Sorry. Long night. Ryder tell you to call?"

"As a matter of fact, he did. He's still a little too worked up to talk to you just yet. But he's worried about you, Zane."

Zane scoffed and looked around the room. Sometime in the night he'd peeled off those wet jeans, and they now lay in a pile on the floor. Eve's ripped skirt and filthy blouse were tossed over a chair, but the clothes he'd picked up for her yesterday were nowhere to be found.

Anger simmered under his skin, followed by a nasty shot of stupidity. Dammit, he should have expected she'd turn tail and run, but he'd thought—no, he'd hoped—in some way he'd gotten through to her last night. Apparently, he'd thought wrong, but then, when it came to Eve, he was always wrong.

He slouched back into the pillows and pulled his knees up under the blanket, planting his feet on the mattress. A dull ache started in his thigh, one he knew all too well. "I seriously doubt that."

"He's just ticked you went out on your own on this one," Marley said. "He'd have helped you if you'd asked."

Zane fought from scoffing again. "No, he wouldn't have. And he'd have been right to say no." *Shit.* He rubbed another hand down his face. He should have listened to Ryder. He never should have gone after Evelyn Wolfe. At least then, instead of being alone and wanted for a major crime, he'd simply be alone. "Listen, Wolfe's sister is still missing—"

"Miller's on it. We've been in contact. As soon as we have news about Olivia Wolfe, someone will contact you. But that's not the reason I'm calling. The reason I'm calling is because I need you to talk to Wolfe and find out if she knows about something called Project Thirteen."

Zane's brow lowered. "Why?"

"Because somehow, it's linked to everything that's happening." Marley filled him in on her discovery at the State Department, the link to the Guatemala raid, and Humbolt's connection to ADD Roberts in the counterintelligence division.

Slowly, Zane sat upright. "Are you telling me the Guatemala raid was a cover-up?"

"It could have been. Or it could have been coincidental. Whether Aegis or Humbolt was the target, we may never know. For now, we need to know if Wolfe has any intel on Project Thirteen."

Shit. Zane rubbed his suddenly aching forehead. "Well, I would ask her if she was here, but she's not, so I can't."

"What do you mean?"

Zane sighed and dropped his hand. Man, he was so fucking gullible when it came to that woman. "What I mean is, she's go—"

The door to the motel room pushed open, and a breath of cool Pacific Northwest air swept into the room, followed by Eve, wearing slim jeans, a fitted black button-down blouse, and black ankle boots. In her hands she carried a drink holder and several paper cups.

Relief spread through him like fog rolling across the ocean, and warmth seeped into his chest, dousing the ache that had started to grow there from her absence.

"Archer?"

Realizing Marley was still talking to him, he blinked and looked down at the sheet over his legs. "Yeah."

"Where is Wolfe?"

"She just walked in. Listen, Marley, I'll call you back after I talk to her."

"You do know how to keep things exciting, Archer. I will say that for you."

He smiled, feeling better by the second. "So do you."

He hit End on his phone and looked across the room. Eve's back was turned toward him, and she was taking steaming paper cups out of the drink holder and setting them on the round, scarred table. "Who was on the phone?" she asked, not looking his way.

Slowly, he unfolded himself from the bed, snagging the sheet around his waist as he moved. "Aegis."

"Worried about you?"

"Something like that."

He tied the sheet together at his hip, stopped behind her, and drew in a whiff of her familiar scent. Her dark hair was tousled and messy, just begging his fingers to weave through it, and the way her ass filled out those jeans . . .

The blood stirred in his groin all over again.

She turned and handed him a steaming paper cup, then stepped past him, careful, he noticed, not to look him in the eye or touch him. "I couldn't remember how you liked your coffee, so I just left it black."

"Thanks." She was nervous. An odd sort of thrill rushed through him as he took the cup and turned to look after her. "I didn't hear you get up."

She crossed the floor, sat on the end of the second bed, and tugged off her boots. "I couldn't sleep. Look, we're meeting my CSIS contact in a few hours and need to get going. I'm gonna finish getting ready. I got some food in case you're hungry."

She pushed off the bed and moved for the bathroom. Surprise rippled through him when he looked over the selection. "You got me M&M's?"

"I got you oatmeal," she called from the bathroom. "It's called breakfast."

Bullshit. She'd gotten M&M's too. Excitement slithered through his veins. He snagged the little brown bag and followed her into the cramped bathroom.

She was bent over the counter, splashing water on her face, when he leaned against the doorjamb. Water slid down her creamy skin as she straightened, eyed him in the mirror, and reached for the towel. "What?"

A one-sided grin curled his mouth. He ripped the bag open. "Nothing. It's just . . . you got me M&M's."

She rolled her eyes and swiped the towel over her face. "Maybe the M&M's were for me, smart guy. Ever think about that?"

He tossed a handful of the chocolate candies in his mouth, chewed, and moved in behind her. Swallowing, he dropped the open bag on the counter and wrapped his arms around her slim waist. "Mm, they taste good. But not as good as you."

A surprised gasp slipped from her lips. She tensed against him, pressing her hands over his forearms. "Archer—"

He nuzzled her neck, loving the way she felt against him, loving the soft tickle of her hair against this face, loving the silly lift to his spirits just knowing she'd come back. "You have a photographic memory, Eve. You don't forget anything. God, you smell good. Remember what we did with those M&M's in Beirut?"

"I don't know what you're talking about."

Oh yeah, she did. He saw it in her eyes when he glanced into the mirror. "'Melt in your mouth, not in your hand.' We tested that theory, didn't we? All over your body. I wouldn't be averse to trying that experiment again."

"Archer." Her stomach tightened beneath his arms, and when she gripped his forearms and squirmed, her sweet ass ground against his growing erection. "We have things to do today. We don't have time for this."

He breathed hotly over the skin behind her ear, then pressed his lips to the supersensitive spot. A shudder ran through her. Releasing one arm from her waist, he slid his hand down her lower belly and over her jeans to cup her sex. "There's always time, Evie."

Eve sucked in a breath. Muttered, "Shit." Then her eyes slid closed. Her struggling stopped. She rested her head back against him as he palmed her, and she rocked her hips ever so slightly into his hand. "You make this impossible, Archer."

He smiled against her neck and kissed her again. "Make what impossible?"

"This. Telling you to stop. You know this isn't going anywhere, right?" Sighing, she ground against him, caught between his erection and his hand. "Oh God, that feels so damn good."

An uncontrollable urge to prove her wrong whipped through him. He let go of her, twisted her to face him, and then lifted her quickly and sat her up on the counter. Her mouth fell open in surprise, but he pushed her legs open and moved between them before she could close him out. "Look at me, Eve."

Her mouth slid closed.

He braced his palms on the counter on each side of her. "Stop. Okay? Right now, just stop running from me."

She scowled. "I'm not running. I'm here, aren't I? If I'd wanted to run, I'd have ditched you this morning when you were dead to the world."

"But you didn't."

"No."

"Why not?"

"Why not?" she repeated. "Because I told you I wouldn't."

"More."

"Because you saved my life."

"More."

She sighed in clear frustration. "I don't know what you want me to say, Archer. I'm here, dammit. That's enough."

"No, it's not." It wouldn't ever be enough for him. "You're here, but you're still hiding from me. I want to know the real reason you stayed. And don't tell me it was because of last night. Because you could have easily fucked my brains out and then run from me this morning and never looked back. Tell me the truth, Eve. Let me in. Why are you still here?"

She opened her mouth. Looked down at his bare chest. Pressed her lips together.

"Tell me," he said, moving in closer, until the heat from her body swirled around him to make him light-headed.

"I . . . I . . ." Unease trickled through her dark gaze as it focused on his skin. "Because I . . ."

"Because you care about me." Her eyes shot to his. Wide, suddenly frightened eyes. Eyes that told him, *Bingo!* He was right. "Say it, Eve. It's not a bad thing to care about someone else."

"I . . ." Her gaze searched his, and this close, he could hear the rapid beat of her pulse. "I . . ."

He moved even closer, until his hips were flush against hers, his arms were circling her waist, and her legs were sliding around his hips. "Just tell me, Evie. I'm not gonna bite you. Well, not hard, at least."

Her hands landed against his bare shoulders, and she whispered, "I hate you, Archer. I really do."

He leaned in and brushed his mouth gently over hers. Loved the way her whole body tightened against him when he got close. "No, you don't." He pressed his lips to the corner of her mouth. "You're crazy about me. You always have been."

Her hands pressed against his shoulders. "Zane—"

Pain zipped through his wound, but he ignored it. "It's okay if you can't say it. Just seeing how flustered you are this morning tells me everything I need to know." He kissed her jaw. Reveled in the way she started to relax, muscle by muscle. "And I'm a patient guy. I waited for you all these months. I'm willing to wait a little longer until you figure it out on your own."

He skimmed his lips to her ear, then slowly down her neck. And right then he knew what he wanted. Her. Back in his life. This time for good.

She groaned, and tiny vibrations shook her body as he unbuttoned her blouse one button at a time, as he continued to tease her throat with his mouth and tongue and teeth.

"You're certifiable, you know that?" she mumbled, tipping her head to the side to offer him more. "Any sane man would run from me the first chance he got."

Grinning, he pushed the halves of her blouse apart, pulled away from her throat, and looked down at her perfect breasts, spilling from the practical, white cotton bra. "Yeah, well, my psych profile's always been a little fucked up. God, Evie. You are gorgeous."

She straightened her head. Blinked several times. His gaze came up. But when it focused on hers, he didn't see arousal. He saw sadness.

"Zane," she said softly. "You don't know the real me. You know the person I was in Beirut, the one who was pretending not to be investigating you, and you know the woman you blamed for your injury when that op went wrong in Guatemala. But neither of those is the real me. Yes, I care about you, and yes, that's why I came back. Because I don't want to see you hurt anymore because of me. But incredible sexual chemistry—which we have—isn't a real relationship. And it sure isn't a basis for any kind of future. It can't be, because you don't know who I really am."

"So let me know you. Let me in, Eve."

She exhaled a long breath and looked over his shoulder. "I can't."

"Why not?"

"Because I don't like the real me. And you won't either if you get to know her."

He didn't know what she meant. He only knew that she was moving away and erecting a barrier between them. One he thought he'd chipped away at last night.

Carefully, she eased off the counter and moved out of his grasp. "Listen, let's just focus on what we have to do next. I need to finish getting ready, and you need to re-bandage that shoulder. Looks like water got in it last night. The last thing you need is infection setting in."

He didn't care about his shoulder. He didn't care about anything except her. "Eve—"

She held up a hand to keep him from reaching for her and stepped back. "No, don't. Just don't, okay? Let me focus on what I need to do today. That's all I can handle right now."

If he'd seen confidence in her eyes or even challenge, he'd have grabbed her, shoved her up against the wall, and kissed her until all thought rushed out of her head. But he didn't see that. He saw fear. Stark fear, over a truth he wasn't sure how to argue against.

She was right. He didn't know the real her. Not *all* of her. And he'd been wrong about her before. If she let him all the way in and he didn't like what he found, he'd be the one to blame for making things worse for both of them.

But that didn't mean he was giving up.

"This conversation isn't over, Eve. And whether you want to admit it or not, I know more of you than you think. I'm not the one you have to be afraid of."

He moved out of the bathroom, and she quickly closed the door at his back. But before it clicked, he heard her whisper, "You've always been the one I'm afraid of."

Eve's skin felt three sizes too small.

Sitting in the passenger seat of the Taurus, she shifted away from Zane and stared at the scenery whizzing by her window.

She should have left. She shouldn't have come back this morning. The more time she spent with him, the more he pushed her toward wanting a future she was never going to have.

Forget this morning. She should have been smart from the first and left him lying on the floor of that warehouse loft as soon as he untied her from that chair.

Her mind skipped back to the group of men who'd come barreling through that door, then to her meeting with Smith in Seattle. "Chechnya. I've never been to Chechnya. I've never investigated anyone working in Chechnya. So my being the target in Seattle couldn't have been personal."

"Unless you know something you don't know you know."

She harrumphed. "Okay, Dr. Seuss."

He frowned. "You can be a real smart-ass sometimes, you know that?"

The hurt in his voice caused Eve's gaze to slide his way. She watched the sunlight weave through his thick, dark hair, highlighting the strands and the bit of wave. His hair was longer than she'd ever seen it, brushing his collar and skimming his ears, but she liked the shaggy look on him. Liked the sexy scruff on his jaw from days without shaving too.

Focus, Eve.

She looked back out the window. "Yeah, well. It's not easy being a woman in this business." She crossed her arms over her chest. "Whatever was on that drive is more than a simple list of compromised agents."

"What do you know about something called Project Thirteen?"

Eve's gaze shot his way again, this time in surprise. "It's a top secret biological weapons program. Why?"

He still didn't look at her. His gaze was focused out the windshield, and both hands gripped the steering wheel, accentuating the muscles in his arms and the strength in his shoulders. "Adam Humbolt, the target in that Guatemalan raid, was a scientist supposedly working on some top secret shit for the government. Turns out, Humbolt was working on Project Thirteen, but we were told he was a chemical weapons specialist who'd been kidnapped while vacationing in the Caribbean."

"That cover's a little convenient, don't you think?"

"Now? Hell yeah. Especially when I heard from Aegis this morning that ADD Roberts specifically requested Aegis be the one to go in after him."

That didn't make sense. Eve's brow dropped low. "Why would the assistant deputy director of counterintelligence for the CIA be involved in the rescue mission of a US scientist? That would fall under a different division."

"That's what I want to know."

Slowly, Eve looked back out the windshield. There were too many questions. Too many threads to this that didn't align.

As they pulled into the parking lot of Lake Padden Park, where they'd agreed to meet Eve's Canadian contact, Eve's stomach tensed.

The park was wide and green, with tall trees and a broad dog run. A running trail wound away from the parking lot and playground and into the woods. A handful of benches sat scattered through the area. Several young children swung on the swing set and ran around the bark chips near the play structure, and a few rambunctious dogs chased balls and returned them to their masters in the field.

Zane shut off the engine and eyed the park. "Where'd you say we're meeting her?"

"About a quarter mile down the running path. She said there's an old oak and a bench. Can't miss it."

Zane pulled the keys from the ignition. "I have a bad feeling about this."

The fine hairs standing at attention all along Eve's nape screamed the same thing, but this was their best lead at this point.

Grabbing the backpack from the backseat—the one Zane had had stashed in the wheel well of the car—she set it on her lap. She pulled out a Beretta 92G from the bag and handed it to Zane. "Those jam. Be careful."

He huffed as he took the weapon. "Not if you use them right, beautiful."

She rolled her eyes and checked the magazine on her Glock 17. "Her name's Natalie."

He climbed out of the car without responding, and her chest squeezed tight as she watched his long legs filling out the faded jeans and that black T-shirt molding to his strong chest and abs. He holstered the gun at his lower back and pulled the shirt over the butt, then swung the backpack over one shoulder.

He was upset with her over what had happened this morning, and he had every right to be. But it didn't change reality. And wishing she could rewrite the past so she could have a different future was futile at this point.

Drawing a deep breath, she popped the car door and eased out. Cool morning air rushed over her skin, but the sun was shining, a sign the day couldn't be all bad. She holstered her own gun and tugged her T-shirt over the bulge. Then she looked toward Zane over the top of the car. "Ready?"

He grinned her way—a mesmerizing smile that lit up his whole face and warmed her belly. "Sure, baby. You want to swing first or go for a walk?"

He was settling into their cover. Pretending to be a couple in love, out for a morning stroll. And while the thought of holding his hand electrified Eve, it also scared her to death.

Be tough. Be strong. Don't give in to stupid emotions right now.

She worked up her own smile and moved around the front of the vehicle. "Let's walk. I want to be alone with you, handsome."

He tugged on a Mariners cap and took her hand, his skin warm, the pulse beneath strong and steady. But she felt the tension in his muscles. Felt the way he was holding back after everything she'd said this morning.

You have no idea how much I wish things could be different . . .

The words were on the tip of her tongue, but she swallowed them when he tugged her toward the path. A dog barked. Nerves gathered in Eve's belly when she realized heads were turning their direction.

Zane's fingers, intertwined with hers, shifted to her lower back, pinning her arm behind her. Then he stopped, tugged her into him, and lowered his head. "People are looking."

They'd talked about this. About the fact they'd be in a public place. That people would be on the lookout for anyone out of the norm. That Zane's description was all over the news. But her face still hadn't been made public by the CIA, and whatever they could do to keep attention off him as an individual was their only hope of not being caught.

She'd known he might have to kiss her. That she'd have to pretend—again—to be his girlfriend or wife or lover. But the moment his head lowered and she felt his soft lips brush hers, creating a believable cover became the last thing on her mind.

Warmth pressed against her mouth. And memories of last night—when he'd kissed her in the shower, when he'd thrust inside her—filled her mind and sent sharp electrical currents of arousal all through her body.

She lifted her chin, pressed her lips against his more firmly, and tangled the fingers of her free hand in the T-shirt at his chest.

He groaned, and that hand against her lower back pulled her even closer into the heat of his body. And then his tongue pushed between her lips and dipped into her mouth, giving her a sinful, sexy, so-not-enough taste.

She moaned, tried to get closer. He answered by letting go of the hand at her back and sliding his palm down to cup her ass and pull her so close she felt the hard ridge of his growing erection against her lower belly.

This was the way it could be. The way it could always be if she just gave in. If she admitted how she felt. If she opened herself fully and showed him all of her.

He won't forget the things you've done. He won't forgive you.

The hard, coarse voice of reality slapped a hand against her chest and pushed her away from him. She pulled her mouth from his and pressed her face against his chest, frantically fighting for control.

"That wasn't cover," he whispered in her ear.

Eve didn't push away, and he didn't release her. He just went on holding her, breathing warmth over her suddenly chilled skin and rubbing a hand down her back. And though she knew for her own sanity she needed to get out of his arms, she couldn't seem to move her feet.

"That was the real you, Evie. Wanting me the same way you did in that stupid apartment in Beirut. The same way you did last night. I know more about you than you think. I know you can't walk away from me without it tearing a part of you to shreds. Just like I haven't been able to stop thinking about you all these months."

Eve's eyes slid closed, and she breathed deeply through her nose. Focused on the push and pull of air in her lungs in the hopes it would ease the sharp ache growing in the middle of her chest. She'd given up happily ever after when Sam died. Had never expected to be teased with it by another man. And now here was Zane. The person she'd tried countless times to forget and had never been able to. The person who made her want things even Sam had never stirred inside her.

"It's nice to see you two haven't killed each other yet."

Eve stiffened at the voice and whipped around. A man stood feet from them on the path, hands tucked in the front pocket of his slacks, light jacket over his white button-down. His neatly trimmed blond hair blew gently in the breeze, and those deep, familiar blue eyes hinted at mischief.

"Carter," Eve breathed.

James Dietrick's smile widened. "Is that the best you can do, Juliet?"

Whether it was joy over seeing a familiar face or simply relief at getting away from Zane, Eve didn't know. She pulled away from Zane and wrapped her arms around Carter's neck, hugging him tightly. "Oh my God. What . . . ? How . . . ?"

He chuckled against her, squeezed her tight, and then let go. "I figured you guys might need some help. Don't worry. No one from the Agency knows I'm here."

Eve lowered to her feet. "Olivia?"

Carter's smile turned grim. "Nothing yet. We're still looking, though."

A wave of sickness rolled through her belly.

Fingers gripping the backpack strap against his shoulder, Zane reached around her and shook Carter's hand. "It's nice to see you, man."

Carter returned the handshake, then slid on his sunglasses and glanced around the park. The people who'd been watching them earlier had gone back to swinging and throwing tennis balls for their dogs. "Where's this meeting taking place?"

"Park bench," Eve said, refocusing on what she could do now. Miller would find Olivia. Zane had said he was the best of the best, and if he'd been DIA, she had at least a tiny bit of hope. "Down the path."

Carter turned, and she and Zane fell into step beside him.

"You've created a heck of a mess, Eve," Carter said.

At her right, Zane snorted. "The woman has a knack for finding trouble."

Eve ignored him and looked toward Carter on her other side. "I didn't have anything to do with that bombing. If the Agency looks into it, they'll see I have no connection to Chechnya. And Zane was just in the wrong—"

"Eve." Carter stopped and looked down at her. "Five hundred thousand dollars was deposited into your personal account two days ago. Through back channels, the Agency tracked it to a group in western Chechnya. The government has already seized your holdings. In a matter of hours, your face is going to be all over every police station computer screen and news broadcast in the country. That's why I'm here." He tugged off his glasses, and his worried blue eyes met hers. "I think it's time you turned yourself in and got a lawyer."

The earth shifted beneath Eve's feet, and the park started to swirl in front of her eyes.

Strong hands wrapped around her shoulders and tugged her back against a warm, solid male chest. "Hold it together, beautiful. We're in a public place."

Zane's voice echoed in her ears and slowly trickled through the fog clouding her brain. *Hold it together . . . Hold it together . . .*

Five hundred *thousand* dollars.

Anger and disbelief coiled beneath her skin and threatened to explode. She closed her eyes and leaned back into Zane. *Don't lose it.*

Zane's broad hands massaged her upper arms. "Who strong-armed the Agency into awarding that defense contract to Aegis for Humbolt's life?"

"How the hell would I know that?" Carter asked. "That shit's decided by committee."

"Was it Roberts?"

Eve stilled against Zane's chest.

"ADD Roberts," Carter said in a monotone voice. "In counterintelligence. You think he was involved in your failed raid in Guatemala?"

"I've heard . . . whispers," Zane said.

His familiar voice echoed in his chest and vibrated into Eve's body. But it was Carter's silence that set her on edge.

"Christ," Carter finally whispered. "Not here. Let's get further down the path."

Eve opened her eyes and pulled away from Zane, but before she turned, she caught the look on his resolute face. The one that said,

Don't worry, I'm not leaving you. The one that sent ripples of awareness all through her body.

They moved down the path and into the trees, and when Carter
felt they were far enough so that no one could hear him, he stopped
and turned their way. "I could get into serious hot water for this,
but fuck it. You two are already in so much hot water it's boiling.
Roberts is gunning for the deputy director position within the Company. He's got sway within the Agency. Big sway. Whether he had a
hand in Aegis's appointment to that op, I have no idea. But I will
tell you this. He's got no love for your boss Ryder. If you're asking
me on the record if he set Aegis up to take the fall in Guatemala, I'd
say that's bullshit. Everyone in the Company wanted Humbolt back
alive. Off the record, though, I'd say most of us thought it was a
suicide mission. No black ops team has ever infiltrated that cartel's
stronghold without major casualties."

Eve's gaze slowly slid Zane's way.

His jaw tightened, but he didn't look at her. His intense gaze
was locked solidly on Carter. "Did Roberts know Eve had been
tipped off that the op had been compromised?"

"I don't know." Carter frowned. "It's possible, I guess. He might
have known."

So all of this—the Agency coming down on her—she was being
punished because of Zane's connection to Aegis? No. That was too . . .
fucking simple.

She looked up at Carter. "Humbolt is the key to all of this.
What was he working on?"

"I—"

"Eve." Zane's hand against her arm drew Eve around, and she
looked down the path, toward a redheaded woman wearing slacks
and a white blouse rolled up to her elbows, heading their direction.

"That's Natalie," she breathed.

Natalie tucked her shoulder-length hair behind her ears and eyed their group. When she caught Eve's gaze, she nodded, then sat on the bench. But her eagle eyes were watching every move Zane and Carter made, and Eve knew she was surprised to find the players had multiplied.

Eve didn't know the woman well. Natalie was in her midthirties and had been in the business a little longer than Eve, but her agency had always been more than willing to cooperate when Eve needed help, and over the years she'd been a solid contact Eve could count on.

They headed her direction. Sitting next to Natalie on the bench, Eve nodded toward the two men. "This is Carter and Sawyer."

Natalie's dark gaze locked on Zane. "I recognize you."

"Don't believe everything you see or read," he said with a wink. "It's never true."

A wry smile curled her lips. "I never do." Her humor faded as she focused on Eve. "People within your organization are asking questions. My agency's been able to head them off so far, but it won't be long before they discover we met."

"I appreciate that. Natalie, I need to know about the file Tyrone Smith was supposed to sell to me. It's at the root of all of this. It wasn't a list of compromised agents like you led me to believe."

Natalie's wary gaze drifted to Zane, then Carter.

"It's okay," Eve assured her. "They're safe."

Natalie was silent a moment, looking them both over again, and Eve's adrenaline surged over the possibility the woman might not tell what she knew.

Finally, Natalie's gaze settled on Eve once more. "No. It wasn't. I—"

"That was my doing," Carter cut in.

Eve's gaze snapped his way. "What?"

He glanced toward Natalie and then focused on Eve. "CSIS has been in contact with the Agency about this since before Humbolt was killed. When we realized Smith was the middleman Humbolt was using, we needed someone to get close to the file. ADD Roberts suggested you. He thinks quite highly of you, Juliet. Or at least, he did."

Eve's brow lowered. "What does Humbolt have to do with all of this?"

"A few years ago," Natalie said, "a research team at the State University of New York chemically synthesized an artificial polio virus from scratch. You might have heard about it in the news. They started with the genetic sequence, which they found online, then created small DNA strands, which they combined to reconstruct the viral genome. They then added a chemical cocktail that brought the entire pathogenic virus to life. Polio, as you know, is an ineffective biological weapon, but Humbolt was applying their research techniques to other viruses."

"What kind of viruses?" Zane asked. "Ebola, Marburg, Venezuelan equine encephalitis . . . all of those have been considered as biological weapons but ruled out because of a lack of efficient delivery method."

"Correct," Natalie said, looking up at him. "But Humbolt wasn't concerned with those viruses."

"What was he concerned with?" Eve asked.

Natalie focused on her again. "Our intel says one particularly nasty virus that was eradicated more than twenty years ago. One that's officially only stored at two high-security laboratories in the world. One of which is in Russia. And the other—"

Shit. "The United States," Eve breathed.

"Bingo," Natalie answered.

"Smallpox," Zane said, his gaze growing more serious. "You're telling us Humbolt was working on the production of an artificially produced smallpox virus."

"Yes."

"Why?" Eve asked. "Why waste his time creating something for the government they already have access to?"

"Because he wasn't working for the US government, Juliet," Natalie said. "Adam Humbolt was a French citizen. Our intel says he was preparing to shop what he had to the highest bidder for a large sum of cash."

"Holy shit," Zane muttered.

Holy shit didn't even begin to cover it. Slowly, Eve's gaze slid back to Zane. He'd been right. The US government had set Aegis up. They'd needed that op in Guatemala to fail. They'd wanted Humbolt dead. And Zane had been caught in the crosshairs.

Her throat grew thick. She had to focus on the here and now. She faced Natalie again. "So the file—"

"We think it contained Humbolt's research notes," Carter answered. When she glanced his way again, he said, "We knew Smith was feeling out the competition and that Humbolt was ready to sell what he had to the highest bidder. The smallpox genome has over two hundred thousand base pairs, so creating an artificial virus is still years away, but his research would cut that time in half with the right scientists working on what he'd already found. The Agency was concerned and sent you in to get it back."

"Without my knowing."

"Let's just say there were . . . questions"—he glanced toward Zane—"about where your loyalties rested. After the incident in Guatemala, Roberts wanted to make sure you were still committed to the Company. And then all this happened with the Chechens and Sawyer and you—"

Eve's temper shot up. "I'm not in league with any Chechen terrorists."

"I know that," he said on a sigh. "But someone's setting you up to make it look like you are. The big question is why."

Eve's pulse shot up. If anything, this little meeting had created more questions than answers.

That file was going to save her life, though. If she wanted to clear her name—clear Zane's name—she needed to find it and prove her loyalty to the United States. She looked at Carter. "So where is the file now?"

"That, we don't know." He tucked his hands into the pockets of his slacks. "Smith was supposed to make the drop with you. The fact that he didn't leads us to believe someone got to him before we did. Your disappearance from the scene of the bombing led to questions. Originally the Agency just wanted to pick you up to find out what had gone wrong. But after that cash was dumped into your account, and with the file still missing, well . . . let's just say your involvement in all of this has jumped a few notches."

A shriek echoed from the direction of the playground. Zane turned to look. From where he was standing, he had a better view through the trees than Eve did on the bench, but when he muttered, "Fuck," under his breath, she knew a child hadn't simply fallen off a swing or been hit by a Frisbee.

"What's going on?" Eve asked, slowly pushing to her feet.

Zane pulled the Beretta from the holster at his lower back. "We're about to have company."

"Who?" Eve asked, reaching for her weapon. From the corner of her eye she saw Carter and Natalie do the same.

Zane shot her a *we're fucked* look over his shoulder. "Your friends from the warehouse."

chapter 17

Landon stared at the small, well-kept two-story home on a quiet street in the Fremont district of Seattle. The lawn was neatly mowed, the fence was freshly painted, and the iron chairs on the wide front porch were decked out with new seat cushions.

Not your typical safe house. Then again, that didn't mean it wasn't the right place. Every curtain was closed tight, blocking the inside from view, and the fence was taller than your standard six-foot fare, reminding him of that house in Cleveland where those three women had been held captive by a monster for years on end.

His stomach tightened as he sat in the shade of an oak tree and watched the house. When not a single person came or went in an hour, he decided to take a closer look.

His mind drifted to Olivia Wolfe as he crossed the street, and he couldn't help but wonder what she was thinking. What she was feeling. Fear and trauma weren't things that could be measured in time. Whether it was a day, a week, or ten years, a person's life could be changed forever by one single moment. He knew that better than most because usually he was the cause.

He shifted the backpack hanging off one shoulder, climbed the front porch, pulled back the screen, and knocked. It was ballsy, but he wanted to know what he was up against before he went in, guns blazing.

Seconds ticked by, and no one answered. He knocked again. Waited. When still no one answered, he stepped back off the porch and looked up at the second story.

That fucker in Cleveland had left those women chained in their rooms when he'd gone out. Landon tugged the backpack over his other shoulder, glanced toward the fence, and then made his way around the side of the house.

The possibility that there could be guard dogs flickered through his mind, but he pushed the thought aside and quickly scaled the ten-foot metal fence. Dropping to his feet, he eyed the elaborate combination locking mechanism on the inside, then pulled the SIG from his lower back. Someone definitely wanted to keep something or someone inside this place.

He moved quietly through the backyard. Trees rimmed the lawn, blocking the view from other houses. A patio void of furniture led to three small steps and a back door. One look at the wires in the corner of the window told him there was a security system in place.

Landon glanced toward the upstairs windows, looking for any crack or opening. All the windows looked closed, but that didn't mean there was no point of entry.

Choosing the closest tree, he climbed until he could access the roof of the garage. Balancing on the steep grade, he made his way across the roof toward the upstairs window he'd targeted below.

Like the door downstairs, there was a magnetic sensor, but it would be triggered only when the window was opened, not broken. Landon tugged on a pair of gloves from the backpack, then pulled out a folded piece of tinfoil he'd brought for this very reason. Using his elbow, he broke the window in the top right corner.

Pain echoed down his arm, but the long-sleeved Henley protected him from the broken glass. After unfolding the tinfoil, he carefully slid it inside the window and down between the magnetic sensors. Confident it was in place, he reached through the hole in the window and flipped the window lock on the top of the pane.

Moment of truth. He pushed the window up and climbed inside.

The small bedroom was empty except for a neatly made bed, a dresser, and a chair. Gun held steady in both hands, he scanned the room and listened. No alarms rang. No footsteps echoed. Moving quickly through the upstairs and finding it quiet, he eased down the stairs and into the kitchen. A glance at the alarm panel by the back door confirmed the system hadn't been tripped. He turned a slow circle, took in the silent family room and the empty kitchen, and then moved down the hall toward the front of the house.

The place was like a ghost town. No sound, no movement, nothing that indicated anyone had been here in days.

Making a circle through the downstairs rooms, he stopped when he spotted the door beneath the staircase.

He reached out, turned the handle. Found it locked.

Suspicion sent tiny arcs of electricity all down his spine. He holstered his weapon and pulled out his lock pick kit. Minutes later, he pulled the door open and stood staring down a dark, silent staircase.

His adrenaline inched up. He reached back for his weapon again and slowly moved down the first few steps. Wood creaked under his feet. A musty smell hit his nose. The only light came from behind him, spilling down the basement stairs into a pitch-black cavern.

He reached the cement floor. Squinted through the darkness, looking for a light, a switch, anything. Shuffling echoed to his right before he could reach back in his bag and find his flashlight. Heart pounding, he swiveled in that direction and lifted his gun. "Move and you're dead."

Something hard slammed into the side of his head.

The shriek burst past Olivia's lips before she could stop it.

The wooden leg she'd broken off a small table slid against her sweaty palms, but she pulled back, ready to nail the fucker in the head again.

"Son of a bitch." The man yanked the weapon out of her hand. It clattered against the floor across the room. "Don't fucking hit me again."

Olivia scooted as far away from him as the chain would let her go. Bright light burned her eyes, making it hard to see. Her muscles ached, her stomach hurt, and her entire body vibrated with both fear and exhaustion. She couldn't see the other table legs she'd ripped off that small piece of furniture. Wondered how far away they were and if she could reach them before he came at her. She knew she shouldn't do anything more to antagonize the men holding her, but she was losing control. Playing scared wasn't working. It was time to fight back or die.

Kill me. Just do it. Get it over with.

She wanted to scream the words but couldn't seem to make her lips work. All that came out was another pathetic screech.

"Son of a bitch. No. Don't. Shit. Shh . . ."

Fabric rustled. The man standing in the spray of light moved closer. Olivia's terror shot to all new levels. She scrambled for the corner of the room. The chain around her ankle rattled. She looked around for her weapons. All she needed was one. Something . . .

Stay back. Don't touch me . . .

Do it! Just get it over with and kill me!

Conflicting thoughts battled in her mind. She was losing her slight grasp on sanity. The shadow grew larger, closer. Her hand curled into a tight fist, and she shook her head, searching for that elusive place where they couldn't touch her, where they couldn't hurt her, where no matter what they did, they wouldn't win.

"Olivia, shh . . . I'm not here to hurt you. I'm here to help."

She tugged her legs up to her chest. Tightened her other fist. Pain ricocheted all through her body. She'd heard those words before. Had fallen for them one too many times. The screams from the man she'd been talking to through the wall in that other house when they'd dragged him away echoed through her mind.

"Olivia, stop. I'm not going to hurt you. My name's Landon Miller. I work for a company called Aegis Security. Your sister Eve sent me to find you."

One word got through. One thought.

Eve.

"That's right," he said in a gentler voice. "You know Eve. You remember her. She's worried about you. She can't be here right now, but she sent me to get you."

Olivia stilled, squinted, and tried to see his face. With the light at his back, all she could make out was the silhouette of his body, kneeling close to her.

Trust him. Don't trust him. It could be a trap. Her frantic mind searched for something solid to latch on to. Eve could have sent him, or he could be another psycho, this one eager to torment her in new, more sadistic ways.

"Look," he said softly. "All I want to do is get you out of this house and away from these people. But first you have to trust me. Do you think you can trust me, Olivia?"

No. Yes. Olivia wasn't sure. All she knew for certain was that as bad as her captivity had been so far, at the hands of someone else it could be a thousand times worse.

She was still debating her options when the floorboards creaked above.

"Shit." The man tilted his head toward the ceiling. Footsteps echoed, and a door somewhere above slammed shut.

Olivia's heart rate shot up.

"Stay here." He pushed to his feet and quickly disappeared.

Confused, Olivia drew away from the wall and looked for him, unsure what he was doing. Seconds later he was back, kneeling in front of her again. "We need to get moving."

He shifted around, tugged something from his back. Olivia tensed. Then he flicked a switch, and a beam of light spread over her dirty, bare feet.

A flashlight. He was holding a flashlight.

"Hold still." He put the end of the small flashlight in his mouth and tugged something else from his back. Light shone over her butterfly tattoo and the metal cuff around her ankle. A click echoed, and she looked down and watched in surprise as he used a long metal object to pick the lock.

The cuff sprang free. He tucked the lock pick back in his pack and pushed to his feet. He was tall. Really tall. Taller than the others who'd come down here. He held out a hand. "Can you stand?"

Olivia's heart raced. Indecision warred. She was free. Free for the first time in days. With a complete stranger who might or might not be another psychopath.

"Cellar doors lead to freedom, Olivia. You're either with me or you're not. It'll only be seconds before they find that door upstairs open."

Freedom. The word sounded elusive. A fable. A fantasy. She looked down at his wide palm, dimly lit from the light near the stairs, and made her choice.

Her hand slid over his. Warmth rushed into her skin. His fingers quickly closed over hers and tightened, holding her in a fierce grip, tugging her to her feet and closer to his broad body.

His chest was huge. His arms thick and muscled beneath the long-sleeved top. And his legs . . . dear God, they were like tree trunks. Panic consumed her. His other hand landed at her waist and slid around her back. The spicy scent of leather and musk filled her nostrils. The air grew thicker the closer she drew to his body, and her heart rate picked up speed.

She'd made the wrong choice. He was one of them. He was going to hurt her. He was going to—

Shouts echoed from above. His head swiveled toward the stairs, and he muttered, "Fucking A."

Light from the stairs spilled over his profile, and she caught her first glimpse of his face. A nose slightly crooked as if it had been broken once or twice, full lips, a strong chin and sculpted jaw. She couldn't tell what color his hair was, but his skin was shades lighter than the men who'd been holding her in this prison, and even in the dim light, there was something solid, reassuring, hopeful about him.

His gaze snapped back to her, and she found herself wondering what color his eyes were. "I have to let go of you. Don't fall."

She didn't have time to answer. He released her waist and hand and reached back for his pack. Weak, Olivia swayed on her bare feet, but her adrenaline kept her upright. Footsteps pounded above. Running. Growing louder. Growing closer. Her gaze darted toward the stairs.

The man—Miller? Had he said his name was Miller? Or had she imagined that?—pulled something from his pack. His fingers moved quickly in the dark, and then he grasped her at the wrist and pulled. "Come on."

They were heading toward the stairs. Sweat burst all over her skin. He couldn't possibly mean to—

They reached the base of the stairs. A body stepped into the light at the top. One she recognized. The man who'd hit her relentlessly. She tensed. Tried to pull back out of the grip at her wrist. The man yelled in that same foreign language she didn't understand. Miller threw whatever was in his hand up the stairs.

The sound of an explosion echoed through the basement, shaking the walls. A blinding light erupted above. Miller tugged hard on her arm. "Now!"

Olivia stumbled. Gasped. Tried to keep up. He dragged her across the basement, then stopped in front of what looked like a steel door. "Turn away."

She didn't know what he was doing, but she listened. Two more bangs, then the sound of metal shattering. She looked back just as he was shoving his shoulder against the door. It gave with a crack. Cement steps let up to cellar doors, which he quickly pushed open. Then warm sunlight rushed over her body, warming her frigid skin and bathing her in light.

Relief trickled through every cell in her body. She sucked in a deep breath, but the grip on her hand jolted her out of any celebration she wanted to lose herself in. "No time to fuck around," Miller said to her. "We have to keep moving."

Bright light blinded her, but she looked his way and realized he was holding a gun in both hands, scanning the area behind them.

"Head toward the fence," he directed.

Grass pressed against the bottom of her feet as she forced her muscles forward, running for the fence. When she reached it, her heart sank.

The thing had to be at least ten feet tall. And metal, straight up. No footholds. She'd never scale it.

A dog barked. Inside the house, voices echoed and shouted. Footsteps pounded.

"Up, let's go, come on. We're running out of time." Miller holstered the gun and then leaned over and cupped both hands together, creating a step for her.

"I can't—"

"Fuck can't. You wanna live? Then haul ass, woman. We've got seconds before they're here."

Olivia's heart jumped into her throat. She gripped his strong shoulders and slid her foot into his hands. "What about you?"

"Don't worry about me." He didn't even grunt as he hefted her up. Her fingertips grazed the top of the fence, and she clawed for a tight grip. "Throw yourself over."

Throw herself over? She managed to get one leg over the side of the fence, then made the mistake of looking back.

Three, four, no . . . five men spilled out of the house, guns drawn. Somewhere a dog snarled and barked.

"Go!" Miller screamed.

Fear froze every muscle in her body.

Gunfire erupted in the yard.

Zane's pulse shot into the stratosphere as he slid his arms into both straps of the backpack. He'd counted four men heading toward them from the direction of the parking lot, but they were already splitting up.

Eve's hand gripped his shirt and tugged him back into the cover of the trees.

"How many?" Carter asked.

Eve took up space near Zane, gun drawn and ready, eyes scanning the park beyond. She was in black ops mode, and all he wanted to do was shove her behind him where he knew she'd be safe, but he knew there was no way in hell she'd ever go for that.

"Four," he answered.

"Civilians?" Natalie asked, pulling a Colt XSE from her holster.

"They've scattered." Zane squinted through the trees. "I can't see them anymore."

"Let's hope to God they had the sense to get out of here." Natalie gripped the gun in both hands. "Four against four. Those aren't bad odds."

"Four that we can see." Zane glanced her way. "Packing M14s and who the hell knows what else."

She grinned. "Makes it all the more fun."

"You should leave, Natalie." Eve's strained voice met Zane's ears, but he refused to turn and look. "This isn't your fight."

"I'm not leaving the three of you on your own."

Yeah, but they needed Natalie alive so she could help clear Eve's name. "Listen," Zane said, "maybe Eve's right."

Gunfire exploded in the clearing. Reflexes had Zane shoving Eve to the ground.

She grunted as her shoulder and hip hit the earth. Dirt and grass flew up around them. More gunfire ricocheted, this time from Carter and Natalie as they fired back, protected by the trees. A thud echoed to Zane's right, and Natalie groaned. When he turned to look, bright red seeped through the white cotton at her shoulder.

Zane scrambled off Eve and rushed to Natalie. With Eve's help, they pulled her behind another tree. From ahead, Carter hollered, "A little help here!"

Eve was on her feet in seconds, her gun drawn as she joined Carter. Tightness closed around Zane's chest, but he knew he had to trust in her training. Had to let her do what she needed to do. He helped Natalie lean against a tree and pressed a hand over the wound.

"Shit," she gasped. "Maybe I should have listened."

"We're gonna get you out of here." He picked up her good arm and placed her hand against the wound. "Pressure here. You hear me? Don't let up."

She bit hard into her lip. Nodded. "Just get the fuckers."

When Zane reached Eve and Carter, Eve was already switching magazines. Two assailants lay dead in the park, but two more were closing in fast. He skidded to his knees and quickly rummaged through the backpack until he found the flash grenades in the bottom. Jerking the pin free, he threw one into the park. "Go!"

A boom echoed, followed by a flash of light, blinding the attackers. Eve stepped out from behind the tree, lifted the gun in both hands, aimed at the man on the right, and fired. The bullet hit him in the throat. He went down like a board. She swiveled and aimed at the guy on the left and did the same. Gunfire erupted, but the man only got off two shots before he was on the ground.

"Fucking A," Carter mumbled from yards away. "Archer!"

Lifting his Beretta again, Zane swiveled and saw what Carter was staring at.

Two more men coming from the direction of the parking lot. One carrying what looked like a rocket launcher on his shoulder.

"Fuck me," Zane muttered.

Carter whipped around. "We need to haul ass."

Eve stepped out and fired. Missed. Fired again. Bullets thunked against wood. She ducked back behind the tree, just barely missing being hit. "What about—?"

"I'll get her," Carter announced. "Just fucking *go!*"

He was already running for Natalie before Zane could stop him. Before he could argue. The guy with the rocket launcher lowered it to his shoulder and lined up his sights.

Grasping Eve by the collar, Zane pulled hard. "Go, go, *go!*"

Muscles in his legs burned as they sprinted for the far end of the park. Gunfire rang out behind him. He turned to fire one. Twice. Felt like he was in a dream. From the corner of his eye he saw Carter lift Natalie over his shoulder. Saw the blood running down her arm. Saw Carter push his legs into motion and head the other direction.

No. They were going the wrong direction. That would lead them closer to the parking lot. Where they didn't know how many others were waiting.

He opened his mouth to yell for Carter to stop. The rocket launcher hissed.

And then the world exploded.

chapter 18

Dirt and leaves and grass filled Eve's mouth.

She coughed, rolled to her side, and grimaced at the burn in her side. Heat spread over her skin. She pulled her eyelids apart to see the trees, the forest, everything in flames.

"Get up. Gotta keep moving."

Zane's hand tugged on her arm, pulling her to her feet. In a daze she tried to make sense of the explosion. Tried to see through the flames and smoke to what lay beyond. Tried to find—

"Carter!" She jerked hard on Zane's arm, stopping him from pulling her.

"He's dead, Eve."

"No!" Eve struggled against his grip.

Zane's dirt-streaked face appeared right in front of hers, his eyes wide and intense, and she registered his strong arms gripping her upper arms. "He's dead. They both are. And we will be too if we don't get the fuck out of here now."

Dead. They . . . *Oh shit.* Natalie. Carter. Both of them.

Zane yanked her forward. Her muscles reacted even if her mind was having trouble keeping up. Gripping the gun tightly in her other hand, she ran with him through the trees, away from the carnage. Her stomach rolled. Sickness threatened, but she fought it back. Just like every other time an op had gone wrong and someone had died.

But this was Carter . . .

Don't think about him. Don't think about them.

They stumbled onto a golf course. Zane didn't let up on his hold. He tugged her into the trees, around shrubs and rocks and saplings, not giving her a moment to rest. Not giving her time to think. Only time to feel.

Dead.

No . . . Not both of them. Not because of her.

They reached another parking lot, this one for the golf course. Sweating and out of breath, Zane finally released his grip long enough so Eve could double over and suck in air. Her stomach rolled all over again. And then the burn started low and bubbled up.

She stumbled for a bush and retched what was in her stomach. Pain consumed every part of her. Dead. Both of them. All because of her.

"Come on. I got a car."

She registered Zane's voice. Not the words or the tone. Just that it was familiar. He tugged on her arm. "This way."

Wiping her mouth on her sleeve, she stumbled after him toward a Honda. A back window was broken in. He popped the passenger door and helped her in. Tossing the pack in the backseat, he moved to the driver's seat, pulled the panel off the area below the steering wheel, and yanked out a handful of wires.

She wanted to ask him where he'd learned to hot-wire a car but couldn't find her voice. Her throat burned. Her stomach ached. And when she thought about Carter and Natalie . . .

"I'm going to be sick."

Zane shoved her head between her knees. "Breathe."

Seconds later the ignition started. Zane leaned back in his seat. "Hold on."

Time rushed by with the scenery. Eve didn't know how long they drove or in what direction. She heard Zane on his cell phone but didn't know who he was talking to. Couldn't seem to focus on any one thing. All she could see was Natalie hefted over Carter's shoulder, Carter running the wrong way, and then the world burning in a fireball like the one in Seattle. Closing her eyes, she tipped her head against the window and tried not to get sick all over again.

She awoke sometime later. The car had stopped. It was raining. It was always raining somewhere in the Pacific Northwest. Cool air washed over her when the driver's door opened and closed. "I changed the plates," Zane said, settling behind the wheel. Water droplets stuck in his hair and on his shoulders and arms. "And I don't think anyone's following us. At least not yet."

Her eyes slid closed again as he pulled back onto the highway. Tipping her head away from him, she focused on the hum of the windshield wipers. Back and forth. Back and forth. Her stomach hurt, and her head throbbed. She didn't want to think. Didn't want to feel. The hum of the wipers grew louder.

It was dusk when she felt the car stop again. Blinking several times, she looked out the windshield at the monstrous log cabin with its multitude of porches and windows and different levels in surprise. "Wh-where are we?"

"Safe house." Zane popped the door and stepped out into the rain. "Come on."

In a daze, she climbed out of the car and moved for the front porch. Rain ran down her cheeks and beaded on her clothes, but she barely felt it. She climbed up the steps and moved onto the porch after him, waiting while he checked the pots along the side of the house for what she suspected was a spare key.

He disappeared around the corner of the house, and Eve slowly turned to look around. Tall pine and Douglas fir trees rose toward the dark sky. They were obviously in the mountains, though at what elevation she couldn't tell, and since she hadn't paid attention to the direction Zane had been driving, they could be in Canada for all she knew. There were no other vehicles anywhere close. No other homes that she could see, either. Just dense forest growing darker by the minute, and ominous clouds that mirrored her mood.

Dead.

Her stomach rolled again. Pain wrapped knotted, gnarled fingers around her chest. She closed her eyes and breathed through her nose to keep from getting sick once more. Carter was dead. Because of her. Carter and Natalie. Probably Olivia too. If those were the same men who'd taken her sister, there was no hope for Olivia's return now.

She'd dealt with death before, but this hit too close to home. This was too real. This was her fault.

Footsteps echoed close, and Eve managed to open her eyes just as Zane came around the corner. He held something shiny in his hand. "Got it."

Seconds later they were in the house. Light pine floors ran from the massive entryway toward a two-story family room and, beyond that, an industrial-sized kitchen. A curved staircase rose to the second floor. Wide windows covered the entire back wall of the great room, looking out over the enormous back deck, the grass, and the pristine blue lake.

He closed and locked the door behind him, then grasped her hand. "Come on."

He led her into the great room. Plush furnishings surrounded a huge rock fireplace that ran to the ceiling. An elaborate mantle stretched from one side to the other. Above, an enormous flat-screen

TV was mounted to the wall. Past the kitchen on the right, a large round mahogany table sat in a bay of towering windows, looking out toward the lake. He pulled out one of the ten chairs around it and pushed her to sit. Then grabbed the arm of her left sleeve and pulled.

Fabric ripped. Startled by the sound, Eve looked down where he was kneeling next to her. "What are you doing?"

"You're hit. Hold still while I see how bad it is."

The white sleeve was stained with soot and blood and dirt. She stared at the jagged wound across her biceps, swollen and red, not even feeling it.

"It's just a scratch." He pushed to his feet and disappeared. "Stay here."

She looked around the room, feeling numb inside. She should get up. She should be trying to find her sister. She should be tracking those men who'd blown up that park and killed her friends. But she didn't have the energy. Didn't have the drive. Didn't have . . . anything anymore.

Dead.

Zane knelt next to her again. "This might sting."

Something cool brushed her arm, but she barely registered the sensation. He cleaned and bandaged the wound, then pushed to his feet. Seconds passed before he said, "I need to move the car. You gonna be okay for a few minutes?"

Was she okay? She didn't know. She didn't know anything. She didn't answer.

Footsteps echoed across the floor. Then the door opened and closed. Minutes later he was back, shaking the rain from his hair and locking the door once more. When he moved back into the room, she heard him mutter, "God, you're a mess," but she didn't have the energy to fight with him or even look his way.

"Whose house is this?"

He moved into the kitchen and flipped on a light. "A high-profile client. It's a vacation home in the Cascades. No one will find us. We're safe for the time being."

For the time being. That didn't do much to bolster Eve's mood. She turned and looked out at the water. "I thought you weren't speaking to your boss at Aegis."

"I am now."

He didn't elaborate, and Eve couldn't help but wonder what else had happened in the hours she'd been out of it, but she still didn't have the desire to ask.

"Is there"—she swallowed the lump in her throat—"any news about Olivia?"

"No, none. I'm sorry."

None. She didn't expect there to be. Olivia was dead. Just like Natalie. Just like Carter. Just like that child in the street in Seattle.

All because of her.

She closed her eyes again. Focused on the sounds. The fridge opening. A cupboard door slapping shut. A pan landing on a burner. Familiar, normal sounds.

Just don't think. Just don't feel.

A click echoed in front of her, and she opened her eyes to see a plate of scrambled eggs on the table.

"Eat," Zane said.

She didn't feel like eating. And just the sight of food made her stomach roll. He went back into the kitchen and returned with his own plate and two glasses of water.

Water. Water she could manage. She picked up the glass and downed the entire thing.

"There's something you need to know." He waited until she put the glass down before going on. "Jake Ryder, the CEO of Aegis Security, and ADD Roberts went to school together. I don't know all the details, but they don't get along. Aegis was passed over on the defense contract for the Guatemala mission. Ryder got pissed and told the government they could go fuck themselves. He makes enough money off private security where he doesn't need the State Department's kickback. But it was a big deal at the time. And then, surprisingly, a few weeks later, Aegis was awarded the contract."

Slowly, Eve turned to look his way. And a tiny part of her brain kicked into gear. "You're telling me the assistant deputy director at the CIA is the one who set Aegis up to take the fall for Humbolt's death."

"That's the way it's looking."

"And by that theory, ADD Roberts is the one after Humbolt's formula."

"Yes."

"My boss."

"Yes."

Her eyes narrowed. "In counterintelligence."

Zane exhaled a breath and rested his forearm on the table. "Think about it. If he really did set Aegis up because of some vendetta against Ryder, and he sent you in to get the drop from Smith, then his hands are all over a lot of sticky shit."

Eve considered for a moment. She worked for the world's greatest spy agency. She knew there were double agents in the organization. Knew there were compromised agents. Hell, her job was to find them. And though there were a variety of reasons a person could turn, usually they were focused around money, ideology, coercion, or ego. ADD Roberts was, as Carter had pointed out, a mover within the Agency. Eve couldn't see any of the above four reasons compromising his chance at one day being director of the CIA.

"How did you know the op in Guatemala was compromised?" Zane asked.

Eve's brain was suddenly spinning way too fast. She pushed her untouched eggs away, rested her elbow on the table, and rubbed her throbbing head. "I got a call from Langley. A researcher who'd originally helped me pull info on both you and Carter before I went to Beirut."

"And he or she said what?"

She rubbed harder. "That word of the raid had leaked, and that the op was compromised."

"But no info about how or where it was leaked?"

"No."

Zane was quiet for a second and then said, "Ryder's on his way here. He's digging up info on Roberts so we can figure out how to play this."

She dropped her hand, and her gaze snapped his direction. "Here?"

He pushed back from the table and took his plate into the kitchen. "I figure it's time we brought in some help on this."

Eve's stomach rolled all over again. Did they need help? She wasn't so sure. The only out she could see at this point was total surrender. "Carter was right. I need to call Langley and turn myself in."

Zane's plate clattered in the sink. *"What?"*

"You'll have to turn yourself in too, but they're not going to find any involvement in all of this on your part. You'll be released in a couple of days."

"Fuck that. They shot at me, Eve. At you too. They almost killed us, more than once. And one of them has a Chechen terrorist cell behind them. You think you're safe at Langley? You're not safe there. You're not safe anywhere. Look at Carter. You're not safe until we figure out who's really behind this shit once and for all. You go there, and you're dead."

Dead.

Like Carter.

Like Natalie.

Like Olivia.

All because of me.

Eve closed her eyes, and a wave of nausea rolled through her belly.

Footsteps echoed across the floor. Then her chair jolted, and the legs scraped against the floor. "Open your eyes, dammit."

She tore her eyes open, shocked to see Zane leaning over her, one hand resting against the back of her chair, which he'd obviously kicked away from the table. His gaze was as dark and intense as she'd ever seen it, and a fire brewed inside him, one that marked him as dangerous. As deadly. As a force not to be ignored.

"Don't you fucking give up on me now. You want to be tired and sad. Fine. Be that way. But you're not turning yourself in. Not after everything we've been through. People died out there today because of us. We owe them more than that."

Her temper flared, and she knocked his hand away from her chair and stood. "People died because of *me*. Not because of you. Don't tell me what *we* owe them. *We* don't owe them shit." Nausea rolled through her belly all over again. "I do."

The fire in his eyes dimmed just a touch, and he straightened. "What happened out there today was not your fault."

She crossed her arms over her chest and moved to the window, looking out at the darkening view. But that hollow feeling in her chest was growing bigger, more consuming, threatening to pull her under. "I don't see anyone else in the middle of this nightmare. Only me."

He stepped back, but from the corner of her eye, she watched a muscle in his jaw clench. "No, that's right. It's only you. Everything's always about you. It's your fault your sister was taken. It's your fault Roberts set you up. It's your fault Humbolt created that damn file in the first place. Hell, since we're blaming you for shit, I'm sure it was your fault I was stationed in Beirut to begin with."

He was talking to her like she was a child. Like she was an idiot. She glared hard over her shoulder. "Don't mock me."

"Oh, I wouldn't dare." He held up both hands in surrender. "The great Evelyn Wolfe's got it all figured out. She knows how to deal with this mess because, frankly, she started it all. So why don't you do that, Eve. Why don't you just worry about yourself and take care of everything on your own. God knows you've been doing it long enough. Should be second nature by now."

The hurt mixed with sarcasm in his voice made her drop her arms and turn away from the window. "I told you to leave. I told you not to get involved in all of this. If you'd gone when I said, you could have explained your way out of this mess without too many consequences. I *told* you I didn't need your help."

"No, you never do." His eyes hardened. "That's what this is all about, isn't it? The fact you don't want or need anyone's help, not even mine. Well, you know what? That's fine. You made your point, and I'm finally listening. Once Ryder gets here, I'm gone. It was my mistake for sticking with you and thinking you actually cared about someone other than yourself."

He turned for the foyer, and Eve's pulse picked up speed, followed by a sharp pinch in her chest that radiated pain all through her torso. He was leaving. Now. Because of what she'd said. Sweat broke out all over her skin, and a tiny voice in her head screamed, *Stop him!*

But instead of the front door opening and closing like she'd expected to hear, footsteps sounded on the curved staircase that led from the entry to the second floor, followed by a door slamming somewhere upstairs.

Hands shaking, she pulled out a chair and sat, then wrapped her arms around her waist and leaned forward in the hopes it would ease the ache growing in the pit of her stomach.

It didn't help.

The sharp slap of rejection she'd seen in his eyes cut deeper than his words. He thought she didn't care. He thought that all this time she'd been telling him to go because he meant nothing to her. He couldn't possibly know he meant more to her than anyone ever had. She wouldn't be able to survive his death too. Couldn't he see that?

How would he?

That niggling voice in the back of her mind reminded her she'd never told him. That she'd barely admitted it to herself. That she had one chance now to do the right thing where he was concerned. She'd fucked up everything else, but this she could fix. Or at least, end. The right way. Which was something she should have done a long time ago.

But doing it . . .

Her stomach twisted tighter. Doing it meant watching everything he felt for her slowly wither and die.

chapter 19

"I think she's coming around."

Landon looked up at the nurse standing next to Olivia's bed. Pushing out of the chair, he dropped the newspaper he'd been reading on the table at his side and took a small step forward. "Olivia?"

Machines beeped in the small hospital room. The nurse leaned over the frail woman under the thin blanket and said, "Come on, Olivia. Open your eyes."

She'd been unconscious since Landon had brought her to the hospital. When he'd found her lying on the grass on the other side of that fence, completely out, he'd thought she was dead. And when he'd felt her pulse beneath her skin, his relief had been swift and consuming. Losing a hostage in the last seconds of a rescue mission was not an acceptable outcome for him. Though he'd never admit it, he totally understood and condoned Archer's need for revenge after Humbolt had been killed.

Olivia turned her head slightly on the pillow and groaned. Landon's pulse sped up as he waited.

"That's it," the nurse said. "Open up and say hello, why don't you?"

Bruises covered her slim face and bony arms. Her hair was dirty and matted against her head, preventing him from knowing its true color. She was a tiny thing, maybe five four, if she was lucky, and a hundred and ten pounds max on a good day. But dehydrated and malnourished like she was, she'd weighed nearly nothing in his arms.

She hadn't been raped. The doctors had assured him of that after they'd examined her when he'd brought her to the ER, but that was small consolation considering everything else. Remembering the way she'd had trouble standing when he'd tugged her to her feet, how frail her arms had been and how she'd barely been able to pull herself up that wall, part of him wished he could go back and shoot those fuckers who'd done this to her all over again.

"That's it, Olivia," the nurse cooed. "I've got some juice here for you. You like juice, don't you? Everyone likes juice."

Olivia's eyes fluttered and finally opened, and when they did, Landon felt like someone had sucker punched him straight in the middle of the chest.

Green. Her eyes were a piercing emerald green. Not like Eve's at all. As stunning as a highly polished precious stone.

"Welcome back," the woman said to her. "I'm Carol, your nurse. And you recognize this guy, don't you?"

Slowly, Olivia's head rolled on the pillow, and those captivating eyes locked on his.

She stared at him. Didn't move. Didn't speak. And as he studied the emptiness in her gaze, he realized she didn't remember him. Probably hadn't gotten a good enough look to recognize his face, not that his scarred mug was anything special to remember. But considering everything she'd been through, he didn't want her to think he was one of those thugs and unleash another ear-piercing scream on the nurse like she'd done on him. Frail or not, the woman had lungs.

"Hey." His voice was thick. Not his own. He cleared his throat. "Nice to see you're finally awake. We were starting to worry."

Those pretty eyes narrowed and held. After several seconds they widened in shock. "M-Miller?"

"Yeah." Another burst of relief rippled through his veins. That she remembered him. That she knew his name. Relief he wasn't used to feeling. He fought the urge to feel her hand sliding against his like he'd done when he'd pulled her free of that chain.

Which was . . . nowhere close to normal for him. She was a target, not anyone he knew personally. He shoved his hands in the front pocket of his jeans so he wouldn't do something stupid. Like reach for her. "How do you feel?"

"I feel . . ." She pulled her gaze from his and slowly glanced around the white room. "Where am I?"

"In the hospital," the nurse said. "Here, let's get you up so you can have some juice." She fiddled with the bed controller, then the motor hummed and the top of the bed lifted. "You were pretty dehydrated, and you took a nasty fall."

Sitting upright didn't help the way Olivia looked. If anything, the fluorescent lights above highlighted the bruises and swelling around her eyes. Her hair fell to her shoulders, but Landon still couldn't tell the color. It was so dirty, it could be blonde, light brown, or even dark. The nurse handed Olivia the juice, and Landon cringed when her bruised arm lifted from the bed and her weak fingers wrapped around the box. But the sound she made when she sucked on the straw—a moan of pure pleasure—shot a burst of wicked heat all through his body.

He turned quickly away from the bed and scrubbed a hand over his face. Holy shit. Okay, he was clearly losing it. Lack of sleep was obviously getting to him. Forget the fact she wasn't even his type and that he didn't go for skinny, matronly schoolteachers. The chick looked like she'd been used for a punching bag, and her face was so fucked up, he couldn't even tell if she was pretty. But aside from all that, he never got involved with his principals. Never. Even the totally built, superrich, hot ones.

Zoning back into his role, he locked up whatever silly emotions were playing with his head and turned back to face the bed. The nurse finished checking Olivia's vitals, then said, "I'm going to have the doctor come in and check on you in a minute. Just keep drinking that juice, and I'll be right back."

"Okay."

The nurse left the room, leaving the door open, but she pulled the curtain closed. Olivia sucked on the juice box until it made a slurping sound, then lowered it to her lap. A moment of uncomfortable silence passed before she said, "That bandage on the side of your head. I, um, didn't do that, did I?"

He brushed a finger over the butterfly bandage against his temple and chuckled. "You've got some muscles."

She cringed. "I'm sorry. I thought you were . . . one of them."

"It's okay. It's not the first time my face has taken a beating. I'll heal."

Her gaze lingered on the jagged scar across his left cheek, and he knew she was wondering where he'd gotten it, but she didn't ask. Instead, she looked around the room again. "How did we get here? The last thing I remember was those men shooting at you in that yard."

She sounded halfway sane, and Landon figured that was a plus, considering everything she'd been through. Though he wished for her sake she couldn't remember any of it. "I took care of them."

Surprised green eyes darted to his. Eyes that sucker punched him again, right in the chest. "All of them?"

Be cool. She's just a girl. Nothing special. "It's what I do."

"Oh." Her gaze roamed over his body, and tiny pinpricks of heat erupted wherever she looked. Heat he couldn't seem to douse even though he knew he should. "Are you, like, special forces or something?"

"Something like that." He wasn't about to tell this innocent little thing what he'd done for a living with the DIA. And he had to get her eyes off his body and refocused on his face because otherwise . . . yeah, otherwise he wasn't sure what he'd do next. "Olivia, do you remember the men who were holding you? Can you tell me anything about them?"

She closed her eyes and dropped her head back against the pillow. A sick look passed over her features. "I don't want to talk about them."

"I know." The urge to torture those men he'd killed whipped back through him like a hurricane. "But anything you can remember might help."

She didn't answer. Just sat there with her eyes closed. And something in his chest turned over as he watched her. He didn't know what she was remembering. Had no clue what she was feeling. But he knew it was bad. And the need to protect her, to wrap her in his arms and tell her everything would be okay, consumed him from the top down.

Which was ludicrous. He couldn't convince himself of that on a good day, and he'd tried thousands of times. Why the hell did he think he could help someone else?

Suddenly, her eyes popped open, and she lifted her head from the pillow, looking his way, those green eyes, which moments ago had been flat and empty, now vibrant and alive. "There was a man. He was the one who grabbed me at my house."

Finally. Something. "Do you remember what he looked like?"

She shook her head. "He was dark. And tall. That's all I got. But he was nice to me. He kept telling me it would all be over soon.

Somewhere along the way things changed, though, and he wasn't the one in charge. I didn't see him again, but I heard him. Yesterday. I think he was in the room next to me, before they moved me to that last house. He talked to me through the wall. I'm sure it was him."

The guy who'd kidnapped her had been overpowered and then locked up himself? "Did you ever hear anyone call him Smith?"

Her brow lowered, and then she shook her head. "No. But—" She lifted her torso from the bed, sitting all the way up on her own. The sheet and thin blanket fell against her waist, revealing the drab gray hospital gown and her bony arms. "Wait. He said his name was Tyrone."

Bingo. Excitement spread through Landon's veins. "What else?"

"He"—she looked down at her thin legs under the blanket— "he told me that he'd grabbed me to get to Eve." Her worried gaze shot to Landon's face. "My sister's okay, isn't she? Please tell me they don't have Eve."

"Relax." The panic in her voice set his protective instincts into high gear. He sat on the bottom of her bed and rested his hand on her calf. Heat seeped through the thin cotton, but he told himself this was okay. He needed to calm her down. He wasn't touching her for himself. "She's fine. Worried about you. We'll call her in a minute. I wanted to wait until you were awake. Tell me what else Tyrone said."

Olivia relaxed just a touch and looked down at his hand. His fingers felt huge resting against her frail leg, but he forced himself not to pull away.

"He . . . he said she was the target. That they'd grabbed me to draw her out. That she knows too much." She frowned. "But that doesn't make sense. Eve works for a politician. I mean . . . what could she know?"

Eve had obviously kept her family in the dark just like she'd done to Archer. But now wasn't the time to worry about spilling secrets. "Olivia, look at me."

When those pretty, gemlike eyes met his, his pulse sped up, but he ignored it. She'd been through so much, he doubted much more could shock her, but even if this did, he had to ask. "Your sister works for the CIA. There was a bombing in Seattle a few days ago. Eve was supposed to meet a man named Tyrone Smith and obtain a file from him. Something went wrong, and a car bomb went off not far from their meeting place. The authorities think Eve was involved in the bombing, but we know it's all linked to your kidnapping. I need to know if Tyrone said anything else. Anything at all that might help your sister."

Olivia's brow dropped low as she processed his words, and then her eyes grew wide. Wide and—oh fuck—absolutely mesmerizing. "Western Avenue."

"What?"

"We have to get to Seattle." She threw back the covers. "There's an athletic club on Western Avenue."

"Wait." His brow lowered as she tossed her legs over the side of the bed. "What? Hold on. Now you want to work out?"

She pushed to her bare feet. Wobbled. The hospital gown fell to her knees, but she was so small, it all but swallowed her whole.

"Olivia." He was in front of her before he even realized it, wrapping his arm around her waist and giving her his body to use as a crutch. "Dammit, don't fall."

Her hands landed against his chest, and warmth bloomed beneath her palms. Against his belly he felt her tiny breasts and—oh shit—hard nipples.

Cold. She's fucking cold in that open gown, not turned on. Get a grip, Miller.

He stilled and tried to get his head back in the game. Clearing his throat, he managed, "You need to sit back down. You're in no shape to go anywhere. I'll take you to Seattle when you're better."

"No." She lifted her chin and looked up at him. "I have to go now. Don't you understand? We have to get it before anyone else."

"Get what?"

An exasperated look crossed her face. "The item in the locker at the athletic club. He said it was the only thing that would help Eve."

Landon stilled. And even though his pulse was still roaring in his ears being this close to her, his brain was slowly coming back on line. "What's the locker number? I'll go."

"No. She's my sister. I'm going."

And right then he saw a glimpse of something he hadn't seen before. Strength. Rock-solid strength. The kind that proved she was a survivor and not a victim. She wasn't thanking him for saving her life. She wasn't whining and crying about what had happened. She was trying to walk out of a hospital she desperately needed to be in, more concerned about her sister's well-being than her own.

Those gemlike eyes turned hard and resolute. And he pictured her in front of her class, when she had a rowdy student, laying down the law, not taking shit from anyone. A lot like him when he was in black ops mode. "Either take me to Seattle, Miller, or I'll find a way there myself."

Landon stared down into her strong, beautiful eyes. And his heart picked up speed. Because right then he knew Olivia Wolfe was not like any other principal he'd ever gone after.

And that meant he was in deep shit.

Eve's stomach was a knot of nerves as she made her way up the curved staircase toward the second floor.

The house was beautiful. That fact, at least, took her mind off what she was about to do. Old timbers that spanned the high ceilings, gleaming wood floors, and plush, expensive carpets. Whoever owned this place was loaded. But then, she knew Aegis Security was the best of the best, and they had numerous high-profile, wealthy names on their client list. Names that could afford this as a second, third, or even fourth home.

She couldn't fathom having money like that. Didn't know what she'd do with it even if she ever had it. Someone thought she'd sold US secrets for money? They obviously didn't know her very well. Her life was as simple as it came. At least it used to be.

She breathed deeply as she moved onto the second floor. An archway led to a huge game room, decked out with couches, a pool table, and a bar. Beyond that were four bedrooms and a theater room with a gigantic movie screen. All the rooms were empty, though, and right now she didn't care about checking out the amenities. She had something more important to do.

Making her way to the far end of the hall, she pushed the double doors open and stepped into the massive master suite. Water ran in the bathroom somewhere to her right, and steam spilled from the open bathroom door. A monster king-sized bed, covered in expensive fabrics, took up space near the left wall, but it was the view out the gigantic windows that spanned two whole walls that stopped her feet. Not just of the darkening lake, but in the distance, the steadily fading view of an enormous mountain.

Sam would have loved this. He'd loved hiking, skiing, being in the outdoors. For a second, she tried to picture him here, but found she couldn't. He didn't fit. And the more she tried to conjure his image, the more she realized his face wasn't the one she longed to see.

She sank onto the end of the bed and let the soft cotton and billowy comforter cushion her tired body. Let it give her strength. Her stomach knotted with every second the shower ran, but she held her ground and told herself that if she did nothing else for anyone ever again, she could at least do this.

The shower cut off. She heard Zane moving around in the bathroom. Her pulse sped up, and she tangled her fingers in the bedspread at her sides while she waited. Seconds later, Zane stepped out of the room, wearing nothing but a towel wrapped low around his lean hips. Water glistened on his sculpted chest and abs, and when he rubbed another towel over his dripping hair, the muscles in his arms flexed and released, reminding her what it felt like to be surrounded by him.

He made it three steps before he realized she was there. His feet stopped. His hand stopped its frantic rubbing. Slowly, he looked in her direction. And butterflies took flight in her stomach.

"I owe you something."

A frown pulled at his mouth. "I'm not in the mood to get my ass handed to me again, thanks."

She couldn't stop the corner of her lips from curling. Even hurt and pissed at her, he could still make her smile. "I didn't mean that. I meant—" Moment of truth. "I meant, I owe you the truth."

He looked away from her, walked toward a chair across the room, and dropped the towel in his hand. "You don't owe me any explanation, Eve. Let's just call this what it is. Over."

Her chest squeezed so tight she could barely breathe. "I was engaged."

His hand stilled against the back of the chair. He didn't say anything, but she knew she'd shocked him. And honestly, she'd shocked herself. She'd never told anyone this.

"It was in college," she said, before she could change her mind. "He was a few years older than me. He was this computer whiz, and he worked for a company in Silicon Valley. We hadn't told anyone we were getting married. I was in my senior year and was finishing up fall term. We'd planned to announce to our families at Christmas. It just . . . never happened."

"Why not?"

The fact he asked told her he was at least a little curious. She steeled her nerves and went on. "He left for a meeting in Hong Kong a couple days after we got engaged. His plane was hijacked and diverted to Manila. You might have heard about it. Fifteen passengers were killed before authorities took control of the aircraft."

He lowered himself to sit on the arm of the chair and crossed his arms over his chest. "I remember. Happened about twelve years ago, right?"

She nodded. "He was one of the fifteen." She looked away from his face, not wanting to see pity in his eyes. She didn't deserve it. "I lost focus after he died. Couldn't seem to pull it together. My friends were worried, my parents talked about sending me to therapy. Luckily, they were in Idaho so they didn't see how bad I really was, but . . ." She drew another breath. "I wanted to die. I didn't know how I could go on. And then one day I was walking by the student union and saw there was a job fair. I went in for no reason and realized the CIA was there, educating students about what they do. I saw it as my way out."

Her hands grew sweaty, and she swiped them against her dirty jeans. "I started out as an analyst but then moved over to counterintelligence. I needed something to do. I couldn't sit behind a desk all day. And I loved it. I loved the travel and the challenge and being out of my head. Working for the Agency saved me when nothing else could have. And I was doing good. Really good. Until I met you."

She looked up. He hadn't moved from his position on the arm of the chair, but he was watching her. Closely. She willed herself to go on.

"I knew as soon as I met you that you weren't the mole. You didn't fit the profile. You were too honest. And just being around you, I knew you were the kind of guy who'd joined CIA for the *right* reasons. To make a difference, not to hide, like I'd done. And I knew I should have stayed away from you, but . . ." She lifted her shoulders and then dropped them. "I couldn't. Because your energy was contagious. And after just a few weeks, I realized I was . . . happy. For the first time since Sam's death. Even in a miserable country that devalues women. With you I felt . . . safe."

He didn't say anything, and she had no idea what he was thinking. All she knew was that her pulse was pounding and her hands were sweating, and that as hard as all of that was to admit, what she had to say next would be worse.

"And then . . . do you remember that merchant we were staked out watching? The one we were trying to connect to those arms deals in the Middle East? Remember when he ventured out, and the three of us followed? We thought he was making a drop somewhere and that we could finally catch him in the act. Only he tricked us, and you and Carter and I had to split up to try to find him."

She pressed a hand against her chest, remembering the fear she'd felt that day. "When that car bomb went off and blew up part of the street you'd disappeared down, I couldn't breathe. I was sure you were dead. *Sure* of it. And then when I found out you were alive, I was so relieved. You have no idea what I felt in that moment."

"Eve—"

"And then . . . then I was pissed and scared all at the same time. And I knew I had to get away from you. See, I gave up everything for the CIA. Everything I'd wanted before. A home, a family, a future. I never wanted to go through the kind of pain I went through when I lost Sam. And in one moment, in one microsecond, I was right back there. Only this time it was worse because what I felt for you was a thousand times stronger than what I had ever felt for Sam."

Those hard, wary eyes that had been watching her since he'd stepped out of the shower softened, and he pushed off the chair. "Eve."

Eve quickly rose to her feet and held up a hand, blocking him from touching her. "No." She had to get this out. If she stopped, she'd never finish, and this time she was determined to tell him everything. "I hated you for that. For making me feel something again. And I hated myself even more for letting it happen. With you I was losing focus. I didn't need the CIA, and that scared me. So I pulled back. And when you wouldn't let me, when I knew I wasn't going to be able to make a clean break without something dramatic, I set up that meeting with that arms dealer, and I made sure you saw."

She stiffened her shoulders and met his gaze head-on, knowing this wasn't something she could back down from, no matter how much she suddenly wanted to. "I wanted you to think the worst of me so I could get away from you, so I set it up to look like I was trading information with him. And then . . ."

She drew a deep breath. "And then I let him go, even knowing all the things he was rumored to be a part of, because I wanted you to hate me."

chapter 20

Zane didn't know how to answer. Didn't know what to say, for that matter.

From the moment he'd walked out of the shower and found Eve sitting on the bed, he'd been speechless. After their argument downstairs, he'd expected to barely interact with her before Ryder showed up. And now here she was. Telling him things he'd never in a million years expected her to divulge.

So much now made sense. The way she'd started distancing herself after that bombing in Beirut. Her antagonistic tone when he'd tried to talk to her about what was wrong. Her animosity the night he'd confronted her. "Eve—"

She stepped back, out of his reach. "You're not like me and Carter and everyone else in the Company. You believe that one life has value, whether that life is a child or an adult or an innocent or even a suspect. And you have a clear dividing line between right and wrong. It's why you left the Agency. Not because you weren't good— my God, you *are* good, and Aegis is lucky to have you. But you left because there is no gray area for you."

He had. She was right. The life of a spy had not been what he'd expected, and by the time he'd gotten to Beirut, he knew he was going to leave. He'd been planning to turn in his resignation when his tour there was up. And then he'd met Eve, and his world had turned upside down.

"My whole life is gray areas," she went on. "There is no right or wrong for me. There's only what's needed to get the information for the next op."

"That doesn't mean—"

She moved back again, and disbelief coated her features. "Don't you get it, Zane? I've sat back and watched things most people hope never to see. Prisoners being tied up and held in stress positions for hours on end, being subjected to hypothermia, sleep deprivation, even waterboarding. I stood by and watched when they were screaming for mercy. And I did it because it was acceptable—they were the bad guys and we were the good, and that made it okay. But it didn't stop there."

She paused, and he could see that there was more. Something she didn't want to tell him. Regret brewed in her beautiful eyes. "The contact you saw me with in Beirut. . . I knew he was planning to hit a high-profile target somewhere in the city. I knew, and I let him go anyway. I was waiting for more information from him about the mole. I made the decision that a few people dying in a random car bombing didn't matter in the long run when I was facing a compromised officer who could be feeding US secrets to terrorist cells. I made the choice. Me. No one else."

The school. That bastard had gone on to blow up a school US aid had helped rebuild. Dozens of children had died. And she could have stopped him. His words to her in that warehouse, when he'd accused her of being a traitor, filled his head and wrapped ice-cold fingers around his heart. "Eve—"

"No, don't." She took another step toward the door. Toward

freedom. "You said it wasn't my fault what happened to Carter and Natalie? Maybe it wasn't directly, but indirectly it was. They were in that park today because of me. They're dead now because they tried to help *me*. Not you. Not anyone else. And if something were to happen to you because of me"—her voice caught, and she closed her mouth briefly—"I couldn't live with myself."

Warmth filled his chest and radiated outward through his limbs. In a moment of panic, when he'd had her tied to that chair in the warehouse, she'd admitted that she'd once loved him. But he hadn't believed her, not really. Now he did. Now he knew that what held her back wasn't lack of emotion, but the exact opposite.

He crossed the space between them before she could run, wrapped both arms around her waist, and tugged her close. Her hands landed against his biceps. Confusion crossed her features. She was strong, and, in her mood, fired up enough to take him down, so he backed her against the wall and closed in at her front, trapping her with his arms and legs so all she could see was him.

"What are you doing? Let me go."

She pushed at his arms, but he only held her tighter around the waist. "Not on your life. Never again."

"Archer, goddammit—"

"I love you, Evelyn Wolfe."

She went still as stone in his arms, and wide, shocked eyes darted to his. "No you don't. You can't. Didn't you hear any of what I just said to you?"

"I heard it. And if you'd told me all of this sooner, we could have avoided a hell of a lot of trouble between us the last few days. We could have avoided the entire last eighteen months."

"You—you don't know what you're saying."

His lips turned up at the corner, and, releasing one arm from around her waist, he swiped at a smudge of dirt across her cheek. "I know that I've been miserable since Beirut. That I don't really sleep,

I just dream of you. I know that as much as I wanted to hate you, a part of me still ached for you. Every hour of every day. And I know that these last few days with you, even though I've wanted to strangle you half the time, have been the best of my life."

Her eyes grew damp, and her fingers dug into his biceps. "Don't say shit like that. I'm not like you. I'm not . . ."

She looked quickly away, blinked several times, and swallowed hard, and in that moment he knew what the big hang-up was between them. It wasn't just that she loved him and was afraid to take a chance again. It was that she didn't think he could ever see past the things she'd done.

He slid his finger under her chin and tipped her face back to his. "Just because I couldn't hack it as an officer in the CIA doesn't mean I don't understand the necessity of what you do, Eve. I know what goes on behind closed doors. I know about enhanced interrogation techniques and the choices you have to make between snagging small fish and big ones. Just because I can't do it myself doesn't mean I don't support those who do."

She closed her eyes. "Zane—"

"I can't judge you for what you've done, and I can't forgive you either. You're the only one who can do that. But you're not the monster you want me to believe you are. And though you might not be able to see the good you've done, it's there. Trust me, beautiful, it's there. You've made a difference in the world, and that's something not a lot of people can say they've done. Me included."

"You do make a difference," she said softly, opening her eyes and staring at her hand resting against his bare chest. "You save people. That's more than I've done in ten years."

"The people I save wouldn't need saving if they'd just learn to stay out of trouble in the first place. And besides, I don't work for Aegis anymore, remember?"

"Ryder's an idiot to let you go."

"He didn't have a choice. I left to find you. I'd do it again in a heartbeat too."

Tears filled her eyes. Tears filled with so many emotions, he could feel them vibrating in the air between them. "I don't love you," she whispered. "I don't even know what that word means anymore."

"Yes, you do." His heart swelled, and he lowered his head, kissing the corner of her mouth so very softly. "You've loved me for years, you're just too stubborn to admit it. If you didn't, you would have left me on that rooftop. You would have ditched me on that island. And you wouldn't still be with me now, telling me things you never had to tell me, making me love you even more."

"Zane . . ." She closed her eyes. But she didn't pull away. Instead she tipped her chin up and to the side, letting him kiss her jaw, her cheek, shivering when his lips moved toward the sensitive column of her neck.

"We're gonna work this out, you and me. I'm not about to let you take the fall for something you didn't do. And there's no way I'm walking away from you now." He pressed his lips to the sweet little mole just beneath her jaw. Loved the way she trembled at his touch. "Tell me you believe me, Evie."

Her whole body tightened, and her fingers lifted from his arms and threaded into his damp hair. And then her hands were pulling his head toward hers, her fingernails digging into his scalp while she lifted to her toes and fit her mouth to his. "Kiss me."

Her tongue pushed past his lips and dipped into his mouth. And the taste of her—heat, life, love—filled his heart. He deepened the kiss, stroked his tongue against hers, trembled himself when she arched into his growing erection and the soft mounds of her breasts pressed against his chest.

"Need you," she whispered against his lips. "Need you now."

Her fingers dropped from his hair, streaked down his body, and tangled in the towel at his hips. Cool air rushed over his overheated skin just before she pulled her mouth from his, pushed him back a step, and dropped to her knees in front of him.

He was already hard, and he knew if she touched him there with those sinful lips, he wouldn't last. And he wanted this to be about her. Before she could wrap her lips around his cock, he dragged her to her feet and closed his mouth over hers.

She protested, tried to pull away, but he kissed her deeper. Then he wrapped his arms around her, cupped her ass, and lifted her feet off the floor.

She groaned into his mouth and kissed him slowly, deeply, until he was aching to taste all of her.

He carried her to the bed and laid her out. Her dark hair fanned around her as she hit the mattress. He eased away long enough to tug her shirt off, mindful of the bandage around her arm. She wriggled out of the garment and lifted her torso off the bed, reaching for him. Her fingers slid along his jaw, drawing his mouth back to hers, and then her lips were there again. Kissing him softly. Teasing him until he saw stars.

Emotions filled his heart and soul and mind. This wasn't about sex. This time it was about so much more, and he wanted to prove to her it always would be.

He kissed his way down her neck to her collarbone. One hand closed around her breast and squeezed. She moaned and arched into his touch. He flipped the front clasp of her bra and slid lower, dragging his lips down her sculpted chest, and then he finally brought her breast to his lips and circled the nipple with his tongue.

"Oh, Zane."

He loved the sounds she made. Loved the way when they were together—whenever they were together like this—the real her came out. The one he'd known years ago. The one he'd rediscovered on Bainbridge Island. The one she could never hide from him.

"I want to lick you everywhere like this, Evie."

She groaned at his words. Moaned when he moved to her other breast, licked and laved and finally sucked. Her legs spread open, and she made room for him. He rocked his hips against hers, pressing his erection right between her legs where he knew it would drive her absolutely crazy.

He moved back up to her lips, nipped and licked and suckled there too. She arched into him and kissed him back. Her fingers slid back into his hair, and her nails scraped along his scalp. But it didn't hurt. If anything it only amped his need more.

He flipped the button on her jeans, pulled away from her mouth, and dragged them down her legs. Then he groaned himself when he saw the lacy black panties. "Oh, Evie. You naughty girl. You're wearing the crotchless panties for me."

A red tinge darkened her cheeks. She pushed up onto her elbows and looked down her half-naked body toward him.

"Spread your legs."

Her cheeks turned a brighter shade of red, but slowly she lifted one knee and then inched her legs open.

She was already slick and swollen, and he needed to taste her there. To feel her come apart in his mouth.

He grasped her hips and dragged her to the edge of the bed. She gasped and tried to hold on to the comforter. "Zane—"

He dropped to his knees, spread the opening in her sexy panties, and ran his tongue up her slit.

"Oh, God." Her head fell back. She raised her feet and planted them on the edge of the mattress. When he did it again, she lifted her hips slightly. Helping him. Urging him on.

Blood rushed to his groin, and his erection grew harder. Hotter. More insistent. He swirled his tongue around her clit, then dipped down to her opening and did the same. Her body trembled. Another moan echoed from her throat. He licked back up to her clit and circled until her elbows went out from under her. And then he suckled.

Her entire body shook. He knew her orgasm was rushing in. Knew the signs. He ran a finger down her slick center as he tormented her with his mouth, then pressed inside until he found her sweetest spot.

The moan that shook her body echoed through every part of him. She tightened around his finger and rode the wave against his lips as it crashed over her. And when it receded, when she was putty in his arms, he kissed his way back up her body, continuing to tease her with his lips, his tongue, his fingers between her thighs.

"Zane . . ."

He loved that breathless, needy voice. Could listen to it forever. He stripped her of the panties, then leaned forward, pressing his hips between her legs until his cock slid along her hot, slick center.

She groaned. Reached for him, grasping his hips and pulling him closer.

God, she was sexy. And hot. And his. All his. Whether she could say the words or not, she'd only ever be his. Pushing both of her knees up and back to open her even more, he rocked his hips forward, circling her clit with the tip of his cock, loving the sight, loving even more every gasp and groan and sexy little moan she made. "Open your eyes, Evie."

She blinked several times but finally managed to tear her eyes open. And when they were focused on him, when he knew he was all she could see, he slid lower, to her opening, then pressed forward and filled her.

"Oh . . ." Her tight walls clenched all around him. He groaned and lowered his mouth to hers. Slid out and back in. Her knees pressed against his hips, and her hands clamped down on his ass, pulling him into her. "Kiss me. I need you to kiss me."

He closed his lips over hers, and the taste of her filled his mouth and heart. His tongue stroked hers as he thrust into her again and again. He tried to take it slow, but every rock of her hips against his, every time her fingernails dug into his ass, every time she tightened around him, he lost a little more of his self-control.

"Eve . . ." Sweat broke out all over his skin, slid down his spine. His balls grew to bursting. He planted a fist against the mattress and drove deeper, faster, harder, needing to take her, fill her, mark her as his own.

She pulled her mouth from his. Groaned, "Do it. I need it. I need you. Come for me, Zane. Now. Right now."

As if she had some magical control over him, his orgasm raced down his spine, shot through his balls, and exploded through every part of his body. He plunged deep again and again, unable to stop, and then he felt her tighten everywhere and heard her cry out his name when she peaked.

Breathless, he collapsed against her, unable to move. Unable to think. Her legs fell open. Her hands slid up his sweaty back and closed around his shoulders while he fought for air. He felt her lips pressing against his temple, felt her heart racing against his cheek, felt her tantalizing fingers tracing light lines over his back, but it was the warmth closing in around his heart that he focused on. A warmth he'd convinced himself he'd never have. A warmth that came only from her.

Slowly, he pushed up on his hand and looked down at her. Her hair stuck out at all angles, her mascara was smeared beneath her eyes, and she still had dirt and blood and soot across her cheeks, her shoulders, different parts of her sexy little body.

And staring at her, he knew it was more than that "just fucked" look that flushed her cheeks and made her look sexier than any woman he'd ever met. It was everything she'd admitted to him earlier.

A one-sided smile slid across his lips. "You're a mess."

She brushed her fingers over her cheek. "I didn't have a chance to shower like some people."

His smile widened. Easing back, he slid out of her, then grabbed her around the waist and lifted her off the bed.

"Archer!" She gasped. "What do you think you're doing now?"

"Taking you to the shower. I've been fantasizing about a repeat of what we did last night."

She sucked in a breath, but the look in her eyes said she wasn't about to protest. She glanced down at his naked chest as he carried her into the bathroom. "I don't see a belt on you anywhere."

"Oh, baby. If it involves leather and bondage, you know I'll find a way to make it work."

She chuckled as he reached into the massive stone shower with multiple showerheads and flipped on the water. A sigh slid from her lips when he stepped in, still carrying her, and the hot liquid slid over both their bodies. "I'm probably going to regret this tomorrow."

"Never, Eve." He lowered her to her feet, lifted his hands, and brushed the wet hair away from her face. "With me, you are never, ever going to regret this. That, I promise."

Olivia leaned against the wall outside the men's locker room at the Seattle Athletic Club and looked right and left. Nerves danced in her belly, and she checked each face that passed, reassuring herself none were the men who'd abducted her.

The club was located only a few blocks from Pike Place Market, and the people coming and going in the early evening hours were yuppie city people, not terrorists or kidnappers or any kind of threat.

Her fingers shook as she adjusted the big sunglasses Landon had bought for her, pulled the baseball cap lower over her eyes, and tugged the long-sleeved T-shirt down, hoping no one could see her bruises.

He hadn't been happy when she'd checked herself out of the hospital, but she couldn't stay there. Every moment in that room made her feel like a victim, and she refused to be one. She was alive. She'd survived. No matter what they'd done to her, she'd won. And she wasn't about to let a few days rule the rest of her life.

That's what her head told her. Her heart was another matter. *Stay tough. Stay strong.*

She looked toward the locker room door again, then down at the phone Landon had given her when he'd gone inside, searching for anything to take her mind off remembering. He was everything she should be afraid of after her ordeal. Big. Muscular. Scarred in numerous places. With huge hands he could use to crush her in a second if he wanted. And when she remembered the way he'd gone after those men in that yard before she'd fallen over the fence, she knew she should be terrified of him. But she wasn't. There was something about him that comforted her. Something that made her feel alive. And right now, she didn't care who or where that came from. She was hanging on to it like it was her last lifeline.

"Everything okay?"

Her head shot up at the sound of his voice, and she exhaled a breath of relief when she found him standing right in front of her. She hadn't even heard him come out of the locker room. But she was so glad he was here now. More relieved even than when she'd been freed. "Yes. Did you find it?"

His smile was pure victory when he patted his pocket. "Bingo."

He closed his hand over her elbow and turned her back toward the front of the club. Heat tingled across her skin. She liked his hands. Liked them against her. Liked the way they made her feel.

People glanced their way. She knew they made an unlikely pair. Her, bruised and frail, and him, buff and muscular. As they moved into the lobby, she found herself wondering if he was married, if he had a girlfriend, or even what kind of woman he was interested in.

Probably one like that brunette over there in the tiny spandex shorts and skimpy sports bra. One with a small waist, huge rack, and voluptuous hips. Not a skinny, small-breasted schoolteacher from Idaho.

She was suddenly aware of the way the clothes he'd brought her at the hospital hung off her frame. She'd always been thin, but she'd lost quite a bit of weight this last week—more than she'd thought. And glancing over the hard bodies around her, she was also achingly aware of the sallowness to her skin, her dirty hair beneath the ball cap, and the fact she wasn't wearing a stitch of makeup.

No, she definitely wasn't his type, and she was smart enough to know that what she was feeling for him was hero worship. He'd saved her life. On a normal day, he wasn't the kind of guy she'd even look twice at. She didn't even *like* muscles.

They exited the club and stepped onto Western Avenue. Damp, fresh air from the earlier rain filled her lungs. She looked up the hill to where the car was parked two blocks away.

"Are you okay?" Landon asked at her side.

"What? Yeah." She wasn't going to lean on him. She'd already done that too many times to count, and she was determined to be her old self. She started walking. Halfway up the hill, her lungs grew thick and her breath labored. They passed a storefront window, and from the corner of her eye she caught their reflection, but she forced herself not to look closely. She couldn't, because she knew she wouldn't recognize the face staring back at her. Right now she needed to focus. Needed to think about Eve. Needed to do anything to keep her mind away from the past.

"We can stop if you're tired."

"No," she huffed, pressing her hands against her knees as she leaned forward and forced her feet to keep moving up the hill. "I'm . . . fine."

"Son of a bitch."

Strong arms wrapped around Olivia from behind, and she gasped as her feet left the ground and she found herself cradled against Landon's muscular chest. She pressed a hand against his bulging pec and then regretted it. It was big. Strong. Safe. "P-put me down."

"Why? So you can fucking collapse on me?"

Moments in the back of that van rushed through her mind, and she slammed her eyes shut, shaking her head back and forth, digging her fingernails into his muscles. "Don't swear. Don't . . . I can't . . ."

"Okay. Okay, just breathe. I'm sorry. I'll be more careful. That's it. In and out. You're okay."

The city seemed to swirl around Olivia, but slowly she realized her feet were on the ground, she was leaning into Landon's muscular body, and his arms were wrapped tight around her, his hand running up and down her spine in a languid motion, his voice right at her ear, reassuring her with his words and warm breath.

She opened her eyes and blinked several times. He'd stopped in the middle of the sidewalk and was now leaning back against the wall of a building while she tried to work her way down from a panic attack she couldn't remember starting. People passed on the busy street. Several glanced their way, but no one stopped. She focused on the push and draw of air in her lungs and the soft brush of his fingers against her spine. Told herself she was safe, that she wasn't in that van, that she wasn't going back there. Ever.

"That's better," Landon said softly in her ear. "That's—"

Something in his pocket vibrated. He let go of her and pulled out a phone.

"Damn." He cringed. "Sorry. I need to take this."

Olivia nodded and tried to back out of his arms, but he held her tight, not letting her move, and part of her was grateful. She sank back into him while he lifted the phone to his ear and said, "Miller."

Her cheek pressed against his chest. Warmth seeped from him into her, and the strong, steady beat of his heart calmed her in a way nothing else could.

"Yeah." His voice echoed through his chest and into her, sending vibrations all through her body. "I know where that is. No, I've got her. No, I don't think that's a good idea right now. I'll have her call from the car when we're on our way."

They—whoever he was talking to—were discussing her. The independent thirty-year-old inside told her to suck it up and stop leaning on him, but her body wasn't listening. And though she knew this was hero worship at its finest, she didn't care. He smelled too wonderful, felt too good, and for a moment, she needed the comfort.

"Okay. Will do." He tugged the phone from his ear and slipped it back in his pocket, and then his other arm came around her, holding her close all over again. And she couldn't fight the sigh that slipped from her lips, or the way she snuggled in tighter and just let him hold her.

"Wh-who was that?" she asked against him, not making any move to pull away.

"My boss," he answered, not giving her a chance. "Your sister's at a safe house north of here. If you want to see her, I can take you to her."

Olivia lifted her head and looked up into his eyes. They weren't just brown like she'd originally thought. They were a warm, rich chocolate with flecks of gold and green, all swirled together in a mix that made her wonder which was the true him. The way he'd taken her captors out in that yard flashed in her mind, contrasting so strongly with the way he was holding her now, like she was made of glass, like she was the most fragile thing in the world. Part of her could barely believe he was the same person.

But he was. The jagged scar across the side of his face and the other near his chin proved he was more than just her comfort. He was a force not to be crossed. And soon she'd be home, and he would be out of her life for good.

She swallowed hard, not wanting to think about that too much just yet. The thought of going home—to that small house where she'd been grabbed in the first place—left a hole the size of the Grand Canyon right in the middle of her belly. "You'll take me to Eve?"

"Yes. On one condition. You eat something. Those fluids at the hospital weren't enough. You need energy."

Her stomach rolled at the thought of food, but she nodded. She did need to eat. She needed to get stronger. Needed to get better. Needed to forget everything that had happened, so she could stop leaning on him once and for all. "Okay."

"Okay." He released her, then swept her into his arms all over again.

This time she didn't try to wiggle free. "I can walk, you know."

"I know. But I like this better. Humor me."

She liked it better too. And if she was going to be with him for only a few more hours, she was going to enjoy every last second.

She settled into him and sighed.

chapter 21

Eve stood at the counter in the massive kitchen, chopping vegetables for the stir-fry Zane was making. Someone had recently stocked the refrigerator as if they knew the house were about to be used, which seemed so strange to Eve—having people who rushed around preparing things for your arrival. She'd gotten so used to doing things on her own over the years, she couldn't comprehend relying on others like that.

Soft lips pressed against the nape of her neck, and the knife stilled in her hand as she felt Zane move in at her back. He threaded one arm around her waist and up under the shirt she'd grabbed from the master closet. Something else she couldn't comprehend. He'd said this house belonged to a client, but when he'd told her to find something clean to wear in the closet, she'd been startled to discover a variety of women's clothing, in all different sizes.

Zane's palm pressed against her bare lower belly, and he splayed his fingers, sending tiny tremors of heat all through her body. His other hand reached around for a yellow pepper from the cutting board. "Don't cut me, beautiful."

He popped the pepper in his mouth and chewed, and a chuckle vibrated at her back when he kissed her nape again. "Tasty. But not as tasty as you."

He eased away, and as she heard the sizzle and pop of the wok at the stove, she closed her eyes and tried to tell herself she hadn't just fucked things up royally by sleeping with him again—correction, by making love with him. But a tiny voice in the back of her head said she had. That if she'd hoped to save his life, it was going to be near impossible now.

"Are those almost ready?"

His voice dragged her out of her wandering mind and back to the moment. Setting the knife down, she lifted the cutting board and took it over to him at the stove. "Here."

She wasn't the least bit hungry, but she knew she needed to eat. Plus, making a meal kept her hands busy and her mind off her sister and Carter and everything else she couldn't change now.

"There's wine in the cellar," Zane said, stuffing one hand into the front pocket of his low-slung jeans, using the wooden spoon in the other to stir the steaming vegetables. "Why don't you go pick one out?"

"Really?" Eve wiped her hand on a dishtowel and lifted her brows. "The owner won't care?"

Zane chuckled. "Trust me, he won't even notice it's gone."

Curiosity got the best of her. She leaned a hip against the granite counter. "What kind of guy has women's clothing in different sizes hanging in his closet? Whose house is this?"

Zane lifted the pan and shook the vegetables around. "You listen to much rock music?"

"Some."

"What about reality TV?"

Eve's brow lowered. "Not much. Not a lot of it overseas."

"A few years ago there was this guy on one of those singing shows who tore up the charts. Really made a name for himself. He didn't win, I think he placed like third, but he was the big story of the season."

Eve didn't watch a lot of TV in general, but she did like to page through magazines in the airport. She thought back to what she knew about those voice competition shows, and when she realized who he was talking about, her eyes flew open wide. "Tate Kendrick. You're saying the front man for Kendrick, the wildly popular rock band that's exploded these last few years, owns this house?"

He nodded. "Aegis did some security work for him. After his success on that reality show, his band totally took off. He's got a place on Whidbey Island. This is just his ski chalet."

"His ski chalet." Eve glanced around the enormous great room with its great everything. "I can't imagine what his real house looks like."

Zane chuckled and stirred the veggies again. "He likes Ryder, though why, I don't know. Gave us free reign of the place, including the wine cellar." He pointed toward a door at the far end of the kitchen. "Why don't you go see what you can find?"

If Eve expected to find a couple bottles of chardonnay in the basement, she'd thought wrong. When she flipped on the light and climbed down the cool, polished wood stairs, she found herself gasping at the four full walls decked out in rows and rows of racks, each one filled with a different bottle.

Holy cow. She turned a slow circle, not knowing where to look first. This kind of money wasn't even something she could comprehend. As she stared at the collection, something Zane had told whispered through her mind.

After he'd been injured in Guatemala, he'd gone to Mexico to recover. To some compound. She hadn't thought much about it then, but now she couldn't help but wonder who it had belonged to and how well he knew these people with money coming out of their ears. His life now was completely different than it had been before.

He hobnobbed with the rich and famous. Aegis had to pay him well. A lot of guys who left government work went on to make a killing in the private security field, and he'd inherited a good chunk of change when his grandparents had died. By staying with him, she wasn't just jeopardizing his safety; she was jeopardizing a future that could be extremely successful for him.

Her chest tightened. Hand shaking, she grabbed the first red she came to, pulled it off the shelf, and headed back up the stairs.

The kitchen was empty when she stepped out of the cellar and closed the door. The vegetables hissed in the pan, but the wok sat on a cold burner, and the stove was turned off. Voices echoed from the front of the house. Voices Eve didn't recognize but immediately guessed had to belong to Jake Ryder and whatever people he'd brought from Aegis.

Her stomach knotted, and she immediately thought of the failed op in Guatemala. Of Zane's menacing voice when she'd called to make sure he was still alive. Of the hate she'd heard in his words. Others at Aegis had to hate her too. For over a year they'd believed she was a traitor, just like Zane had.

He doesn't believe that anymore. He loves you.

That knot in her stomach twisted tighter, and perspiration broke out all along her skin. Hate she knew what to do with, but love . . . ? Love was a foreign emotion she knew she didn't deserve.

"You look like shit, Archer," a man's voice said from the foyer. "I suppose it wouldn't be fair to kick your ass right now, so I'll save it for later."

"Let's not destroy Kendrick's house, shall we?" a woman said. "He was nice enough to let us use it. I think the least we can do is make sure it's still in one piece when we're done."

"See what I have to put up with?" the man said. "She's no fun at all. Where's Wolfe?"

"Through here," Zane answered.

Eve stiffened. Seconds later, Zane appeared in the great room, followed by a dark-haired man wearing jeans and a blue button-down, and a woman in black slacks and a pale yellow sweater, with blonde hair tied back in a neat tail and wire-rimmed glasses perched on her small nose.

"Eve," Zane said, "this is my ex-boss, Jake Ryder, and Marley Addison, his conscience."

Marley snorted.

Ryder frowned. He crossed the floor and held out his hand to her. "Current boss. Jackass over there never formally submitted his resignation."

His grip was solid, his eyes a dark brown, almost black, and Eve recognized the edge he held, marking him as former special forces. Eve released his hand. "Archer doesn't seem to do anything anyone wants him to do."

The corner of Zane's lips turned down. He rested his hands on his hips, then looked toward Marley. "I think they're ganging up on me already."

Marley chuckled and set the bag she'd had slung over her shoulder on the ground at her feet. "Don't look at me. He was in a mood all the way out here. I'm not getting in the middle of this one."

Ryder glanced toward Eve at the stove. "You cooked? Oh man, a chick with a gun who's not afraid of a kitchen. Forget about all the terrorist crap and you might be my fantasy woman yet."

Marley snorted as she pulled a folder out of her bag. "Your idea of the perfect fantasy woman changes every five minutes."

Ryder shot Marley a perturbed look, and as Eve glanced from face to face, she relaxed, just a touch. While she could definitely feel the tension between the two men, they were both working hard to keep things civil, and Marley was a good buffer. Plus the fact that Zane's boss—ex or not—had flown all the way out here from Kentucky meant he was committed to helping. And that he cared. Which was a hell of a lot more than she could say for her superiors.

She pushed that thought aside and tucked the hair tickling the side of her face behind her ear. "Sorry. My cooking skills are limited to the microwave, and I'm not even good at that. Zane cooked."

Ryder's surprised gaze shot to Zane, then landed on Marley. "He is trying to butter me up."

Marley lifted her brows. "I warned him ahead of time." She glanced Zane's way. "Three double Crowns on the plane helped. But food was a good idea."

"I get no respect." Ryder took the bottle of wine from Eve's hands. "Why don't I open this? I think we all need more alcohol."

Zane moved into the kitchen, opened the cupboard door, and reached for a stack of plates. "Rice should be done in a few minutes. Then we can eat."

Marley stepped toward the dining room table. "Shouldn't we wait for Miller?"

Eve's heart skipped a beat, and she froze, for a moment unable to think. "Miller's coming?"

Marley looked Ryder's way. "You didn't tell them."

He poured wine into four glasses and flashed Marley an annoyed look. "I wasn't sure we should share that just yet."

The sound of an engine cutting off echoed from out front. Heart in her throat, Eve bolted for the entry.

"Eve," Zane said. "Wait—"

Her bare feet skidded to a stop, but Zane's hand against the door prevented her from opening it. "Move," she said.

"Hold on." His hand landed on her shoulder, warm, solid, supporting her. Everything she always felt when he was close. "He might be alone. You need to be prepared for that. But if she is with him, don't crowd her. Give her room. After what she's been through, she might not be able to handle it just yet."

"She's my sister."

"I know, but . . . she's been missing for several days. I just . . .
If she's there—and I don't know that she is—I want you to be prepared for the fact she might not . . . be her normal self."

Sickness rolled through Eve's belly, and images of what Olivia
could have been through pinged rapid-fire through her brain. But
more than that, she was blindingly aware that even now Zane was
worried about her. About how she would react and feel when she
saw her sister. Not about himself or the situation or even what she
was doing to his future. His only concern was for her.

If she hadn't believed his declaration of love earlier, she believed
it now, and it sent a host of butterflies fluttering all through her
already queasy stomach.

Nodding slowly, she closed her hand around the door handle.
"I-I'll remember that."

He pressed his lips to her temple. "I'm right here with you.
Don't forget that either."

How could she? Her pulse raced, and her heart felt like it grew
every time he touched her.

Steeling herself for what she'd find, she pulled the door open
and stared through the light drizzle toward the black sedan parked
in the driveway. A man sat in the driver's seat, but more than that,
there was a passenger next to him. Someone small. A woman.

Eve stepped out onto the porch, and her heart lurched into her
throat. "Olivia."

Landon cut off the ignition and looked up at the lodge-style house.
He'd been here only a few weeks ago with Kendrick. He had not
planned to be back anytime soon.

He glanced toward Olivia in the passenger seat. She was eyeing
the house like it might just jump out and bite her. "You ready for this?"

"Eve's in there?"

She'd slept during the drive up here, and he'd thought about calling Archer to let him know they were on their way, but he hadn't wanted to wake her. The swelling had gone down a little on her face, but dark circles had taken up refuge under her eyes, and he guessed she hadn't slept in days. "Yeah. Along with some other people I work with. You don't have to worry. You're totally safe here."

Her gaze slid his way, and when those rich green eyes landed on his, he felt that punch to the gut all over again. "Eve will freak out when she sees me. I-I didn't think about that until right now. I-I don't want to have to explain things, you know?" Her voice dropped to a whisper. "I don't want to have to talk about it."

He laid his hand on hers, resting on her lap, and squeezed. To his surprise, she didn't flinch, only opened her fingers and squeezed his hand back. "I'll run interference, how about that?"

She exhaled a long breath and swiped her free hand over her face. "I'm such a mess. I'm sorry. It's not your job to babysit me. I'll be fine. I just"—she tried to pull her hand away—"I'll be fine in a minute."

"Olivia." He gripped her fingers tighter. "Look at me." Tears swirled in her eyes when she looked his way, and something in his chest knotted. Something he'd thought had died a long time ago. "I know what you're going through. I've been there. You're not a mess. You're a hell of a lot stronger than any woman I've ever met. Remember that."

She blinked several times. Movement on the front porch drew his attention. She looked in that direction just as the front door opened and Eve stepped out on the porch, followed by Archer.

For a heartbeat, he held her hand and wished they could go on being alone. But that was impossible—and totally fucking unrealistic. Olivia Wolfe was not the kind of woman who'd be interested in a man like him, especially not if she knew about his past. And as much as her pretty eyes might get to him, he knew it was lack of sleep and adrenaline that had him feeling crazy things for her. She wasn't his type. He didn't do relationships. And by tomorrow, he knew he'd no longer care.

"Time to face the fire," Olivia whispered.

She let go of his hand, and cool air washed over his palm, dousing his spirits. But before he could think of a reason to stop her, she popped the door and stepped out into the rain.

Moving away from him for good. Which was exactly where he needed her to go, for both their sakes.

- - - - - - - - - - - - - - - - -

"Oh my God."

Zane didn't stop Eve from rushing down the porch steps and into the rain. Didn't even think to try. As soon as the slim woman climbed out of the car, relief flooded every cell in his body.

His biggest fear was that Miller was going to show up alone. Eve had already survived that bombing, the deaths of her CSIS contact and Carter. Even though she put on a tough face, he didn't think she could make it through one more major blow. And losing her sister would have been that.

The two women hugged. Eve cooed over her sister, checking every inch of her. He couldn't tell what they said, but he knew from Eve's body language that her sister wasn't in the best of shape. But she was alive, and right now that was all that mattered.

Miller climbed out of the car, stuffed his hands in the front pockets of his jeans, and jogged up the front steps of the house. Shaking the rain from his hair, he looked back toward the car. "That woman should be in a damn hospital. She's weak as shit, but she refused to stay there. She's got a hell of a lot of fight in her. Like her sister."

If she was anything like Eve, Zane could only imagine. He turned toward Miller and held out his hand. "I owe you, man."

Miller returned the handshake with a frown. "Yeah, you do. Don't fucking forget it."

Zane waited while Eve wrapped an arm around her sister and ushered her up the steps and into the house. She was a whole head taller than Olivia, but the slope of their noses was the same, the shape of their eyes. He could definitely see the family resemblance. Closing the door at their backs, he watched while Eve took the light jacket from her sister and threw it over a bench in the entryway.

"Give me your hat too," Eve said. "It's all wet."

Olivia clamped a hand over the top of her head, and as she did, her shirtsleeve pulled back just enough so Zane could see the multitude of bruises on her arm. "No. My hair's a mess. It'll dry."

Eve twisted her hands together, like she didn't know what to do, but there was a light in her eyes Zane hadn't seen in all the time they'd been together, and warmth bloomed in his belly while he watched Eve's face soften and heard her whisper, "I'm so glad to see you."

She drew her sister in for a tight hug. Olivia stiffened at the contact and cringed, as if she were in pain, and when she lifted her face and looked his way, Zane saw the bruises around her eyes.

At his side, Miller tensed. "Hey, is Ryder here already? Jacka—"

Olivia eased out of Eve's arms and looked his way.

Miller closed his mouth and frowned. "Idiot owes me money."

Zane looked between the two, sensing . . . something.

Eve swiped at her eyes and threaded one arm through her sister's. "Yeah, he's here. Zane made dinner. Liv, you're hungry, right?"

Olivia pulled back on her arm, stopping her sister from drawing her into the main part of the house. "No. What I'd really like is a shower."

"Sure," Eve answered, eyes wide. "Yeah. We can do that. Come upstairs with me."

Instead of letting Eve pull her toward the stairs, Olivia drew her arm out of her sister's grip. "I don't need you to coddle me right now,

Eve. I know you're trying to help, but you can't. I just need . . ." She sucked in a deep breath. Let it out as if it could calm her. "If you just tell me where it is, I can do it alone."

Surprise rippled over Eve's features, and then that light Zane had just watched jump to life dimmed. "I-I'm not trying to coddle you."

Olivia closed her eyes. "I know. I'm sorry. I just . . ."

Her voice trailed off. And at Zane's side, he sensed Miller tense all over again.

Helpless. They were all helpless. Only time was going to heal this wound.

Zane stepped up to Eve and squeezed her shoulder. "This place is pretty big, Olivia. I keep getting turned around in here. Why don't you let Eve show you where the shower is, and you can come down when you're ready."

Olivia's gaze snapped his way, and in her green eyes he saw relief. And thanks. She nodded.

Eve, he could tell, wasn't sure what to do or say. She twisted her hands together again, swallowed, and then moved for the stairs. "This way."

When the girls were halfway up the curved staircase, Zane said to Miller, "She's not okay, is she?"

From the corner of his eye, he watched Miller's jaw tighten. "Would you be after a week with a bunch of psychos?"

No, Zane figured he'd be pretty well fucked up.

"She doesn't want to be smothered right now," Miller said, still looking up the staircase. "Tell Eve not to bring up what happened to her."

Frustration welled inside Zane. He understood that the poor girl had been through a major trauma, but they needed answers. "She might know about—"

From his pocket, Miller pulled a small zip drive and turned his way. "About this?"

Zane's heart skipped a beat. "Tell me that's real."

"Tyrone Smith was locked up in the room next to her. He stashed this in a locker at an athletic club in downtown Seattle and told her where to find it. That's why she checked herself out of that damn hospital."

Miller eyed the drive in his hand. "Something tells me this puppy is what everyone's looking for. Whatever's on here is worth killing for."

chapter 22

Eve knew she should be focused on what Marley was currently doing with the zip drive at the laptop on the dining room table, but she couldn't stop looking toward the archway for Olivia.

Her sister had been upstairs for at least a half hour. What if she needed something? What if she was too weak to get out of the shower on her own? When Eve had seen those bruises on her face, she'd nearly come out of her skin. And every second since, she'd fought an overwhelming urge to go up there and help. She just didn't know how.

Heat brushed her back where she stood in the kitchen, leaning against the counter while Marley fiddled with the encrypted file at the computer, and Ryder and Miller hovered over her. She felt Zane press up against her, felt his muscular body try to wipe away the chill that had spread over her since Olivia's arrival, but nothing totally helped. Yes, Olivia was alive, and Eve should be elated over that fact, but all she could see in her mind were those bruises. And she knew if it weren't for her, her sister wouldn't be upstairs suffering right this very minute.

"She's okay," Zane whispered. "Just give her space."

His warm breath fanned over her skin, but it didn't ease the chill either. "I know."

Both his hands landed against her shoulders, and he pressed his talented fingers into her muscles, slowly kneading at the tension gathering there. Instinct made her want to pull away, but with so many people around, she knew it would only cause more problems she couldn't handle right now, so she stayed where she was. But she hated that she enjoyed it. Hated even more that while Olivia had been suffering, she'd been screwing around with Zane, reigniting something that never should have been ignited in the first place.

"I think we have it," Marley announced.

Thankful for the excuse, she pulled out of Zane's hands and stepped toward the table. One look over Marley's shoulder at the pages scrolling by sent a hitch straight to her stomach. "That doesn't look like notes to me."

"That's because it's not." Elbow braced on the table at his side, Ryder shifted in his seat to look Zane's way. A grim look passed over his face. "He'd already figured out the damn formula."

That chill went ice-cold.

Zane moved to her side, his own eyes wide with disbelief. "Holy hell. Do you know how much something like this is worth?"

"More than a deputy director's salary at the CIA," Ryder said.

Eve's stomach tightened. "We still don't have any proof Roberts is the one behind this."

"Marley and I did some digging while you two were out gallivanting through the Pacific Northwest." He reached across his assistant for the folder at her side. Slapping it open on the table, he spread out several papers. Some looked like bank records. Others phone records. And beneath those were a handful of pictures.

Eve stepped forward and shifted one of the papers. The records showed repeated phone calls to and from a number in Seattle, days before the bombing. A number that wasn't hers. She glanced toward the bank records. It was for an offshore account in the Caymans, under a name she didn't recognize. But it was the photo at the bottom, the one of Roberts with Smith, obviously discussing something of importance in what looked like a park, that stopped her heart. "H-how did you get all this?"

"Illegally," Marley answered, turning to face her. "We've got connections, but none of this would probably be admissible in any court." She reached for the picture. "These are ADD Roberts's phone records. And the bank account belongs to this man. I'm guessing you know him?"

Slowly, Eve nodded. "Smith."

Ryder crossed his arms over his chest. "Tyrone Smith's real name is Michael Cross. He's a spook with the CIA."

Eve's mouth fell open. "No. I don't believe that."

Marley handed Ryder another file, which he opened and turned so Eve could see the Agency photo attached to Cross's dossier. It was the same man. "He's been with the Company for eight years."

Eve snatched the file out of his hand and scanned his employment record. A sick feeling began in her stomach and inched its way higher. No wonder he'd looked so damn familiar. "Cross and Roberts were in on this together."

"Looks that way," Ryder said slowly.

Eve shook her head. "I don't believe it. ADD Roberts can't be the mole." She glanced toward Zane at her side. His grim expression said anything was possible.

"Let me tell you something about Ian Roberts," Ryder said, drawing her attention again. "He and I went to school together, and even back then, he was a son of a bitch who cared about only two things: power and money. He has the first at the CIA—*if* he gets the promotion he's looking for—but that's a big if when you consider he's been passed over twice already."

Eve had no idea Roberts had been passed over for promotion

already. But then, she never paid much attention to what went on above her.

"This deal started well over a year ago," Ryder went on. "Even if he is in line now for the deputy director position, he's got to either go through with the deal or cover up all the evidence. And when you start looking at the body count in this thing, the last option seems like the simplest answer."

Occam's razor. The simplest answer was usually the right one.

Eve's mind spun as she thought about everything that had happened. But still, in her gut, she didn't believe Roberts was the one at the root of it all. Though he might be the only person able to shed some light on the truth.

At her side, Zane rested his hands on his hips. "I'm thinking we need a sting operation to catch Roberts in the act."

From his spot at the end of the table, Miller scrubbed a hand over the stubble on his jaw. "I didn't catch a whiff of Cross when I went after Wolfe's sister. Trust me, I was looking. For all we know, the fucker's already been hard-boiled."

Marley's gaze narrowed on the picture. "Finn Tierney's a dead ringer for Cross. We put Tierney in a hat and sunglasses, from a distance, he could totally pass for Cross."

"Who's Tierney?" Eve asked.

"Another operative," Ryder said. He focused on Marley. "Tierney's Irish accent will give him away."

"So we coach him. Plus, Miller has Eve's cell phone. I bet if we scroll back through the messages, we'll find Cross's voice. It should be enough for me to play with. I could create a recording."

Ryder crossed his arms over his chest and chewed on his lip. "It's ballsy."

"Aren't my ideas always?" She peered up at him over her glasses. "And am I ever wrong?"

He frowned, then brushed his hand over his mouth, still thinking.

"Look," Marley said, "the longer we wait, the bigger the case the CIA will build against Eve and Zane."

Several long seconds passed before Ryder looked toward Zane. "What do you both think?"

Zane's eyes hardened. "Tell me what you need from me. I want to bring this fucker down."

Ryder's gaze slid to Eve. "Wolfe?"

"I—"

"Holy shit," Miller muttered at the end of the table.

Eve's gaze darted his way, and when she realized he was looking past her, toward the archway that led to the entry, she turned. Then drew in a relieved breath.

Olivia stood in the doorway, her shoulder-length blonde hair tousled around her face from the blow dryer, her skin clean and fresh. And she was wearing the jeans and green V-neck sweater Eve had left for her in the bedroom.

The jeans were a full size too big, and the sweater seemed to swallow her whole, reinforcing how much weight she'd lost in such a short amount of time. But even with the bruises still evident around her right eye, for the first time since she'd walked into this house, she looked like the Olivia Eve remembered.

She went right to her sister and hugged her tight. Told herself not to take it personally when Olivia tensed in her arms. Keeping one arm around her sister's waist, she ushered Olivia into the room and introduced her to Zane and the others.

Zane shook her hand. "It's nice to finally meet you. Officially. Eve's been worried sick about you."

Olivia slanted Eve a look, and Eve couldn't help but remember the last time they'd seen each other, at their dad's funeral, and the argument that had followed. She gripped her sister's waist tighter, hoping to bridge the gap, wanting to make up for so many things she'd done wrong.

Ryder offered his hand too. "You gave us all a little scare."

"Not me." Marley turned in her chair and rested a hand on the back while she smiled up at Olivia. "I always knew Miller would find you. He's the best of the best."

Slowly, Olivia's gaze slid to Miller at the end of the table. His eyes were locked on Olivia, and the look that passed between them . . .

Eve had seen that look before. The one that said, *I won't let anything happen to you.* From the man on the other side of her sister. Her gaze drifted to Zane. And she saw it now as he stared over her sister's head toward her.

Her heart picked up speed. Perspiration broke out along her spine. Tearing his gaze from hers, Zane smiled, looked down at Olivia, and said, "How about some food? I think we could all use some fuel right now."

He stepped by Eve, squeezed her hand, and moved into the kitchen. And Eve hissed in one calming breath, then let it out. She definitely needed fuel. Because what she now knew she had to do tonight would take every last bit of strength she had left.

If someone had told Zane a month ago he'd be camped out at Tate Kendrick's mountain lodge with Evelyn Wolfe and Jake Ryder, tipping back a bottle of wine and laughing about old times, Zane would have thought they were nuts.

No, he would have thought they were fucking high.

"So Archer's cable snaps," Ryder said. "It's like this random, fluke thing, but of course, it happens to him. And he's got a hold of the zip line with two hands. Luckily he's wearing gloves, but at this point he's barely hanging on. And he hears this noise and glances back, and here comes Tierney, barreling toward him at top speed, screaming at the top of his lungs to drop. 'Drop! Drop! Fucking drop!' in his Irish accent. And Archer hollers back, 'You fucking drop, you psycho!'"

Everyone at the table laughed except for Olivia.

Eve glanced Zane's way. "This sounds like some team-building experience. What did you do?"

"I fucking dropped." More laughter. "If he'd hit me at that speed, I would have lost an arm. As it was, I only broke a leg."

Eve's eyes widened. "You broke your leg?"

He shrugged and reached for his wine. "It was a pretty long drop."

"He was off for two months," Marley said. "It was right after we'd hired him. And then four months after that he was injured in that raid in Guatemala." She glanced Ryder's way and tipped her head. "I'm thinking he's costing us an awful lot in insurance. Are you sure you want him back?"

Ryder's dark eyes narrowed on Zane. "He and I have some shit to discuss about his risk assessment."

Marley chuckled. Miller lifted the beer in his hand toward his lips. "You're in trouble now."

Olivia pushed back from the table. "I'm tired. If you all don't mind, I'm just going to go to bed."

Miller immediately stiffened. "You okay?"

"Yeah." She pursed her lips. "Yeah, I'm fine. Just . . . tired."

But she wasn't. They could all see it. The last week was catching up with her.

Eve immediately jumped to her feet. "I'll go with you."

"Eve, I don't—"

"Humor me, would you? If I stay down here, Archer will start telling stories about stupid stuff *I've* done to get the focus off of him. And trust me, I'm not in the mood." She smiled Zane's way, and her voice was relaxed, almost a soothing tone, but something was off. He knew she was just trying to make Olivia feel at ease, but Zane sensed something was bothering Eve. He'd sensed it all through dinner. Even before that really. Since they'd made love.

Something in the bottom of his gut tightened. A familiar warning shot of fear he knew all too well. "Don't go far, beautiful."

Eve rolled her eyes and headed for the stairs with her sister. "Where would I go all the way out here? There's no need to handcuff me since we're in the middle of nowhere."

True. It'd be virtually impossible for her take off on her own. But with Eve, *impossible* was never a word he used lightly.

When they were both gone, Ryder lifted his brows. "Handcuff?"

Zane's cheeks warmed. He downed the rest of his wine in one swallow. Pushing back from the table, he said, "Law enforcement technique."

"You were never in law enforcement, dumbass."

Zane grinned. "Whatever works, right?"

Ryder stood. "Let's you and I get some air, Archer."

Marley rose as well. "Miller, that means we're on dish duty."

"Aw, Mom," Miller groaned. "Do I have to?"

She smiled and moved into the kitchen. "We'll make a game out of it. For every Ryder joke you can come up with, I'll clean two dishes to your one."

He bolted from his chair. "Done."

Ryder shook his head. "See the shit I put up with?"

Zane couldn't help it. He smiled.

The cool mountain air felt good against Zane's skin, and as they stepped out onto the back deck that overlooked the black lake, he filled his lungs with sweet, mountain air. The rain had stopped, and breaks in the clouds filtered just enough moonlight to shimmer like ribbons of silver across the surface of the lake.

Ryder leaned his forearms against the railing. "You think Wolfe will go along with our plan?"

Zane shoved his hands in the front pockets of his jeans. That unease was still there about Eve, but after their heart-to-heart earlier, he knew they'd turned a corner. "She doesn't have many other options. She'll go along with it."

"I talked to Tierney just before dinner. He's in New York at a photo shoot with his wife. He'll meet us in DC day after tomorrow."

"You don't think Roberts will be suspicious?"

"Of course he will be, but we'll use that to our advantage. I know the way the guy thinks. Which brings me to you." He turned, still leaning against the railing but this time with one elbow. "I have no fucking clue how you think. And that's usually a liability."

Zane stiffened. "I already told you I quit. You don't have to worry about—"

"I don't want you to quit. I didn't want you to quit a year ago. Tell me this. Did you know Wolfe was innocent? Did you have any hunch before you went after her?"

Zane thought about his answer. And knew lying right now wouldn't do any good. "I wanted her to be. But no, I didn't think she was."

"And yet your instincts still said to go after her." Ryder turned back toward the railing, rested both forearms on the damp wood, and looked out at the sparkling lake. "I can teach tactical maneuvers. I can teach an operative how to read a situation and analyze a threat. What I can't teach is instinct. I'm not happy about the way you went about it, but your instinct on this one was right."

He slanted Zane a look. "Just, next time, tell me what you have fucking planned before you go off the reservation. It'll sure as hell save me an ulcer."

Zane's muscles relaxed one by one, and a slow and easy smile spread across his face. "Will do."

He turned for the door.

"Archer."

One hand on the door handle, Zane looked back over his shoulder. "Yeah?"

"Don't fuck things up with Wolfe tonight. We need her on our side on this."

Zane huffed a sound that was half laugh, half disbelief. "Don't I know it."

The kitchen was empty when he went back inside. Marley and Miller had obviously gone to find rooms of their own. Since the lodge boasted eight bedrooms, there was plenty of space for all of them to spread out, but Zane didn't want a room of his own. He wanted Eve. And he wanted to make sure the distance he'd felt her drawing between them was just his own damn insecurities and nothing more.

He found the master bedroom empty too. Turning back for the hallway that ran to the other end of the house, he peeked into the first bedroom and found it quiet. Miller's duffel bag sat on the bed in the second, and water ran from the adjacent bathroom. He was just about to try the third door when it opened and Eve drew up short with an abbreviated gasp. "Zane." She pressed a hand to her chest. "Geez, you scared me."

"Sorry."

He moved back just enough so she could step out into the hall and pull the door closed behind her. "Everything okay?"

"Yeah, she's fine. Sleeping, finally. I made her take the sleep aid the hospital sent home with her."

He nodded and studied her closely. "How about you?"

"Me? I'm fine. Why wouldn't I be fine?"

He brushed a lock of hair back from her temple. "Eve," he said softly.

She closed her eyes and. "We argued. The last time we talked. At our dad's funeral. Did you know that? I'd flown all the way back from Turkey for the service, and she laid into me about never being around. And I was already feeling guilty enough about not being there with him at the end. I was so mad at her. I just . . ." She shook her head. "I just had to get out of there. So I left. I left her to take care of it all. And when I think about that, and then about the fact that none of this would have happened to her if it weren't for me—"

"Stop." He couldn't let her beat herself up anymore. "Olivia's alive. Everything is going to be okay."

"Kinda hard to believe that when I look at the bruises on her face and arms."

He tipped her chin up with his hand. "Open your eyes, Evie." He waited until she did, until her amber irises focused on his. "She's alive because of you. Because you didn't give up on her and because you sent Miller to get her. And speaking of Miller, something tells me he's not gonna let anyone get within ten feet of her."

She swiped at her cheek. "I saw that too. And I'm more than a little worried about that fact. Miller's an ex-assassin."

"Can you think of anyone better to protect her?"

Eve frowned, and a sexy little crease formed between her eyebrows, one he wanted to kiss away. "That's not funny. Don't try to make jokes right now."

"I'm not. I'm being perfectly serious."

She looked away, then ran a hand through her hair.

"Look, if it makes you feel any better, your sister isn't Miller's type. He likes his women long-legged, big-breasted, and short on brains."

Eve huffed. "That's definitely not Olivia."

One side of Zane's lips curled. "No, it's not. Whatever's going on between them has to do with the rescue and nothing more. Miller's not stupid enough to get involved with one of his principals, no matter how sweet she might be. And honestly, I'm pretty sure the DIA trained any kind of real emotion out of him long ago."

Eve's gaze met his. "I just wish Olivia knew that."

"She will. Trust me. By tomorrow, anything you thought you saw between them will be long gone. Miller will make sure of it."

Eve frowned like she wasn't sure, but she heaved out a breath. "I'm too keyed up to sleep right now. Maybe I need to go for a walk."

He lifted her off the floor and threw her over his shoulder. "I think we can find another way to tire you out."

"Archer." She pressed a silky soft hand against his lower back. One that warmed him from the outside in. "I'm not really in the mood right now."

He dropped her on her feet, kicked the master bedroom door closed, and then tugged her into his arms. "You will be." Before he was done, he planned to make sure that distance between them vanished for good. He lowered his mouth to hers and reveled in the soft sigh that slipped from her lips just before she sank into the kiss. "Give in to me, Evie."

Her fingers threaded into his hair, and her hips pressed flush against his. "I already have, haven't I?"

He needed to make sure she always would. He walked her back toward the bed. "Do it again."

chapter 23

Eve waited until Zane was sound asleep before she eased quietly out from under his warm, naked body.

The clock read 2:00 a.m., which meant she didn't have many hours until daylight. Tugging on a long-sleeved shirt and slim jeans, she bit her lip to keep from groaning at the ache in her muscles. This was a sweet ache, though. From Zane's adventurous lovemaking, which had lasted way longer than she'd expected.

Warmth rolled through her belly and hips when she remembered his hands, his lips, the wicked things he could do with his tongue. As she sat on a bench in the walk-in closet and pulled on a pair of hiking boots, then reached for a light jacket from a hanger, she reminded herself she wasn't running. Not like the last time. She was doing this for him.

Yeah, he'd be ticked when he awoke and found she was gone, but she wasn't about to let one more person she cared about get hurt because of her. Even if they thought they had a foolproof plan. Because there was no such thing as a foolproof plan in this situation.

She checked the magazine on the Glock she'd set on the shelf in the closet when they'd first arrived, then holstered it at her back. Her gut said Roberts was not the mole.

And if you're wrong?

Well, then she'd be the one to take him out.

Quietly, she stepped out of the closet and paused in the middle of the bedroom. Zane's rhythmic breathing echoed from the bed. She moved to the end of the mattress and stared down at him. He was lying on his side, his cheek pressed against the pillow, his hand up near his face, the blanket low against his lean hips, showcasing the muscles in his belly and chest and arms, making her ache to slide back in next to him and forget her stupid plan.

But it wasn't stupid. And she was done sitting on the sidelines waiting for things to happen. Olivia was safe. She knew Miller and the others would protect her. Now it was her turn to protect the people she loved.

She didn't kiss him goodbye. Knew if she did and he woke up, she'd lose her chance to make a clean break. Pulse racing, she stepped out of the room, took one last look, and then closed the door softly at her back.

The keys Zane had left sitting on the dresser in the bedroom jingled in her pocket as she made her way downstairs. She paused on the bottom step, waiting to see if anything moved in the house. When only silence met her ears, she crossed to the dark kitchen, scribbled a note, and then folded it and left it on the entry table.

He'd parked the car in the adjacent garage building. Her eyes grew wide when she opened the door to the garage, stepped inside, and flipped on the light. Four shiny snowmobiles, a pristine tractor outfitted with a snow blade to clear the drive, two dirt bikes, and a Range Rover. Top-of-the-line, of course. So new it looked like it had hardly been used.

She bypassed the toys and headed for Zane's Taurus.

It took a little maneuvering, but she was able to put the vehicle in neutral and push it outside. After closing the garage doors, she got out and gave the car a push, then rushed back to the driver's side and jumped in. The door closed softly at her side. She coasted down the driveway. When she was a hundred yards away, she finally turned the key in the ignition.

A quick look in the rearview mirror assured her no one had turned on the lights in the house. No one even knew she was gone.

And that was good, because where she was going, she didn't want anyone to follow.

Zane sat straight up in bed. His heart pounded hard. His skin was slicked with sweat. He wasn't sure what had woken him, but the tightness in his chest screamed that whatever it was, it wasn't good.

Early-morning light speared through the wall of windows that looked out toward the lake. Water sparkled in the distance, and blue-green mountains rose on every side, but he didn't see the beauty around him. Leaning back on his hands, he looked around the quiet room while his heart beat a staccato against his ribs. "Eve?"

No answer.

Panic crept into his chest, taking up space. He darted a look toward the bathroom. The door was pushed partway open, but no light spilled from the other side. "Eve?"

A cold chill spread down his spine. Throwing back the covers, he tossed his legs over the side of the bed and reached for his jeans from the floor. After tugging them on, he crossed the floor and pushed the bathroom door open wider.

The lavish bathroom was dark and empty. He flipped on a light and looked around. That panic condensed, growing with every silent second.

Moving back into the bedroom, he headed for the master closet and found it empty as well. But Eve's gun was gone from the shelf.

Panic rolled to disbelief, then downright betrayal. "Son of a bitch."

He snagged a shirt and pushed his feet into his boots, then rushed down the stairs. Marley and Olivia were sitting on the couch quietly talking when he entered the room. Miller and Ryder were in the kitchen, arguing over a griddle of what smelled like burning pancakes. All four looked up when he entered. There was no sign of Eve.

Son of a . . . goddammit. He'd caught the signs last night, and he'd all but ignored them. He was either the biggest fucking idiot on the planet or . . .

He clenched his jaw. No, there was no "or." That was him to the letter.

"She's gone," he announced.

Olivia's eyes grew wide, and she pushed up from the couch "*What?* What do you mean by 'gone'?"

Ryder set the spatula on the counter, his brows dropping low. "Are you sure?"

"Pretty damn." Zane raked his hand through his hair. He'd fallen asleep after their lovemaking, and the whole time she'd been plotting to run. Had the last few days not meant anything to her? He hadn't missed the fact she hadn't told him she loved him. Obviously, he was still nothing more than a means to an end to her.

"I'll check outside." Miller moved for the back door.

"Maybe we're jumping the gun." Marley pushed up from the couch and stepped into the kitchen. Her hair was loose around her face, and the glasses she always wore were currently sitting on the table next to her laptop. "Maybe she's just out for a walk."

"Out for a walk. Right." Zane rested his hands on his hips. No, she was long gone. And he wouldn't find her until she surfaced, which could be months—years—later. No one was better at disappearing than Evelyn Wolfe. "Her gun's missing."

"Um, Zane?"

Zane looked toward the archway where Olivia stood. In her hand she held a slip of paper.

"What is it?" Ryder crossed the floor and took the note from Olivia's fingers. He scanned it, then looked up at Zane. "It's for you."

Zane took the paper and stared down at Eve's handwritten scribbles across the sheet.

Sawyer—
I lied. It's the only thing I know how to do well. Forget about
Roberts. If you're smart, you'll disappear, just like I plan to do.
—Juliet

His heart thumped hard while he read the words again and again. But this panic wasn't clamping down over the fact she'd left. This time it was fear over what she planned to do next that caused his pulse to soar.

He caught Ryder's gaze. "I need to get to DC."

Miller thrust the back door open, and a wave of cool air washed into the house. "Vehicle's gone."

"She'll be hours ahead of you," Ryder said.

"I don't care. I just need to get there."

"I don't understand," Olivia cut in. "Why DC? The note says she plans to disappear."

"Because she's going after Roberts herself," Marley answered before Zane could. Slowly, she shook her head. "She's trying to protect you."

Yeah, Zane had already figured that out. He looked toward Eve's sister. "She's lying. She doesn't believe Roberts is the mole, so she's planning to confront him herself."

"Stupid woman," Ryder muttered. To Marley, he said, "Get on the horn to Mack and get our plane fueled and ready to go." Then to Zane, "She can't have more than a three- to four-hour head start. Flying private, we might beat her. If we hustle."

Zane wasn't so sure. When Eve put her mind to something, she found a way to make it happen, then and there.

"I still don't understand," Olivia said. "She can't show her face anywhere. The government's watching for her."

Olivia obviously didn't know the extent of Eve's career. "She knows that. And she'll find a way around it. She has a stash somewhere in Seattle—money, passports, disguises—in case things went wrong." He focused on Ryder again. "If she went back for that, then yeah, it's possible we might beat her. But probably not. This is Eve we're talking about."

He headed for the stairs, already cataloging what he'd need to take with him. Ryder's voice stopped him. "Archer."

With one hand on the newel post, he looked back. Ryder stood in the archway between the entry and great room. "Yeah?"

"Is she worth it?"

Eve had asked him the same thing. In that motel. And then he hadn't been able to give her an answer. His gut told him she'd run this time because she loved him, not because she was trying to end things. But there was always the possibility he was wrong. Was she worth getting his teeth kicked in again if he found out he really was just a means to an end?

"I loved you, you son of a bitch."

Confidence swirled in his chest. "More than worth it."

Ryder nodded. "Then I'm in. Get your gear. We're gone in ten."

Eve stood in the trees outside ADD Ian Roberts's brick colonial on the banks of the Potomac in Alexandria, Virginia. Dusk was just settling in, and no lights had come on inside the house yet, but that didn't mean he wasn't home.

Common sense told her surprise was her best friend at the moment, but her mind kept second-guessing her decisions. She knew Archer was probably spitting nails right now, but she didn't want him to walk into another situation that could possibly get him killed. Not when she was the reason, and not when she could be the one to end it.

She'd gotten the lay of the land earlier. The big old colonial was at least three stories, with tall white pillars that rose from the front steps all the way to the roofline, and a balcony that stretched above the double-door entry. A daylight basement and multiple decks opened to the back, and more windows than she could count gazed out at the wide river. Beyond the patio sat a swimming pool, a dock, and a forty-foot sailboat bobbing on the river.

The more she looked around the lavish property, the harder it was for her to deny the fact the man had money. More money than she'd expected. That didn't mean he'd gotten it selling Company secrets, though. He could have inherited his money, like Archer.

Yeah, right. When, during this entire ordeal, have you been right about anything?

Pushing aside the doubt, she tried the doors on the bottom level and first deck. All were locked. Thankful for the dimming light, she climbed the closest tree, then jumped to the roof. Her boots crunched on the roofing material. She paused, waiting to see if anyone came running out. When nothing happened, she climbed over the peak, then dropped to the third-floor balcony and reached for the door.

The handle turned without resistance.

Exercise equipment filled the rectangular room. A flat-screen TV was mounted high on the wall.

She moved to the door and quietly opened it. The third-floor hall was quiet and empty. Moving down the steps, she pulled her Glock from its holster at her lower back and held it in both hands.

Wood creaked under her boots. She paused steps from the second level and waited, her heart pounding in her ears.

Again nothing moved. No sound echoed through the house. But the sudden tightness in her chest brought her feet to a stop at the bottom of the stairs.

"You don't have to do everything on your own."

How many times had Zane said that to her? More times than she could count. More times than she deserved to hear. Against the handle of her gun, her palms grew sweaty, and the air seemed to clog in her throat.

Understanding pushed pinpricks of heat up her neck and cheeks. What the hell was she doing? Whether Roberts was the mole or not, she shouldn't be here alone. If the last few days had taught her anything, it was that they worked better together than apart. And Zane was right. She didn't have to do everything alone. She could lean on him and not lose a part of herself in the process. She could love him and not have to fear the future. Because she was a better person with him than without.

Of course, right now he was probably seeing only red because she'd run from him again. He couldn't possibly know that's what she'd needed to do to realize she couldn't live without him.

Warmth unfurled in her stomach and spread all through her body, and a completeness—one she hadn't expected to ever feel again—took up space right in the middle of her chest.

Slowly, she backed up the stairs. No, she wasn't doing this alone. She'd leave, call Zane, try to make things up to him. Then come back *with* him and do this right.

Wood creaked on the stairs. When she reached the top step, she turned back for the exercise room.

A hand wrapped around her mouth and jerked her back into a hard, solid body. "Not the smartest move you've ever made. Not even close."

chapter 24

The muzzle of a gun pressing against the base of Eve's skull caused her entire body to stiffen. "Drop the gun, Juliet."

Eve knew that voice. Knew it well. And knew it meant business.

Disbelief at her utter gullibility whipped through her like a tornado, sending her stomach into a hard, tight knot. She'd missed the signs. Hadn't even seen this coming, even though she knew better than to trust the people around her. She'd clearly been blinded by emotion on this one.

Slowly, she lowered her hand. When it was at her side, she released her hold on the weapon. It clanked to the floor at her feet with a deafening thunk.

"Good girl. I always knew you were smart."

Carter.

Sweat broke out all over Eve's skin as she lifted her arms in surrender. "Y-you staged that scene in the park to make it look like you were dead?"

"Things were getting too hot," he said at her back. "I couldn't have people looking my way. And it would have worked too. If you'd died there like you were supposed to. Your will to live keeps fucking with my plans, Juliet. Where's Archer?"

Her mind spun. "H-he's not here. I left him in Washington."

Carter was silent at her back, and she knew he was contemplating whether she was telling the truth or not. Finally, he said, "I want you to know I tried, Juliet. I really did. I tried to get you to back off, but you just wouldn't. All you had to do was let Archer die in Guatemala so I'd know you wouldn't be a problem, but you couldn't even do that. I never wanted to involve you, but you left me no choice."

From the shadows at the base of the stairs, a woman stepped into the fading light coming through the windows, the end of a Colt pointed right at Eve's chest. Beneath the hand covering her mouth, Eve swallowed hard.

"I'll take that." Natalie climbed the stairs and picked up Eve's gun from the floor, then holstered it at her back. Both hands gripping her gun, she looked past Eve toward Carter. "I warned you she was a problem."

"I didn't know she was going to show up here."

"If you'd done the job correctly the first time, Archer would be dead and none of this would be a problem. And if you'd followed through in Seattle, they'd both already be out of the picture." Natalie's voice rose a notch. "Don't talk to me about not knowing. It's your job to think ten steps ahead. Now she knows we aren't dead, and we're not going to be able to pin this on her like we'd planned."

Eve's adrenaline shot up. Her mind rushed back over that meeting in the park followed by the chaos after. She'd been so wrapped up in Zane, in finding out what was going on, that she'd let down her guard and hadn't noticed when Carter had gone after Natalie instead of letting Zane help her. Or that he'd gone the wrong direction, on purpose.

"It'll still work," Carter said. "Relax. Where's Roberts?"

"In the den."

Carter lifted his hand from Eve's mouth and slid the gun to the middle of her back. "Move. Toward the stairs. And go slow, Juliet. Don't think I won't shoot you right here if you do anything funny."

Eve's pulse raced as she stepped past Natalie and her smug expression. The stairs creaked under her boots with every step, and her mind ran with options. Zane had been the target from the beginning, not her. "Why Archer?"

"Don't answer her," Natalie snapped.

"Shut up," Carter said at Eve's back. Then to Eve, "Because he knew too much. He overheard me on the phone with Cross one night when we were in Beirut. The only plus in all of this is that those Chechens already killed Cross. Even if Archer didn't remember, I had to make sure he never would. And if he'd died in Guatemala like I'd planned, all of this would be a moot point."

They hit the first set of stairs, heading for the main level. "And the bombing in Seattle?"

"Cover-up. Kill two birds with one stone. I knew Archer was in Seattle looking for you. Hell, I even leaked information to him through a third party as to where you were. I knew he'd come after you. The dumb fuck was way too obsessed with finding you these last few months. And if Cross hadn't messed that one up, you'd both have died in that blast, and we wouldn't be here now."

He pushed her into the den. In the corner of the room, Roberts was handcuffed and gagged, leaning against the dark oak wall paneling, blood dripping down his forehead. His wife and ten-year-old son were also bound and gagged next to him, eyes wide and frightened.

Memories bombarded Eve. The kids in that school in Beirut. The child on the street next to her in Seattle. This boy.

Her pulse picked up speed until it was rapid-fire in her ears.

"So this is how this is going to go down," Natalie announced. "Roberts is going to tell us where he stashed Humbolt's file, and we'll kill you all quick and painlessly. There's no reason for anyone to have to suffer here."

The boy whimpered and closed his eyes. Horror reflected in the wife's eyes. Beneath the gag, Roberts mumbled something Eve couldn't decipher.

Natalie glanced toward Carter. "We'll use Wolfe's being here to our advantage. It'll look like she came after the file, killed his family, and Roberts shot her before she could get away. By the time anyone figures out what's going on, our Chechen friends will have the file, and we'll be billionaires."

"A nice, neat bow," Carter mumbled.

"Better than yours."

Natalie crossed the room and yanked the gag from Roberts's mouth, then moved behind the wife and pushed the muzzle of her gun against the woman's nape. "Start talking, Roberts."

Roberts's wife screamed beneath the gag. The boy sobbed louder.

"Carter," Eve said in a low voice, "you can't do this."

"Shut up, Wolfe."

"I don't have Humbolt's file," Roberts sputtered. "I never had it."

"That's a lie." Natalie shoved the gun harder against the woman's head. "We know Cross got cold feet and sent it to you. Tell us where it is or your wife dies."

"Carter," Eve hissed. "You can't let her kill innocent people."

"Shut. Up." Carter growled.

"You've got five seconds," Natalie hollered. "Five—"

"I don't know," Roberts screamed.

Adrenaline surged through Eve's body. "He doesn't have it," she yelled. "He doesn't have it because I do."

Natalie's head came up. She glared hard Eve's way. "Where?"

"Kill any of these people and you'll never know."

Fury flashed in Natalie's eyes. She shoved Roberts's wife to the floor, stepped over the woman's crumpled body, and lifted the gun to Eve's head. "Where's the fucking file?"

Beyond the glass doors that led from the den to the patio, a shadow moved.

"Natalie!" Carter yelled.

"I won't ask again," Natalie said in a calm voice. "Five—"

"Goddammit, Natalie, if you kill her, we'll never know where it is."

"Yes, we will. We'll find her fucking boyfriend and get it out of him. Four, three—"

"Dammit. Tell her, Eve." Carter's panicked voice echoed through the room. "She's not fucking around. I can't stop her."

"Two—"

Eve tensed. No way was she telling this chick where that file was located.

A gunshot sounded. Eve jolted. Glass shattered. Natalie yelped, and her gun went flying.

Carter let go of Eve and swiveled away. Realizing the shot had come from outside, Eve didn't turn to look at what he was doing. She arced out with her fist and caught Natalie with a right hook to the jaw. The woman fell back into the desk. Paper and pens went flying. Her body hit the ground with a thud.

The crack of fist against bone met Eve's ears. Wood splintered. Some kind of fight was going on behind her, but before she could look, she heard voices. Carter's. And Archer's.

"Son of a bitch," Archer muttered. "You should have stayed dead."

He'd come after her. Even after she'd left him with that stupid note. Even after all the things she'd done to try to fuck things up between them.

Her hand dripping blood where she'd been shot, Natalie pushed to her feet and used her good arm to swipe at her bloody mouth.

"He should have killed you a long time ago." She reached for Eve's gun at her lower back.

Eve swiveled and kicked out. Her foot connected with Natalie's jaw and then knocked into the hand lifting the gun. The gun went sailing. Eve threw two more punches and shoved Natalie into the fireplace. Natalie's head smacked against the mantle. She grunted, then sank to the floor.

Eve checked Natalie's pulse and found she was still alive, just unconscious. Carter and Archer were gone, though, and she couldn't hear them anymore. Her adrenaline shot up even more. Grabbing scissors from the desk drawer, she stepped up behind Roberts.

"I didn't know Cross was compromised," he said while she cut the zip ties around his wrists. "How did you get Humbolt's file?"

Eve moved to his wife. "Cross had a change of heart. He didn't know Natalie and Carter were going to blow up a city street. When the Chechens realized he'd stashed it and wasn't playing fair, they locked him up next to my sister. He told her where to find it."

"Is she okay?" Roberts pushed to his feet and reached for the gag around his son's mouth.

"She's alive. Okay is another matter." Eve grabbed her gun off the floor. "Stay here with them." She nodded toward Natalie. "She's out, but she'll be awake soon."

"I've got it. And, Wolfe." When Eve looked back, he nodded once. "Thank you."

Eve didn't want thanks right now. She wanted Zane.

Gun in both hands, she moved out into the foyer. Her heart pounded, and sweat slicked her skin. She rounded the corner and scanned the empty kitchen and family room.

"On your right."

She swiveled and nearly swallowed her tongue. "Ryder," she breathed.

From his spot near the stairs, Jake Ryder scowled over his own gun and whispered, "Just don't fucking shoot me. I'm not in the mood for a hospital right now. Is the redhead down?"

"Contained," Eve said quietly, lifting her gun again and scanning the room for any kind of movement. "Was that you outside?"

He nodded.

"Nice shot."

"Be thankful for big, tall windows."

Eve was. They passed through the dining room and kitchen. "My sister?"

"With Marley and Miller. Don't worry. She's safe."

Eve nodded, one tiny part of her relieved. "Archer?"

He shook his head.

Eve's worry shot up. They circled back to the entry hall. Eve nodded up toward the second floor, then pointed down to the basement. Ryder nodded. Gun held in both hands, he moved slowly up the stairs.

Eve did the same, moving slowly down the steps into the daylight basement. A wide bonus room complete with big-screen TV, wet bar, and pool table filled the space. But it was the open slider door that sent her heart rate up.

Shadows from tall trees surrounding the backyard fell over the pool and lawn chairs. The fading light of dusk made it hard to see as she stepped out onto the patio, but in the distance, she heard a commotion.

She took off running, heading for the dock. A groan met her ears. The crack of fist against bone. The splintering of wood. The thunk of a body hitting something hard. Panic closed in.

"Enough!" That was Zane's voice. Her feet hit the end of the dock. "It's over, Carter."

The growing darkness made it hard to see, but she could just make out Carter pushing himself up to his feet at the far end of the dock. Beyond, city lights flickered over the dark waters of the Potomac.

"You couldn't just die like we wanted." Carter swiped at his mouth. "Always had to be the hero. Well, you're not going to be the hero this time, Sawyer."

He lunged for Zane. Zane grunted and went down. Arms and legs flailed as they wrestled across the dock. Both had lost their weapons in the struggle somewhere. Heart in her throat, Eve stopped fifteen feet away and lifted her gun. But there was no good shot. "Freeze, Carter."

Zane's head came up, and Carter used the opportunity to slam his fist into Zane's jaw and take the upper hand. He whipped behind Zane and dragged him to his feet, using Zane as a shield. Zane's hands gripped Carter's forearm, but Carter had Zane in a headlock. From his ankle, Carter pulled a Guardian semiautomatic pistol and held it up against Zane's temple.

"Stay back, Juliet!" Carter yelled.

Sweat broke out along Eve's nape. She took a step closer on the dock. "Let him go. You've got no out here, James. You kill him, I kill you. If you do the smart thing, we all walk away from this."

Sweaty blond hair fell into Carter's eyes. He shook it back. "Walk away in cuffs, you mean. I'm not going to prison." He took a step back, toward the end of the dock, dragging Zane with him. "I'm not going down for this. It was Natalie's idea."

"It doesn't matter whose idea it was anymore." Eve inched closer, keeping her voice calm and her weapon trained on Carter's forehead, trying not to look at Zane. If she did, she might not be able to hold it together.

"No." Carter shook his head. Sweat and blood ran down his temple. He shifted to the left, closer to the docked sailboat. "He's coming with me. Back off, Eve. Back off before you make me do something I don't want to do. I'll kill him. I swear to God I'll kill him. Then I'll kill you."

From the corner of her vision, she saw Zane shake his head. Saw his eyes widen. Saw him mouth the words, *Shoot me.*

Disbelief and panic spread beneath Eve's ribs. She'd read that wrong. He couldn't have meant . . .

Shoot me.

He did it again, and her fingers grew wet around the handle of her gun.

"I'll fucking kill you all," Carter screamed, inching closer to the boat. "Back! Off!"

They were out of time.

Zane's eyes grew even wider. *Shoot me!*

Eve shifted the gun and fired.

chapter 25

Zane grunted as the bullet pierced his leg, and Eve's heart shot into her throat as she watched.

The force of the shot knocked off his center of balance, and Carter couldn't hold on. Zane's body hit the deck with a *thunk*. Trying not to focus too much on what she'd just done, Eve shifted her gun back up. Before Carter could dive for the boat, she fired once, twice, three times.

Carter's gun went flying. His body sailed backward. A splash echoed when he hit the Potomac. Sprinting forward, Eve looked over the end of the dock into the dark river, but she couldn't see Carter's body in the fast-moving water.

"Holy hell, you shot me."

She rushed back to Zane, dropped to her knees, and rolled him to his back. His pants were ripped at the right thigh, and blood was already seeping from the wound. Heart in her throat, she set her gun down on the dock and ripped the denim wider so she could see the damage.

Air filled her lungs. "I grazed you. The bullet didn't go in." She whipped off her jacket and pressed it against the blood. "You're okay. You're gonna be okay."

He cringed and pressed his palms back against the dock so he was partially sitting up. "You fucking shot me."

Relief warmed the icy-cold space that had formed in her chest when she'd seen Carter holding a gun to Zane's head. "You told me to."

"I know, but . . ." He frowned up at her. "You don't have to look like you enjoyed it so damn much."

Eve couldn't help it. She smiled. He wasn't dead. He wasn't mad at her. He was here. He was . . . hers.

"Where's Carter?" he asked.

"In the water somewhere. I can't see him. I hit him three times in the chest. No way he survived that."

"Dumb dead bastard," Zane muttered. "It didn't have to end like that."

Eve didn't care about Carter anymore. She only cared about the man currently beside her.

Holding the jacket against his wound, she caught his face with her other hand and kissed him. Hard.

"Don't ever make me do that again." Breathing fast, she rested her forehead against his. Her heart felt like it was about to jump out of her throat. In the distance, the faint sound of sirens echoed on the breeze.

"Don't run from me ever again," Zane said quietly.

Easing back, she stared into his dark eyes, knowing she had so much to make up for. "I shouldn't have. I'm sorry. I knew as soon as I got here that I needed your help, but by then it was too late. I just . . . I didn't want you to get hurt."

"And look how well that worked out."

He was making jokes. God . . . She closed her eyes and just tried to breath. "I wasn't running from you, Zane. Not like before. So much of what I've done, I did to try to keep you safe, and it turns out that all along you were the target. Not me. I was a stupid idiot." Tearing her eyes open, she looked deep into his. "I've done things on my own so long, I . . . I don't know how to rely on someone else."

"Well, you're gonna have to learn. I'm not going through this again, Eve. No more running."

"No more running," she whispered. Her heart filled, and tears burned the backs of her eyes. "You followed me."

"Like a pathetic puppy dog." He frowned. "I'll never hear the end of it from Miller and Ryder."

She smiled, leaned in, and rested her forehead against his once more, her heart growing with every second. "I'll make it up to you. I promise."

"Sexual favors," he mumbled when she kissed him again. "Lots of them." Voices echoed from the direction of the house, and footsteps sounded on the dock. "I'll make you a list."

She laughed, for the first time in months—years, really—feeling nothing but happiness. "I have no doubt you will."

Zane leaned back against the bench outside CIA headquarters in Langley and crossed his arms over his chest in the midafternoon sunlight.

People passed along the pathway as they entered and exited the building, and above, the leaves of a giant maple swayed in the breeze.

He shifted, feeling the scratch of the bandage on his leg beneath his jeans. Luckily, Eve had shot him in his bad leg, and a lot of the tissue there was already numb. He had to hand it to her. She could have done big-time damage to his already-fucked-up leg, but she'd made sure he wasn't seriously injured.

A slow smile spread across his lips. The throb in his leg would always be there, but he hadn't needed pain meds in days. And, he realized, a lot of that need had been a crutch, trying to deal with the loss of losing her, not true physical pain. Since she'd come back into his life, he'd been stronger, more agile, and though he still wanted to shake her sometimes, happier than he'd ever been.

His smile faded as he looked toward the entrance again, wondering when she was coming out. Wondering what the hell she was going to say when she did. They'd both been questioned separately, but the Agency was doing an in-depth debriefing with Eve, and he hadn't seen her since federal agents had shown up at Roberts's house. A tiny place inside couldn't help but worry what two days' separation had done to her.

The double doors at the building's entrance slid open, and a woman in a dark suit and crisp white dress shirt stepped out into the sun, her dark hair blowing gently in the wind. She slipped on sunglasses and looked around, and when her eyes found him, she froze.

Moment of truth. His pulse kicked up. Things said or done in a moment of extreme duress couldn't exactly be counted on. He might have teased her about making things up to him with sexual favors, but whether or not she ever paid up was another matter entirely.

She jogged down the front steps and headed his direction, stopping a foot from his bench. "I didn't expect to see you here."

Play it cool. "A little bird told me you'd be done today."

"Roberts."

"Yeah." He couldn't see her eyes behind those dark shades. Couldn't read her expression. Pushing to his feet, he said, "How did it go?"

"Okay. Natalie's finally talking, filling in some needed gaps about how she and Carter hooked up and how they brought Cross into their plans. Cross is really the hero in all of this. If he hadn't turned on them, both of us might not be here now."

Zane nodded. "You give them the file?"

"Yes. But you won't hear any of this on the nightly news. It's being covered up. Humbolt's discovery, Carter's involvement . . . The Agency's burying it in the name of national security."

Zane figured as much. He slid his hands in the front pockets of his jeans.

"The bombing in Seattle's being blamed on a Chechen terrorist group. By tonight it'll be all over the media. Along with the headlines: WE CAUGHT 'EM."

"What about Carter?"

Eve crossed her arms over her chest. "They found a bulletproof vest a mile downstream with three slugs in the front chest plate. But no sign of Carter."

That didn't exactly put Zane at ease. But James Dietrick was no longer his worry. "They'll find him, Eve. It's what the Agency does best." He tipped his head and narrowed his gaze. "And what about you?"

"Me?" Eve exhaled a long breath and uncrossed her arms. "They're moving me out of CI. Giving me my station of choice. Anywhere in the world."

His heart felt like it stopped, right in the center of his chest. For a CIA operative, that was the ultimate dream. To pick where you wanted to work. He couldn't remember the number of times in Beirut he'd heard Eve say she wanted to be stationed in Paris or Madrid or Rome.

He forced his lips into a smile when inside he wanted to scream. No way could they make this work with her halfway around the world for months—years—at a time. She'd told him once she never planned to marry because the life of a CIA officer caused too much strain on a relationship with time and distance separations, and he knew from their week together that her thinking on that point hadn't changed. And why he hadn't remembered that until right now, he'd never know.

"Congratulations." His voice was rough. Strained. *Screw it.* If she didn't want him, he wasn't gonna beg. He cleared his throat. "I know that's what you wanted."

"I never said that's what I wanted. I said it's what they offered." He wasn't sure what she was saying.

A wry smile turned one side of her lips, and she held out her hand to shake his. "The name's Evelyn Lenore Wolfe. *Retired.* I think this time we should start from the beginning, without all the aliases."

For a second, time stood still. And every cell in Zane's body vibrated with disbelief. Followed by a tiny voice in the back of his head whispering, *No way. You have to have heard her wrong.* "Wh-what?"

Her smile widened, and with her free hand, she tugged off her glasses. "No 'what' about it. I turned them down."

Relief was the sweetest emotion, whipping through Zane's body with the force of a hurricane. He snagged her hand, closed the distance between them, and tugged her in tight. His arms closed around Eve's waist, drawing her trim, toned body flush against his. "Lenore, huh? That one I didn't see coming."

Glasses dangling from her fingers, she pressed her hands against his T-shirt and smiled. "*That's* what you caught from my whole info dump there?"

"I'm trained to pick out the most important pieces of information." His expression sobered as he looked down at her amber eyes. "I didn't want you to quit, beautiful. Not for me."

"I didn't quit for you. Geez, it's like you think the world revolves around you or something."

He tightened his arms around her. "It does. Where you're concerned."

Her smile faded, and she looked down at her hands. "I did it for me. I'm ready for a change. Ready to do something that matters. I don't want to be responsible for innocent children dying anymore."

"Evie." He let go of her waist with one arm and tipped her face up to his with a finger under her jaw. "That kid in Seattle lived. The news updated this morning. No fatalities."

"Oh, thank God." Her eyes slid closed.

He wrapped his arm around her waist again, loving the feel of her next to him. Loving that this was the start of something incredible, not the end like he'd feared. "You really quit?"

She laughed and rested her cheek against his chest. "Don't sound so shocked."

"I can't help it. You never do anything I expect."

"Ha. In a few weeks you'll be wishing I'd stayed. I have no job now, and I haven't been without a job since I was fifteen. I'll probably drive you nuts until I find something else."

"Baby, you can drive me nuts anytime, anywhere." And suddenly, he could think of a hundred different ways.

"We're going to have to start over on a lot of things, you know. I mean, I don't even know where you live."

"In Colorado. I've got a house there."

She looked up in surprise. "You do?"

He smiled. "Remember all that money I inherited? I had to do something with it. It's a great place in the mountains outside Aspen, but it could definitely use a woman's touch."

Unease flashed in her eyes, but it quickly faded and was followed by a slow, warm smile. "I think I might be able to help you out there. As long as you do the cooking."

"Deal."

Sighing, she sank into him, and he smiled into her hair, holding her close, treasuring every single second. All those long, lonely nights after she'd left him, he'd never once thought it could possibly end like this. But it wasn't the end. It was the beginning. And he vowed here and now not to screw up their second chance.

"You know," he said after several seconds, "if you're serious about a job, I might be able to help you out there."

Her head lifted, and she eased back to look into his eyes. "What kind of job?"

He shrugged. "I know this security company that's always looking for the best of the best."

Her eyes narrowed. "I thought you and Ryder were on the outs."

"Nah. Ryder loves me too much."

She laughed and wrapped her arms around his neck. "I'm glad someone does, because I hate you. I really do. I always have."

"No, you don't." He smiled as he leaned down and brushed his lips across hers. "You love me."

She sighed against his mouth and tightened her arms around his neck. "I'm pretty sure that love will be the death of me."

"No way. Those sexual favors you owe me, though? Yeah, those might be."

She barked a laugh and rose up on her toes to kiss him. "Then you better hold on, Archer. Because I'm unpredictable in a variety of ways."

His lips curled against hers. "I can't wait to see what you do next."

about the author

Photo by Curtis Almquist at Almquist Studios

Before topping multiple bestseller lists—including those of the *New York Times*, *USA Today*, and the *Wall Street Journal*—Elisabeth Naughton taught middle school science. A rabid reader, she soon discovered she had a knack for creating stories with a chemistry of their own. The spark turned into a flame, and Naughton now writes full-time. Besides topping bestseller lists, her books have been nominated for some of the industry's most prestigious awards, such as the RITA® and Golden Heart Awards from Romance Writers of America, the Australian Romance Reader Awards, and the Golden Leaf Award. When not dreaming up new stories, Naughton can be found spending time with her husband and three children in their western Oregon home.